MW00860511

MURDER UNDER THE OAKS

Bouchercon Anthology 2015

MURDER UNDER THE OAKS

Bouchercon Anthology 2015

EDITED BY
ART TAYLOR

To Laurie
Hope you enjoy
the wide range of
stories here!

DOWN&OUT
BOOKS

Compilation copyright © 2015
Story Copyrights 2015 by Individual Authors
First Edition: October 2015

All rights reserved. No part of the book may be reproduced in any form or by any electronic or mechanical means, including information storage and retrieval systems, without permission in writing from the publisher, except by a reviewer who may quote brief passages in a review.

Down & Out Books
3959 Van Dyke Rd, Ste. 265
Lutz, FL 33558
www.DownAndOutBooks.com

The characters and events in this book are fictitious. Any similarity to real persons, living or dead, is coincidental and not intended by the author.

Cover design by Eric Beetner

ISBN: 1943402000
ISBN-13: 978-1-943402-00-7

To Librarians,
who feed both the mind and the soul

.

CONTENTS

CONTENTS

Introduction
Art Taylor

Whenever people ask about my favorite mystery writers, usually with an eye toward recommendations about who to read next, I often come back with a question or two of my own: Which writers do they already admire? Or even more to the point: What exactly do they mean by *mystery*?

While many people still define that word *mystery* in its narrowest terms—the fair-play whodunit, the traditional detective story—crime fiction (the term I personally prefer) covers a much broader and continually expanding territory. It's not just the cozy at one end of a spectrum and the hardboiled tale or the darkest noir at the other, but the full range of subgenres that...well, not that fall between those extremes (it's not a continuum, not at all) but that push the boundaries of the genre in so many different directions. The PI investigation and the police procedural. The caper, the con game, the courtroom drama. Spy stories, wartime espionage, international derring-do, romantic suspense. The historical tale and the techno-thriller. The legal thriller. The forensic thriller. The paranormal thriller. Serial killers and more serial killers. The classic locked room set-up. And that supposed line between literary and genre has long since been blurred. It's not just that some of the best *plots* can be found in crime stories today, but also the sharpest prose.

Similarly, that deceptively straightforward phrase *short story* can represent a wide variety of styles and structures and even sizes. A crisp bit of flash fiction can illuminate a moment's importance so intensely that a reader might glimpse a character's entire world or history or future. And at the further reaches of the word count limits, the novella can interweave several seemingly divergent storylines into a richly layered whole. The traditional linear story is only one available structure: a chain of events falling out cause and effect in a chronological format. Modular storytelling—assembling disparate bits of story into a complex and coherent mosaic—can juxtapose multiple perspectives, vault across great expanses of time, or shift tone radically across a simple section break. A piece of short fiction might sustain itself on a burst of mood or on a significant glimpse of character or lend itself to experimentation in ways that a novel, at such greater length, simply can't.

Just as each year's Bouchercon provides an umbrella—or, more suitably this year, perhaps an oak canopy—for the breadth of the crime writing community, so too do I hope that *Murder Under the Oaks*, the 2015 Bouchercon Anthology, will offer a sampling both of the subgenres and of the stylistic and structural choices available to today's writers of short fiction.

The stories in these pages include both invited contributions by distinguished guests and a dozen tales chosen from more than 150 blind submissions. Together, they form a vibrant and eclectic mix and represent both veteran mystery writers taking fresh risks and at least one newcomer making a striking debut. While most of us know best the award-winning novels of MWA Grand Master and Bouchercon Lifetime Achievement Award winner Margaret Maron, we shouldn't forget that she began her career as a short story writer and continues to push the boundaries of the form; when she submitted "Spring Break" here, she admitted that she was trying something new with the story: "Just to see if I could do one that's all dialogue with no narrative." Likewise, International Guest of Honor Zoë Sharp noted in her email to me that she "went a little out on a limb" with "Kill Me Again Slowly"—incorporating quotes by Groucho Marx, Oscar Wilde, Dorothy Parker, and Marilyn Monroe, each of whom has a cameo in a blissfully dizzying dinner scene with Sharp's series heroine Charlotte "Charlie" Fox. Meanwhile, J.D. Allen earns her very first mystery publication with "Grasshoppers," a six-part story that shuttles between three perspectives to tell an unforgettable story of revenge and redemption.

Several of the tales here center on investigations, whether by the police (Detective "Roc" Rozinski in Kathleen Mix's "Another Day, Another Murder"), by private investigators (Justice and Mercy Givens in Britni Patterson's "Mall Rats"), by other authorities (Judge Lu in P.A. De Voe's "The Immortality Mushroom") or by determined amateurs (the now-legendary group of University of Virginia students at the core of Kristin Kisska's "The Sevens").

De Voe's and Kisska's stories—set in Ming Dynasty China and early 20th-century Virginia, respectively—contribute to the range of historical periods represented: "Christians" by Bouchercon Guest of Honor Tom Franklin charts the aftermath of a killing in the post-Civil War South; "Death of a Bible Salesman" by Guest of Honor Sarah Shaber unfolds in World War II Washington, DC; and Karen E. Salyer's "Childhood's Hour," set in the early 19th century, features the father of detective fiction, Edgar Allan Poe himself, as a young child seeking answers about his troubled family history. He might not get them, but we do.

The shortest of the stories here, the tense, taut "Praying to a Porcelain God" by Bouchercon Toastmaster Lori Armstrong, reveals how much energy and anger can be packed into a small space. The longest, J.L. Abramo's "Walking the Dog," weaves a seemingly loose collection of conversations, reflections, and memories into a suddenly tight narrative—no stray threads, no unnecessary details, nothing wasted. Armstrong's story and "Driftwood" by her fellow Toastmaster Sean Doolittle may be among the darkest of the batch here, with Ron Rash's somber and urgent "Time Zones" exploring darkness of a different sort. But even some of those with a lighter or more humorous bent can take some sharp and unexpected turns. The narrator of Robert Mangeot's "Crack-up at Waycross" had me laughing out loud, the black comedy of Graham Wynd's "Life Just Bounces" struck me as decadently delightful, and there are different levels of amusement and surprise and emotional depth in the raise-the-stakes adventures of the title character in Karen Pullen's "#grenadegranny," in the face-off between Perko and Mongoose in Rob Brunet's "A Good Name," and in the interplay between two American tourists and a Spanish pickpocket in Robert Lopresti's "On the Ramblas."

To cap off my claims about diversity within the crime short story, two of the stories here ultimately feature no significant crimes at all—but you won't know which until you finish them, and that absence hardly compromises the suspense or the success of either.

While *Murder Under the Oaks* was never intended to be a themed anthology, several trends did present themselves. If a search for justice might predominate, the spirit of revenge—justice's close kin—courses even more menacingly through the collection. Family features prominently in several stories—both the lengths someone will go to protect family and the dysfunctions and even dangers that can lie at the heart of such relationships. Friendship plays a similarly recurring role, most notably in the escalating game of truth or dare between B.K. Stevens' "Old Friends." Older characters appear frequently as victims or criminals, and the plight of aging is perhaps nowhere more eloquently explored than in the showdown between Andy Griffith (yes, *that* Andy Griffith) and the widowed schoolteacher in Toni Goodyear's "Down Home." And speaking of Sheriff Andy, while the collection was also never meant to be geographically centered, the prevalence of stories that ended up being set in North Carolina as well as Virginia and Georgia does help to commemorate this first Bouchercon in the South—and thanks, in that regard, to UK writer Sharp for bringing not just herself but her character for a visit to Raleigh.

I'm pleased to have been chosen to guest edit this anthology, and it's been a great pleasure to work with all the authors included here, but a collection like this relies on many more people than those listed on the table of contents. Great thanks go to Karen Pullen, a fine short story writer and anthologist in her own right, for her tremendous organizational efforts and stamina getting this project going and keeping it going, and to Amy Funderburk of the Cameron Village Regional Library for her work logging the blind submissions, communicating with the authors, and organizing their manuscripts for judging. I also want to thank Eric

Campbell of Down & Out Books, Janet Reid of Fine Print Literary Management, and several of the organizers of Bouchercon 2015—including Al Abramson, Ingrid Willis, and Stacey Cochran—plus give a quick personal thanks to Dana Cameron, editor of last year's Bouchercon anthology, for bits of advice and guidance along the way.

Finally, no celebration of the writers here would be complete without a celebration of the readers themselves, who've picked up this anthology and will hopefully search out the works of these authors elsewhere too. In that spirit, I want to close with thanks to *you* reading this right now and also with a big shout-out to the beneficiary of this anthology: the Wake County Public Libraries, who, along with all libraries, continue the mission of bringing writers and readers, all of us, together.

Spring Break
Margaret Maron

"Hello?"

"Oh, thank goodness you're there, Granna! I'm sorry if I woke you up. I know it's late, but Mom's not answering her phone and I can't tell Dad. He'll kill me!"

"Susie? Is that you? What's wrong? Where are you? What's happened?"

"Promise you won't tell Dad?"

"Tell your dad? What are you talking about?"

"I'm in so much trouble."

"Honey, stop crying and tell me what's happened...Susie? Are you there?"

"Hello? Mrs...is it Foley?"

"Yes. Emma Foley. Who are you? Where's Susie?"

"This is Sergeant Monroe of the State Highway Patrol. Are you her grandmother?"

"I am. What's this all about?"

"I'm sorry, Mrs. Foley, but I have to make sure you really are her grandmother before I release any details. She says you live in Cameron Village up there in Raleigh. Is that correct?"

"That's right. Wait a minute! You said *up there?* Where are you calling from? What's happening with Susie?"

"I'm sorry, ma'am, but your granddaughter's just been arrested down here in Georgia for possession of a controlled substance."

"Controlled substance? You mean drugs? That's crazy. Susie's never used drugs."

"I'm sorry, ma'am."

"Let me speak to her, Sergeant."

"Granna?"

"Susie? I don't understand. What on earth are you doing in Georgia?"

"It's spring break, remember? My roommate and I came down to Tybee Beach for some sun and fun and it's turned into a nightmare. The drugs aren't mine, Granna. Honest! They were under the seat of our rental car and I don't know how they got there, but they're going to lock me up if I can't post a bond for twenty-eight hundred dollars... Granna?...Granna?...Are you still there?"

"Sorry, honey. I was sound asleep when you called. The doctor gave me a sleeping pill and my brain's still in bed. Twenty-eight hundred?"

"Please, Granna. The trooper says if you wire it to me right away, I won't have to spend the rest of the night here in jail. I'll call Mom first thing in the morning and get her to pay you back. Just don't call Dad, okay? He'll totally freak."

"Oh, Susie."

"Granna? Are you crying? Don't worry. *Please!* I'll be okay. They say I can go just as soon as someone sends the money to cover my bond. Please don't cry."

"Let me speak to that officer."

"Sergeant Monroe, here."

"What do I have to do, Sergeant, to get my granddaughter released?"

"The magistrate has set her bond at twenty-eight hundred, ma'am. If you want to wire the money here, I can give you the details."

"The thing is, I never go out at this time of night anymore and I haven't the faintest idea where a Western Union is."

"I'm sorry, ma'am."

"Wait! Don't hang up. I have that much cash here in the house. I just don't know how to get it to Georgia. Maybe I should call Susie's mother and—"

"Your grandmother wants to call your mother...ma'am? Miss Foley's shaking her head and begging you not to. I'm sure Western Union must be in your Yellow Pages."

"I'm an old woman, Sergeant. It's almost midnight. I can't go roaming the streets of Raleigh at this hour. Isn't there another way to do it?"

8

"What do you suggest, ma'am?"

"I know it's asking a lot, but couldn't you get a police officer here to come get the money and then wire it down to Georgia? As a professional courtesy? Don't you law enforcement officers do things like that for each other?"

"That's highly irregular, ma'am."

"Do you have children, Sergeant? Or a grandmother? Please?"

"Let me see what I can do. I'll call you back."

"Hello?"

"Mrs. Foley?"

"Sergeant Monroe! I was beginning to think you'd changed your mind."

"Sorry. It took a while for me to set this up. I have an old Army buddy with the Raleigh PD. He's going off duty and he's agreed to pick up the money at your house and wire it to the courthouse down here. He says it'll take him about twenty minutes to get over to Cameron Village. His name is James Morris and he'll show you his badge."

"Morris? Oh, that's wonderful! Tell him I'll leave the front porch light on. Let me give you my address."

"Mrs. Foley?"

"Are you Sergeant Monroe's friend?"

"Officer Morris, yes, ma'am."

"Do come in, Officer."

"If you don't mind, ma'am, it's been a long day for me. If the money's ready, I'll just take it on over to the Western Union on Capital Boulevard."

"Certainly, Officer. Here it is. Twenty-eight hundred dollars. I hope you won't mind signing a receipt for it. These are such strange times and my accountant always tells me to get a receipt for everything."

"No problem, ma'am. You have a pen?...Here you go."

"What nice handwriting you have. Thank you so much...Is that enough, son?"

"That'll do just fine, Mom. Cuff him, Bob."

"Hey! Where'd you guys come from? Who are you? *Ow!* Easy with those handcuffs!"

"James Morris? Or is it Sergeant Monroe? I'm Mrs. Foley's son and my partner and I are *real* Raleigh PD officers. You're under arrest for attempted fraud and for impersonating a police officer. Anything you say can and will be used against you in a court of law. You have the right to an attorney—"

"Yeah, yeah. Save your breath. You—Grandma. What tipped you off?"

"*Your* Susie kept saying she didn't want her dad to know when—"

"*Ow!* Hey! What'd I say? What'd I do? Oh, my God! Is that *blood?* Is my nose bleeding? Police brutality! You just bought the city of Raleigh a lawsuit, mister."

"Get him some ice, son. And you, Mr. Morris or whatever your name is, you're lucky he didn't break your nose. He's Susie's uncle. As for what gave you away, Susie—*my* Susie—posted about her spring break on her Facebook page two days ago and I posted for her to have fun and be safe. Is that how your girlfriend knew to call me Granna?"

"What if it was?"

"One of you should have checked Susie's page tonight before you called. You would have known from all the condolences that she wasn't still in Georgia."

"Huh? Condolences?"

"Her dad—my other son—died in a car wreck this morning."

The Immorality Mushroom
From Judge Lu's Ming Dynasty Case Files
P.A. De Voe

Judge Lu enjoyed his visits to the Temple of the Enduring Oak. He had discovered a sympathetic soul in its head monk Tsu Fei-long. When possible, Lu would slip away from his duties in order to share a cup of tea and the pleasure of an afternoon filled with philosophical discussion. Such visits provided him with relief from his busy and stressful schedule as magistrate of the local province.

Today, however, they had just begun their discussion when a monk entered the room and whispered in Tsu Fei-long's ear. Fei-long nodded and glanced at Lu. "Come with me, Your Honor, there is something you need to see." His tone was solemn.

They followed the young monk out of the temple and past its namesake, a massive oak, which –because of its age and size—represented longevity, a good luck omen. Within a short distance, they reached a river.

Two saffron-robed monks stood on the banks directing a young fellow who strode hip deep into a swirling eddy. He skimmed the water's surface with a net. A cry went up when he snagged something and started dragging it toward shore.

By the time Lu and Fei-long reached the trio, one of the monks cradled the object in his arms. Bending, he gently laid it on a square piece of cloth draped on the grassy banks. Lu recognized a tiny, puffy body covered unevenly with reddish blotches. He turned his head and closed his eyes against the sight. A drowned newborn.

Fei-long spoke quietly to his monks. They wrapped the body and carried it up the slight hill.

"You can examine it in the shade of the temple," he said to

Lu. As they turned to go, he added, "That's the second little one we've found this month."

Lu frowned. "The second?" *Why hadn't he been told?* he wondered.

Before he could ask, however, Fei-long said, "We find several every year. Their parents, too poor to feed another mouth, drown them rather than have everyone else in the family suffer even more deprivation, possibly even threatening the lives of the other children."

"It was a girl child," Lu said, a statement, not a question.

Fei-long sucked in his breadth. "Yes. We rarely find a boy child. Boys are too precious, even in times of want."

Lu understood what he meant. Girls were expendable. They married and became a part of someone else's family, producing their descendants. Boys, on the other hand, were essential to the survival of their family line. He knew the girls' families didn't make these decisions easily, but if there was a choice about which child to abandon, a son or a daughter, there was no choice. The family line must survive.

Pu-an was a large district. By any standard most of its citizens had enough to eat; a good percentage were even well off. However, there were always those families on the margins. The working poor and the abject poor. Lu knew it was useless to go looking for the infant's parents. No one would say anything; no one would admit to knowing anything. Infanticide was a moral quagmire, but he also realized the monk was right: the cause was not callousness or uncaring parents; it rose from a fear of want, of hopelessness, of true poverty.

Riding back to the yamen with his two personal guards Ma and Zhang, Lu thought about the temple giving each of the little victims a burial. He was called Father of the People. What could he do as their magistrate? How could he eliminate the killing of innocent babies?

Deep in thought, he rode through the town unaware of the merchants' calls and the excited bargaining voices of buyers and sellers. He ignored it all as he rounded the last corner and the yamen's massive wood gate rose majestically ahead of him, drawing him in.

"Sir! Honorable Sir!" a high-pitched voice rose above the street's cacophony.

Zhang immediately thrust out his spear and sharply tightened his reigns. The woman—arms flailing and her loose, untamed hair flying—ignored Zhang and continued rushing toward the judge. Ma moved closer, placing his horse between the judge and the wild figure.

Lu, however, instantly recognized her as Widow Han from a previous case. He pushed thoughts of the drowned babies away and concentrated on this new development. He told his guards to let her pass.

Breathing rapidly, she stopped within an arm's distance of his horse, rested her hand on her chest, and gasped for air. Catching her breath, she lifted a saddened and wrinkled face toward him and then announced, "Your Honor, Master Chou is dead. Someone robbed and killed him."

Lu scowled down at her. "Master Chou? Who is he and where did this happen?"

"He's the bell doctor who lives on Dong Jie," she said, referring to the itinerant doctor by the local term. He walked the streets ringing a bell alerting people about his presence in case they needed his services. "I went to visit him and happened to arrive at the very moment his son found him dead in their house."

"Lead us to Master Chou's," Lu ordered the widow.

She didn't hesitate or turn to see if they were following as she sped back through the streets; she moved at a surprising speed, belying her fragile, if erratic, appearance.

A crowd had already started to form around the bell doctor's door. A strongly-built man of medium height, with small eyes and prematurely thinning hair, stood just inside the house and kept the crowd at bay. The crowd parted as Lu and his entourage approached; Widow Han strode straight up to the man. "Chou Xiao-zei, I've brought Magistrate Lu," she said in a loud voice.

He frowned down at her, but then, looking up as the judge dismounted from his horse, the frown passed and he said, "Honorable Sir," while bowing in Lu's direction. "Please come in."

As Lu stepped through the doorway, he was wrapped in a pungent gloom. He paused and looked around, letting his eyes become accustomed to the room's dimness. Shelves overflowing with jars and bottles stretched along two walls. In the center stood a long table with three stools pushed under it; another small, square table filled out the remaining space. On the latter, Lu noted a cutting board, a chopping knife, and mortar and pestle sitting on its rough, work-worn surface. Master Chou's body lay stretched out on the long table, a light cloth covering him.

Lu wanted to be mindful of the pain and shock he was sure Master Chou's son was feeling at his father's sudden and horrible death. Nevertheless, it was imperative he proceed as quickly as possible, before details were forgotten or altered. Plus—and this he tried to ignore because it could lead to bringing closure at any cost and, thereby, subverting impartiality—Lu was also too keenly aware that his superiors expected the murderer to be discovered and apprehended within days of the death. Anything longer than this and the magistrate was suspected of mishandling the case; there would be repercussions, perhaps even dismissal. Lu tried not to let such thoughts determine his actions; he concentrated on bringing justice to the victims, not on protecting his own position.

He stepped to the table and pulled back the cover. As he bent to inspect the body, he was aware of Widow Han's slipping into the room and taking up a position behind the open door. He ignored her, allowing her to remain. Looking at the victim, Lu immediately discovered the cause of death: a fractured skull. No other signs of trauma were visible.

"Where did you find him?" Lu asked Chou Xiao-zei.

"There," he said pointing to a narrow space between the square table and the shelves.

"He was already dead?"

Xiao-zei passed a hand over his eyes. "Yes. I was bringing in firewood and found him slumped on the floor. He didn't have to die like that."

"Did he have any enemies? Anyone he was fighting with?"

"No. No one I knew. Of course, he was a doctor and

sometimes people died, no matter what he did to save them. Sometimes families blamed him. But I don't know of anyone who'd kill him."

Lu glanced around the room, "Was anything stolen?"

"Nothing."

Lu heard a sharp intake of breath from Widow Han, but he didn't glance in her direction. "Are you sure? There are a lot of jars around here."

"I work with my father. I know everything in this room. Nothing's missing."

"Did he have any appointments today?"

"Not that I know of. As I said, I was out fetching wood, so if anyone stopped in, I wouldn't know it, but I don't think he had any appointments. He was preparing his medicines."

After closely inspecting the room, Lu again returned to the body. Pushing down a sense of revulsion, he gently moved his fingers through Master Chou's matted hair, feeling the skull's wound in more detail.

The late afternoon sun sent a narrow stream of light through the window as if highlighting the bloodied mass. As he pushed hair out of the way, he felt a few chunks of matter. He picked them out, wrapped them in a handkerchief, and placed the evidence in his sleeve. Continuing to carefully examine the wound, he noted the fracture was a rounded depression.

Lu surveyed the room once more. His eyes rested on the pestle used for pounding herbs and such into powders. He picked it up and gently held it close to the victim's wound. It was a match. It had been wiped clean, but it matched the injury.

Xiao-zei watched Lu. "Do you think that's what killed him?"

Lu handed the pestle to his guard. "Very likely."

"A thief came in and killed my father, thinking he could rob him. But we never had any money here." He smiled grimly. "Bell doctors don't make much."

Lu ran his hand over the table's rough surface, dislodging a couple of pieces of vegetable matter from its crevices. He put those into another handkerchief and dropped them gently into his sleeve along with the first handkerchief.

Later, back in his office, Lu sat with his two guards and his brother Lu Fu-hao, who served as his secretary. They were discussing Master Chou's death. The killing seemed random; there was no motive and no suspect. Yet, such a violent murder suggested a degree of passion—from what? Fear? Anger? Desperation? The fact that Master Chou had his back turned toward the killer indicated he wasn't afraid of him. Perhaps he even knew his killer and trusted him. They all thought it had to be a man; none of them believed a woman would have the constitution for, or be physically strong enough to commit, such a murder.

As they sat sifting through the scant information Lu had gathered that afternoon, his servant announced Widow Han was outside, requesting an audience.

Lu slipped on his court robes and returned to his desk.

Widow Han wandered into the room and it wasn't the first time Lu wondered at her mercurial behavior. She appeared to go from aggressive assertiveness to mistily drifting in and out of consciousness. Watching her, he wondered at her sanity. He sighed and waited.

When she arrived at the desk, she stopped and looked around her as though surprised to find herself in the office. She cocked her head to one side and—as if continuing a conversation—said, "You know, Master Chou also talked to that farmer from the eastern hillside; the one who comes to town to sell vegetables on market day with the stall across the street from Chou's shop."

Lu and Fu-hao exchanged glances.

"When did he talk to the farmer?" Lu asked.

"The same day he found the mushrooms." She glanced around the room. "He might have told the farmer about the mushrooms. He told me." She stopped and stared up at Lu.

He shifted his weight in his elaborate high backed chair. "And what is it that he told you?"

"Why that he'd found them, of course. Although I suppose

it would have been better for him not to mention anything to anyone. Not even me." She shook her head and bit her lip.

Lu cast a brief look at Fu-hao who was sitting at a side table. His brother widened his eyes and shook his head in a silent comment on her behavior. Lu shifted back into place.

"Are you saying he'd found mushrooms? That's what he told you and the other farmer?" He wondered why mushrooms would demand secrecy.

Widow Han looked up, eyes bright. "Yes. The Immortality Mushroom."

Lu started. Had he heard correctly?

She hurriedly went on, words tumbling over each other as she related her story. "I met him on my way back to town. I'd been out gathering herbs, just as he had been. He was looking for lichen and mushrooms in the woods—the one with a stand of old oak trees in it." She licked her lips. "There they were— three of them—growing on the side of an oak stump."

"Are you sure? How did he recognize them? The Immortality Mushroom is extremely rare."

Swaying rhythmically from side to side, she smiled. "Rare, yes. The golden treasure. Any herbalist would be able to identify one; they are distinctive with their bright red color and broad, flat shape. Even one would bring a lifetime of comfort. It's what we all hope to find as we hunt for herbs. And, Master Chou found three." She smiled as if in awe at his luck. "He was delirious with excitement. When he saw me on the road, he had to tell me the whole story of his looking for lichens, of finding the mushrooms. While he was telling me the tale, Farmer Xiong came along. I warned Master Chou not to say anything more. He was walking around with a treasure and anyone could steal it."

She held Judge Lu's gaze. "It may be Farmer Xiong heard enough to know Master Chou had something of great value."

"Do you think he knew it was the mushrooms?" Lu asked.

She shook her head. "No, probably not. And he wouldn't recognize the importance of the mushrooms—at least I don't think so. Who really knows what someone else knows?"

"When was this?"

"Four days ago. I went to Master Chou's place today

because I was sure he would have prepared the mushrooms for sale by now, drying them and grinding them into a powder."

"Wouldn't he sell them whole, thereby assuring the customer he was getting a real Immortality Mushroom?" Lu asked.

"They are too powerful. They need to be mixed in with special vegetables and longevity noodles and eaten over several days."

Lu fingered the tiny, dried chunks he'd taken from the wound. "Look at these, Widow Han. What do you think they are?"

She stepped up to the desk, pressed her nose close to the pieces, and sniffed. Lifting her head slightly, she studied them, and turned them over with her index finger. "Immortality Mushrooms," she said with conviction.

Lu pushed his shoulders back and stared down at the fragments. "So he might have been grinding the mushrooms when he was struck down." They didn't look like much, just brown and reddish bits, nothing worth murdering for. "The killer must have known how valuable they were. The table and mortar were thoroughly cleaned."

Crinkling her wizened features, she nodded at the bits on his desk. "Even those few pieces are worth a half a year's wages."

"Thank you, Widow Han. You have been most helpful," he said and was about to dismiss her when she said, "One more thing, Your Honor."

He inclined his head indicating she could continue.

"Chou Xiao-zei must have known about the mushrooms. I doubt his father could have kept such great luck from his son. Yet, he said nothing was missing."

"Yes," Lu said, lightly drumming his fingers on the table, waiting for her to finish.

"Of course, that doesn't make him guilty of murder," Widow Han went on. "No insult intended, Your Honor, but he could be hiding the mushrooms in order to protect his wealth when this case goes to court. It's possible Master Chou was killed for other reasons and then, when Xiao-zei found him, he hid the precious mushrooms to sell later."

He grimaced. She was right. Any involvement with the law brought disaster to all, whether victims or criminals. Once a case came to court, bribery was rife at every level, from those who delivered messages—even court documents—to the cost of paper for writing necessary court affidavits, to protecting the accused person's home from vandalism. The amount of bribery exacted at each and every level depended on how much money people thought the victim's family had. Hiding such new-found wealth would be reasonable. Master Chou's son could easily be penniless at the end of this unfortunate and deadly event. Nevertheless, Lu had to identify the guilty party.

Lu spun around toward his personal guards. "Ma, bring in Farmer Xiong immediately for questioning. Zhang, I want you to go to Master Chou's neighborhood and talk to everyone you can. Find out who might have gone into his house or who was nearby. Find out if there was any gossip about his having the Immortality Mushrooms. Report back as soon as you can."

Early the next morning, Judge Lu sat behind his official court desk. Soldiers lined each side of the room. Fu-hao sat at a table to the side and behind the soldiers. A dark, dense liquid filled his ink stone and his brush rested in his hand perpendicular to the rice paper, ready to record the interrogation.

"Farmer Xiong," a young man in a long, dark robe announced from the back of the court. Almost immediately a burly soldier led in a lean man of medium build, wearing a plain, short jacket over baggy pants. With wide, staring eyes and hunched shoulders he kept bowing even before he reached the judge.

Lu watched him come forward. The farmer was clearly terrified and overwhelmed. Lu was satisfied, confident fear would ensure honesty in the proceeding.

"You were on the road four days ago and met with Master Chou and Widow Han. Tell me everything about that meeting," Lu ordered.

Farmer Xiong had grasped his hands so tightly together his knuckles were a shiny, pallid color. "Yes, sir. As I came down the road I saw Master Chou talking excitedly with Widow Han."

"You know the Widow Han?"

"Yes, sir. Everyone knows her. She's taken care of most folks' families at one time or another, same as Master Chou."

"Go on," Lu said.

"I'd never seen Master Chou so stirred up. He's an honorable man, quiet. That day he was almost hopping in the street, waving a bag around. Widow Han was laughing and seemed to be congratulating him."

"Did they tell you what he was so happy about?"

Farmer Xiong pouted. "No. When they saw me coming up to them, they both stopped. It was as if they were hiding something. I said hello and they said hello, but they obviously didn't want me to hear what they were talking about."

"What did you do?"

"Me?" He shrugged. "I went on my way. I had a load of vegetables to sell, and the sooner I got to market, the sooner I'd go home."

Lu observed the lanky farmer as he went through his description. Although the man was clearly anxious at being in court, Lu could not detect any signs of disingenuousness or trying to hide information. Unless he was extremely clever and an adept liar, Lu believed him to be no more than he appeared: a simple man giving simple, honest answers.

After releasing Farmer Xiong, Lu returned to his office and waited impatiently for Zhang to return. He hoped his guard had discovered something useful in this case. How could a man be robbed and killed without anyone knowing about it?

He tried to divert his attention by going over old files from his predecessor, familiarizing himself with cases involving chronic small-time criminals. Having a list of names of such people would help him in future cases. They could provide him with either insider knowledge of the district's underworld or a list of possible criminals for new cases.

As he went through the documents, a name caught his attention: Chou Xiao-zei. He'd been involved in a couple of rowdy situations where the police had to come and arrest the combatants. He'd also been arrested once for theft, but his father compensated the victim and Xiao-zei was let off with a beating. *Hum. So Master Chou's son had a history of violence and theft. Interesting,* Lu thought. Closing the stack, he saw Zhang step inside the office's door.

"Good. You're here. Come and tell us what you've discovered," Lu said, waving toward a chair next to his brother Fu-hao and Ma.

As Lu's servant poured tea, Zhang bent his large frame onto the sturdy chair, while keeping his back straight, as if at attention.

"Everyone I talked to respected the doctor. He'd helped most of them at one time or another and was known for his generosity. He'd care for those who couldn't afford to pay or could only make partial payments. He always said he was building merit. No matter how I asked it, no one indicated they knew anything about his finding the Immortality Mushrooms or even having anything of value. It seems Master Chou managed to keep his treasure a secret."

"How about his son, Xiao-zei," Lu asked.

Zhang's lips thinned in an upside down smile. "Now that's another story entirely," he said. "Almost to a man, they agreed his son, from the time he was a young man, was the bane of Master Chou's life. Chou's wife managed to keep the peace between her husband and son when she was alive, but when she died two years ago, the relationship between them became even more strained. Master Chou had trained his son to be a bell doctor, but because of his violent reputation and thievery, people didn't trust him. Finally, Chou threw Xiao-zei out of the house about a year ago."

"And yet, he was there, at the house, yesterday," Lu said.

"Perhaps he was trying to reunite with his father," Ma said. "Xiao-zei did say he'd brought wood for him."

Lu nodded. He tapped his fingertips on the table while he

ran over yesterday in his mind. Finally, he asked, "Do any of you remember seeing a load of wood at Master Chou's?"

They all shook their heads. Zhang added, "I'd peeked in the back room as well, in case there was any one hiding there. There were only a couple of sticks near the stove."

"Zhang, Ma, arrest Chou Xiao-zei. Don't bring him to court; take him directly to jail and place him under the head jailer's care."

The two men nodded and strode from the room.

"Is that wise?" Fu-hao asked. "You know what the head jailer will do."

"Yes. He'll threaten torture unless Xiao-zei can pay him off," Lu said leaning back in his glossy, highly carved, wood chair. He sipped his tea and then held the cup up, silently examining the porcelain's luminescent design.

Fu-hao grinned. "Ah, yes. To get the bribe, Xiao-zei will have to get one of his cronies to sell some of the Immortality Mushroom. He'll lead us right to them, proving he stole the mushrooms," Fu-hao said, then muttered, "and implicating himself in his father's death."

Lu sadly nodded. "It's the most serious and monstrous crime anyone can commit: patricide."

"How could he have done such a thing?" Fu-hao asked. But they both knew there was no answer, the crime was too overwhelming, too horrendous. It was against all the rules of nature. "He deserves to be tortured," Fu-hao added, anger tingeing his voice.

Two days later, Lu had Xiao-zei brought before the court. Most of the people living in Master Chou's neighborhood were in the back of the great hall, ready to hear the proceedings.

Barely able to walk, Xiao-zei shuffled in, half carried between two soldiers. Large patches of sweat marred his clothing. His matted hair formed a skullcap on his head. When he raised his eyes, they were devoid of light. He was a defeated man.

Lu never liked to use torture. The law permitted it,

expected its use. His superiors believed it was an efficient route to achieve justice. Evidence might indicate who was guilty, but—by law—no one could be convicted and sentenced of such a heinous crime if he did not confess. Therefore, torture was considered an important tool for producing confessions and obtaining a moral balance once more.

"Chou Xiao-zei, confess to your crime of murdering your father, Master Chou, and stealing the Immortality Mushrooms," Lu thundered.

"I..."

"Louder! So all can learn of your evil transgressions," Lu said.

Xiao-zei began again. "I struck my father on the head with a pestle. It broke his skull and he died. I didn't mean to kill him. I needed money and he wouldn't help me. I knew he had the Immortality Mushrooms. He'd told me; he was so proud of it; said it would make us rich. Still, he wouldn't give me any money right then and I needed it.

"I was so angry I didn't think about what I was doing. I just grabbed the pestle and hit him." He looked around, eyes empty. "I really didn't mean to hurt him. I was just angry."

He bent his head, then looked up again. "Once I saw he was dead, I took the mushrooms. He didn't need them anymore. I did."

Lu had Fu-hao read out Xiao-zei's confession and Xiao-zei put his mark on it.

Back in his office, Fu-hao asked his brother, "What are you going to do with Master Chou's Immortality Mushrooms?"

Lu studied his brother's face for some time before answering. "Master Chou and his wife had no other children. There is no one to take care of their spirits in the afterlife. I am going to confiscate the mushrooms and his property, which would have all gone to their son Xiao-zei. That will provide the basis of a foundation for an orphanage for abandoned babies.

"Poor families will not have to kill their babies anymore;

they can leave them without question at the great oak tree outside the Temple of the Enduring Oak. We'll get volunteers from our community to provide food and clothing. And we'll hire wet nurses. Twice a year, on this day and on Tomb Sweeping Day, a great feast will be offered to the spirits of Master Chou and his wife in thanks for providing life to so many newborns."

Fu-hao nodded solemnly. "Such a decision will earn you merit as well, my brother."

Lu didn't answer but bent his head as he wrote out his decision.

#grenadegranny
Karen Pullen

It's not difficult to rob a bank. The hard part is—*cue drumroll*—getting away with it.

How'd I get to this point in my life? I admit to a colorful past, but felonies weren't part of it. A few misdemeanors in my youth, a DUI last year, but overall Martha Sue Bly obeys the law. I even declare every penny of income from my laundromat, the Wishy Washy, to the IRS. You'll agree that's the very definition of honesty. Of course, since my quarters are deposited in the bank, which then reports them to the IRS, I don't have much choice.

Quite a racket, this coziness between banks and U.S. Government. When a bank can't pay what it owes, it's *too big to fail* and U.S. Government steps in with a bailout. When you or I run into financial misfortune, we get slapped with overdraft fees, repossession, foreclosure, and bankruptcy. Recently I was headed in that direction, with good reason to ponder the unfairness of this cozy relationship.

A few months ago I got a death sentence. Oh, not those words exactly. The doctor used terms like *rare, difficult to treat, aggressive. We can try this, Martha. Or that. No guarantees.*

It's not easy to obtain *this* or *that* when you've got no health insurance. Yup, I'm one of the unlucky North Carolina residents who earns too much for Medicaid, not enough for government subsidies. (Read that sentence twice. Because it doesn't make sense.)

I went through the Kübler-Ross stages in about three minutes flat: the lab musta made a mistake. But if they didn't—the doc's old, pushing sixty, so why not him instead? But since I got it—there's a chance, isn't there, with chemo and stem cells? Aw, there's no hope and I'm just gonna lie on the floor and cry for the rest of my short life.

It looked like forty-four years might be it for *moi*. What did I have to show for my too-short moment on this planet? A born-again evangelical daughter who said I was headed straight to hell to burn for eternity. A string of sorry men, evidence of a weakness for looks over brains, money, or character. Tattoos and cellulite.

Not very much. Somehow, that fact was even worse than my diagnosis.

The Wishy Washy is conveniently located in a strip mall right outside my neighborhood, Evergreen Hills, where the only hills are speed bumps and "green" is furnished by plentiful crabgrass, algae growing on our vinyl siding, and water in last summer's wading pools. The entrance is marked by a splintery sign that some hoodlum teenager took a mallet to, knocking off letters so that it now says " v rg n Hills."

Three weeks into chemo, I pulled into my driveway with groceries and seven hundred dollars' worth of pills—thank you, AmEx. I was nauseated, tired, bald, and broke. My medical bills resembled a Wall Street bonus but the only hedge fund I knew of was my neighbor Robert's. Robert came back from Afghanistan with a limp and a four-square-inch plate in his head. He was big as a fridge and good with tools, but simple. He earned money as a handyman—cutting grass, painting, spreading mulch, any little repair job you could think of. He lived at 312, next door to me, with his mom Annie, who used to be my best friend.

Robert was edging his sidewalk. "I almost didn't recognize you, Miss Martha," he said. "Where did your hair go?" Gotta love him.

"Don't know," I said. "It just fell out one day."

"You look real different. I never saw a bald lady before."

"There's a first time for everything. Your momma still working at the bakery?"

"Um, no. She was laid off. She's sleeping. Should I wake her up?"

"Let her sleep. I'll stop by later." A big fat lie. Annie and I weren't speaking. She claimed I stole her fiancé but if you ask me, I did her a favor. Smitty was lousy husband material. When I got sick, he slithered away quicker than a bobcat onto his next prey—a dropout he found at the soft serve ice cream window. My feelings survived that blow, so should Annie's. I missed her, though, and most days I wished I had a friend like she used to be. I sighed and turned to get my grocery bags.

Robert laid the edger down. "Let me help you, Miss Martha."

"Bless you." I hadn't the strength of a newborn those days. He grabbed all five of my bags with one hand and jogged in front of me to get the door. "Lemonade?" I offered, once we were inside.

"Oh no, thank you, ma'am, I've got to get back to work. You need any help with your yard?"

My heart slipped in a sad direction as I pondered the boy. The man. He was about twenty-five, weighed over two-fifty, so tall he ducked going through doorways as a matter of habit.

I barely had enough for the phone bill but money was starting to look less and less important. "My beds sure do need weeding," I said. "And spread some mulch. I know you can make it look nice out front."

Too tired to put my groceries away, I lay down on the couch for a rest, until the phone rang. My spirits sagged when I saw it was Isabella with her dutiful-daughter weekly call. Is the average mom pleased to hear from her lovely daughter who lives in Charlotte in a million-dollar mansion with her perfect preacher husband and brilliant infant? Yes, of course she is.

Me, not so much.

"Hi, darling," I said, drumming up a bit of vocal enthusiasm.

"Mom, how are you?" Isabella meant, *Are you sober?* I hadn't told her about my health problems because she would imply they were divine retribution for my lifestyle.

"Good, I'm very good. How are you?" I braced myself.

"You got the package, right?"

Take a moment to imagine what a wealthy daughter might send to her cash-strapped mom. A fruit-and-cheese arrangement, perhaps, with a selection of fancy crackers and soups. A gift card for a dog groomer—my mutt's appropriately named Scruffy. Or what I really need: a note that says "please send me the roofer's bill once he's fixed that leak into your bedroom."

But Isabella's package had contained religious tracts. Flimsy paper booklets, the end of the world (coming soon!!!), the wages of sin, who gets into heaven and who doesn't. She'd underlined passages and written in the margins: *It's never too late. So important. His love will save you.*

"Thank you," I said, gritting my teeth. "Very thoughtful."

"Jesus loves you, Mom, no matter what you've done."

She didn't know the half of what I've done. Perhaps Jesus did, though. "I'm glad to hear that, honey. Kiss the baby for me." And a prayer wouldn't hurt either. I hung up, sighed, and turned to Scruffy for some puppy love. Though shaggy bangs covered his dark expressive eyes, he managed to find my face for a sloppy kiss. Why did Issy's calls make me feel so lonely? My bones ached as my thoughts skittered from one regret to another.

Coulda been a better mom, not shuffled Issy off to her dad's to be indoctrinated by his holier-than-thou second wife.

Shoulda gone to college. Was having too much fun pouring drinks at Spanky's.

Woulda been happier (and wealthier) after my divorce if I hadn't married Trevor on the rebound. Trevor was smooth as glass, confident, and charming. How was I to know he made a living scamming snowbird seniors? Seasonal work. Each May he'd come back to North Carolina for six months. We were currently separated; neither of us could afford the price of a divorce.

Regrets, I had a few. I closed my eyes, tried to clear my brain and dozed off until my doorbell rang.

"Come see, Miss Martha," Robert said. He'd trimmed the holly hedge, weeded the flower bed by my front steps and even planted impatiens, red, pink, and white. With dark mulch, mine was the nicest house on the street. "I'll water these the next few days," hc said. "No charge."

"Wonderful job, Robert." I paid him fifty dollars plus cost of the supplies. Mostly in quarters and ones, but he was happy, trotting home to show his mother.

I was putting my groceries away, slowly, when Annie knocked on my back door and walked right in, bearing a box. She's built like a fireplug, a look tempered by abundant black hair, dimpled chin, and a rosebud mouth currently set in a frown. Awash with joy at the sight of my friend, I wrapped my arms around her for a full minute. "I have no words," I breathed into her ear. "Missed you."

She took my face in her hands. "You didn't tell me you were getting chemo. And look at those cheekbones—you're not eating enough. Here, I made you some cupcakes."

I opened the box and gasped. "These are beautiful!" Each fat cupcake was perfectly swirled with frosting and decorated—blue with a white daisy, lime-green with chocolate hearts, lavender with silver sprinkles. Just seeing them lifted my spirits.

"Made with cannabis butter. I hear it helps with chemo. Don't tell Robert." She took over, efficiently sorting my groceries into fridge, pantry, fruit bowl.

"Oh my God, Annie, pot cupcakes. You are the best friend ever. And I'm sorry about Smitty."

"Not to worry. You did me a big favor, actually. Now taste one. I'm on a diet, can't even sample them. They're low dose but *go easy.*" She creased each grocery bag and folded it into a rectangle.

It was hard to decide. "What's this one?" White frosting speckled with orange zest and shaved chocolate.

"Chocolate cake, orange-infused buttercream." Annie picked up a pencil and started wandering through my house, making notes. I wasn't too curious, being occupied with *going easy.* Meanwhile, the cannabis (which I couldn't taste) soothed my stomach, the chocolate and orange fired up my brain's pleasure centers, and this homemade gift eased my soul.

"Robert told me you were laid off," I said. "You could sell these online. Minus the pot."

"I've thought about it. Takes cash, honey. Licenses, website, supplies. We're barely existing on my unemployment." She shrugged, and her face looked worn. My moment of happiness faded as I realized how little I could do for Annie in return.

Over the next few days neighbors dropped by. People I knew by sight, from brief chats at the Wishy, from patting their dogs when I was out with Scruffy.

Peter Jensen pushed his wife's wheelchair right up to my front steps. I'd never met her before. He'd always come to the Wishy by himself, towing a shopping cart of dirty laundry. He was a gentle quiet man. She was—well, neither.

"I'm Rosie," she said. "You've never met me because he can't hardly push me up the street in this thing." She pounded on the arms of her wheelchair. I murmured some pleasantry. "They sawed off my foot, you see?" She lifted the wool throw covering her legs, revealing a stump wrapped with stretchy bandages. "Diabetes. Couldn't afford the supplies, the food. But now it's the medical bills killing us, phew." She eyed me suspiciously, like I might be after her husband. Ha.

I wondered why they were here. To make me appreciate my feet?

"We brought you something," Peter said.

Rosie handed me a package wrapped in tissue paper. "I can't help or cook you nothing. But this I do."

I open the package. Inside, four knitted beanie hats, in pastel shades, variously trimmed with buttons, a tassel, ribbon. I blinked back a spurt of tears at her thoughtfulness. "Oh, Rosie, thank you."

"I picked colors for your skin tone," she said. "You're a spring. Or were." Referring no doubt to my sickly hue and lack of locks. "Will be again."

Dawn showed up later. She was a fifty-ish woman who always talked with her hand covering her mouth because her teeth were blackened, crooked, or missing, like Rosie's foot.

"Can't afford a dentist," she'd told me. She was renting a room from Peter and Rosie and looking for work. "But it's hard to get hired when you can't smile at people. Can't hardly let them see you talk." She asked to borrow Scruffy for an hour. He went willingly—he never met a stranger he didn't adore. She brought him back bathed and trimmed, with a jaunty red bow in his hair. This time I took deep breaths and didn't weep; I was getting used to kindness.

The next day I was at the Wishy, a no-longer scruffy Scruffy at my feet and a pink tasseled hat warming my skull, when Annie came in and asked me for the key to my front door.

I held it up. "Why?"

"Just trust me."

"I don't want you going in my house. It's a mess." I'd been too exhausted to wash dishes, hang up clothes, or vacuum. Dog hair was second only to dust bunnies in square foot coverage.

"Relax." She took the key and left.

I settled down to counting my week's take, wondering what Annie wanted to do in my house. Maybe she was going to leave me another half-dozen pot cupcakes, bless her little baker's heart. I tried to think about what I could do for her in return, or for Rosie and Dawn. Maybe a Wishy Washy gift card.

I came home to a sparkling clean house. My clothes had been washed, ironed, and put away. Gone were the dog hair and dust bunnies. The kitchen counter, normally strewn with dirty dishes and unread mail, was scrubbed clean. Someone had even washed my windows and arranged a bouquet of tulips on the dining table. I knew those tulips—they came from Celina Robles' front yard. She and her husband José worked all hours selling fish tacos from their food truck. I called her to say thank you.

"Martha, you are very welcome. I hope you are not offended that I clean your house?"

Words failed me. Finally I managed to say, "Of course not.

You didn't go out in your truck today?"

"Oh no, is broken. Something about engine rod throwing. So you see I have plenty of time and cleaning is easy for me. Look in your oven, we put some tamales."

Those damn tears. I choked out a "gracias" before checking the oven. Finding not only chicken tamales, but also some little tortilla things filled with apples and drizzled with Nutella. How did she know Nutella was my favorite condiment?

Oh, right. Annie. The woman was born to organize.

Lest I fail to mention—someone had fixed my roof too. I didn't know who.

The next morning I spent a half hour making up my sallow face into almost-pretty, getting ready for my weekly trip to the bank, looking forward to flirtatious innuendoes with the extremely hot teller Joshua, a thirty-something with manly stubble.

At the bank, I was filling out a deposit slip when a brouhaha broke out. Annie's son Robert wanted to cash a check he'd received from a client.

Joshua sounded apologetic. "Sorry, sir. We can't cash a third-party check for more than your account balance. Bank policy."

Robert was clenching his jaw, snorting through his nose, and working up to something he'd regret. I didn't blame him one bit—the raging unfairness of institutional coldness grabbed my attention. On impulse I reached around Robert and handed my bag of change and small bills to Joshua. "Put this in his account," I said.

Joshua looked startled, then at Robert for affirmation. The crazed look in Robert's eyes dimmed, was replaced by—tears? This six-foot man, tough as nails, tattooed with serpents and eagles and Semper Fi, rubbed his eyes. "Nicest thing...I'll pay you back next week." he mumbled.

It occurred to me he had probably fixed my roof; I'd seen him on top of his own house nailing down shingles. "No, no. Keep it," I said. Joshua started counting quarters, tension dissipated, Robert gave me a hug, like a cuddle from a grizzly. Need I say how good that felt? If I'd kept the money, it would've gone to pay my VISA bill, no happy feelings for anyone. But here I bought a smile and a hug with it. A new sensation, a bit of joy. When you don't have a future, what's money for?

That's when I decide to start robbing banks.

I didn't intend to get caught. Not that I would've minded much—hello, free health care—but I had goals to meet first. I made a plan.

The bank had to be at least thirty miles from my house. It needed to have ample parking, a layout so I could make a quick getaway. The bank itself: not crowded—I didn't need witnesses or heroes who might interfere. A weekday morning to miss the lunch crowd, the closing rush.

The night before, I stole a license plate from a random car in a grocery store parking lot. How often do you check whether you still have a license plate? Never, right? The next morning, I screwed the stolen plate onto my beige Camry, the most common car in America. Every third car is a beige Camry.

I put on brown baggy pants and a baggier top, grabbed a small pillow for stuffing and a wig of short white curls. I'd bought an assortment of white wigs—chemo gave me an excuse. I slathered on an exfoliating facial mask that drew my skin into wrinkled cracks.

My target: a branch bank in a Winston-Salem shopping center. I parked in a quiet corner, tucked the pillow into my waistband, straightened my wig. Orange lipstick, a fake wart on my chin, and a fake grenade in my pocket— I was ready to rob and roll. Hunched over a little, walked kind slow. There's no one more invisible than a respectable granny.

Invisible, that is, until I reached the head of the line, showed the teller my metal pineapple, my pinkie tucked in the ring-pull, and handed her a note: *No bait, no dye pack. Just twenties, fifties, and hundreds, missy, all you got, spread 'em out where I can see 'em. Thank you very much and have a nice day.* ☺

The teller frowned. "Is this a joke?" she said.

"No, don't be rude." I waggled the grenade at her and she grew pale, got busy pulling bills out of her drawer.

"On the counter first," I said, "then slide them over here." I lowered my voice, spoke hoarsely.

She followed directions, I stuffed bills into a paper bag, and a minute later I walked out with over six thousand dollars. No one followed me as I got into my car and drove out of the lot, onto I-40 for the drive home. Trembling a little from thrill and adrenaline, I patted the bag. "I have plans for you," I said.

A video of my robbery was on the News at Ten. Exciting! The security camera had filmed a roundish elderly woman. Very wrinkled with a noticeable wart. My own daughter wouldn't have recognized me.

I washed off wrinkles and the wart, dusted my eyelids with smoky eyeshadow, and took the bills to my bank. I handed them to Joshua. "Will this buy me a night with you?"

"Martha, I would pay *you.*" He winked. "Laundering real cash today?"

"That's right. Give me half of that in a cashier's check." Neither of us mentioned that my deposit was four times the usual amount.

A few days later, entering a bank for the second robbery, I looked entirely different. Black leather jacket, tweed skirt, black boots. White hair in a severe bob, lots of red lipstick and too much blush. Same grenade and note, however. Why change what worked? I escaped with four thousand plus change. Bought another cashier's check, deposited the rest, and went home to bed. The chemo still took its toll, though Annie's cupcakes helped with the worst symptoms.

For the next four banks I was variously a hippy with long white hair wearing a tie-dye caftan; an old lady lumberjack in one of Trevor's flannel shirts and red suspenders; a stylishly unconventional senior in leopard-print leggings, a crocheted tunic, and braids; and a punk granny, all in black, with a purple stripe in my white hair, showing cleavage and a dolphin tattoo.

A website went up with all my robbery videos and soon I even had my own hashtag. I'd never had so much fun. Not even when I was drinking. And the best came next.

I started spreading the cash around, anonymously. After each robbery, one of my neighbors would make a pleasant discovery.

In his driveway, Robert found a gently used Ford van, painted shiny orange, with *Robert's Handyman Services No Job Too Big or Small* in green. On the front seat was a gift card to a home improvement store for $2,000, for tools. I was walking Scruffy when he came out of his house. The look on his face was priceless.

A motorized wheelchair was delivered to Rosie's house. In a side pocket she found a cashier's check for $2,000 with an anonymous note directing her and Peter to hire Robert to build them an entrance ramp and revamp their bathroom. I met her tooling down the street. As she bubbled about her new-found independence, I felt something new and tender inside. I didn't know a word for it. Like an ache was gone.

Dawn received a phone call from a dentist. Her dental implants were paid for; did she want to make an appointment? She was so excited when she told me. "As soon as I can smile, I'm going to call all the vets in town and offer my services as a dog groomer. Will you give me a reference?"

"You bet," I told her. "So will Scruffy."

José and Celina's mobile food truck disappeared. They didn't report it stolen—no insurance—which was just as well, because three days later it re-appeared, freshly painted, with a rebuilt engine, new tires and brakes, a new fryer. They parked their truck outside the Wishy, and I was the first customer, asking for three apple Nutella taquitos.

A package of business cards, brochures, boxes, and bags—

all decorated with a charming logo for Annie's Cupcakery and containing the link to her new website—was delivered to Annie's door. A $4,000 cashier's check for a computer, start-up supplies, and a social media consultant was icing on the cake, so to speak. I was visiting her when she opened it. It was so much fun to watch her go through the box, squeal at each little design detail. After a while she grew quiet and gave me an odd look. "A good fairy has moved to Oak Leaf Court," she said.

"I know! And I'd like to place the first order. A dozen assorted cupcakes. You know, the ones with the *special* ingredient." I shipped them to Issy, warning her not to let the baby have any.

So my goals had been achieved, I hadn't been caught, the chemo had bought me some time. My hair had grown back into sort of a curly pixie, and I'd gained weight, thanks to Nutella taquitos. My cheeks were rosy, my step was light. All was well—as well as possible, anyway—in Martha Sue Bly's world.

Until it wasn't.

The first of May. Annie and I were in my kitchen taste-testing her latest creation, tiramisu cupcakes. "Someone's gotta do it," I joked as I inhaled vanilla bean cake with marscapone frosting, dusted with cocoa. We were having fun, exchanging stories about Smitty, our ex-in-common, when the front door opened and my almost-ex Trevor walked into my house. "Martha Sue, sweetheart!" he said. "Your hair is different. I like it."

Trevor makes an excellent impression with his dark floppy hair, broad shoulders, sapphire eyes. Annie sat up a little straighter and I heard her hum until I whispered, "He's a sociopath. Watch and learn."

I accosted my husband. "Uh, you heard of calling? Or even knocking?" I was feeling sassy. Joshua had asked me to run away with him when he took my deposit that morning.

"It's my house too, remember?" Trevor smiled at Annie. "Nice to meet you, darlin'."

"Not exactly. I make the payments."

"According to North Carolina law—" here Trevor cleared his throat, his intro to all pompous pronouncements. I braced myself. "Half," he said, lowering his head and glaring at me. Just the one word, like I'd know what he meant. I felt cold all over as a stiletto of fear pierced me. Could he know about the robberies? How? All my fun vanished and I asked Annie to come back later because Trevor and I had to discuss some things in private.

She gave me a look—*are you sure?*—and when I nodded yes, she left.

Trevor wasted no time in stating his objective. "You owe me half of everything. Community property, right? I also want my red suspenders and blue flannel shirt back."

Oh no. I'd been so careful to disguise myself, then he'd recognized the lumberjack outfit I wore at bank #4. His clothes. *Dummy!* "I don't know what you're talking about."

"Of course you do, Grenade Granny."

He was right. Though blackmail was a felony, so was robbing banks. "I've given the money away, to my neighbors who've helped me out because I've been sick." I didn't want tell him the details of my illness. Trevor's attempts at fake sympathy would nauseate me.

"Then you need to hit one more, don't you? Make enough to give me my share?"

I sighed, feeling lower than the day I got my diagnosis. "I guess so. Give me a couple of weeks."

"I'll be on your doorstep in two days. Twenty thousand in cash is perfectly acceptable."

So I geared up for one last haul. This time I donned a white pageboy wig, black wrap dress, padded bra, high heels and sunglasses. I was hardly invisible granny but the hair covered much of my face, the glasses hid my eyes, and I added some fake teeth to give me an overbite. I could see the headlines...Grenade Granny Goes Glam. The trembling teller gave me nine thousand dollars, the biggest haul yet.

On my way out of the parking lot, I pulled off the wig and removed the teeth, then stopped at a fast food restaurant to strip off my dress and bra and slip into shorts and sandals. All the bank's money went into an envelope for Trevor.

In a cloud of anxiety I walked up to the Wishy and collected the bills from the change machine, quarters from the washers and dryers. The place was busy, but no one from Oak Leaf Court was there. Maybe they'd all bought washers and dryers with their newfound prosperity. I was frantic with worry over Trevor. Paying him blackmail money might just whet his appetite for more. And if I balked and he told the police I was Grenade Granny, they might figure out where the money had gone. Scandal would rain down on Oak Leaf Court. I had nowhere to turn.

I dabbed on mascara and a red lippy and went to the bank with my regular deposit. My unhappiness must have showed on my face, because Joshua frowned. "Say it's not true," he said, counting my money. "That you've found someone else and you're dumping me." His hazel eyes studied me.

I made an effort. "There will never be anyone else. You smell too good, like pine and lemon and the sea."

"Then what's wrong?"

"Nothing, I'm fine." I forced a smile but he didn't return it. He handed me the deposit slip, on which he'd drawn a pair of hearts linked by an arrow.

For the first time in a year, I felt desperate for a drink. But alcohol wouldn't have cured my ills, only created more problems. I went home and waited for Trevor to arrive on my doorstep.

He never came.

Trevor had been murdered. His body was found that night, underneath the stadium seating at a Greensboro high school. He'd been stabbed four times in the back. Estimated time of death, late morning, so I had an alibi—I'd been seen in the Wishy and at the bank. Not that I was a suspect—why should I be?

His other wife wasn't a suspect either. Yes, it turned out that Trevor was a bigamist with a wife in Florida, which partly explained his six-month absences. She and I commiserated over our similar miserable Trevor-experiences. A detective flew to Palm Beach to interview a few of Trevor's angry scammed seniors, but finally concluded it must have been a mugging, since Trevor's wallet and phone were missing.

I didn't believe it was a mugging, or a scamming victim. I suspected who killed Trevor. And I was grateful.

A week later, on the Riviera Maya. Joshua and I reclined in a private cabana, avoiding the heat of the day, drinking pisco sours. Mine was virgin, but nonetheless tasty. Also tasty was Joshua, who turned out to be even sexier once he emerged from the bank. I'd shown him the ad for this resort as a joke but he thought I was serious, and maybe I was. And here we were, me and my boy-toy.

"Pour me another, please," I said. "All those quips about money laundering. How did you know?"

"I'll tell you but you won't like it." He handed me the drink and rested his hand on my thigh. His hand was warm and brown and very capable. "I recognized you in the first video."

"What? I was invisible granny with a wart!"

"You looked right at the camera at one point. I saw your eyes. These eyes." He leaned over and kissed my closed eyes, left, right. "I didn't know why, but I remembered when you gave Robert your money, and I thought...you were a woman on a mission."

I inhaled his smell, pine and the sea. "Why didn't you turn me in?"

"Guess I liked your mission. Spread happiness."

"Until Trevor showed up, it was working." I told him about Trevor's murder. "Someone saved me."

"Who?"

I remembered how Annie left my house the day Trevor threatened to blackmail me. Did she go home? Or lurk under my kitchen window to listen to us talk? I thought about Annie's amazing organizational skills on my behalf, getting my good neighbors to clean my house, fix my roof, knit me pretty caps, groom Scruffy, cook delicious foods that I could eat, thanks to her pot cupcakes. I thought about the morning Trevor was killed, how none of those neighbors were in the Wishy Washy. What else, who else, had Annie organized?

"It doesn't matter," I said. "Let's go for a swim." I took his hand in mine and we walked across the white sand, into a sparkling turquoise sea.

Praying to the Porcelain God
Lori Armstrong

The squeak of a key turning in the lock echoed through the quiet room, yet she remained motionless.

She knew the drill by now. Wait, stay silent, and pray.

Still, she didn't stop the quick shudder of anticipation when the door opened and his footsteps shuffled across the tile. In the pristine silence the tiny sound became deafening. No white noise was allowed. Nothing registered in the cavernous house but the unsteady clamoring of her heart. She realized if she heard that rapid fire *lub-dub, lub-dub*, he'd punish her. He expected peace and quiet. A gentleman, he claimed, rarely raised his voice.

He wasn't a gentle man.

Eyes downcast, she leveled her breathing. And waited.

He inspected her first, before ridding himself of the stench of the piety of the world in which he worked with gallons of hot, purifying water.

He crept across the carpet with the stealth of a jungle cat seeking prey, lingering behind her, batting at her hair. Sometimes he examined her nails for minute specks of dirt. Upon declaring her filthy, he then scrubbed her fingers until the cuticles turned bloody. If her scalp appeared unclean, he'd dunk her head in the stool.

Tonight he took his time. But she knew he couldn't find fault. Everything was perfect: *she* was finally perfect, even when he'd told her repeatedly, in his patronizing, dulcet tone, she'd never been the woman he'd wanted.

Tonight that would change.

His fetid breath drifted across the nape of her neck, damp and sticky as a dirty sponge. She lowered her eyes as he began to slowly circle the table, searching for proof of her insubordination. When he clapped his hands loudly next to her ear, she didn't flinch.

Did her obedience please him?

No. It never did.

He slid into the captain's chair across from her; the marble between them gleamed as black as his mood.

The table had been scrubbed to a high sheen as was required. He insisted cleanliness was next to godliness.

He wasn't a god.

"Audra," he murmured on an exigent sigh.

Don't look up, don't look up, she whispered the mantra inside her own head, fearful even her private thoughts were thunderous. But the pull to seek his approval was too strongly ingrained. She glanced up and met his dark, taciturn stare.

First, he said quiet disapproval with his eyes. Then with his fists.

Yes. She knew the drill. Wait. Stay silent. Pray.

Except tonight, she refused to pray. It never did any good.

The first incident happened on their one month anniversary. A little wine, a little song, and she'd accidentally charred his steak. She'd actually laughed.

Then punch drunk had taken on a whole new meaning.

After she'd vomited in the bathroom, he'd become enraged in that eerie, hushed manner, taunting her; *Even praying to the porcelain god wouldn't save her from his punishment.*

The penalty had to fit the crime, he'd admonished, forcing her to scrub the toilet blindfolded with undiluted bleach until her fingers had cracked, her flesh peeled nearly to the bone. He believed himself to be a dispenser of justice.

He wasn't a fair man.

Yet, he'd never marred her face, blackened her eyes, or broken her nose. He made certain to hide his marks of possession where only he could admire them. Swollen patches of flesh where he'd pinched until her fair skin protruded in ugly bumps, the red slap of his hand prints on her stomach and buttocks, the crusted skin where his nails scored her until she'd bled, remained out of sight—out of mind.

The neat rows of bite marks were worse in the winter, because they could be hidden under heavy layers of clothing.

He'd been particularly proud of his Valentine's Day gift; a ring of sorts—a ring of purplish black bruises resembling tribal tattoos which circled her upper arms. They lasted two full weeks, much longer than a dozen red roses.

She knew he wasn't to blame, but she hadn't bothered to tell another soul. Who'd believe her? He was beloved, a gentle man, a quiet man, a godly man, a fair man. At first she'd been his equal, a woman reared in a respectable church-going family. With no history of familial abuse, she didn't fit the societal mold, a young, broken girl so desperate for love and attention she'd gotten sucked into a familiar cycle. No, she'd been unlucky enough to start a new cycle all her own.

But tonight that cycle would end.

The promise of summer hung outside her sparkling windows; short skirts, short sleeves, and for her, a short temper.

She fondled the gun perched on her lap. No silencer. Giddy, loud laughter burst forth on the inside. She envisioned red splatters on the spotless white shower curtain before his blood swirled down the drain. Afterwards, she wouldn't bother cleaning up.

Praying to any god—porcelain or otherwise—wouldn't help him.

No. Tonight he'd be the man *she'd* wanted all these years; not a quiet man, not a gentle man, not a godly man, not a fair man.

A dead man.

Childhood's Hour
Karen E. Salyer

Words are weapons. Through the canvas of the tent come swipes of inquiry about creditors and Mr. Allan's failed business venture. Stunned silence follows. Mrs. Allan responds to her tormentor in the local cadence, slow, and melodic, with lengthy details of seasickness. Both women oblivious to the listener so close yet unseen. Ren blinks away sweat, wonders how long she will go on. Brisk business from passers-by began mid-morning, sparse now in the Indian summer heat. A makeshift venue situated across the street from St. John's Church. The others have set up stalls which flank the tent on the grassy common: Maggie with her packets of herbs to be mixed with wine for curing ailments of body or heart, Louis's deceptively simple games of chance. Harvest Faire, they call it. Not the gathering of grain to be celebrated, rather the fleecing of Richmond sheep.

"So I endured a month's voyage after five years of homesickness. Oh, here's my Eddy. He thrived onboard. Learned a number of sailor's songs, some quite rude. Eddy is a brilliant pupil, excels at Latin and French. Writes verses in English as well. He should recite a poem."

"Ma, I know how he moves the pea from under the walnut shell. A fine chance to double my pocket money, please may I?"

The harsh-voiced woman interrupts the budding poet and gambler. "I must speak with the sexton about sinners practicing deceit on our Lord's doorstep. Good afternoon."

Words are coins, likely fewer earned today. The old tabby will have them all gone, with small profit to show. Ren hears the rustling churn of petticoats followed by an indistinct whispered exchange between mother and son.

A thin curtain marking the tent's entrance flutters before the boy pushes through. The pair's clothes are finely cut and a necklace gleams in candlelight from the table. Ren motions Mrs. Allan to the cushioned chair opposite while he perches on a crate, careful not to move much and risk the rough edges. Customers must have their comforts.

"Welcome, madam and young sir." Ren hears his own accent slipping, drifting. Years of roaming the country and forgotten roles played.

The woman tilts her face up at the boy, and he produces silver from his embroidered best pocket. She tugs at her glove. "I'm indulging Eddy. My little gentleman insists having our fortunes told will be a rare treat."

Whiff of laudanum when she opens her mouth. Mrs. Allan has that look about her, the kind who makes illness her constant companion. Eddy twists his grimace into a squint. Her interest rather than his has brought them. The boy seems sturdy enough, though slight in build. His large gray eyes are dark-lashed and inquisitive in a face pretty enough for a girl.

Ren examines the woman's hand with studied care. Palmistry owes more to dramatic art than any science. Reference to her husband's devotion brings a frown. Assertion no other shipborne travel will be required of her, and she mutters softly in relief. Predictions of an unexpected inheritance and a large house requiring more servants brighten Mrs. Allan's demeanor. Vague hints for improved health or additional children since she desires neither.

Satisfied with her future, Mrs. Allan gestures for Eddy. "Your turn, pet."

He folds into the seat, flops both hands on the tabletop where they twitch like small trout. The challenge in Eddy's eyes a test which Ren does not plan to fail.

"You choose. Some say the future is shown in the right, the past in the left. Significance to be found in both."

"Will you charge double then? Last time, Ma's gypsy said the right hand read for men, while the left is read for women." Eddy's London drawl is pronounced. Time enough spent overseas for a child's speech to echo his former schoolmates rather than his Virginia neighbors. Left hand disappears under the table.

Ren glances at the faintly lined palm. "I see numerous trips in your future."

Eddy nods. "Over a great distance, I hope. Explore all of France and Greece and Russia, too. Join the military and lead soldiers into battle. Or become a pirate, like Captain Kidd and Blackbeard." The boy warms to the game of wishes.

"Your talent for languages will serve you well. And a fine singer is welcome anywhere."

Eddy gives a crooked grin and begins. Notes soar clear and sweet, with steady volume to reach the farthest listener. Chorus of seaman slang is more than a little obscene. A moment to speculate if the boy or his mother realize how much. *Not this mother. The dead one. Her voice.*

Singing as if Eliza has strolled over from St. John's graveyard; the resemblance alive in the boy's features while he performs. Ren does not believe in ghosts, yet fears them. It takes all his effort to tamp down an impulse to bolt, put as much distance as he can between himself and this revenant.

"Hush now." Mrs. Allan hovers over Eddy.

Surely Eliza's son observes Ren for what he is, a frightened man attired in a dress and shawl. Children often see through the pretense. Adults seldom look beyond their noses. The littlest ones might smile shyly; older ones would glance away in confusion. Eddy does neither, simply slants his gaze toward the crystal orb resting on the corner of the table. An old prop.

"Please accept my sincerest apologies. My son's manners lack—"

Not your son. Ren goes still and silent, his body an empty shell. Called back by the heavy thump of the glass ball rolling across the table in his direction.

"Gone into a trance, I think." The lilt of amused mischief is pure Eliza.

Thoughts turn into words leaping from Ren's mouth, "Your mam, I knew her. We shared the stage hundreds of times. Eliza married my best mate."

* * *

"She went straight to the sexton, and him to the vicar. Quoted our banishment, he did, 'Thou shalt not defraud thy neighbor, neither rob him.' Reckoned Maggie would fly at the churchman when he began another verse against divination and charms. Thank God, he turned on his coat-tail." Louis gives a shout of derision. "You're not drinking. Are you ill? Is that why you packed up early?"

Ren nods, knowing Louis prefers a lively companion in wine.

Louis continues, "Your final customers, the lady near wrestled her lad from your tent. Halfway to their carriage, he turned back and she started bawling. Tears halted him, secure as a chain. Been a day, all right." Louis sends him a sharp look. When he gets no response, he takes the bottle in hand. "I'll go then."

The room shrinks after Louis's departure. Ren levers open the window for a twilight breeze from the James River. Tobacco and coal carried out on ships, slaves conveyed in by other vessels. He turns away, uses a kerchief dipped in a pan of water to cleanse sweat and paint from his face. Sprawls across the narrow bed and finds his past on the map of stained ceiling.

He had located Eliza's flat stone marker yesterday. Already cracked and weather worn among the many graves on Church Hill. St. John's the place where forty-five years earlier, firebrand Patrick Henry had secured his fame by shouting, "Give me liberty or give me death." Ren heard only silence of the dead. Pushed aside wilted pansies with a scrape of his boot. Fallen to his knees and begged her forgiveness, behavior fit for their most celebrated melodrama. She answered by sending her son.

A scuffle outside in the passageway. Ren waits for the combatants to resolve their problem. October chill has crept into the room. Yells and the distinct sound of a body slammed against wood force him to leave his bed, crack open the door and bellow, "Leave off."

They stagger then untangle at the sight of Ren. His landlord's wife and the boy. Edgar Poe. He still wears the expensive clothes beneath a costume of tattered ill-fitting jacket, a dirty cap on the floor beside them. Child of actors, after all. Edgar exchanges outrage for bemusement when released with a parting shove.

"Caught him skulking. Trifle young for you, eh?" Her leer takes in Ren's nightshirt, the silvered black hair hanging like nautical ropes to his waist. She stumps downstairs.

Should have trusted terror. All we have in the end. Ren confronts the specter, sees instead a youngster puffed up with daring and driven by curiosity.

"How did you manage to find me?"

"When I returned, I found only the vicar. He cautioned me against consorting with your kind." That crooked grin again. "Offended by the herb peddler's wrath—she blamed him for not earning enough coins to spend in a certain tavern." He tilts his head. "Wasn't allowed inside. I waited nearby until the gaming man left that place. He came here but departed soon after. Spied you at the window." Edgar locks his gaze on Ren. "You knew my parents well."

Not exactly his earlier words, no. Ren says, "Wandering the streets after sundown invites danger enough for a man. A boy should be at home. The Allans know nothing of your absence?"

"Ma confined herself in her room with a headache. She takes my interest in my poor mother as an affront to her maternal care. Pa, uh, he is not home. I can guess where...." Words falter then increase speed. "I can run faster than any boy I know. I'm the best swimmer in all of Richmond. Not one can touch me."

Ren's first glimpse of the foolhardy father. Treacherous currents. He retreats to locate his trousers and pulls them on. Closes the window and adjusts the lamp, turns back to find the boy still in place. Makes no gesture of welcome.

Edgar shuffles a step inside the doorway. His eyes inventory the room: bed, battered trunk under the familiar table, and chair which Eddy and Mrs. Allan sat in how many hours ago, the fortune-teller's rags hung on a peg. Ren sits on the mattress. Rotates his shoulder in an attempt to ease the ache, penalty for hauling furniture about.

"Can you tell me even one memory? I know little of them,

their lives together. I have often wondered. Please, if you would do this small thing for me, please." Edgar's abrupt switch to wheedling might work with Mrs. Allan. Ren almost snaps: never beg. Ask. Bargain when necessary, with no trace of desperation.

"The last time I saw Eliza was Christmastime, eleven, no, twelve years past. Met her in a Boston shop. Lovely as ever, she was. Pleased to be living in one place. Carried a small boy on her hip, introduced the tot as Henry. Her cloak didn't conceal the babe growing her belly. She happily shared names already chosen. Rosalie for a girl. Yours, if another son."

Edgar's cheeks grow pink at his plain words. Ren declines to include his second sighting of Eliza, later that same day, towing her drunkard of a husband through a frigid corridor of snow. He points at the trunk. "You'll find memories enough there. Go on."

Edgar practically dives into Pandora's Box. The crystal ball emerges in his hands. He passes it back and forth with the ease of a juggler. Seats himself cross-legged on the floor, leaning forward.

"Our first play together was a patchwork of stolen Shakespeare and the author's own imagining. Eliza's role one of several star-crossed lovers. I wore velvet robes of a wizard. She would dare to snatch the crystal from my grasp high above her head. She was a small lass. Obliged to leap while I turned one way and another. Our dance carried us around the stage. One night I dropped the damned thing. Eliza scrambled after, barely able to contain her laughter. Watched it vanish into the front row where several fellows fought to retrieve and return the prize to her. We added that bit to future performances. A wonder it survived in one piece."

Never has Ren had a more attentive audience. He describes Eliza in glowing detail, her willingness to work long hours on and off the stage without complaint. Her fondness for teacakes and solving riddles. Edgar is entranced. He cradles the glass as if to connect his touch with hers from long ago. Hunched over, the boy looks alone and lonely. Compelled to get up and rifle through the trunk, Ren offers a stack of playbills and yellowed newsprint. Edgar surrenders the ball to Ren and begins examining each page.

"I joined the company when Eliza was fourteen. We traveled Georgia, the Carolinas and Virginia circuits. She was a gifted dancer and singer, performing since the age of nine when she and her actress mother arrived in Boston from England. Knew dozens of parts in every sort of play."

Edgar looks up. "You called him your close friend. My father, David Poe. His father was a war hero, I expect he told you."

Ren is shaking his head before he recognizes the misunderstanding. How could the boy know? "Your mam was widowed before she married your father. Charles Hopkins was Eliza's husband, a player like her. Charley was the one."

"He died, too."

Much that does not need telling to a child. Eliza and Charley, both still in their teens, had come to Ren with a plan for their marriage of convenience. A decade older than Charley, Ren encouraged the scheme to thwart the troupe's new manager. The bastard harassed and humiliated Eliza and threatened to dismiss Charley for speaking against his lechery. Ren witnessed their marriage and watched them present the document. Their enemy turned his attention elsewhere with poor result. That girl's brother shot him.

"Did they have children?" Edgar conveys a mixture of dismay and hope for the existence of half siblings.

"No." They had three years before cholera took him. Ren can conjure up Charley's Irish purr of a voice. His face proves elusive, possibly because of his ability to transform it with the slightest change of expression. Charley was the finest actor Ren ever saw on the stage. Eliza always treated their arrangement as a small joke on the world outside their own. Never seemed to mind that Charley spent more nights in Ren's bed than in hers. Six months after Charley's death, though, she'd married David Poe.

"Where is your brother Henry?" Ren settles into the armchair.

"He lives with our grandparents in Baltimore. He writes

often. He has promised to visit in the spring. My little sister Rosalie—she's called Rose now—lives with the Mackenzies. They adopted her." His grim smile doesn't hide the resentment. Odd behavior for the Poe clan, to take in only the eldest grandson and heir. Edgar's accounting for Eliza's three orphans affects Ren. He plucks at his sleeve to hide the emotion.

"I've heard Ma and Pa argue, she says my name should be Allan, he says to wait." Jolted out of his self-absorption by a sudden realization. "What is your name?"

Ren takes up one of the playbills. Indicates a surname listed several lines below Miss E. Arnold. Mr. G. Renfro. "George is my Christian name. Most call me Ren."

"Your parents, they were not players?"

"Huh, my dad was a miner. Said I could go to the devil when I confessed my ambition to act. I left soon after."

"Pa says after I finish school I will work for him, at 'The House of Ellis and Allan.'" Exaggerated emphasis on the capital letters. "Have you seen their warehouses?" Edgar scowls. "They stink of tobacco."

No doubt Mr. Allan believes they reek of money. Or they did until recently; if the morning's overheard conversation can be interpreted. Ren suspects Mr. Allan's reluctance to adopt Edgar is based on prejudice against Eliza and David Poe's profession. Ren has spent enough years in southern cities to understand their citizens preserve tradition. Society patrons applaud and admire theatrical performers on Saturday evening, then despise the same people as disreputable and immoral on Sunday morning. Mr. Allan would view Edgar in the business-like manner of acquiring a mongrel pup over a pure-bred hound, to be watched carefully for defects in behavior.

"I follow him. When Pa leaves some nights, he does not go to his office as he says. He goes to them. His other family. A woman and a boy, near my size. He smiles and kisses them." Edgar stares into a shadowed corner of the room for a long minute then goes back to sorting the papers in his lap. Ren reserves comment. No doubt the boy has encountered gossip about a mistress. And he did track down Ren. Stalking his guardian might be more truth than imagining.

"Critics were not kind to my father. They filled my mother's notices with praise."

Ren snorts. "Critics aren't in the business of kindness. They couldn't help but notice she was more able and pleasing in her craft. The disparity between them was obvious." He must not go off on a rant about the boy's dead father. David Poe, who couldn't hit the mark, routinely forgot his lines or mumbled, then shouted abuse in response to jeers from the audience. "Your father had little acting experience." Or talent. If not for Eliza's sake, other players would have made life difficult for Mr. Poe. "They married and departed for Boston. She sent word later that I could find plenty of work there."

"Your name is not on these playbills, only theirs." Edgar holds two in each hand.

True, Ren had arrived in Boston nearly a month prior to his meeting with Eliza. "I paid my admittance, same as the rest. Thought to greet them backstage after their performance. I was struck by sudden indisposition." The boy seems familiar with the euphemism for drunkenness. "New England winters drove me south again. I heard occasional mention of Mr. and Mrs. Poe. Met an actor who'd been with them during their time in New York. Word of her passing reached me in the low country of South Carolina."

Weight of fatigue settles upon Ren. He smothers a yawn, sees Edgar catch it and mirror his gesture. The pages are tidied and neat when Edgar moves to return them to the trunk.

"Keep the lot. You've more need of them than me." Ren is finished with carrying the past. Edgar hugs the bundle beneath his coat. Stiffens his spine in what seems an effort to appear taller, older.

"I talk to her, too." Pauses. "You didn't see me. In the cemetery." He waits impassively for the effect of his statement.

Was the damned boy any place he was ever supposed to be? Then the meaning of what Edgar might or might not have overheard sinks in. No fear, no judgment of a confessed murderer in those gray eyes.

"I climb the oak tree next to the church. It's enormously tall. After I visit with her, I wait for sunrise. Or observe the stars. One summer evening, from that height, I watched a storm cloud pass over the river." He adjusts the dirty cap to a jaunty angle on his head. "Good-bye, Mr. Renfro."

Ren considers going after the boy, decides he needs no escort. Edgar will find his own way in the darkness. Unlike his father.

A second war with Britain had halted foreign trade and the economy. By early spring of 1813, enterprising American raiders switched their base from the Chesapeake Bay to various southern ports. Ren had abandoned Charleston for her less grand Carolinas sister, the port of Wilmington. Jacob's Run Tavern recommended as a congenial refuge for newcomers. The room filling up with people, all noise. Conversation around him punctuated a meal of shrimp chowder and ale.

"I understand the change from Royal Oak, with Royal Navy blockades all along the coast. New sign out front must've cost a pretty penny. Who is Jacob running from or chasing after?"

"Run means a stream, same as creek or branch. And Jacob's no privateer. Name of a local architect and builder. His slaves covered over the water with bricks years ago. A whole network of tunnels beneath our feet. All leading to the river."

"Hell's teeth, you've dribbled beer down my best shirt." The speaker rounded on the barman whose abject apologies testified to his own thespian history. His companion fixated on the underground, continued, "Smugglers must use them to their advantage. Why advertise."

"Jacob's Run is a legend hereabouts. It extends from Fourth Street to the docks. Patriot prisoners made good their escape that way from Cornwallis's dungeon in 1781. My grandmother told me. One was her distant cousin."

Gradually a loud voice of complaint had lifted above the din. Cursing his luck, not an uncommon practice, the primary source of the man's woe seemed a lack of money. The drinker beside Ren gave a sneery little hiss. "Dan Dilly himself. The muffin man."

Epithets earned from critics in New York. Ren had moved closer. David Poe was no longer handsome. And recently released from prison. Ren never got the straight of the offense; Poe's famous temper combined with drink brought the inevitable violence. Poe chose to squander his new freedom with blame for his parents and friends in shunning him, and his whore of a wife. Level of self-pity rose to a shout, "How many brats has she birthed in the years since I returned home to find her with child, not mine?"

Ren had followed him out the door. Into the alleyway, waited. Trailed Poe through a grid of streets all sloped downhill toward the water. The full moon slid in and out behind a curtain of clouds, dark, light, dark. Each step was akin to walking a checkerboard.

"Eliza is dead." Ren had no need to raise his voice, which carried as always.

Poe turned. "What?"

"She's gone. Well beyond a year in the grave, while you were away."

"Died in childbirth—what she deserved." His round face mottled with shadow. "I remember you. Never your bastard leastways." His laugh ugly. If Poe had feigned the slightest sorrow...Then again, he'd never been much of an actor.

Ren had leaned in, almost conversational. "Richmond Theater burned the day after Christmas, 1811. Called Boxing Day when I was a child. Fire began during a performance attended by six hundred people." The players' grapevine in Charleston had entwined the two tragedies. Eliza died a fortnight and four days prior. Ren's grief laid him bare when the details were sorted; to compare her fate from lingering illness to agony and flames. "Some seventy people perished, including the state's Governor."

David Poe's eyes had shone with avid interest. Aggressively inquisitive. Calling the false words from Ren.

"She was onstage when the first shouts came. Your sons playing backstage. They'd done the same many nights. A rain of burning scenery fell from above."

Force of will had propelled Ren forward until the man stumbled back, reeling. He must needs go that the devil drives. "Your bloodline ended with a pitiful trio of corpses found in the ruin. All charred together from the fire's heat. The air was thick with smoke and the smell of roasted meat."

"Not true. Not my boys, no." Poe's roar of anguish had answered at last. Silver flash and fierce hurt in Ren's shoulder. Poe launched himself sideways then Ren was the one falling, feet sliding under him on the cobblestones. Sparks not unlike those he'd described exploded inside his head followed by darkness.

He had awakened to a different texture of black. Not blinded exactly, more the complete absence of light. Foolish not to have anticipated David Poe's impulse to murder the messenger. Pain and the stench of sewage. Groans and retches echoed in his ears. *Be silent and listen, same six letters— answer to one of Eliza's little puzzles she'd loved.* A soft trickle close by, liquid onto the cold stone.

When Ren had been a little more aware of what was around him, he wondered if Poe simply assumed disposal of a corpse. Or had he hoped Ren would revive enough to feel the choking despair. Hazy recall of words about streams flowing through tunnels to the river. His fingers which lately explored his wounds and the slimed walls found the water. He would follow its direction.

Progress had been wretched and slow. Unable to stand to his full height, often forced to edge crab-like within the narrow space. Finally reduced to crawling on hands and knees. At one point, the tunnel closed in so that Ren had to suck in breath and slither through on his belly. His body pressed against smaller, furred ones who squealed and scrabbled away. Ren writhed in panic. Madness in the thoughts of himself as feast for rats in this pit forced him onward.

The air had changed first, freshening and heavier with humidity. Dimness transformed so subtly that his eyes ached from strain. Subterranean arches framed the gateway. He nearly fell through it, caught himself with his good arm. Pale dawn silhouetted ships along the wharves in the distance. A dying campfire. A whiskey jug half-hidden in the sand. Two people. Ren reached for a brick from a cairn formed with culls left behind by craftsmen. David Poe's companion fled, his face a mask of horror. Afterwards Ren had felt shivery and light-headed. The river called Cape Fear carried away the dead man. Well named, that.

Another Day, Another Murder
Kathleen Mix

Detective "Roc" Rozinski braked hard and steered his department-issue Crown Vic between the granite pillars at the main road, then up the winding drive of the dead man's estate. Close to the mansion, two familiar vans were parked diagonally on the groomed lawn. The coroner and crime scene units were already on scene.

To his left, a brisk November wind slammed waves born in the Atlantic against an unyielding seawall. He parked and grabbed his topcoat from the back seat. Twenty-five years ago, as a rookie patrol officer newly relocated to North Carolina from Florida, he'd enjoyed being outdoors on Beaufort's crisp fall mornings. Now his bones ached at the prospect of being bitten by wind-driven cold, even if he'd only have to endure the attack for the fifty-yard walk from his spot on the circular drive to the massive front doors of Seaspray Manor.

He climbed the ten steps to the entrance of the sprawling two-story, Spanish style house, nodded to the officer stationed at the door, and paused to don booties and gloves in the domed foyer. When he stepped into the office where the body still lay, the odor of recent violent death assaulted his nostrils.

Evidence collection was already well under way, and he hung back, waiting for the photo technician to finish recording the state of the room. Reluctant to waste a minute, Roc scrutinized the layout and furnishings of the office. Everything in the neat room screamed wealth and comfort. The victim's fully clothed body was slumped on an overstuffed, beige-leather sofa positioned opposite a glossy oak desk. Wooden tables at each end of the sofa held matching lamps. An oil painting that had to be four feet high and five feet wide occupied the wall behind the corpse. At the far end of the room, long shelves holding books, photographs, and memorabilia butted up against a six-foot long marble-topped bar. Behind the desk, a bank of windows lit the blood-splattered scene with bright, incongruous sunshine.

His gaze traveled back to the body partially hidden behind the county coroner, a competent man Roc had worked with dozens of times before. He itched to hear the details of this death but bit back the questions lining up in his head. He'd get a full report in due time.

The oil painting drew his attention again. The type might be called a landscape. Several oaks towered over an emerald lawn and dropped a stream of brown leaves as the branches shook in the wind. Beneath the trees, a lone man in workman's clothing labored with a rake, piling the leaves that blew away as quickly as he struggled to gather them together.

Roc snorted. The guy could rake forever and never make any progress. He might as well be a homicide detective. Over the years, the bodies had never stopped coming, and Roc had learned that, like the guy raking against the wind, his work would never be done.

The coroner secured bags over the victim's hands to preserve any evidence on the skin or under the nails, then stood and turned. His gaze landed on Roc. "Detective. You're certainly looking a little world-weary this morning."

Roc nodded. "Late night wrapping up my last case. What have we got?"

"Cause of death appears to be a single bullet to the right side of the head. On the surface, it looks like a suicide."

"And beneath the surface?"

The coroner shrugged his bony shoulders. "Maybe I'm just too suspicious. We shall see."

"Anything in particular poking your suspicion bone?"

"Maybe just envy and frustration. A billionaire is supposed to be on top of the world and the happiest guy alive. He could have anything he wanted. Why would he blow his brains out?"

Roc looked hard at the body. "We all have inner demons. Maybe his were more than he could handle." He met the coroner's gaze. "But just in case his demons were mortal, let me know what you find as soon as you can."

"Of course."

"What's our approximate time of death?"

The coroner glanced at his watch. "About nine hours ago. Between eleven and midnight would be my best guess."

"Thanks, Doc." Roc turned to a patrolman nearby. "Were you the responding officer?"

"Yes, sir."

"Who found our victim?"

A woman's voice came from behind Roc. "That would be me."

He turned and inspected the slender woman who stepped closer and extended her hand. Mid-thirties, maybe five foot two, short blonde hair pinned back away from her face, no obvious make-up but naturally attractive, chin up in such a way as to exude composure and confidence.

"I'm Margaret Appleton," she said. "I am—was—Mr. Mortensen's personal secretary and administrative assistant. I discovered his body when I came in at seven-thirty this morning."

He shook her hand. "Detective Rozinski, Ms. Appleton. I'm sorry for your loss."

"Thank you."

"Do you feel up to answering a few questions?"

"Of course. He was my employer. Naturally I'm saddened by his death. But our relationship was purely professional, so I'm not overly distraught."

No tears shone in her eyes. Roc had the urge to comment on her cool attitude but remained silent. The two things he hated most about working homicides were telling shocked families a loved one was gone and dealing with the people who lacked the decency to grieve the end of a human life. His distaste for those who couldn't care about the dead was part of what drove him to give every victim his honest best. Someone had to care. Although caring killed his soul and some victims were difficult to like, he would make darn sure that, whenever warranted, justice was done.

Studying Ms. Appleton, he reminded himself to reserve judgment when it came to those who appeared cold. Some truly didn't care, some pretended not to care, and some cared so deeply they'd been driven to murder. The trick was to get all the facts before drawing any conclusions.

He pulled out a notebook and pen and jotted down her name. "Do you know of any reason Mr. Mortensen would want to take his own life?"

"No. He has the usual business problems of a highly driven and successful man, but no crises or scandals, if that's what you're thinking."

"When was the last time you saw him alive?"

"Last night at eight-fifteen. I completed reviewing a contract for him and turned in my analysis before going home."

"Do you normally work that late?"

"No. The contract was late arriving, or I would have finished much earlier."

"Other than Mr. Mortensen, who was here when you left?"

"No one. He was alone."

Roc looked up from his notes. "No staff? Not even a cook or butler?"

"Everyone else leaves at seven. I leave when my work is finished and return before them in the morning to bring him his coffee at seven-thirty. The cook comes in about that time and has his breakfast ready precisely at eight. The housekeeping staff starts work at eight. His financial advisor reports at nine."

Roc glanced at his watch, and then the responding officer. "Has everyone reported in this morning?"

"Yes, sir. They're all in the parlor waiting to be interviewed."

Roc nodded his approval. "Anything else you can tell me that might be significant, Ms. Appleton?"

She sighed and gave him a sad smile. "Only that Mr. Mortensen was left-handed."

Roc stopped writing. "Left, you say?"

"Left."

He glanced at the body then gave Ms. Appleton another look. Her chin was quivering and she no longer seemed as composed.

The passing of Mr. Jonathan Oliver Mortensen officially became a homicide when the coroner announced his determination concerning manner-of-death. But Roc was already working the case. A left-handed man committing suicide didn't hold a gun to the right side of his head.

By the next morning, he'd interviewed every person who'd worked at the estate, viewed the deceased's autopsy, and made several calls to the evidence techs, hoping to prod them to work faster and provide him with a lead on the identity of the murderer. At noon, he had nothing but a throbbing headache to show for his efforts. He popped two aspirin and, for the second time this week, thought fondly of the option of retirement. He could pack it in any time. After twenty-five years on the force, he'd get a good pension. Why not move back to Florida and take up fly fishing? Why keep coming in every day and banging his head against the wall working cases where nothing made sense?

Lacking a good answer to either question, he put aside the retirement fantasy and moved forward with his investigation.

None of the deceased's employees or associates had seen or heard anything suspicious. No one had a concrete idea who had killed him. No one knew squat. Or so they said.

As Roc probed deeper with question after question, he made no attempt to hide his skepticism. A killer always made a mistake, and someone always knew something. He just had to find the key piece of evidence or data that would crack the case.

His best bet for finding the key seemed to be linked to Mr. Mortensen's business. He ran an empire built on the publication of a sexually explicit magazine he called a *journal of artistic expression* and had published several sex manuals for those seeking help with their techniques. What he defended as *art* was pornography pure and simple, but a stable of lawyers kept the monthly magazine issues coming despite the scorn and objections of hundreds of critics.

One of those critics could have wanted the publications stopped enough to kill the man who personally selected every word and image distributed by his printers. The big question was: of the many people who might have a motive, who also had means and opportunity?

Deciding to take a closer look around the estate and fill in some blanks, Roc called Ms. Appleton. "Would you be able to meet me at the crime scene at four this afternoon?"

"Of course. I'll do whatever I can to help."

At three thirty, Roc slid from his car and once again donned his topcoat. Waves walloped the seawall with a booming rhythm. The cutting wind still howled across the water and swirled around the house and outbuildings in the compound. Instead of easing as forecast, it seemed to have intensified.

He muttered a curse, flipped up his collar, and focused on his job. Cold wind or not, he had to examine the exterior of the house, imagine the killer's route in and out, and analyze the security. As he circled the huge house in a clockwise direction, the wind pushed at the back of his legs and cold dove down his neck. He shivered and felt like an old soldier weary from war.

He paused in his circuit. The bank of windows behind the desk in the victim's office included a door that opened onto a wide patio. The door showed no signs of forced entry, but Mortensen's staff had reported it was frequently left unlocked.

Roc shook his head in wonder. For a man so disliked by a large slice of the general public, his security had been seriously lax. The house had an alarm system that would alert the local police of a break-in, but it was rarely armed. Security cameras that should have monitored the doors and approaches to the house were aimed wrong. Lack of maintenance and vigilance had rendered the system ninety percent useless.

Obviously Mortensen hadn't been afraid. Or if he had been, he'd had a fateful or resigned attitude. His open-door policy seemed to say: if they want me bad enough, they'll get me sooner or later, so why try to hide? Someone had gotten him, so he'd probably been right.

Nothing else of significance jumped out at Roc as he completed his journey around the house, so he entered the front door and ducked under the yellow crime scene tape strung across the door to the victim's office. He stood inside the doorway with his attention focused on the spot where the body had been found.

Based on physical markers like dilated pupils and blood chemistry, the coroner believed Mortensen had been soundly sleeping just before he'd died. He'd been lying on his left side on the sofa when his killer had crept into the room, put a gun to his head, and fired. A gap in the blood splatter pattern revealed where the killer had stood by the sofa. As blood and brain matter sprayed into the air, his body had prevented the rug behind him, or her, from being stained. A trail of slightly disturbed droplets indicated the killer had exited through the door to the patio.

A lack of gunshot residue proved the gun with Mortensen's prints had been pressed into his hand post-mortem. Roc snorted at the lame attempt to fake suicide. The killer needed to watch more episodes of *CSI*. Any devotee of the program would know the deceased's hands would be tested for GSR.

He wondered about the killer: stupid, over-confident, or acting in a fit of temper? State of mind could be significant. He shrugged. His job had become more difficult as fictional and real-life crime shows instructed viewers in how *not* to leave evidence, so he was thankful for the physical clues left by a killer who watched too little TV.

Roc pictured a figure standing over the victim, firing his or her gun, lifting the dead man's hand and pressing each limp finger onto the gun grip, then letting the gun drop and land where it may. A human life ended in an instant. A bold killer savoring or regretting the thing he'd done.

Nausea churned in Roc's stomach. No one deserved to die violently no matter what his perceived sins in life, but there was never a shortage of new victims. He glanced up at the man working in the painting hanging over the sofa. "Damn frustrating, isn't it? We keep plugging away, but just like the wind, the killers never seem to stop."

A female voice came from behind him. "That's one of the wonderful things about art. Everyone sees something different. I see the workman as representing the depths of human persistence, not frustration."

Roc turned toward the speaker, spotted Ms. Appleton standing on the far side of the crime scene tape, and shook his head. "Looks to me like he's been working forever and about to burn out. Seeing persistence is a positive slant. Maybe I should buy a copy of this thing and put it over my desk. It might remind me not to be so negative."

"I doubt you'll find a print available for your office. Mr. Mortensen paid nine point six million for *The Groundskeeper* at a Paris auction a week ago, and works of its stature are rarely copied."

Roc whistled and looked back at the painting. "He must have really liked it to fork over that kind of cash."

Ms. Appleton shrugged. "He might have loved it, might have hated it. Either way, the purchase was strictly an investment. An investment one his advisors strongly disapproved of, I might add."

"This advisor didn't think it was worth the price?"

"Not at all. It's a famous piece and well-worth nine point six. The advisor, Mr. Partesean, simply didn't want Mr. Mortensen to put money into art. He felt it would be short-sighted."

"How so?"

"He argued that any painting hung in this house would be a poor investment because it was likely to decrease in value as a result of being associated with Mr. Mortensen's business. The dirt would rub off, so to speak. He phrased his objection much more diplomatically, of course. But that was the gist."

Roc pursed his lips. "Interesting." He thought about that for a second, then squared his shoulders and moved on. "Thanks for meeting me, Ms. Appleton. I asked you here because I was hoping you could help me out. I've been wondering who would know the layout of the house and grounds beside the help and your boss's business associates. Did you keep a record of Mr. Mortensen's guests? People who have been in the house recently?"

She nodded. "I have meeting minutes and guests lists, of course. But I'm afraid they won't help much."

"Why's that?"

"Twice in the last year, major magazines have done features on Mr. Mortensen. He gave the writers unlimited access and free rein to include anything they chose, including photos of the estate, inside and out."

Roc's stomach twisted like a pretzel. "I suppose they told the world his schedule and habits, too."

She smiled. "Right down to the detail that he spent nights alone and frequently slept in his office."

"Both these magazines have a wide circulation?"

"Naturally. And for anyone who didn't subscribe, the articles were also posted online."

Roc sighed and ran his fingers through the thinning hair on the top of his head. "I'm feeling my frustration building again."

Ms. Appleton blew out a breath. "Sorry to discourage you."

He tried another tack. "Would you be able to make me a list of the people who criticized your former boss most vigorously?"

"Certainly. I'll get started on it right away. Unfortunately, a list like that could get lengthy. How many names would you like?"

Roc considered how many hours and days he had before he'd get yanked from exclusively working this case and be assigned one or more new victims. "The top dozen or so should do." She nodded and started to turn away. He stopped her. "One other thing."

"Yes?"

"Has your boss received any hate mail recently?"

She motioned down the hall. "Follow me."

He ducked under the tape and walked several paces to where Ms. Appleton stood by an open door. Looking inside at the stacked cardboard boxes, he swore silently.

"Would you like the entire collection or just the boxes from the last couple months?"

Roc stayed up all night researching Mr. Jonathan Mortensen's life and business. Ms. Appleton's list was in his inbox when he checked for email messages at eight the following morning. The list she'd compiled included fourteen names, each followed by a short explanation.

He scanned the names and was surprised to see *Margaret Appleton* at number thirteen. Her explanation for including herself followed.

I submitted my resignation a few days before his murder, giving a week's notice. The man and his business were disgusting. I understand I've set a record for longevity, since most assistants last less than six months. I worked for him for nine before becoming too sickened to go on. I pride myself on dispassion and professionalism, but my tolerance for his language and methods proved to be lower than I anticipated. After he insulted me with an inappropriate sexual remark in front of several guests, I was furious and made my decision.

Reading her words, Roc pursed his lips and nodded. She went up another notch in his estimation. He understood how she could attempt to be dispassionate yet be unable to deny her emotions. Plus he appreciated her honesty.

The last name on the list, number fourteen, was Lorenzo Regarde, the artist who'd painted *The Groundskeeper*. According to Ms. Appleton, Regarde had been appalled to learn that his painting had been purchased by Mortensen and would be hung in the man's office. She had included a pertinent quote as a means of explanation.

"I don't care how much he paid. To have my painting in his possession, hanging in the very room out of which he spews those disgusting magazines, is an insult to my art," the

artist had told a reporter when asked to comment on the exorbitant purchase price.

Roc scratched at the stubble on his chin. Mortensen seemed to have had a talent for insults. Had he insulted someone who owned a gun?

He printed a copy of the list and tucked it in his pocket for later. Right now, he had to shave and change his shirt then conduct his first interview of the day.

Mr. Mortensen's legal work had been handled by the firm of Blynn, Frasier, and Crowe. Mr. Crowe had personally overseen the crafting of the deceased's will, and Roc was anxious to know who benefited most from the victim's death.

After Crowe made Roc wait for fifteen minutes in an elegant outer office, he offered him coffee and a velvety chair, then sat with his fingers steepled on his huge cherry desk. He was middle-aged, with a streak of gray at each temple. He navy suit shouted tailor-made, and his perfectly formed, overly white teeth shone as if they'd been tailor-made too.

"What can I help you with, Detective?"

"I'd like to know who profits from your client's death."

"I can't reveal the total contents of his will without an appropriate warrant, of course, but I can tell you several individuals and organizations will be enriched by his passing."

"For example?"

"Two cousins are now many millions richer. In addition, Mr. Mortensen made various smaller bequests to a dozen other people and groups, from his cook to the Museum of Fine Art."

"Any chance you could give me a list?"

"I'll have my secretary send you some names."

"You'll profit from his death too," Roc pointed out to gauge whether the lawyer had a motive. "Your firm stands to collect thousands in fees for handling the estate."

"Not as much as we collected when Mort was alive. You'd be amazed at the number of hours we billed every week keeping his smut available to the public."

Roc nodded. He'd seen some of the magazine covers framed and hanging in the mansion's foyer and had no doubt the figure was substantial. "Any hunch as to who would kill your client?"

Crowe smiled a lawyerly smile. "No, but mention our name if you arrest someone, would you? Blynn, Frasier, and Crowe has an excellent criminal defense department."

Roc's second interview of the day was a follow-up with Roger Partesean, former financial advisor of the deceased. They'd spoken at the mansion the morning of the murder, but that was before Ms. Appleton mentioned the opposing opinions of client and advisor.

"I understand you disagreed with your client's decision to purchase art," Roc began. "Did he often act against your advice?"

"More frequently than I liked. He lost ten million on a dot com investment last year after I warned him the company was shaky. The old goat wouldn't listen to reason. He considered himself to be smarter than me and could be as stubborn as my grandfather's donkey."

"Mistakes like that would affect your professional reputation, I guess. It reflected badly on you when he lost money, because other people were unaware it wasn't your doing."

"Exactly. If he hadn't been my biggest client, I never would have stayed with him. But what could I do?"

"You could have murdered him so he wouldn't make you look incompetent any longer."

Partesean snorted. "Why would I kill a man who paid me generously whether he took my advice or not? Wrong tree, Detective. If I were you, I'd bark up the one near that loud-mouthed feminist, Brenda Temple."

"You think she disliked Mortensen enough to murder him?"

"She hated his guts, claimed his magazine demeaned women. She'd top my list of suspects if I were making one."

Roc asked a few more leading questions, then left.

Partesean liked money and Mortensen had paid him extremely well. If he was the killer, his actions were fueled by resentment or professional pride. Roc was a student of human nature and knew people had killed for much less. In his estimation, Partesean was still a suspect.

As for Brenda Temple, he had an appointment to interview her at two that afternoon. Ms. Appleton's list had her at number four.

The lawyer's list of heirs was looking like a dead end. Both Mortensen's cousins were giddy with joy, like they'd won a mega lottery. They didn't even bother to fake grief, and their lack of compassion for the dead man rubbed Roc the wrong way. He would have liked to keep them at the top of his suspects list, but they both had iron-clad alibis. Their finances were being scrutinized. So far, the department's forensic accountants had found no evidence either had paid a hit man, but money was always a strong motive, and Roc still had hope.

The rest of the people who'd inherit got smaller stipends, and even though he checked them out, his gut told him none of them had fired the gun.

Roc had interviewed the top ten candidates on Ms. Appleton's list. Brenda Temple admitted hating the deceased and expressed joy and relief at his passing. But she wasn't his killer. She'd been speaking in front of forty people then hustling attendees for donations to her charity during the hours when the fatal shot had been fired.

For a few hours, number six on Ms. Appleton's list, a born-again Christian who had once been arrested for threatening an abortion doctor, seemed like a hot prospect. That hope evaporated when the man's lawyer informed Roc, "My client spent the night of the murder locked in jail for disturbing the peace during a protest."

A week passed with no break in the case. Roc added names to his notebook and crossed off other names one by one. He got down to Ms. Appleton's name on her list and sat her down for a grilling too. He doubted she was a murderer, but couldn't assume anyone was innocent. Her name was the only one that appeared on both her list and the one from Crowe. And a smart woman, which he had no doubt she was, might steer him toward someone else, hoping her helpfulness would keep her above suspicion.

She smiled when he stated that theory. "Thank you for the compliment, Detective, but I'm really not that crafty. I'm trying to help because that's who I am, the perennial helpmate and assistant to everyone, except myself."

"You could have an accomplice you're protecting and have left the name of the guilty party off your list intentionally, hoping to throw me off."

"I could have, but I didn't. We're two of a kind, Detective. No friends or loved ones. Straight shooters with too many morals. Worker bees who keep working no matter what."

"Is that why you know so much about persistence and frustration?" he asked.

She pursed her lips. "I suppose it is."

On the eighth day after the murder, Crowe, as executor of the estate, formally requested the crime scene be released so he could bring in a crew of cleaners.

Roc balked at the request. "He doesn't need access to the room to get the estate into probate. I'd like to keep it sealed for a couple more days."

The Chief of Detectives, mindful of Roc's high percentage of case closures, hedged. "Crowe has friends in high places, so I can't stall too long. But Mortensen's murder is high profile, and I want it solved. I'll give you another twenty-four hours."

Feeling the pressure of a ticking clock and unable to quiet the voice of doubt nagging inside his head, Roc drove the familiar route back out to the estate. Bracing himself against the unrelenting wind out of habit, he entered the house once more.

He stopped in the doorway and looked around the office. Something wasn't right. He could feel it in his gut. Somewhere he was missing an important clue.

He studied the room, mentally reviewed his notes, and

replayed interviews in his mind. Half an hour passed and still nothing jumped out at him as overlooked and important. He heaved out a frustrated sigh and glanced at *The Groundskeeper*. Maybe the twisting in his gut wasn't caused by the existence of a missed clue. Maybe it was nothing more than a developing ulcer warning him to stop being stubborn, throw in the towel, and retire.

He stepped closer to the painting and peered at the little man working so diligently against the wind. "What do you think, buddy? A clue or indigestion from last night's pizza?"

The perfectly formed figure on the painting went on with his work. His fingers were wrapped tightly around the straight wooden shaft of the rake, the only breaks in the shaded woodgrain. Every strand of the workman's black hair was distinct against the leaves and grass in the background. Roc noticed the clarity of the details and frowned.

He drew back and examined the blood-splattered wall next to the painting's frame, then the similarly-speckled frame. Puzzled, he leaned forward and looked closer at the painting. A smile tugged at his lips as he reached for his phone to speed dial an evidence tech.

"Well, I'll be damned."

"It's been cleaned, all right," the tech reported after examining the painting with a magnifying glass. "I found a few traces of blood along the very edge of the frame, and a couple tiny smears in the corners. Whoever wiped it down did a pretty complete job when you consider the whole bottom quarter should have been sprayed with blood, judging by the level of the splatter pattern on the wall." The tech spread a large sheet of plastic on the carpet. "Help me get it down and into my van. We'll go over it in more detail at the lab."

Roc put on vinyl gloves and grabbed hold of a corner. "How was it cleaned? Water?"

"No. If water had been used, moisture would have collected along the bottom by the frame and either blurred some of the paint at the edges or leeched into the wood and stained the frame. There's no evidence of either."

"What then? An alcohol wipe? One of those packaged hand cleaners they give out in restaurants?"

"I'll have to confirm it in the lab by analyzing the residue, but my guess is it was wiped with a dilute alcohol solution, probably thinned fifty percent with turpentine."

"Thinned alcohol? Why would that be?"

They laid the painting on the plastic sheet and stopped to rest. The tech explained, "Straight alcohol is a solvent and likely to damage paint. I don't see paint damage, so it was probably thinned. The turpentine acts as a slowing agent and keeps it dilute, so only the dirt or varnish coating, or in this case, blood splatter, would be removed. Years ago, I worked for a guy who restored antique paintings. He could remove the dirt of centuries without any damage to the original paint. The secret is in the percentages in the solution."

Roc rubbed his chin. "In other words, whoever cleaned the painting knew their way around artwork, didn't want to do any damage, and even brought along a container of cleaning solution in case it was needed."

"Bingo."

Roc pulled out his lists of suspects. One name on each list jumped out at him.

The Museum of Fine Art would be the painting's next owner, according to Mortensen's will. People there would know how to clean a painting, but he doubted any museum employee would kill for the privilege of adding it to their collection.

He switched his focus to the bottom of Ms. Appleton's list. Number fourteen. Lorenzo Regarde. The artist who'd toiled to create *The Groundskeeper*. He'd know how to clean a painting. Who had a better reason to want the painting undamaged as well as a motive to want the current owner dead? The odds were excellent that he'd once owned a gun and had no alibi.

As Roc walked to his car a few minutes later on his way to locate and arrest a killer, he felt warm in his topcoat and realized the wind had suddenly died. He spoke aloud to the toiling groundskeeper in Regarde's painting. "Looks like your persistence paid off, buddy. You outlasted the wind."

He removed his coat, tossed it onto his back seat, shook his head in wonder, and smiled. Who knew? Maybe someday his persistence would pay off too and he'd outlast the city's supply of killers.

Crack-Up at Waycross
Robert Mangeot

Up on the ridge like we were, I heard it before I saw it, the growl of a diesel rig from down at the shelling plant. I shushed Deke and bolted up straight in the passenger seat.

"Like clockwork," I said. "Saddle up, brother."

Deke and I both had beers to kill, which we did just as the rig came lumbering for the main road, headlights sweeping through the leaf-bare orchard. Piled in its double trailer was the mother lode of Georgia pecans, fifty tons of Old Lady Whitlock's bumper harvest. An early cold snap had hurried along the fall drop and left her swimming in surplus nuts, and of fine quality.

Tonight like usual, Deke and I had parked overlooking the orchard for our after-shift libations. Like usual, Old Lady Whitlock had worked us overtime. Not like usual, we drank up in my uncle Grissom's Ford Super Duty, borrowed as not to have our personal rides spotted while jacking a double trailer. My uncle might have objected, but he had skipped the U.S. of A. back in June. Something about Feds and mail fraud, what I'd heard.

As mastermind-in-chief I would handle the maps and general reacting to events. I had made sure to stock the cabin with beers on ice and a bag of golden fancy pecans. We would need sustenance. Also, hidden under canvas we had Deke's paintball rifle, a halogen flashlight each, one blackjack, our ski masks, and some rope. I tuned the radio to arena rock, for kickass tailing music. Deke churned plenty of clay getting the Super Duty off the track and onto the county road. Soon up ahead the rig's tail lights blazed out as if guiding us home.

I said, "Ease off the gas, brother."

We fell in a hundred yards back, which I calculated was an

innocuous distance. In short order the rig turned east on Highway 37, and we tracked it slow and steady.

The plan was to bide our time until Jermaine, the driver on schedule tonight, stopped for hash browns. Everyone in our stretch of Georgia knew Jermaine liked his hash browns scattered, smothered, covered, and often. The first Batter Hut east of Albany was outside Moultrie. There in the parking lot we would assess over beers how best to snatch the unguarded trailer. I'd do the rig-snatching, having taken informal tractor-trailer lessons over the last few months.

Quick thinking, a test of genius.

Another test was complex arithmetic. The simple math said making off with Old Mrs. Whitlock's nuts a lunch cooler per theft would yield me one bushel a week, a ton in nine months, and a fifty-ton truckload by the time I cashed my first social security check. A genius, though, would boost fifty tons in one brilliant swoop. A buck-and-a-half per pound resold on the QT fetched three grand per ton. Times fifty tons. That kind of math multiplied up quick, and it equaled the good life.

Ahead the trailer slowed for a hard left where 37 angled around yet another old-growth orchard. The sign dangling off its mailbox read: *Whitlock Farms, Doerun.*

"See that?" I said, and I opened fresh beers and the golden fancies. "That right there is what I've been saying. She's minting coin while we get squat."

"That's not true," Deke said. "Second shifts she pays time-and-a-half. And profit-sharing, don't forget."

Here was why Deke still worked the cracking line while I had moved up to quality control. Her idea of profit-sharing was to gather everybody at the loading dock and give us each fifty dollars cash, plus the very one-pound bag of golden fancies that I snacked on. She had gripped my hand in that gravedigger's shake of hers and said in a nicotine-soaked voice, "Keep at it, son."

Quality control, that was where repetition honed genius. Only a discerning mind could spot the withered and diseased rejects among a conveyor belt packed with nutmeats, at speed, all day. First thing I'd noticed was every year a boatload more nuts vibrated across my station, thanks to Old Lady Whitlock gobbling up orchards all over the surrounding counties. This, I confirmed through researching the business headlines, both print and internet. Then there were the record prices. Nutrition experts somewhere had declared pecans a superfood, and ever since Asian folks bought them up as fast as we shelled them, like Asia had gone on a full-fledged nut bender. In life, just as at quality control, you had to pay attention to get ahead.

Deke tipped his bottle neck toward my bag of pecans. "Those'll ruin your beer."

I made a show of crunching a fat nut. "She thinks she's the pecan queen of Georgia. Well, after tonight we're halfway to being the kings."

"Seriously, Bray. One time I ponied up for Millers in the black bottle and had them with some nut mix. Now I like the black Miller and I like nut mix, but together they went down like salted tar."

"Won't be long before we're front page of whatever the Atlanta paper is, you and me and our Falcons cheerleader wives buying up another pecan farm."

"Never could figure out which nut," Deke said.

"What are you talking about?"

"That ruined the black Miller. It was that mix with only fifty percent peanuts guaranteed, but everybody knows peanuts and beer are plain made for each other. There were walnuts, cashew halves, Brazilians, all that. Any one of them could have spoiled it."

Here again was why more than once I had warned Deke not to wear loose-fitting shirts near the machinery.

Up ahead the trailer plowed on toward Moultrie and hash brown heaven. "Check it," I said. "It's like we thought. He's making for the 133 bypass."

Deke wiped his face with his sleeve. "Sorry, but I can't steal nothing from a Batter Hut. That's sacred ground. I mean, where do I take Mom from now on?"

I fixed him with my senior partner grin. Not that I'd stolen much before, other than the rubber-armed inflatable skydancer from the Tifton Dodge. I'd break that bad boy out for our first pecan harvest.

Talking up those big harvests and that skydancer calmed Deke a little. For a while we drove on through orchards and scraggly pines and such. Sure enough, west of Moultrie the rig grumbled around onto the 133 bypass. I popped open a celebratory Natty Lite and a microbrew for Deke. Except Jermaine didn't stop at the Batter Hut. East of Moultrie the trailer cranked around onto Highway 37, toward the interstate.

"Guess he's not hungry," Deke said.

"Drop us a back a ways. Jermaine there is getting ahead of schedule, that's all. You watch, he's stopping at the Hut in Adel."

"Mom hates the coffee there," Deke said. "Says it's like burnt sludge."

"Then you won't mind jacking the rig there, will you?"

"We don't really have to steal those nuts, do we? We got a whole orchard growing."

More like a sinkhole. For years Deke had slipped tree cuttings out of Whitlock Farms. We split the cost on soil and plant food, me every month at Ace Hardware buying pails of kelp emulsion and probably climbing a terrorist watch list. We kept the works at his mom's greenhouse. No doubt she believed it all a cover somehow for our growing weed. Come morning, fifty tons of pecans appearing in her barn could only arouse further suspicion. Well, she hadn't turned in her baby Deke over a suspected pot operation, with exotic chemicals, so then no chance, no way, no how was she turning in her baby Deke over health food. Besides, who'd carry her to church and brunch?

And like that, I was back imagining fat bank accounts on the horizon. My uncle Grissom, while still in country, had connected me to a buddy over in Savannah who exported pecans for international tycoon folks. In-shell or shucked, with bills of lading or just a wink, the buddy didn't give a rip how he came into the nuts, so long as the price was fifty percent or better off wholesale. Thing was, he only bought a batch at a time so he could fudge the paperwork. What nuts we couldn't milk through that angle, Deke and I would sell roadside in Florida or Alabama, or we'd set up a virtual stand on-line, like that eBay thing some people did, and you know most of that junk was stolen, too.

"Bray?" Deke said. "I don't think he's stopping."

No, he wasn't. The trailer thundered into Adel, past the Batter Hut, past the airstrip and motels, past the Pilot stop, past the interstate ramp and on into the Georgia night. I snapped off a string of words that left pecan bits pasted on the windshield.

"Maybe we turn back," Deke said.

"Just let me think a minute."

East of town the fields turned drier, sandier, and Spanish moss took hold on the pines. Canals glistened from moonlight and probably gator eyes. An armadillo scuttled down the highway shoulder. A bug the size of the sausage link Jermaine should have ordered by now latched on my window. The map confirmed the obvious: ahead for an hour was nothing but boondocks.

I scooped up pecans for brain food. "All right then, if he's headed this way, so be it. Lonely out here. What we do is spring a trap. Whang him on the head and get his keys."

"No way." Deke gripped the wheel. "No, sir. We've got the saplings back home. We can keep feeding them, and nobody gets their head busted."

"I told you, braining him does him a favor. Otherwise the cops figure he's in on it. That'd get them all suspicious about everybody at the plant. That don't help nobody, does it?"

Deke went quiet, but I could tell he was mulling the idea over by how his nose twitched in the dashboard glow.

"Carpe diem," I said. "I don't like taking a blackjack to Jermaine any more than you, but this is how empires get forged."

Deke took a slug off his bottle. He shot me a sideways glance. "How are those nuts sitting with your beer?"

"Get past him," I said. Truth was that pecan film greased my mouth. "But casual. Then we pretend engine trouble. I'll be ducked under the hood, like there's a hose gone bad. He stops, you come out of the trees, and bammo! You whang him."

"Me? I can't bash Jermaine like that. I can't. Last year his wife baked me oatmeal cookies on my birthday."

I suffered then the frustration of genius stalemated—temporarily—by oatmeal cookies. To speed things along, I agreed Deke would play stranded motorist, I'd jump out from the trees, and that when we were serious pecan moguls, we'd hire Jermaine on for life at a good wage.

Deke stepped on the gas, and the pines and live oaks zipped past in a green-brown mash-up. We cruised around the trailer, and when our lead time hit one minute, I had Deke pull off after the next blind curve. He slammed on the brakes and spun the Super Duty square onto the shoulder, gravel dust wafting mad in protest. Into that grit he switched on the hazards.

"Get the hood," I said. "I'll put down the tailgate. That way he can't read the plates."

We made quick work setting the trap, then I took my ski mask and blackjack and a Natty Lite into the scrub. I carried a steel rake along too, in case I woke any cottonmouths.

I settled in where the trees were thick but not too thick. Cedar branches pricked at my neck and hands, and I coughed away a cloud of swamp gas and dried sap. Damned if no-see-ums didn't find me despite the chill, or maybe that was my skin steeling for battle.

High beams lit up the forest edge. The sound of a big diesel downshifting followed its headlights our way. I knocked back my beer, chucked the can into the brush, and ducked low in the cedars. The trailer came around the turn dark and growling like a flint-skinned dragon.

Jermaine didn't slow up, not a lick. If anything, from the bellow of gears and snort of exhaust, he had put the hammer down. The rig clattered inches past the Super Duty, Deke under the hood and all, and continued on hell-bent for Lakeland.

I trudged out from the brush, a phantom rumble still vibrating my feet. Down the highway bats flickered across the road, and the night re-settled in the trailer's wake.

"That's just cold," I said. "You could have been stranded out here for real."

Deke banged the hood shut and slid into the Super Duty. I

barely had the rake stowed and the tailgate up when a luxury SUV whipped around the curve. Deke pulled down his hat and went stiff, and I managed to jam an entire ski mask into my back pocket.

The SUV eased up alongside. The passenger window glided down, and suddenly there was a put-together woman of a certain age flaring her nostrils at me. Behind the wheel sat a clean-cut man in his fifties. Mr. and Mrs. Landed Gentry checked out the Super Duty and shot me a pair of scrubbed and quizzical faces.

"Everything's dandy," I said. "We had a rake get loose, is all."

Mrs. Landed Gentry lifted a manicured eyebrow. Mr. Landed Gentry leaned over and said, "You find it?"

I patted the tailgate. "Back safe and secure."

"Steel or plastic?"

"Say what now?"

"Steel rake comes loose, that'll scuff the tarnation out of a bed liner."

"Steel," I said, "and yeah, we got off lucky. Don't know what shook it loose."

"Somebody might have got hurt," Mrs. Landed Gentry said, brow cocked so high it carried her lip along for the ride.

I took her expression and the adrenaline whoosh in my ears as cues to bring discussion to a close. "No injuries to truck or person, I swear. You all have a good night now."

Whatever they planned the rest of the evening, they didn't need to get there in a hurry. Mr. Landed Gentry took the SUV through some kind of launch sequence, checking his dash and pedals like he hadn't just now used them. Eventually they puttered off at Sunday Driver speed. We gave them a head start before Deke got us going again, and I had him keep two hundred yards behind the SUV so that Mrs. Landed Gentry didn't report us as persons of bad intent.

We nursed our beers while the SUV kept toddling along the highway, five miles per hour below the limit. The rock station had gone out, and Deke found us a country gold channel. He rambled on and on about his mom's grading system for Batter Huts, but I had stopped listening. Outside

Lakeland we passed a strip mall with a *Coming Soon* banner for a Whitlock Farms Pecan Experience store. *Whitlock Pecans*, the banner declared, *The Taste of Georgia*.

Something foul and salted belched up my throat.

"Told you," Deke said.

"Shut it."

Finally, Mr. Landed Gentry turned into a brand new Circle K somebody had put up, and Deke poured on the speed. On the far side of Lakeland we caught up to the rig still barreling ahead, tail lights gleaming like twin evil eyes.

"What's got into him?" I said. "Hell, it's regulations or something he's supposed to stop now and then to walk off the thrombosis."

"That's what you said."

"No, that's what Jermaine told me. Regulations. What's on ahead from here?"

"Homerville. Mom says the Batter Hut there does the best eggs around, but eggs ain't worth driving two counties over for."

I ignored him and checked the map. If the trailer kept on course, and Jermaine seemed bound and determined about that, further east of Homerville a mess of state routes merged into a hub at Waycross. Rail line markers ran from the town in all directions like Georgia had needed stitches.

"That's it," I said. "Waycross. They got the big hump yard there, freight trains coming every which way."

Deke gave me a look. I chose to ignore that and everything else about him until finally he floored it past the trailer. I figured it would take a mile tops before he stopped that under-his-breath grousing. It took him two.

We set up the roadblock on the Ware County line. The highway narrowed there, one tight shoulder an irrigation canal, the even tighter shoulder a pecan grove crowding up to the state route. *Whitlock Farms Cane Creek*, the gatepost sign read.

La-di-da, Mrs. Whitlock. La-di-da.

Deke got the Super Duty crossways on the road and again put on the hazards. For courage I issued him the paintball rifle and a cold microbrew.

"We go with duck-calling," I said, "once we're in position. No texting, no matter what. He'll spot the screen lights."

"Ducks won't work. November they're all down in Louisiana or Mexico or south like that."

"Not every damn duck."

"Most of them, and anyway it's awful late for ducks to be calling."

"Well, you got a better plan, spill it."

"Let's do coots. They're honking twenty-four seven."

The solid idea locked me up momentarily. "Fine, but nothing complicated. One call, it means you're ready. I'll answer. Anybody gives a second call, it means hold position."

Deke nodded and hustled off into the darkened orchard. The night swallowed him up good and quick. Soon a *Waaak aak puhk-cowah* came from somewhere in the trees and gloom.

I grabbed the blackjack and my ski mask and plunged into the high grass along the canal. When situated I gave a return *pkk pkk waaakaak*. Behind me something I hoped was a bull frog late for hibernating plopped into the water.

From west on the highway the trailer headlights punched a glare in the night. It came on relentless, big diesel yammering, horn yowling, and I thought sure Uncle Grissom would be in the market for a replacement truck until Jermaine laid hard on the brakes. There was another rustle and splash behind me, louder, say like gator-sized. That did it. I was cracking Jermaine good and hard for dragging us out into the swamps.

The rig groaned to a halt beside my patch of grass. Way up there—way, way up there—at the wheel might have been Jermaine, if since lunch he had grown six inches, bulked up to linebacker size, and gotten prison tattoos over his face and neck.

Pkk pkk waaak, I wanted to call, I did, but my throat had seized up.

Big Dude cranked the rig onto the shoulder as if to nudge past the Super Duty, or shove it into the canal. With a thump of warping plastic, the truck edged off the center line, but Big Dude had strayed onto wet ground and the double-trailer neared tipping over into the drink. By then I was coot-calling like crazy, but no coot ever hatched could call louder than a diesel roar. Big Dude backed the rig up and tried the other shoulder, but the mammoth tires almost bogged down in the ditch.

The engine cut off. The air brakes released with a mighty hiss. Big Dude swung out great big legs covered in great big jeans and great big boots. Steel shone from their tips. He hopped out and landed hard on the asphalt, and no question the highway got the worse of it. I needed a double-take to process the aluminum glint of his shotgun.

"You will move your vehicle," Big Dude shouted, accent thick and European, like from wherever it was they ate goulash. He chewed his lips as he strode toward the Super Duty. "I repeat that you are to move truck. Now!"

"*Pkk pkk waaak?*" I called low and raspy.

Big Dude racked shells into the gun. "You will come out from there."

My bird-calling may have stunk, but my staying put had never been better. Hunkered down in the grass, I might have outlasted the guy, but then Deke in his ski mask appeared from around the trailer.

"Hey," he said.

Big Dude spun on him and leveled the shotgun. To Deke's credit, nobody had to warn him about bringing a paintball rifle to a gun fight. He yelped and beat it full sprint back into the orchard.

The silence that followed made me wish it was warm enough for katydids, so I'd feel safe to sneak a breath. I felt good about my continued hunkering though, what with the tall grass and darkness, or I did until Big Dude yanked me out by my hair. I looked up at him, and when that spotted only broad chest, I looked up some more. Then my eyes met his flat stare, and I regretted all that looking up.

"Who has sent you?" Big Dude said. "Hashimoto? He thinks he can cut me out of the load? I rip out his lying tongue and eat it while he watches."

"Nobody sent us. We're just out stealing nuts same as you. We would have let things be if we knew you already had them."

Big Dude wrenched my mask off and shook me like a Magic Eight-Ball that damn well better rethink its answer. I said, "There's a couple beers left if we want to talk this over."

Big Dude cuffed me across the cheek. My butt planted on the highway, and I sat there reeling pretty good. Big Dude patted me down and relieved me of my keys, wallet—tonight sans ID—and the blackjack. He jabbed the shotgun between my shoulder blades, which I did not take as friendly. Then off I went force-marched into the grove, which seemed downright hostile. My shoe kicked pecan husks rotting where the shakers had left ruts in the dirt. Peat hung thick in the air. We were some ways into the orchard, under a shroud of night and bare limbs, when Big Dude fell a few steps back.

"Halt here," Big Dude said.

I could have halted like he said, but right there looked like a good spot for dumping bodies. Instead I broke out running. Low branches snagged my clothes and scratched me up good. The beer and that bag of nuts didn't help much while booking it for my life.

Likely owing to a form of paramilitary training, Big Dude reacted fast and closed on me faster. I ventured a glance over my shoulder and there he was, breath puffing and legs pumping like an armed track star. Instinct sent me screeching on a zigzag through the pecan rows. I heard him trip snarling into the mud. Man, I thought, superior brainpower had gotten me home free. Then I ran smack into a split rail fence somebody had put up. Down I went butt-first again onto the ground.

Across the next field, a porch light blinked on at a previously-darkened cottage. Excellent. Buck shot crossfire.

"Move nothing," Big Dude said. He limped out of the trees toward me. The shotgun was trained noticeably in my direction. He steadied both barrels, grimaced and said, "Ouch."

I nodded, certain I was about to cry out something along those lines myself. Big Dude touched his backside, and his hand came back glopped in pastels. Wherever Deke was, he had opened up with whatever color ammo he had.

What happened next was a surge of war barks inbound from the pasture. My experience with dog packs had been getting the hell out of their way, so I clambered for the nearest tree. Big Dude must have had similar experience. He hop-stepped it out of there fast as likely paramilitary training taught somebody.

I had climbed pecan trees all my life, often after my share of beers, so I hoisted myself up around the bare limbs double-quick until the branches threatened to give. I waited there in my catbird seat to see who or what might have the honors of doing me in. Damned if I'd didn't choke up some over missing out on pecan glory.

Three German Shepherds zipped in like fur-covered missiles. Up high I watched the pack chase Big Dude off through the orchard and into the midnight haze. The fading sounds of hot pursuit had the ring of turning back my way soon enough.

Something whizzed past my ear. Next thing red paint splattered a limb near my head.

There Deke was down by the road, swinging his paintball rifle and coot-calling like mad. I about broke my ankles and neck scrambling out of that tree. Beer and adrenaline helped me shake off the pain and leg it quick to the highway. Waiting there sat the double trailer, driver door open, engine idling, fifty tons of in-shell glory unattended. I laughed sweet relief climbing up into the cabin. Big Dude had left paperwork that might pass as legit if an inspector wasn't inclined to make a few calls. It was hello to pecan fortunes and trophy wives.

I had Deke toss me a Natty Lite before he tore off in the Super Duty. Beaten up as it was, the truck rattled in protest when he got it going west for home. I'd pay Uncle Grissom back the repairs money out of future profits.

I tortured the gears and motor trying to get the rig going. A cockpit of buttons and pedals stymied me, and those hours practicing at the shelling plant seemed about a million years gone. Eventually I got the trailer into a crawl, the crawl into a creep, and creep into a veer off the road, and the veer into a wet slide into the canal. Muck grabbed hold of the tires, and the rig settled into a ten-degree list.

In the muddy water below unseen things kept bubbling and splashing. Thus why I was still holed up in the cabin when the Georgia State Patrolman waded out from the highway.

I summoned up every scrap of genius I could. What I told him was, "I rescued this truck here."

The trooper sighed. "You been drinking, son?" he said, which I had, but not so much that I answered his question.

The judge gave me eight years at Valdosta State Prison. Felony theft by taking, he called it, despite me not having taken a damn thing. This was after Mr. and Mrs. Landed Gentry both testified about my suspicious nature and after the Georgia troopers handed me over briefly to this bunch of Feds in black windbreakers. They asked in direct fashion how I'd gotten mixed up in some international nut theft ring and how I knew a Bulgarian gangster found cornered in a tool shed by angry dogs. They asked me why I had the rig headed west, the wrong way from the planned drop in Savannah. I told them the only drops I knew about were pecans, every fall, and that I'd cooked up the trailer-jacking there at quality control. Soon the agents turned off their audio-video equipment and filed out, not even asking about Uncle Grissom or that seaweed emulsion.

I liked Valdosta. Out in the prison yard, the musk of pecan orchards scented the breeze, and trailers carting nuts on their first leg toward Asia rumbled past the razor wire. Prison management gave me a job counting parts for the tool shops, where my accuracy earned me points with most everybody. At Christmas Old Lady Whitlock herself dropped off a pecan pie each for us convicts. They lined us up in the auditorium for handshakes, and she grabbed me in her fish-skin grip and said, "Keep at it, son."

Nobody ever fingered Deke. Every visit he showed me the latest pictures of our saplings bursting out of their pots. Some would be ready for planting in a year or two. The public defender said with good behavior I could be a free man by then.

At my sentencing, the judge assured me that I was getting off easy, that if the Feds had pressed charges then I couldn't count as high as the max sentence. I thought about those pecan saplings and didn't tell the judge that I could count pretty high.

Grasshoppers
J.D. Allen

One

Carla's legs didn't touch the ground as she sat on the tailgate, the cool metal biting into her tailbone through her tight jean shorts. For this occasion she'd chosen the black ones that showed off her legs. Two cars had stopped to offer assistance in the last thirty minutes. Both were sent away with a *Thank you, I'm fine.*

She sipped on an open beer and checked the clock on her cell for the fifth time in twelve minutes. Had to be getting close. Bar closed half an hour ago. She glanced over at the ground where her tire was lying on its side, her jack out and opened. She'd abandoned the tire iron in the grass below her feet. Sweat threatened to bead on her upper lip. Its only dissuasion was a soft breeze that offered an occasional break from the humid night.

Grasshoppers and cicadas sung to the darkness, tickling an almost lost memory. The ballad was once one of her favorite things, she and her sister would lie in bed unafraid to be caught talking past lights out because the midnight serenade would muffle their hushed voices. Mom once said the grasshoppers would sing until they die.

Clearing that thought, she mentally checked her cover. ID in the glove box, her small revolver tucked in her holster in the over-tight waist band of those shorts. It pressed hard against her spine. It was going to leave a bruise. Carla didn't care. Nothing like being bait.

Her heart rate rose as yet another set of headlights swung around the bend toward her disabled truck, the sound of the engine recognizable before the make or model of the auto housing it. Finally. The fish had entered the pond. The engine whined as the driver downshifted. Slowing.

As the car approached, a familiar tingle crawled up the back of Carla's neck. Fear. Anticipation. Maybe even excitement over this one. She'd waited long enough.

The screaming-red '80s Trans Am pulled next to her, not leaving the road. He didn't kill the engine. Nonchalant. Darrell Stone leaned over and eyed her through his passenger window. She knew what he saw. Woman alone. Late at night. No one around. Dark woods to veil his evil deed. A cheap smile crawled across his once-handsome face. Every nerve in her body was screaming at her. Get him. Not yet.

"You need a hand with that tire, baby doll?"

She chugged down the last bit of the warmish beer to calm her nerves and tossed the can over her head. The aluminum rattle drew a slightly more genuine smile from Darrell. She pushed herself up, getting a dizzy rush from standing too fast. "You got a hand, hotrod?"

He nodded, revved the engine on the aging muscle car then pulled in front of her truck. He stretched out of the car. His thin, lanky legs stumbled a little as he turned her way. As she had hoped, he'd been at Rack Daddy's hustling pool for hours. "Stuck out here in the middle of the night?"

His head swiveled as he checked around them, Carla knew exactly what he was doing. He'd want to make sure no one saw exactly what kind of help he had in mind. Carla steeled her nerve. This had been a good decision.

"Phone's got no bars. Spare tire's stuck up under the truck. I can't get it to release."

The flat was left on the ground. He checked up under the tailgate, pushing on the spare mounted there. He glanced back at her.

"And I broke a damn nail trying."

She moved closer to show him the evidence, stumbling against him on him in the process. He righted her but didn't let go of her arms when she was steadied. He glanced in the bed and saw the empties, and then looked back toward the club. "You've been here a while. Seems to me someone would have stopped for a looker like you."

"I know!" She let her head fall back as she looked up him, keeping her eyes unfocused. "I was worried no one would come to my rescue." She smiled at him, trying her hardest for cute. "Are you my hero?"

"I don't know about hero." He pulled her toward the line of trees, yanking her arm hard. "But I can make this a night to remember."

"Easy, dude!" She made it slur. Her Keds slipped as he spun her towards the woods. She screamed, knowing no one was within earshot. She struggled as his stronger body dragged her out of the safety of the open road and close to the darkness of the trees. Her heart was pounding. The bead of sweat that threatened earlier burst forth.

"Hold still." He shook her hard and produced a knife from the holster on his belt.

"Fuck you." She relaxed, quit struggling for an instant. They'd not moved that far into the woods. Despite the huge oak trees surrounding her, she might still be heard. She yanked her shoulders, trying to get free. He took her momentum and wrestled her into a chokehold. She twisted. He had her right hand. Her shooting hand. Not that big a deal, but it was quite a bit harder to get to her weapon with her left. After stretching her arm behind her, she managed to retrieve the snubby from the holster. After all, it was point blank range. Left-handed shouldn't be a big deal.

Two

Darrell Stone screamed. And he didn't give a flip if he sounded like a little girl. Searing pain tore through his side, his skin tearing as the bullet exited. His back spasmed, hurt more than any motherfucking thing ever had. He instinctively covered the entry wound with his hand, looking down at his stomach with disbelief. He'd been in Afghanistan and fought off men several times this little bitch's size. Nothing. Nothing had stung him like the hole she put in his side.

"You fucking shot me."

She pushed the little revolver toward him and pulled the trigger again. A second bloom of blood appeared within two inches of the first. "Stings like hell, don't it?"

He stumbled back, trying to keep breathing. Black dots enveloped his vision. Blinking hard and breathing deep, Darrell fought his body's urge to pass out from the pain. He wasn't dying. He knew that. Had to be a small caliber. But he was in the woods with bullet wounds and what appeared to be a very pissed off redhead. His mind raced through countless faces trying to place her. He'd fucked plenty of reds. Supplied shit to some others. Smacked around a few. No telling what her beef was. "Who are you?"

She checked to see if anyone was around. No such luck for him. That gun didn't waver as she stalked closer, holding it like a pro.

"You hurt my feelings, Darrell." She rubbed her forehead as if it hurt. He felt no sympathy. She marched over and grabbed the tire iron off the ground by the tailgate arrogantly, not caring if he got up or tried make a run for it. On the way back, she scooped up the knife he'd dropped when she shot him. With a flip, she closed it and clipped that to her shorts. She spun the tire iron like a majorette until it stopped mid-twirl and pointed at his nose. She motioned him into the woods as if it were a casual invitation.

"We've seen each more than once. You knew my sister very well. Remember Terri? You met her on a night just like this. And me...you met me at the trail." She lifted an eyebrow and said nothing more.

It clicked. His brain scrambled. But seeing her here didn't make any sense. This was a nightmare. How was he supposed to stop a fucking cop? And who would believe him if he managed to get away and say she attacked and shot him?

"You...you can't do this!"

"That's prime coming from you, cretin. I've been watching you for a while." Her face scrunched up. She shook her head. "Pathetic really. I can't believe you've managed to live this long. Someone should have killed you years ago."

He desperately looked around for anything to use as a weapon. Nothing but twigs and leaves within his reach. He kept moving backward. Surely he'd get the upper hand at some point. His side hurt like fuck but this was instinct, fight or flight mode. That little slut was not going to get the best of Darrell Stone.

She kept grumbling. Some of it he wasn't sure he understood. Most if it was about the sister. Maybe she was high. She poked his gut with that tire iron. That got his attention.

"You pick on old men. Bully your way into fights with much weaker foes to make yourself look good. Women are worthless to you." She cocked the little revolver again. He backed up faster. "Someone was bound to shoot your stupid ass sooner or later. After some consideration, I figured I deserved that satisfaction."

He stumbled into a clearing and tripped on uneven ground, landing on his ass. She rushed him. Before he knew it, her gun pressed hard against his temple. He started to shake. "Bitch."

"That's brave, Darrell. You haven't seen bitch yet, but you will." She tilted her head. An old tobacco barn sat at the far side of the clearing. "Move."

She ushered him to a splintered post out in front. "Sit. Put your hands behind you."

"Fuck you. You're not going to get a confession. I had nothing to do with what happened to your sister."

Black metal slammed against his forehead hard enough to push him back on his ass right where she'd asked. He looked up the slick, short gun barrel and saw hell in her eyes. The crazy bitch wasn't kidding. He relaxed and held out the hand that wasn't pressed into his gunshot wounds. "Okay."

She pulled some kind of plastic strips out of her pocket and tied his arms behind his back. The stretching pulled at his gut wounds. Excruciating. The burning had been replaced by intense, throbbing blasts of pain. Sweat stung his eyes. The stench of gunpowder filled his nostrils. What a fucking nightmare. He glanced around as she pulled a lantern out of the dilapidated wood shack and flipped it on. No idea how to get out this mess came to mind.

"I was acquitted." He would have to try and reason with her. It was his best chance. "Double jeopardy. You should know that. So if you're hiding some kind of camera around here..."

She squared directly in front of him and squatted on her heels. Eye level with him. The woman was nuts. "God, you're dumb. A camera? To record me shooting you, kidnapping and coercion, maybe murder. What would I do with it then?" She stood again. "I am not here to get a confession from you."

She closed her eyes and rolled her head around, loosening up her neck. He tried to move his hands to relieve some of the tension on his stomach.

Wasn't happening. Pulling on the plastic ties only made his wrists hurt worse. They bit into his skin with each tug. His heart was pounding like he'd just snorted a couple of lines. He wished he had. No way she'd have got the best of Darrell Stone if he'd been speeding. He needed to get himself under control. A deep breath didn't help. He was afraid to ask but couldn't stop himself. "What the hell are we here for then?"

Three

Carla eased the knife from her waistband. "Do you know what the word *retribution* means?" She said it slow, enunciating each syllable to make sure he heard the word correctly.

She snapped the knife open. Long. Sharp. He looked up at her with blank eyes, saying nothing.

"I didn't think so. Retribution by definition is a punishment. One that is considered to be morally right and fully deserved. I believe *that* is what we're doing here." She considered for a moment then bent down to get back in his personal space. She was enjoying this. Maybe more than she should. But Carla was morally right in this case. The law had failed her. And there was no time to wait for him to get busted doing something else. And he would get busted again. And again. Habitual. "Revenge is to inflict hurt or pain on a person for the wrong done to oneself. And you didn't actually hurt me, did you?"

He shook his head. He looked confused more than frightened.

"So this is a retributive exercise, Darrell." She stuck the knife in the ground just out of his reach, and tapped him on the head with the barrel of the gun again. "Your punishment. The state of North Carolina made a grievous error when they put you back on the street. I am simply correcting it for them."

"You can't do this. You're a cop." He was shaking. Tears formed in his eyes. Carla imagined her sister had felt the same fear Darrell was experiencing. That feeling of dread that comes with understanding you have no way out of a terrifying situation.

Carla shuddered at the thought. At the memory of Terri's body on the table. The photos displayed for the court. *No guilt.* When the time came, her conscience would be clear. No badge. Nothing to make her consider stopping this exercise. She'd shot him twice as it was. Not turning back.

"Ah...You see, Darrell, that's no longer the case. I gave up the badge weeks ago so I could concentrate all my efforts on you. I stand before you as plain ole' Carla Sanders. The woman whose sister was brutally raped and stabbed to death. An innocent young woman that we needed dental records to identify because you saw fit to mutilate her face."

He paled even further. Tears and dust left trails down his cheeks. The big arrogant man she'd watched throughout the trial was gone. This was the scumbag. The coward.

"You can't get away with this, bitch."

Carla couldn't help bark out a laugh. And it felt good. She couldn't remember the last time something really stuck her as funny. "Don't you think a trained officer can get away with murder if a dumbass like you can?"

He spit at her. It missed.

She reclaimed the knife and traced the line of his jaw with the blade. "Now. Where'd you cut her first? Her face?" She slowed when he closed his eyes. "Or maybe it was her genitals."

"You can't." His voice was a high-pitched screech. "You're a cop. This is crazy!"

"No, Darrell. It's retribution."

Four

As Roland stepped out of the worn sedan, he glanced back at the empty passenger seat. The one Carla had occupied day in and day out for the best of seven years. The last of the night's insects sang in the morning glow. It was going to be a beautiful sunrise. He looked to see Carla. She was clean and neatly dressed but still looked like shit. Thinking back, she'd had that same lost look since the trial. He'd watched as her spirit withered when that creep called Terri a slut. Darrell had yelled and cursed at her and every cop in the place. Screaming he'd been framed by the police as they walked him walk out of the courtroom. "A free man," Carla had said it so quietly Roland almost missed it.

A patrol car pulled up and parked by the curb behind him. Two uniforms clambered out, urgent, intense. Roland approached slowly, not fearful but damned unsure what to say to her, still unclear of his own feelings. He understood on a baser level, but she'd gone off the reservation in a huge way. Anger wouldn't help at this point. Luckily, the captain had let him be the one to come.

He glanced back at the two very young officers who trailed a few feet behind. One had his gun holster unlatched and his hand at the ready. As if she would shoot at her partner or any officer for that matter. It was protocol but she looked more like a child in that swing than a suspect. Roland stopped short of her porch. "Give us a minute."

One of the younger officers considered the two veteran detectives and nodded. "Don't give me a reason to regret it," the officer warned as he shot Carla a stern glare. The warning was not needed. Roland didn't look back at the uniforms but heard them move away.

She was dressed in loose jeans and a tight T-shirt, unarmed and set for her fate.

Roland eased up in front of her. She stopped the swinging so he could sit. For a moment, they both stared into the sunbeams peering down though the leaves of the giant old oak in her front yard as the swing made its journey to and fro a couple of times. He scratched his chin. "Is this why?"

Her head tilted and she seemed to consider the question. "Why what?"

Roland realized there were several things he wanted an explanation for. "You gave up the badge."

She glanced at him. The resignation in her red-rimmed eyes burned down to her soul. In his own gut, he knew the answer even if his personal code of disagreed with it. The entire force had sympathy for her. Maybe some even had relatives who had been vics at some point. The savagery Darrel had inflicted on Terri was the worst the department had seen in Raleigh in years. Not surprising she went over the edge.

"I didn't see this coming. Maybe I should have. I thought you'd take a few months off and come back." He shook his head still reeling. "That's what I'd hoped anyway."

She looked at her feet. "Really? I saw it coming. I knew it the moment he walked out of that courtroom. Darrell would get exactly what he gave and I'd be the one to get to deliver it. Nothing you could do."

"Shut up." He looked over at the uniforms. They were most likely out of earshot, but. "You know better than that. Don't say anything else. Those boys will report anything you say." He turned to her. "I called a friend in Charlotte. A big-shot attorney who owes me a huge favor."

She took a sip from the lemonade at her side. Suddenly, Roland stopped the motion of the swing.

"Innocent until proven guilty. Remember?"

They both knew better in this case. "Bullshit. And you know it."

"Not gonna ask why you did it. We all know the why. You didn't even try to cover it up, did you? Jesus, Carla, you left your gun there."

She pushed the swing back on its journey. "I quit the job because I felt like there was no point any more. There's always *another* monster. No matter what we do on the job, there'll be someone else stepping up. We bagged our share, but I couldn't even protect my own sister. But I could...do that. I could punish him. I killed *that* monster. There's no denying blame here."

"You could have just beat the shit out of him and left him

there. I could have pinned that on half the county and made it a good case."

"Nope. No matter what I did he'd still point back to me. And since I did leave his tongue," she shrugged, "he'll use it." She had almost grinned.

"Didn't leave much else." Roland let his own snarf of laugh out.

"He's alive."

"Barely."

"He'll recover. I made sure of it. He won't want to look in the mirror and he'll have to sit to piss, but the asshole's alive."

Both the uniforms were looking away. She used her foot to slide a black case sitting under the swing his way. It rested heavy against his leg. "This is for you. Lock it away. Forget you have it until you're ready to hang it up."

"Carla. We'll get you out of this. You'll need th—"

She put her hand on his leg and gave it a firm squeeze. Roland's heart skipped a couple beats. It hurt. Like he was losing a family member, his own sister. He probably was. "Not this one. No way out now." She glanced at the two vehicles in front of her house. "Thanks for coming in small. I knew you would."

He shook his head and took a big drink of her lemonade. "Yeah, well. Don't be too thankful. They won't be far behind. CSI. IA. Not to mention the media. Gonna be national news all over this, I bet. CNN will be talking about you. Maybe even Wolf Blitzer. Not looking forward to the headlines or the sounds bites."

No sooner had the words come out of his mouth than the criminalist's truck pulled up, followed by the captain's car.

"I wish you'd talked to me about this first." He put his hand over hers and squeezed. How were her fingers so cold?

"Not your burden, Roland. You're a dammed good cop. Stay that way. Move to the desk. Retire early." She tapped the case with her toe. He shook his head, wanted to say no but the two uniforms were headed back their way with the captain right behind.

The quiet moment under the oaks was about to give way

to a media circus. "Ready for the side show?"

"It's not a show." She leaned over a let her head rest on his shoulder for just a moment.

She stood to meet the uniforms as they come on the porch. Her head was held high, her posture tight. She looked so calm given her actions over the last twelve hours.

"All the evidence is in the shed out back." She tilted her head in the proper direction. "Truck, weapons, everything." She turned and let the uniform take her into custody. Her eyes were glazed, staring forward. Dead.

Roland had to turn his head away. He couldn't take the sight of the silver cuffs on her wrists. "I still can't figure how it came to this."

"Neither can I."

Five

She tried to hustle out of the building, but Jack Bridges was hot on her tail. He grabbed her arm and spun her around. Her brain didn't work as fast her body and Carla lost her balance. She caught herself on the wall before she went all the way to the ground. The florescent lights in the courtroom had done a number on her head. It hurt. She wanted something to ease it. But there was nothing. Next best thing was a quiet, dark corner.

"It was all I could do to keep you from going right back to lockup, Sanders." Not so quiet in there. She'd thought she could take it. She was painfully wrong. "Your service record is the only thing between you and spending months in jail waiting for this trial. And once the prosecutor starts throwing around pictures of Darrell and that crime scene, we may be back in front of that judge fighting to keep you out anyway. I need a little help from you. Show some remorse. Something."

Carla pinched the bridge of her nose to stop the pounding. All she needed was a little more time. Then she could manage to think through the next few weeks. The sensational nature of the case had garnered a quicker first appearance than she had expected.

Jack walked off, dragging her by the arm They slipped in a small waiting area that was almost empty. It was quieter, the lights softer. A little better. "I can't defend you without an insanity plea. You cut the man's nuts off and left him to bleed out. I strongly recommend you consider what I'm asking here."

The wounds had not been as bad as the ones Darrell Stone had given to her sister. But men seem to have a strong connection with their balls. The court system was filled with men. Seemed they could only see *that* as her crime. The papers had a field day with it too—headlines and sound bites were not kind. Whatever. "I called the ambulance. He wasn't left for dead. I have a plan. You need to trust me."

"You are insane, Sanders. It's like you want to be a martyr. Listen to me. I can convince any jury the state can come up with that you lost it over Terri's death. Some time in a mental facility will be the worst you will serve. But you stick with not guilty, and you're going up."

He wasn't going to back off. And she didn't care what the charges were. But he may actually have a point. "Fine. Put in an insanity plea. It fits as good as anything. You have to promise me delays though. Postponements. Five or six weeks at least until I have to show in court again. That's what you guys do, right?"

His shoulders fell. She wasn't sure if it was relief for her agreement or his exasperation at her oversimplification of his profession. "Yes. That is what we all live for." He put his hand on her shoulder. "I think you should voluntarily seek help. Now. Inpatient somewhere."

She sighed. "If I do, you can keep the media away?"

"Yes."

Quiet. Peace. That's what she wanted. She should have thought of it in the first place. "I could use the escape from the cameras and reporters. They've camped out in my yard. I can't piss without it being reported. My head hurts. I suppose you have someplace in mind?"

Six

Roland Bridges looked out the hospital window. His partner lay behind him. She'd made it only two weeks in the psych bed before the first of the seizures. Inoperable brain tumor, the doc had told him when he'd rushed to her side.

She coughed softly.

"Prosecutor found out about the tumor, Carla." He turned back to her. She looked so much smaller in that bed. Thin and weak. Not the woman who could handle a two hundred pound drunk with just her stick. She'd been larger than life on the job. "They're holding a press conference."

She opened the mouth, but it was clearly hard for her to speak. She had to swallow hard to get the words out. "My brain tumor is making prime time? Sweet. And my dad always said my looks would get me noticed before my brains."

Her joking about losing her mind had not really amused him. But he understood the coping mechanism for what it was. Brave girl. "I asked the chief to send over some uniforms to get them out of here."

"Now it really becomes a circus. *Dying cop castrates her sister's rapist.*" She closed her eyes and he thought she was going to sleep. "But you kept my secret as long as you could. I knew it was inevitable. Things like that can't stay hidden long. Probably someone from the hospital got pay day for that info."

He looked back out the window. "It would have been better if you'd told me sooner. Before."

"You'd have stopped me."

Would he? She got to slay her monster. To get the bad guy the system let slip. "I'm not so sure."

It started to rain. The rivulets forged ragged tracks down the tinted glass. "Prosecutor's gonna want to speed up the trial. She's saying the tumor proves premeditation. As if the back road sting didn't."

"Doesn't matter." She groaned softly. Mumbled something.

He went to her side. Her eyes were still closed. "How you doing?"

"I'm dying. How are you?"

Her bitter sense of humor was one of the things he loved about her. "Was it worth it?

"Worth?" There was a slight raise of eyebrows but she didn't open her eyes.

He sat in the hard chair next to the bed. "We all feel it. We all want to do it. Throttle that scumbag you just caught beating his kids. Every father of a rape victim, every husband of a wife who gets mugged on the street, killed." He pushed his hair back. "You did it. You got your revenge."

"We missed that one before." Her voice seemed light, playful.

He eased her hand into his own. It was thin. Dry. "The system let Terri down. You didn't."

"Agreed." It was little more than a whisper.

"Are you worried about your soul?"

Carla let her head fall to the side. Wires and sensors were taped to her forehead and at the base of her skull. A nurse came in and started fussing over her. Checking her blood pressure.

Then she giggled, still not opening her eyes. "Put the cup over him, Terr. You have to be fast. They can really jump."

He looked at the nurse as she dabbed at the sweat beading on Carla's forehead. She smiled as she did it. "Grasshoppers. Girl's been chasing grasshoppers with her sister all morning. Told me the story just yesterday."

The woman shook her head. Her eyes were sad. "She's losing so much of her memory, she's fighting to hold onto a few favorite images." She tucked Carla's hand under the covers. "You been lucky, Detective Roland. She's been lucid a good bit today. That tumor's chewing away at her brain like a rabid dog with a bone."

Roland didn't like the imagery of the nurse's statement. But he understood the information to be accurate.

She patted Carla's hand under the sheet. "Doc says she won't have any memories at all by the end of the week." The older woman winked at Roland. "Not one. Might be good for woman like that to die with nothing on her mind. Don't you think?"

Carla wouldn't die tortured over Terri's death. Nor would she have to face uncertainty or guilt over Darrell Stone. That made Roland smile. He stood. Kissed her on the head. "No sense me hanging around here, bringing any of those thoughts back..."

He knew he was crying. Didn't care. He kissed his partner on the forehead. "You keep chasing those grasshoppers, sweetie."

Time Zones
Ron Rash

On a gray December afternoon when the midwestern sky is as flat and wide as what lies beneath it, my daughter speaks from South Carolina, a place far enough away that we can't even share the same time, her voice an hour ahead of me, fifteen time zones soon, she informs me.

"Australia," I say, the word a name for the farthermost place. A long word, its very length threatening, like anaconda.

"Did you know it's summer there even in winter?" she asks, too excited to let me answer. "And they have koala bears. Dan said he'll get me one for a pet."

"That's nice, honey," I say. "Let me speak to your mother a minute."

"Mommy," Laura shouts, turning her mouth from the phone. "Daddy wants to talk to you."

I close my eyes and it's like holding a conch shell to my ear. I hear that same steady sibilance—the sound of distance. In my mind I follow black-coated wires strung on telephone poles like clotheslines, mile after mile of them, headed south out of the wide sprawl that is central Illinois, then swerving east, across the Appalachians to South Carolina where my daughter cradles a phone to her shoulder. It's a miracle we can hear each other at all—our connection dependent on six hundred miles of woven copper. I remember the static of the baby monitor placed above Laura's crib and the second monitor on the table next to our bed. I'd get up every night and walk blind down the hall, lay my finger on Laura's lips to feel her breathing, unwilling to trust a machine to communicate the twelve feet of unseen distance between us.

As I wait for my ex-wife to pick up the phone, I realize again that a man's claim on his child is so much more tenuous than a woman's. He is, except for the briefest of moments, outside the creation. A man can only guess what grace a woman feels when that new presence first stirs inside her. How can two hearts in such proximity, hearts that share one blood, not be forever entwined? A man can't have that. For nine months a man's outside, waiting for that child to became a part of his life. And when that child finally comes red and squalling into his hands and he cradles it to his chest, that heart finally pressed to his own, there are already arms outstretched—doctor, nurse, wife—to take the child away from him.

"Good morning, Brad," Keri says, her tone a measured neutrality—a tone meant to convey more clearly than any words that what she feels toward me is not love or hate but indifference, that the only thing we share now is a biological fact.

"Why didn't you tell me about any of this?" I say, unable to mimic her tone.

"We weren't sure it was going to happen," Keri says. "As a matter of fact, we didn't think it was going to happen. Someone backed out at the last minute, so they called Dan Thursday. They gave us twenty-four hours to make a decision."

"Don't you think I should have had some input."

"No, Brad," she says. "As a matter of fact I don't. This is a once-in a-lifetime opportunity for Dan, for Laura too. How many kids get to live in a foreign country? Think what that would have meant to you when you were a child."

"Not much if it meant being half a world away from one of my parents."

"You're being selfish," Keri says. "It's two years, Brad, not forever. Can't you tell how excited she is."

"She believes it's always summer there. She believes she's going to have a pet koala bear."

"Look," Keri says, her tone no longer indifferent. "We're trying to make this easier for all of us."

No, not for all of us, I think.

"Look," Keri continues. "If I didn't think this was the best thing for Laura I wouldn't do it. Give me enough credit for that, Brad."

"How long before you leave?" I ask.

"Twelve days."

"Then I want to see her next weekend. I'll bring her Christmas presents."

"I don't think that's a good idea," Keri says. "We're going to be incredibly busy around here."

"So," I say. "I can take Laura and let you all get more done."

"Dan believes it will make it harder for Laura if you come," Keri says. "I think he's right."

"So it's better to pretend she's not going to be on the other side of the world for two years. Just act like she's going off to camp for a week."

"I didn't say that, but, yes, maybe it is better. I'm with Laura every day, so I think I know more than you what's best for her."

"I'd be with her every day too, if you hadn't moved back to South Carolina."

"Why are we talking about this again?" she asks. "What good can it do either of us?"

"I'm going to call my lawyer," I say. I feel like a man grasping for an out-of-reach limb even as he's falling farther away.

"You'd ruin this for Laura just to spite me," Keri says, her words not so much a question as a challenge. "And since when can you afford a lawyer," she adds. "I thought you were broke?"

I say nothing for a few moments. Keri knows as well as I do that I'm bluffing.

"Let me speak to Laura again."

"She's outside with Dan."

"Well, go get her," I say, sounding peevish even to myself.

Keri lays the phone on the kitchen counter, and I follow her footsteps down the hallway, follow her through the one-story farmhouse she and I lived in during grad school, a house loaned to us by her uncle on the condition I reshingle the roof.

I no longer hear her footsteps as Keri passes the bathroom and then the back bedroom where Laura was conceived, where Keri and I once slept curled together like question marks, my hand on her waxing belly. After the divorce Keri's uncle let Laura and her move back in. A year later Dan joined them.

"Yeah, Dad," Laura gasps, out of breath, a little impatient with my calling her back in to talk.

"I just wanted to tell you I'll get your Christmas presents to you before you leave."

"Okay," she says.

"I'll talk to you soon, okay."

"Okay," she says, and I know her elbow is already tensed to lay the phone back on its cradle.

I check my billfold, eighty dollars and a charge card not quite maxed out. I know where I'm going, but I don't know why or what I hope to accomplish other than to see my daughter's face when I tell her goodbye.

I don't bother to lock up the apartment, just get in the car and head out of town and into the huge, flat emptiness that spreads like calm water. I'm glad the dark conceals what surrounds me. I grew up where trees and upthrusts of land keep a person from seeing too much of where he's going, where he's been.

As I drive into the future I daydream that old sci-fi fantasy of going back in time, turning the car around and racing west across the country, back through Mountain and Pacific time, hours like waves I break through until three, four years have been recovered and Keri and I are married and Laura is still a baby and we get it right this time. Because that is the worst thing, the fear that it could have worked out if only a few more moments of wisdom, grace—even love—had intervened. Perhaps only one moment.

Neither Keri nor I had wanted to move to Illinois, but it was the only full-time teaching job either of us had been offered. By then fault lines had appeared in our marriage—we too often cherished our grievances against one another, as if they were medals awarded in a battle where we had been heroes. We too often looked for the worst in one another and too often found it.

The ten-hour drive to Illinois was a harbinger of what was to be. Keri and I had been up past midnight packing the U-Haul. We loaded the car the next morning, sweaty and exhausted as we buckled Laura in her back seat and headed north on what the radio announced would be the hottest day of the year. We were only two hours out of South Carolina and already arguing about when to stop and feed Laura, our decade-old Ford struggling up the high mountains of North Carolina toward the Continental Divide. The orange and white U-Haul trailer swayed and jolted in the rearview mirror, slowing us like an anchor someone had forgotten to raise. The temperature gauge rose, and I cut off the air conditioner, rolled down my window, but we were going so slow little air came in. Sweat beaded my brow, slickened the steering wheel.

"I'm hot," Laura whined.

Keri looked back at her. "She's covered in sweat, Brad. Turn the A.C. back on," she said.

"The car will overheat," I said. "It's just a few more minutes and we'll be going downhill."

Laura started crying.

"Turn it back on," Keri said.

"Okay, damnit," I said and yanked the control lever to A.C., punched the On button. The cool air poured over us as the temperature gauge rose.

We almost made it. Continental Divide One-half Mile, a blue-and-white sign said. The temperature indicator wavered like a compass needle in the red part of the gauge, but the car kept moving, and it seemed for a few moments luck might announce itself in our lives—I would be wrong, Keri would be right, and we would both be glad.

"I'm sorry I snapped at you," I said, about to reach for her hand when the radiator hose burst.

I pulled the car off onto the shoulder and hitchhiked on across the mountain, leaving Keri and Laura in the grass beside the car. Two hours passed before I was able to get back with a mechanic. Keri and Laura waited where I'd left them, their arms and faces sunburned. I reached out my hand to help them up but Keri got up by herself, lifted Laura into her arms.

"You're glad this happened," Keri said.

Our marriage found its metaphor on the Illinois plains, for you could not shake the feeling of an abandoned country, that Indians, settlers brought in covered wagons, had lived here once but moved on, leaving a vast loneliness for the eyes' wide stare. Even what appeared close was actually distant. You'd see a silo and drive miles and still not come to it—as if it were only a mirage shimmering on the horizon, as much an illusion as that point where land and sky met.

We lived in a farmhouse five miles from town, our only neighbor a morose old man named Eli Brown, who informed us a previous tenant's wife had hanged herself in our barn.

"Desolate," Keri said after a few days. "I never knew what that word meant until I came here." Keri and Laura stayed there while I drove into town each morning to teach. Keri rarely took Laura outside. She was as uncomfortable as I with that landscape. On the warmest, brightest fall days, she and Laura huddled inside the farmhouse like fugitives. After a month I suggested, then pleaded, that we move into town, but Keri refused. We were like armies maneuvering for an inevitable battle.

Keri made monthly trips with Laura back to South Carolina, and by November the trips were no longer weekends but weeks. Winter came and Keri and I lay in bed with our backs turned to each other and listened to a wind that nothing stood up to for a hundred miles in any direction. It slammed so hard against the wood I half expected the farmhouse to rip apart plank by plank and scatter like matchsticks across central Illinois. That spring when Keri told me she wanted a divorce, it seemed like an afterthought.

I cross the Indiana line at seven o'clock. I have no Christmas gift for my daughter. The bike I have bought for her is too large to take to Australia, too small for when she returns. On the outskirts of Vincennes I leave the interstate, find the inevitable Wal-Mart just past the city limits sign.

I don't know what I'm looking for, except that it must be small. I prowl the toy aisles for a few minutes but end up in the jewelry department looking at watches, passing over the ones with mice, dogs, cats, superheroes. I buy a watch with a blank face, its band coated in gold.

The miles between states are smaller now, and soon I leave Indiana and enter Kentucky, then Tennessee. Between Nashville and Chattanooga I cross the Cumberlands. I am lost in time, for somewhere out in the passing darkness an hour vanishes like blown sand, an hour I could use, for the two lanes I follow from Chattanooga to Greenville wind slow through the Appalachians, the turn-offs often unmarked, easily missed though I've driven them once a month for three years.

I stop at a Waffle House in Murphy, North Carolina.

"What can I get you, honey?" the waitress drawls, and I know clearer than any state line that I'm back in the South. I haven't eaten since lunch, so I order eggs and grits, a waffle on the side, a cup of coffee to keep my eyes open.

The only other customers are a man and child in a booth. They're dressed like they've just come from church, the man wearing a bad-fitting brown suit, the girl, maybe ten or eleven, in a blue cotton dress and overcoat, but even Pentecostals wouldn't be worshipping this late at night. On the child's plate a half-eaten waffle floats in a swamp of syrup.

"I want to go home," the child whines, and for a moment I wonder not so much where they've been but where they are going. Then a woman comes out of the bathroom, sits down beside the child.

"It's almost midnight," she tells the man. "We need to get her home."

I eat quickly, get a cup of coffee to go. In a few minutes I dip down into Georgia, then drive east, passing the Welcome to South Carolina sign, still hours away from where my daughter sleeps. I hit the four-lane near Greenville and can let my mind wander again as I move toward the heart of the state. I imagine a series of motel rooms where the curtains are always closed, diners and service stations where I look away as I thrust bills into palms belonging to people I'll never meet again. It's a dream where my daughter and I are never caught, never run low on money, the car never breaks down and strangers are always kind. I can imagine all this. What I cannot imagine is Laura willingly packing her suitcase in the whispered dark of her room, hugging me as she says, yes, I'll go with you.

It is past three when I skirt Columbia. Then I'm on a two-lane, almost there. Maybe it's fatigue, or just the fact that I'm the only one traveling this road so late, but the telephone poles seem to be rushing past me, not me past them, as if the rest of the world is caught in a current that I am not a part of.

I turn off my lights the last hundred yards, park in front of the mailbox, RADVICH printed on its side. I walk down the half-mile drive that leads to the farmhouse. Century-old pecan trees line the road, narrowing the sky, moon and stars leaking just enough light through the branches to keep a dim outline of the drive in front of me. In summer tree frogs and insects would be making a racket in the high grass and trees, but the land is silent now, only the wind's slight rustle. I can hear the soft crunch my feet make on sand left by a receding ocean eons ago.

I feel like a man sneaking into his own home as I creep around hedges to Laura's room. But I am no Odysseus, neither wily nor especially brave. Dan is a vegetarian. It seems incongruous that a vegetarian would own a firearm, much less use it, but nevertheless I raise my face to Laura's window like a man peering out of a foxhole. A nightlight bathes the room in a soft yellow haze, the darkness held at bay in the corners. I see Laura's body huddled under a quilt, only the top of her head visible. I press my palms under the window and shove upward, knowing the house was built when people worried less about protecting themselves and their possessions. The window gives with a rasping reluctance. I wait but no light comes on in the front bedroom, no feet pad down the hall to Laura's room. I raise my leg like I'm straddling barbed wire, use my hands to pull the rest of me inside. I listen, hearing only my heart knocking against my sternum. Someone stares at me from across the room, someone I'm not even sure I know anymore, an intruder. I walk toward him, raise my hand and touch the bureau's mirror. Laura stirs in the bed, says something I can't decipher as I lift up and examine what lies on the bureau—a hair barrette and brush, a porcelain dog with a missing front paw, a picture book titled *Down Under*, and a pencil box—Laura printed on the top, after the A an L partially erased, made into a K.

I sit down on the bed, pull back the quilt enough to see her face. I touch her cheek.

"Laura," I say, then again and she opens her eyes.

"Daddy," she says, her voice soft, unsurprised, her eyes unfocused. I am still part of a dream.

"I wanted to see you before you went to Australia," I say.

"Okay," she mumbles.

I take the watch from my pocket, but even as I do I know I will not give it to her, not now at least. A man who breaks into a house that isn't his own shouldn't leave evidence behind.

"I brought you a present," I say, and hold out the watch, the gold band lambent like distant fire in the nightlight's glow. Her eyes widen, grow more focused. "Not for now," I say, "for later when you're older."

"Can I put it on?" she asks, "Just for a minute?"

She holds out her thin wrist and I snap the clasp. The watch hangs loose as a bracelet.

"Too big," she says and yawns, lays her head back on the pillow.

"I'll save it until it fits," I say.

Laura's eyes flutter and close.

"Okay," she says.

I tell her I love her, for no other reason than the fact it is the truth. She nods but does not open her eyes, even when I remove the watch.

I sit on the bed a while longer. I listen to Laura breathe and believe that come morning this will have all been just a dream to her. I tell myself that years from now I will give her this watch to show her how dreams can sometimes come true—and I think what a shabby attempt at magic that will be, an illusion that time can be tricked by mere sleight of hand.

I kiss her, then crawl quietly through the window like the

intruder I am. The moon and stars are fainter now, first light sipping through on the horizon. The wind has picked up. I hear it move through the pecan trees like waves. In the fading dark, sand crunching under my feet, it is easy to believe I am at the edge of an ocean, an ocean that stretches out as far as I can see before curving away from me, distant as time.

I'm almost to my car when headlights round the curve and wash over my face. The truck slows, only a few feet away as it passes. I recognize the truck, the man inside the cab. Once, in the early months of my marriage, I'd given him a ride when his truck stalled on this same road. He had told me his name, a name I no longer remember. He speeds up, but not before raising his hand in a manner that argues I belong here, am a part of this place. Perhaps he believes I have never left this place or sees in his rearview mirror a shadowy far traveler who has finally made it home. Or is his act of kinship something else? Is he a person of broad sympathies, one who would understand why a man might break into a home that is no longer his, might wake a child only to say goodbye?

Kill Me Again Slowly
Zoë Sharp

I knew something was wrong when the waiter arrived before the punch-line. Up till that point, things had been going well.

Bizarrely, it has to be said, but well.

I was sitting at a table for six in *Rick's Café Américain* in Casablanca. The dry southeasterly wind, the *chergui,* pushed gently across Morocco from the Sahara, adding a warm lilt to the evening.

On the café stage, Glenn Miller led the jazz band with Wynton Marsalis giving it his all in a trumpet solo. I had to look twice to recognize a down-dressed Elton John at the piano.

The place was packed with beautiful people in immaculate clothes, a mix of uniforms and evening dress. All of them were having the time of their lives. Nobody was raucously drunk, nobody sent back their plate to the kitchen, and for once the haze of smoke that hung beneath the vaulted ceiling did not get right up my nose.

Best of all, nobody was paying too much attention to the other people at my table.

To my left Oscar Wilde lounged elegantly in his chair. Next to him was Marilyn Monroe, while further round sat Groucho Marx and Dorothy Parker. And directly on my right, next to Mrs. Parker, the final player in our little sextet was my host, Asher Campbell Cooper III.

He was dressed in a white tuxedo jacket, snowy white shirt, black pants and a bow tie that was just imperfect enough to be perfect. He looked about thirty, wide of shoulder and narrow of hip, with startling blue eyes and long tanned fingers that toyed with the stem of his champagne flute as he launched almost diffidently into the joke he never got to finish.

At that point his audience was listening with absolute attention. I caught the curve of Dorothy Parker's lips in what appeared to be genuine amusement. Even Oscar Wilde's languid pose had stilled, his brow creasing with the effort of searching fruitlessly for a witty retort to follow.

"So the three nuns, the Russian drug dealer and the clown are being pursued through the food hall of Harrod's by the Japanese ABBA tribute band, when the clown's cellphone rings—"

The waiter, Emile, materialized at Asher's shoulder and cleared his throat.

"Excuse me, sir," he said, bowing slightly, "but there is a telephone call for you. The party pressed upon me to convey that it was most urgent."

Asher shut his open mouth, sighed heavily and flicked me a glance.

"See?" he demanded, buttoning his jacket as he rose. "If you'll excuse me, ladies and gentlemen? I'll be back to finish my story momentarily."

"This suspense is terrible," Oscar Wilde drawled. "I hope it will last."

Groucho Marx waved his cigar expansively, reached around the beaded lamp in the center of the table for the champagne bottle and offered to top up Dorothy Parker's glass. She shook her head.

"One more drink and I'll be under the host."

I stood also, fell into step alongside Asher as Emile shepherded us through the crowded tables toward the bar. On it I could see an old-fashioned black telephone with the receiver off the hook.

"Is this how it usually starts?" I asked.

Asher nodded. "Or something similar. Damn shame. That's my best joke."

"There'll be another time."

Next to the bar was a narrow curtained doorway. As we passed I flicked the curtain aside. Nobody lurked behind it.

Asher grinned at me over his shoulder as he reached for the receiver. "You packing?"

I spread my arms to indicate my strapless, backless, practically arseless dress—his choice, not mine. "And where, exactly, did you expect me to hide a piece in this outfit?" I shot up a splayed hand before he could respond. "No, don't answer that."

He was still smiling as he picked up the phone. It didn't last.

"Yeah, thanks, Brant, but I'd kinda guessed as much," he said and slammed the receiver back onto its cradle.

"Trouble?"

"Uh-huh. Brant's rounding up the usual suspects."

As we weaved back toward our table, I murmured into his ear, "If it all goes bad, you know what to do."

"Yes, ma'am."

I let my gaze wash across the patrons, the staff and the musicians. Nobody was watching us too closely, or trying too hard to avoid doing so. Nobody's attitude had changed. But I was only too aware that I was in a situation where nothing could be trusted.

"If you want to know what God thinks of money," Dorothy Parker was saying to the table at large as Asher politely handed me into my seat, "just look at the people he gave it to."

Marilyn Monroe gave a breathy giggle and said, "Oh, I don't want to make money, I just want to be wonderful."

Dorothy Parker rolled her eyes.

Airily sipping his champagne, Oscar Wilde said, "Who, being loved, is poor?"

Groucho Marx rested his elbow on the table, his chin on his cupped palm, and gazed at Marilyn Monroe. "Marry me and I'll never look at another horse."

"Oh!" Marilyn Monroe glared at him, threw down her serviette and leaped to her feet. "Respect is one of life's greatest treasures." Her eyes were bright with unshed tears. "I mean, what does it all add up to if you don't have that?"

She leaned down for her purse, but when she straightened there was a bolo machete with an eighteen-inch blade in her right hand and she held it like it wasn't her first time. With an inarticulate war cry, she used her chair as a springboard to launch herself across the table aiming straight for Asher's head.

What the...?

Hurling myself sideways I sent him, chair and all, sprawling backward. The slashing arc of what should have been a deadly blow sizzled the air where Asher's throat had been only moments before. I pivoted with my hands on the front edge of his seat, scissored my legs and kicked one of the world's most beautiful women full in the face. In slow motion, I saw her nose fracture and the blood spray out.

She screamed, letting go of the machete. It bounced away under one of the neighboring tables. Landing in a crouch, I grabbed the legs of Asher's chair and wrenched it out from under him. Then I swung it through a hundred and eighty degrees like a hammer thrower going for Olympic gold. It connected with the side of Marilyn Monroe's head and she crashed off the side of the table, taking the beaded lamp with her, and showed the room exactly what she was wearing under that famous white dress.

The place was in uproar by then. Dorothy Parker had leaped to her feet while Groucho Marx dived under the table. Oscar Wilde was fumbling inside his tailcoat.

Some premonition just gave me the time to mutter, "Oh shit..." from between clenched teeth before he pulled out an Uzi machine pistol on a shoulder-strap and grabbed for the trigger.

Dorothy Parker went down flailing in the first burst. I dived on top of Asher, taking one round in the left arm and a second just above my left hip in the process. Both stung like a bastard.

Cursing, I rolled with him under the overhanging cloth of the next table, discovering—painfully—where Marilyn Monroe's discarded machete had come to rest. I hefted it in my right hand, which was the only one still functioning. Above us, the panic was full scream ahead, accompanied by the sounds of a mortally wounded piano and a symphony of breaking glass.

Asher saw the blood and paled. "Charlie—!"

I growled, "Stay down," gripped the machete and low-crawled out into a lethal forest of running feet.

A woman's stiletto heel stamped into the back of my right hand, momentarily skewering it to the floor. I let out an unheard roar of pain. Oscar Wilde was still spraying the room with nine-millimeter rounds at a rate of nine-hundred-and-fifty a minute. Somewhere under that coat he must have had a stack of spare magazines.

I flexed my injured hand. I could still just about make a fist, but trying to wield the machete with any force or accuracy was a non-starter. Instead, I reared up from behind the table and flung it awkwardly at the gunman like a boomerang I prayed wasn't going to come back.

At the last moment Oscar Wilde caught sight of the weapon flashing toward him.

He ducked and spun.

It was the wrong move.

The blade was honed like a razor. It sliced straight through the carotid artery at the side of his exposed neck. He lost his grasp of the Uzi and dropped to his knees, already starting to fade.

"Alas," he muttered, "I am dying beyond my means..."

Staying low—Okay, sagging—I checked the room. As far as I could tell everybody was running away rather than charging toward us.

"Okay, Asher," I called. "Show's over."

No response.

Oh shit...

Clumsily, I dropped to one knee and lifted the edge of the tablecloth. All I could see of Asher was a pair of black-clad legs ending in leather-soled shoes without a hint of wear. I jerked the tablecloth off completely and saw the rest of him on the far side. He had ignored my warning and followed me out into the line of fire. Blood oozed from the bullet holes in his jacket. Those blue eyes stared right through me.

I slumped to the floor and found myself at eye level with Groucho Marx who was lying under the next table, still clutching his cigar.

"Well, I've had a perfectly wonderful evening," he said. "But this wasn't it."

I surfaced through a glutinous morass with a tube down my throat, fighting the overwhelming urge to vomit.

"Take it easy, Charlie," said a calm voice somewhere above me. "Just gotta unhook the main sensor umbel-ical...Okay, you're all clear. Welcome back."

I sat up, dripping the pale green slime that was, so I'd been told, some kind of conductive fluid "to enhance the full-body experience." I ripped the tube out of my mouth with a hiccupping heave like a cat bringing up a fur-ball.

As I did so I realized I'd used both hands. I spread them out in front of me. No holes, no blood, and only a distant twinge.

The technician, Sherwin, grinned at me expectantly.

"So, what did you make of your first virtual reality trip? Pretty awesome, huh?"

I rubbed reflectively at my hip. "Are things *supposed* to hurt that much?"

"Ah, the boss had me ramp up the pain replication inputs so if you take a hit you can *really* imagine what the real thing feels like."

"It would have been nice if he'd mentioned that going in." I half-climbed, half-slithered out of the immersion tank. "Because some of us don't need to use our imagination, thanks."

He paled a little and suddenly found the need to give his full attention to wiping the gunk off the sensors and coiling them into a sterilization tray. For a few moments the only sound was the immersion tank draining like the last of the bathwater disappearing down the plughole.

We were in a small room with soundproofing material covering the walls. Apart from the tank, the overhead umbilical feed, and a steel trolley like you'd find in an operating theater, it was empty of other equipment. I supposed that having spent a good chunk of his considerable fortune developing this VR technology, Asher wanted the brains of it kept well away from prying eyes or fingers.

"Speaking of the boss," I said at last, "where is he?"

"Oh, um, I guess his nurse has taken him back to his quarters. He'll be okay in a half-hour or so," Sherwin said cheerfully. "It always takes him a little while to get over being dead."

Showered, dressed and feeling almost in touch with reality again, I found Brant, Asher's head of security, waiting for me in what I'd heard referred to as the den. It was more like the library of a very upmarket gentleman's club, complete with mahogany-beamed ceiling, clusters of wingback chairs, and flock wallpaper so deep you could wade in it. All that was needed to complete the picture was for some elderly colonel to quietly snuff it behind his copy of the *Financial Times.*

Brant did not seem entirely at home in such surroundings. He was an ex-Navy SEAL—a fact you could tell just by looking—but it was not his job to blend. Brant organized the highly visible security around the mansion on the edge of Falls Lake, just north of Raleigh in North Carolina, and the ten acres of grounds and gardens that went with it.

From what I'd seen on the way in, he was doing a damn good job. The surveillance gear was high grade and well positioned. His team of former military or law enforcement personnel knew what was expected and could be relied upon to think on their feet.

And beneath the more noticeable patrols of men with guns and dogs were layers of covert electronic security that meant a mouse would have a hard time sneaking through. The only extra I could think of was real-time satellite tasking, and I wouldn't put it past Brant to call in a few favors if he felt the need.

All this to protect a man who hadn't set foot outside the property for sixteen years.

As I strolled toward Brant, I reminded myself not to limp from the phantom gunshot wounds. Wasn't *so* long ago I was trying not to limp from the real ones.

"Handled yourself okay in there," Brant said by way of greeting, and although he didn't add the words "for a woman" I heard them all the same. "Not your fault the boss can't take orders."

"Is today typical of the kind of thing that's been happening?"

He nodded. "Just about every visit to La-La-Land over the past month, he comes out in a virtual body bag."

"Has the system been hacked?"

"Sherwin's the guy you'd have to ask about that. He starts talking schematics and I understand maybe one word in ten." He ran a frustrated hand over his close-cropped hair. "What I *do* know is, the whole system's standalone, completely unplugged from the 'Net. Only way anyone could insert a virus would be from *inside* the perimeter."

"Getting in is as close to impossible as makes no difference," I agreed—flattering, but true. "You've got this place sewn up tighter than a fish's armpit."

He showed his teeth briefly in satisfaction. "Watertight."

"So, what do you think is going on here?"

"It would be speculation on my part, but I'd guess somebody knows they can't get to him out there in the real world, so they're trying to take away the only thing he's got left."

A low hum preceded Asher's arrival, his electric wheelchair moving fast enough across the tiled floor that the uniformed nurse at his shoulder had to move briskly to keep pace.

"Hey, Charlie," he rasped, "how're you feeling?"

The irony of having my "dead" principal enquire after the health of his bodyguard was not lost on me.

Asher Campbell Cooper III was still a force of nature regardless of the circumstances of the meeting. According to the background dossier I'd read before heading down from New York, back when Asher was nineteen he'd inherited a modest amount from his father. He used the money to launch himself into the rapidly expanding world of the Internet in the early nineties and within ten years was running one of the largest service providers of wireless, satellite and cable on the Eastern seaboard.

From the file, the appearance he'd chosen for his VR avatar was based pretty much on the way he'd actually looked in younger days. Something of a playboy, he'd married a beauty queen and taken up motorsport. Had his cake, eaten it, licked up the crumbs, and gone back for more.

The pessimists would have said it couldn't last.

It didn't.

A high-speed freak racing accident, a structural failure, a high-temperature engine fire, and a methanol explosion. They all combined to produce the man in the wheelchair with an irreparably damaged spinal cord and third-degree burns that covered more than half his body. He'd lost the fingers of his right hand as well as his right eye and ear. Because he no longer had a recognizable nose, a permanent oxygen supply had been tubed into his chest to boost his seared lungs. Despite enduring years of surgical procedures, his face still had the appearance of an ice sculpture left out in the sun.

Yeah, the irony of *him* enquiring after *my* health was definitely not lost on me.

"I'm fine," I said now. "A great improvement on the last time I was shot—or stabbed for that matter."

He laughed. It sounded like a handful of grit thrown into a blender.

"Not many people get their head around it so fast. Nice job."

"It would have been better if I'd kept you alive in there," I said. "At least to the end of the first day."

"Well, at least you got to experience the craziness firsthand."

"Before we went in, you said it would be 'dinner with some old friends'," I said. "I assume the cabaret wasn't part of the plan?"

"Marilyn Monroe going postal on my ass? No, ma'am."

I paused. "How far do you trust your tech guy, Sherwin?"

"All the way," he said without hesitation. He swiveled the eye that worked in Brant's direction.

"Sherwin passes all the regular polygraph tests," Brant said. "His financials are clean and there are no threats to his family."

"Who else has the expertise to engineer that kind of scenario?"

"Maybe a handful of people in the world. But you forget—I use the technology for my own...diversion. I'm nobody's competition. They gain nothing by sabotaging my system."

"So, who *might* gain something?"

Asher's shoulder gave a convulsive twitch that might once have been a shrug. "I have no idea."

"What about the staff? Friends, family, business associates?"

"Brant vets everyone who works for me."

I didn't ask who vetted Brant—probably the CIA.

"Plus everyone who enters the house undergoes a covert scan for weapons, bugs or other electronic devices," Brant put in.

I didn't rise to that one. "You hired me for personal protection and that means cure as much as prevention. I'm going to need to talk to everyone, including your family."

"Yeah, well. Good luck with that."

Having struck out with the staff—as I'd known I would but still had to go through the motions—I moved on to the family. And working on the theory that sibling rivalry can be the most vicious kind I started with Asher's younger brother, Michael.

On the surface he seemed a viable suspect. Ten years younger, not as good looking, not as much of a go-getter. Michael was a solid kind of guy who would have been the pride of his parents...had his parents not also had a son like Asher to invite unfair comparison.

But after the accident Michael got promoted to the

number-one spot. He was now in command of the Internet giant his brother had started. The reports showed he had the smarts to know his limitations and surround himself with the right people. The business was sound, showing steady growth and the ability to innovate without overreaching itself.

Asher made the introductory call, and Michael's PA squeezed me in between meetings at their offices in downtown Raleigh.

"I'm sure you're anxious to get to the bottom of this," I said carefully as we shook hands. "Thanks for seeing me at such short notice."

"Well, Ash still has some pull around here," Michael said. Rather than returning to his desk he guided me to a cluster of low sofas overlooking the skyline. The building was impressive without being flashy, set in the heart of the city amid wide tree-lined streets.

I sat and raised an eyebrow. "I thought he was out of the company?"

"Oh, he is, don't get me wrong. He's a majority shareholder but draws no salary and he doesn't interfere with the direction I want to take things. Even so, he was the boss for a long time." He gave a shrug. "Old habits."

"If anything should happen to your brother, who gets his shares?"

"The family." He flushed. "I get some, if that's what you're driving at. The rest are split between our sisters—one in West Virginia, the other in Paris France. And Mother, of course."

"But you would have a controlling interest?"

It took him a moment to answer that. The flush regrouped around the collar of his shirt and put up a second wave.

"Look, I realize you have your job to do, but please be assured I am *not* trying to kill my brother—in this world or any other."

Behind us, the office outer door opened and Michael's PA hovered expectantly in the gap. He nodded to her and rose, buttoning his jacket.

"Like I said, Ash doesn't interfere. I can't say that would

be the case if my sisters took control of his shares." He shook my hand again, held on a moment longer. "I'll level with you, Miss Fox. I cannot imagine what it must be like for my brother to be the way he is, but I hope I'll be forgiven for praying the poor bastard lives to a grand old age."

"I stayed by his side and nursed him as far back as he was coming, then I left," said the former beauty queen. You could still see it in the arrangement of her features, the slant of her bones.

"Why no divorce?" I asked.

She smiled, causing a dimple to appear in her right cheek. "Partly to spite his mother," she admitted easily. "And partly because we're Catholics and, old-fashioned as it may seem in this day and age, we don't hold with divorce. Besides, there's no need. Ash and I already live our separate lives and he was more than generous."

She waved an elegant hand to indicate the corner penthouse condo in the PNC Plaza building—one of the tallest in Raleigh. It was airy and modern, with cherry-planked floors and high ceilings. Worth a fraction of the Falls Lake mansion, but well outside my price bracket.

"And if your husband should die?"

To her credit, a flicker passed across her features that I didn't think was faked and the smile turned wry.

"Then our arrangement ends and I get zip," she said. "Mommy dearest saw to that."

"A most unsuitable match," Mrs. Campbell Cooper sniffed, sitting rigidly upright in her chair. "I said she would never stay loyal to my son and I was not disappointed."

Looking at the old woman, her face deeply etched with decades' evidence of disapproval, I could believe it.

"Can you think of anyone who might wish to disrupt Asher's forays into virtual reality?"

She was too ladylike to snort, but it was a near thing. "Video games," she uttered with icy contempt. "All he has left is a first-class brain and he's rotting it playing *video games*. It's a shameful waste of his talents."

If I squinted hard I could just about see her point. Before this job the only contact I'd had with computer simulations was tactical weapons training. But for someone with Asher's permanent injuries I reckoned she could have shown a little more compassion. First-class brain or no.

"What would you rather have him do?" I asked. I did my best to keep my voice neutral, but she heard the implied censure even so.

"*Do?* What do you *mean* what would I have him do?" she demanded. "What is he fit for?" She refolded her hands in her lap, the upper gripping tight to the one beneath as if to prevent it yanking at her own hair.

"So why not let him spend his time however he chooses?"

"Do you honestly think *I* have any say in the matter?" she shot back. She paused, but I'd succeeded in poking her with a sharp enough stick to provoke an outburst. She rose, preparing to sweep out of the room in that wonderful state known as high dudgeon. At the last moment she hesitated just long enough for me to see the genuine anguish through the cracks in her formidable façade.

"We called him Asher. It means fortunate, blessed, and for a long time it seemed he was," she said. "But there isn't a day goes by when I don't wonder if they were gravely mistaken to pull him from the wreckage of that crash."

"Just about anyone could upload some kinda virus if they were told how to go about it," Sherwin said a shade defensively. "And hey, it was me took this whole thing—the glitches that kept occurring in the program—to Brant in the first place. You've met the guy. Why would I go poke an angry bear with a stick if I didn't have to?"

I hid a smile at the outrage in his voice. "How real a danger could Asher be in from these 'glitches'?"

He shrugged. "Kinda hard to say. I mean, if somebody really had it in for the boss surely they'd just find a way to override the safety protocols instead?"

"Which would do what, exactly?" I asked.

He cast me a slightly disbelieving look that I had to ask. "Well, when he gets shot, or run down by a train, or trampled by wildebeest, or pushed off a cliff—all of which have happened recently. There was this one time—"

"Focus, Sherwin!"

"Oh, um, yeah. Well, it would be theoretically possible to induce such physical shock to his system that it would sent him into cardiac arrest."

"But that's not the way the system's been hacked?"

He shook his head. "It's just the scenarios that are totally messed up." He looked about to say more but flicked me an unhappy glance instead.

"This whole thing is totally messed up," I said, "so if you have anything you want to share, however bizarre, please go ahead."

"Well, it's almost like whoever's doing this is not trying to kill him," he said unhappily. "This is more like...torture."

"I think I have a handle on what's going on," I said. "We need to meet."

"You have? That's great," Asher said, the damage to his voice making him hard to read over the phone. "I have just the scenario. You're gonna love it."

"Real world, real time, Asher."

"My dollar, my call," he responded. "Besides, you're in North Carolina. You can't leave without seeing the best it has to offer."

I bit back a pithy retort. "Well you're the boss."

"Yes, ma'am," he said. "Have Sherwin get you kitted out and I'll see you on the other side."

The grit of sand against my teeth was driven this time by a biting northeasterly rather than a gentle Saharan wind. I stood alongside Asher on a vast open stretch of dunes with a grey

Atlantic ahead and a grey sky above. Both of us wore overcoats, hats, and gloves.

"Any of this seem familiar?" Asher asked.

I glanced around. The land rose steadily behind us. The only buildings nearby were wooden shacks, their timbers bleached silver by the elements. What appeared to be a bed sheet flew from one of them like a huge flag.

Then, from the far side of the largest shack, a group of half a dozen men appeared, hauling a contraption that looked both heavy and flimsy at the same time. It was half hang-glider, half children's kite, held together with string and bicycle chains and mounted on a pair of wagon wheels.

"My God," I murmured. "The Wright brothers. We're at Kitty Hawk."

Asher nodded. "Kill Devil Hills on the Outer Banks, to be precise. Kitty Hawk is a couple of miles further up. It's December seventeenth 1903 and we're about to witness the dawn of the aviation era."

I didn't point out that this was a mere virtual reconstruction, no more real than watching a play.

"You wanted to talk, so talk," Asher invited. "Don't worry, they won't do anything momentous until we're ready."

It was hard not to be fascinated as we strolled closer. The men wrestled the machine onto a narrow wooden rail in the sand and lifted the cartwheel bogeys out from under each wing.

"I talked to your family," I said. "Your mother has taken your condition hard."

I caught no glimpse of emotion on the smooth features of Asher's avatar. His eyes were on the two brothers, Wilbur and Orville, fussing round their craft. Wilbur was the taller of the two, clean-shaven and balding. They shared only a passing resemblance.

"Mother was always my greatest supporter and my sternest critic," Asher said at last. "I know how difficult it's been for her to see me as I am now—on the outside."

"She thinks you might have been better off if they'd left you in the burning wreck."

I watched his face as I spoke and saw he'd heard this all

before—probably from the lady herself. She didn't strike me as the kind who'd keep a grievance silent.

He glanced down at me. I'd noticed before that he'd programmed himself with extra height. Either that or made the rest of us shorter.

"She's never had any trouble speaking her mind. Mostly, it's refreshing. Besides, you must have thought the same thing, first time you laid eyes on me."

"Your mother's a daunting woman," I said, side-stepping his question. "Maybe, subconsciously, you're trying to please her."

"By trying to kill myself?" He laughed, a far more melodious sound than in real life. "If I truly wanted to die in here, then I've sure had plenty of opportunities."

"But you were always a thrill seeker, weren't you Asher—a risk taker? Where did it get you?"

"It got me a business empire. If I hadn't taken risks the company would never have gotten off the ground." He nodded toward the Flyer as the Wright brothers swung the propellers and the engine spat and coughed and roared its way to life. "It's amazing *that* thing ever did."

I ignored his attempt to change the subject. "The company has continued to prosper with your brother in charge, and I've never met a man more conservative. Must be tough to watch, especially for someone who considered himself indispensable."

Asher said nothing.

"It would be enough to make anyone wonder what had it all been for?" I went on, just loud enough to be heard over the Flyer's raucous exhaust note.

"You think I *want* to keep dying in here?"

"I think the prospect of dying is, for you, the last great adventure," I said. "I think it's all you have left to live for."

Orville Wright climbed through the tangle of bracing struts to lie on the lower wing. He took the Flyer's control levers, revved the engine and released the wire holding him onto the track. The craft lumbered forward and wobbled slowly into the air.

A cheer went up from the assembled ground crew. Asher and I watched as the bi-plane gradually gained both altitude and airspeed.

After a moment I nudged his arm. "If you *are* serious about your health, we should move." And when he blinked at me, frowning, I added, "How long was the first powered flight supposed to last?"

"Around twelve seconds..."

Above us the bi-plane went into a high banked turn and swooped downward with increasing agility.

"I get the feeling this has suddenly turned into the crop-duster scene from *North By Northwest*," I said. "Move! *Now!*"

There wasn't a handy cornfield to hide in, but the wooden hangar where the Flyer had been stored was standing open and empty. I dragged Asher inside by the lapels of his overcoat and almost flung him against the back wall.

The bi-plane buzzed the roof low enough to make the whole building shudder and raced away to make another run.

"Are you hoping that if you die in here often enough, one day it will really happen?"

"You're crazy," he said. "If I was trying to kill myself I could have removed the safeties and been dead long before now."

"But where's the sporting uncertainty in that? Where's the thrill?" I threw back. "And you're forgetting—a man who won't go against the Church to divorce his wife certainly wouldn't countenance the sin of suicide."

I'd nailed it. I could see it in his face. I let go of his coat and stepped back.

"Take this as my resignation," I said. "Now get me out of this pantomime."

"Please, Charlie—"

I silenced him with a glare. "I can work with a client who doesn't want to die," I said. "But there's fuck all I can do with one who doesn't want to live."

Walking the Dog
J.L. Abramo

I don't remember hearing the gunshot, but the bullet nearly killed me.

The last thing I could remember hearing before I woke up in a hospital bed twenty days later was a voice calling from behind. I can remember stopping to turn—feeling as if I knew the voice but unable to place it. The moment I came out of the coma, the thought briefly grabbed me and then let go.

There are only two things that scare me more than death.

Most frightening by far is the thought of something truly horrible happening to one of my children.

My son had disappeared for two hours one summer. Charlie was six years old and had strayed from the area where we had been camping. It was a fairly desolate spot, so we weren't afraid he would be abducted. We were terrified he might take a dangerous fall or discover a lake to drown in. Frantically we searched and called out for him, praying darkness wouldn't fall before we could locate him.

Finally, there he was. A good half-mile from our campsite. He was surrounded by fallen tree branches, a kind of makeshift fortress. Sitting there, piling small stones he had gathered to create a squat tower. Totally at ease and fearless—completely glad to see us. I told him what a nice job he had done with the stones, asked him if he was ready to leave, scooped him up in my arms and carried him over to his mother.

It was at least a week before I slept well again.

Next on my list of personal terrors, lurking between concern for the well-being of my children and my own mortality, is the thought of losing my sight or the use of my legs.

Two of my childhood friends had lost their legs, one to diabetes and the other in an automobile accident. One crawled away from life toward an early death while the other passionately embraced life with both arms. I fear my approach would be much more like the former. It is impossible to describe what went through my mind when I found myself in a hospital bed with no feeling at all below my waist.

When I came out of my twenty-day sleep they were all there—my wife, my son, and my daughter.

The moment I opened my eyes Annie, who is thirteen going on thirty, said, "Gee, Dad, you must have been very tired." For an instant I could hear the voice that had called from behind me the night I was shot, and then it was gone. I was happy to see my family. When I discovered I had no feeling below my waist I asked my wife what was going on.

"Don't be afraid, Johnny. The doctors say it will be okay and you shouldn't worry."

Nice try.

I was born on the first day of October, 1973. While my mother was in labor, my dad was in the maternity ward lounge with other expectant fathers watching the baseball game. My mother would often tell us how my father came running into her room bubbling with excitement and cried, "The Mets clinched the East, how are you doing?"

When I came out of the coma, my son Charlie ran and jumped up onto the bed, landing on my knees. I didn't feel a thing.

"Hi, son," I said, "getting excited about the Mets' home opener?"

"That was two weeks ago, Dad."

That was when I asked Maggie what week it was.

Charlie asked me if he was too heavy. I told him he was as light as a feather and to stay right where he was. He laughed and asked me what kind of feather. I was doing whatever it is you do with your mind when you want to move your toes. I began to feel lightheaded and must have passed out.

When I woke again my family was gone and had been replaced by two men in white lab coats and stethoscopes. One held a silver clipboard in his left hand while he twirled a pen like a baton in his right. The other was stroking his chin like a Rodin statue and self-consciously dropped his arm to his side when my eyes popped open.

As I looked up at them they smiled simultaneously.

I anxiously waited to find out which of these geniuses would be the first to speak.

After a barrage of mumbo jumbo from the Thinker, about where the bullet had entered and exited and how a bone fragment was affecting my ability to feel the entire lower half of my body, he turned it over to medical mastermind number two. Using his clipboard for protection he assured me the condition was almost surely temporary.

Almost surely?

I wondered why doctors insisted on using terms that were absolutely meaningless to their patients. Being a gambler myself, I told him I would prefer simple odds. He said we were looking at a touchy operation but one that was not without a good rate of success and worrying about it would only make my situation more difficult. I wanted to kick him but I couldn't move my leg. As they turned to leave the room they promised they would return soon to complete the touchy operation consent forms and reminded me that all of the resources of the great City of New York were at our disposal.

"The mayor has been here to see you, twice," said Clipboard.

If I had been doing something more in the line of duty than walking my dog in the park on the night I was shot, I suppose the Governor may have popped in also.

I asked them to thank His Honor for me, twice, and to please send my wife and children back into the room.

When my family returned, I asked Maggie to find Sam and beg him to get over to the hospital as quickly as humanly possible.

* * *

I met Maggie during my senior year at Queens College. It was the fall of 1995 and on the minds of most Americans was the O.J. Simpson trial. Margaret Kelly sat behind me in a Political Science class called *Law and Social Change* and was constantly voicing her extremely emphatic opinions over my left shoulder. She predicted that innocent or guilty Simpson would be acquitted. I personally couldn't call that one, but every other student and the professor strongly disagreed.

I bumped into her in the cafeteria the next day and worked up the nerve to approach her as she sat down to her lunch.

"Mind if I ask you one question?" I asked.

"That is a question. Was that the question?"

"Okay, can I ask you another question?" I asked, and then quickly added, "I mean beside this one?"

"Sure, sit."

I sat.

"Do you really believe Simpson will beat the rap?"

Not exactly out of the book on how to pick up girls.

"Yes, I do. And what's more I never say what I don't believe."

"Never?"

"Never, now did you want to ask me out?"

"Yes."

"Then why don't you ask me, before you run out of questions?"

Simpson was found not guilty a few weeks later.

The night of the verdict Maggie and I were sitting in my Bonneville.

"Well, you nailed that one. Are you always that good at predicting the future?"

"Try me."

"Will we both get into Law School?"

"Yes. Though maybe not the same Law School."

"Will we both become lawyers?"

"You will if you really want to."

"Fair enough. Here's one," I said. "If we were married someday, would we be happy together and have lots of kids?"

"Very happy. Two children, but only after I get done with school, and you'll have to help a lot with the kids so I can practice law before I'm an old woman."

"Fair enough."

Margaret Kelly was right about everything. She was accepted into Columbia Law School, completed her studies, passed the New York State bar, had two beautiful children, and was now a prosecutor in the New York City District Attorney's Office. I graduated with a degree in Political Science and Criminology, but I guess I must not have really wanted to be a lawyer, so here I was instead, lying half-paralyzed in a hospital bed waiting to hear from my partner Sam.

Maggie had to take the kids home to feed them and then drop them off with my sister Barbara so she could get back for an evening visit alone. She said she would try to track Sam down as soon as she reached the house.

After they left, I had one thought and one thought only. I wanted a cigarette. Whether smoking was allowed in the hospital room was not an issue. I couldn't care less. The problem was finding a cigarette, particularly a Camel straight.

The chances of finding one in that room were not good. In fact, even if there was a pack two feet from me I would not have been able to reach it in my condition. There was no denying I was going to need some help.

I am not exactly proud of the fact I smoke cigarettes. It is an unhealthy habit and a tough one to kick.

I am, nevertheless, resolved to the fact. I concluded long ago that one thing I am, among many others, is a smoker. I am an Irish-Italian-American, a very good cook, a loving father, a faithful husband, a devoted son to my cantankerous old man, a better than average softball player, a fair harmonica player, a great Pinochle player, an avid reader, a moderate drinker, an opera lover, a lousy car mechanic, a gun control advocate, a movie addict, and a cigarette smoker.

I pushed the button that was pinned to my gown. This would theoretically summon a nurse to my side. The theory was empirically confirmed when two minutes later a nurse whose nametag identified her as Mary Campanella walked into the room.

"Can I help you, Mr. Sullivan?" she asked.

"I hope so."

"I'll do my very best."

"Do you mind if I smoke?"

"I don't care if you burst into flames," she said and then added, "Sorry, just joking. I've always wanted to say that."

"What are the chances you could get me a Camel cigarette?"

"Slim and none, and slim already left town."

"Let me guess, you've always wanted to say that?"

"No, that one I use every time a patient asks me for a cigarette."

"No exceptions?"

"Well, there is one. If you can give me a really good reason why I should break the rules and bring you a cigarette so you can break the rules, I might give your request some consideration."

"I work with your Uncle Pete."

She walked to the foot of the bed and glanced at the chart hanging there.

"Oh," she said, "you're *that* Mr. Sullivan."

"John."

"Camel you said?"

"Yes."

"Non-filter?"

"Please."

"Give me ten minutes."

"Thank you."

"Don't mention it."

"Don't worry, I won't."

I suppose the cigarette was a little too much for me after almost three weeks cold turkey because the next thing I remembered was opening my eyes to a room lit only by the glow of the television screen on the opposite wall. I don't know how far I made it with the Camel before I fell asleep, but I did notice in the faint green illumination that the ashtray and all other evidence of my transgression had been deftly removed from the scene of the crime. I was reaching for the buzzer on my chest to call for some light when a voice out of the darkness almost got my legs working again.

"How are you feeling, son?"

"Not half bad, Pop," I said. "Why are you sitting in the dark?"

"Didn't want to wake you, want a cigarette?"

"No thanks, I think I just had one. Pete Campanella's niece was good enough to smuggle one in for me."

"Mary?"

"Yeah, she's a real sweetheart."

"She have a boyfriend?"

"She's a little young for you."

"I was thinking about your cousin Jimmy."

"Forget it. She's a nurse, not a psychiatrist. Where's Maggie?"

"She took the kids over to Barbara. I asked her to drop me off here first. Who shot you, son?"

"Don't know. I'm hoping Sam will show up soon with some ideas."

"When I find out, I'm going to kill the bastard."

My father wouldn't hurt a fly unless the fly was involved in an armed felony.

"Thanks, Dad, but maybe we can just rough him up a little."

"Are you going to be able to walk again?"

"That's what they tell me. I certainly hope so."

"Can I do anything for you?"

"Yes, as a matter of fact. Next time you come, bring one of Aunt Tillie's veal parmesan sandwiches on Sabatino's bread and keep Jimmy away from the Campanella girl. And could you change the television station? I think *Jeopardy* is on. And turn on the lights so I can see you."

The lights revealed what was totally hidden from his voice. My tough-as-nails father had clearly been crying. It was almost enough to get me going myself, but I controlled my emotions. I could do that well. After all, I had learned from him. Or maybe I was just saved by the bell, because just then Maggie walked in.

"Hi, Counselor. Thanks for dropping Dad off."

"I'm surprised you two aren't smoking your brains out."

"Did you get hold of Sam?"

"Left a message for him to hurry down here. He's out on the job somewhere."

"I'm missing all the fun."

"Don't worry—there will still be work when you get back. There's never a shortage in your business."

"Hallelujah."

Alex Trebek read the categories for Double Jeopardy.

Maggie and the old man kept the conversation light during their visit. That and the pain medication for the parts of my body that could still feel pain made me sleepy again. I had heard from the hospital grapevine that the operation was tentatively scheduled for the day after next. The theory was that a small bone fragment, which was pressing against my spine, would be carefully removed through a touchy operation and my almost surely temporary lower body paralysis would be history. Terrific theory. And certainly one worth subscribing to. Maggie and Dad said their goodbyes and left me to drift into sleep. I was fighting to stay awake until I heard from Sam, but lost the battle.

In my dream I was reading a book in bed when I heard my father's 1982 Ford Galaxy start up in the driveway. It was October 1986, and Dad was taking my brother to the sixth game of the World Series against the Red Sox at Shea Stadium. The Mets were down three games to two.

Frankie was the logical choice to go with Dad.

Frankie was a diehard Mets fan. I was a Yankee fanatic, but the last time the Bronx Bombers had been in the Series was in 1978, and at five I was too young to go. Regardless of allegiances, I was as jealous as a thirteen-year-old could be that his nine-year-old brat of a brother was going to get to the big game before I did. But in the dream it felt as if something else made me want to jump out of the bed, run to the car, and tell Dad not to take Frankie with him that day. Tell my father to take me instead, and leave Frankie home with Mom. But in the dream I couldn't move my legs, as desperately as I tried, and I lay there helplessly as I listened to the Ford pull away.

When the phone woke me, I was soaked with sweat and I was shaking like a leaf.

Fortunately, the phone was within my reach and I grabbed it after the third ring.

"Spook house," I said.

"Did I wake you?"

"Yes, and I can't thank you enough," I said. "Where are you?"

"I couldn't begin to tell you, partner. It's such a mess that to call it ridiculous would be a gross understatement. I wish you were here."

"I wouldn't mind."

"Margaret tracked me down. How are you feeling?"

"Not bad from the waist up."

"I'm not going to get out of this one soon, but I'll come straight over when I can cut loose. Get some sleep. If you're asleep when I get there, I promise to wake you up."

I wasn't anxious to fall asleep again and pick up my dream where it had left off. I knew all too well how it ended. I wanted another smoke pretty badly, but not enough to bother the nurse again. I turned the television on and flipped through the channels until I came across a martial arts movie already in progress. I watched with the hope that soon I'd be up and kicking again myself.

I was dreaming again. The car was pulling out of the driveway. I was trying to get up from the bed but my legs wouldn't work.

"You will not believe this one." I snapped awake.

The booming voice ricocheted off every wall in the small room and reached my ears with the subtlety of a slap in the face. This is how Sam wakes you. Not like Prince Charming with a whisper and a kiss, but like a hostage negotiator with a bullhorn.

It's one of the character traits that make him so lovable.

"I'm ready to believe anything," I said.

"Picture this, if you will. A guy calls in a pizza delivery order from Di Fara's on Avenue J. Sausage, onion, and green pepper."

"I appreciate the attention to detail."

"It's important. The delivery kid knocks on the door, it's the upstairs of a two-family house on East Fourteenth Street, and the guy opens the door. He keeps the kid waiting on the landing while he goes to get his wallet.

"Cat comes back with a slice on a paper plate, he holds it out to the kid and says, 'Take a bite and tell me if this is sausage, onion, and green pepper'. The kid says he's not really very hungry and he can tell just by looking that it's pepperoni and mushroom. The guy pulls a forty-four Magnum and insists the kid taste it just to be certain."

"He forced the kid to eat pizza at gunpoint. Is that a felony?"

"It gets better," said Sam. "The guy forces the poor kid into the apartment and ties him into a chair. Clothesline. Then he calls the pizzeria and he tells the manager it's the third time they've fucked up his order and if they don't get the right pie up to him in twenty minutes he's going to blow the delivery kid's head off. So much for don't shoot the messenger."

"Unbelievable."

"What'd I tell you? The manager calls the owner at home and the old man calls it in to the precinct. So me and Stevie O'Brien—this is who they put me with because you had to go and get plugged—run over to the pizzeria. O'Brien throws on a smock covered with red sauce, and we take a pizza over to Fourteenth Street."

"I can't stand the suspense."

"Wait. We get to the place, O' Brien knocks on the door, I stand out of view of the peephole. The guy says through the door, 'You look a little old for a delivery boy.' Not to mention that O'Brien looks less Italian than I do, his skin is the color of Elmer's Glue-All. Anyway, Stevie starts winging it, rambling about how he owns the joint and he's Irish, the name Di Fara's is a cover but don't tell anyone because it could hurt business and the hostage in there is his sister's son and she'll murder him if anything happens to the kid, and the pizza, which absolutely has sausage, onion, and green pepper and is by the way on the house, is getting cold."

"I'm exhausted just listening to this. Does the guy make the exchange?"

"He opens the door. He's got the forty-four pointed right at O'Brien's head."

"Oh, boy."

"I've got to admit Stevie stayed cool. He takes a step toward the guy and starts to open the pizza box. The guy asks Stevie what the fuck he's doing and O'Brien says he wants to show the guy that the toppings are correct so he can get his nephew the fuck out of there. Meanwhile, I've got my gun out and I'm wondering when this guy is going to take a peek over and spot me. The next thing I hear is screaming. I jump into the doorway and this guy is trying to get hot mozzarella out of his eyes while O'Brien is tackling him to the floor, the weapon drops neatly into the pizza box, Stevie is trying to handcuff the guy, both their hands are slippery with marinara, and I don't know whether to try to help O'Brien or grab a slice."

"You arrest the guy?"

"Oh, yeah. When I left the station they were still trying to figure out the charge. The gun wasn't registered, but it wasn't loaded either. If we call it a kidnapping, the FBI is going to make us hear about it until the end of time. And all along the guy is yelling about how he's going to sue the city for burning his face with hot tomato sauce. His cheeks look as if they were used to wax a car. So how are you doing?"

"Better than some. Anybody have any ideas about who put the bullet in me?"

"Not a clue, probably someone you locked up once or twice. Maybe we could sit and brainstorm for a while. Can we smoke in here?"

"What are they going to do, arrest us?"

* * *

After graduation I had a decision to make. Maggie had been accepted by the Columbia School of Law, but no law school in the city was interested in me. There were a few out-of-town schools that were interested, but the thought of leaving New York City and Margaret Kelly was unacceptable. I enrolled in the Master's program at the John Jay College of Criminal Justice instead. Two years later, newly married and with Maggie still studying, it was time to begin earning a living. The obvious choice, maybe the only choice from the very beginning, was to join the police force.

I met Sam on my first assignment as a homicide detective. When I arrived he was already at the scene.

"Sullivan," I said, holding out my hand. "John to my friends."

"First homicide call?"

"It is."

"You look Sicilian," he said.

"My mother. My dad was another Irish cop."

"Then we could be distant cousins." He smiled, his white teeth sparkling in his huge black face. "Name's Samson, Sam to my friends."

"Good to meet you, Sam."

"We'll see, John. Gotta minute?"

"Sure."

"Follow me."

He led me into the adjoining room. In the middle of the room was a large bed. In the middle of the bed was a small child. Ten months old maybe. A year at most. A little boy, though you couldn't tell it from his face which looked as if it had been used for soccer practice.

"Welcome to Homicide," Sam said.

That night my father was over for dinner. I asked him what he considered his worst experience in all his years on the job. He reminded me it was the time he came very close to shooting a teenager in the A&P supermarket.

Sam went on and on with a blow by blow recapitulation of all the fun I had missed during my three weeks in limbo.

After an hour and a half of non-stop narrative, Sam fell asleep in the middle of a sentence. It was getting on toward eight in the morning. I decided I had best wake him. I expected Maggie to drop in on her way to the office and figured it was time Sam got some real rest.

If I could have reached him from the bed I would have used a gentle shake. Instead I bopped him off the forehead with an empty paper cup.

He opened his eyes and looked at the cup that had landed neatly in his lap.

"Fine shot."

"Go home and get some sleep."

"Good idea," he said, slowly rising. "I'll be back later. Want me to bring you anything?"

"Anything on my assailant would be nice."

"I'm not very optimistic, but I'll do my best," Sam said. "I'm very glad to see you back among the conscious, partner."

Maggie ran in and out just long enough to give me a kiss and a little squeeze between my legs to see if there had been any miracles overnight. Nothing, but I appreciated the gesture.

Soon the Bobbsey Twins materialized with a third person in tow. He was a good-looking kid with all the trappings of a doctor—lab coat, stethoscope and clipboard. He was introduced as Dr. Levine, an intern working with them on my case. Levine looked so young it was all I could do to stop myself from asking if he was looking forward to his bar mitzvah.

The three stooges took turns round robin style going over the operation planned for the next morning. What it would entail, what I could expect, and what the desired outcome would be.

"If all goes well"—they let Dr. Levine do the closing argument—"we will eliminate the source of pressure on your spine and you should be able to walk out of the hospital at one hundred percent."

I loved it when they use words like *if* and *should*, straight from the handbook of medical disclaimers.

"Will I be able to tap dance?" I asked Levine.

"I see no reason why not," he answered confidently.

Except for the fact I could never tap dance before.

And, believe me, there had been many times I'd tried.

They turned to leave but I pulled them up short.

"Aren't there some papers I need to sign?"

"Oh, yes," said Moe, or was it Curly, "how silly of us, we almost forgot."

You *did* forget, Einstein, I said to myself. And did he say *silly?* Oh, boy.

I was hoping they would remember to wear their silly little rubber gloves the next morning.

It was still not even nine in the morning, and I had at least twenty-four hours to wonder if I would really be able to walk on my own two legs again. The choices for distraction were *Rachel Ray, Live with Kelly and Michael,* or the paperback Maggie had dropped off. I opted for the book. A murder mystery.

There were visitors coming and going all day. They must have waived the limited visiting-hours policy because I was a hero. Lucky me. When you're a cop and you get shot they always try to make you a hero, no matter what you were doing when you got shot, even if you were walking your dog or holding the weapon in your teeth when it happened.

My father was there most of the morning and the early afternoon. He was taking advantage of my condition, telling me stories I had heard a hundred times since I was four years old. He had a captive audience.

And he had nowhere else to go.

Frank Sullivan was a lonely man, even in a room full of people, particularly since my mother passed away.

It had been proven at many a gin mill and family get-together.

Sam showed up just before noon, looking as if he had slept for a week and needed at least two more. He rescued me briefly by taking Dad down for lunch.

There were others in and out. Other cops, some suit from City Hall bringing best wishes from the mayor, the dynamic duo with more papers to sign, Sam to re-deposit Dad by the bed before he had to "get back out on the street and go do good," the Campanella kid to check up on my nicotine cravings.

It's amazing how popular you can become just by taking a bullet in the back.

Look at Jesse James.

My sister came to drop my kids off after school and collect Dad.

Charlie had a baseball bat and asked if he could bat my legs to see if I would feel anything. I said, "No, but thanks for asking."

Anne, she insisted her days as "Annie" were officially over, scooped up the mystery novel and went straight to the last chapter.

Maggie showed up after work and took the kids home for dinner, and came back for a few hours in the evening.

Nurse Campanella came in at around nine insisting I'd need my rest for the morning's appointment with the knife. She encouraged my wife to leave without too much coaxing. The Counselor was exhausted.

Maggie kissed me goodnight, asked me not to worry and assured me she would be at my side throughout.

Not long after Maggie left, Nick Ventura walked into the hospital room holding a large flat box with Totonno's written all over it.

Nick and I grew up on the same Brooklyn street. He was a private investigator who tried roping me into his fiascos a little too often.

"Did you bring beer?"

He placed the box on the bedside table and pulled a Sam Adams out of each pocket of his jacket.

"There's a slice missing," I said when he opened the box.

"Bribe to Mary Campanella to let me in after visiting hours."

"If you're here to ask for help on one of your hopeless cases, I'm sort of on sabbatical."

"I just came to see how you were. Carmella sends her regards."

"Have Carmella and the boys got the beauty shop up and running again?"

"Why? Do you want to get your toenails done?"

I had to laugh.

"Did you hear about Sonny Balducci?" Nick asked.

"They find him?"

"A Boy Scout troop stumbled on a shallow grave when they were digging a fire pit at Camp Pouch in Staten Island. When the forensic guys dug him up they found three red snappers sitting on his chest."

"Nice touch."

"What do you think?"

"Good riddance."

We ate pizza, drank beer, smoked Camels, and reminisced about all of the lines drawn and the choices we were forced to make growing up in the Borough of Churches.

"Do you remember my brother Frankie, Nick?"

"Of course I do. He was a sweet kid."

"Yes, he was," I said.

"Everyone is saying you're going to be fine."

"What if everyone is wrong? What if this is it, and I can't dance at my daughter's wedding?"

"Remember junior year when I broke my ankle sliding into third base last game of the season?"

"How could I forget, they could hear you screaming in Yonkers."

"I thought it was the end of the world."

"You were safe at third, the pinch-runner scored, we won the game, and we made it to the Borough Championship."

"It didn't matter to me, I was inconsolable. Two weeks later I was in a cast up to my knee on the day of the championship. My father planned to take me to the ball field. I said I wouldn't go and I locked myself in my room. He warned me if I didn't unlock the door he would bust it down and break my other ankle. I believed him and let him in. He asked me why I wouldn't want to see my team play for the title. I told him I didn't think I could handle it, that it would be hell to be there and not able to be out in the field. My old man never said much worth repeating but what he said that day got me out to the game."

"What was that?"

"When you're going through hell, keep going."

Nurse Campanella came in to chase Nick out and feed me a pill to help me get to sleep.

"Yell if you need anything," Ventura said.

"Could you leave a few of those cigarettes?"

He placed the package of Camels on the pizza box. He stopped at the door.

"John?"

"Yes?"

"How come no one told me little Annie was engaged to be married?"

"Cute," I said, smiling. "I appreciate you dropping by, Nick."

The pill kicked in quickly and I was nodding out before the second commercial break on an old rerun of *NYPD Blue.*

I remember wondering if I would grow up to be like Andy Sipowitz or Larry Flynt. I remember wondering why all the female cops looked like movie stars.

I remember wondering why David Caruso and Jimmy Smits had given up such a great job.

I remember wondering, as I asked a little favor of God, whether the answer was going to be yes or no.

I remember waking up the next morning and being thrown onto a gurney.

I remember being wheeled into the Operating Room with Maggie's hand clutched tightly in mine.

I remember Doogie Levine MD smiling down at me just before I went under.

Then it was 1986 again and I heard my father's Galaxy start up in the driveway below my bedroom window.

I could hear the Ford pulling out of the driveway taking my father and brother to Shea.

Just as I heard the Galaxy back out onto West 10th Street, my legs suddenly came back to life.

I jumped out of bed, ran down the stairs and rushed out the front door onto the stoop.

I could see the Ford crossing Avenue S.

I could run pretty fast but I knew I'd never catch them before Dad turned onto 86th Street toward the Belt Parkway.

I was almost back into the house when I heard someone call my name from a few doors down. I turned toward the voice to find Bobby Leone yelling for me.

"Johnny."

"Hey, Bobby."

"Get over here."

"What's up?"

"Hurry."

I walked over to where Bobby was pounding on Nicky Ventura's door.

Ventura was up in his window saying he couldn't come down and Bobby was saying if Nicky didn't come down he was going to get the crap beat out of him.

And I was wishing I had stayed inside.

"They stole Tony's bike," Bobby said.

"Who?"

"Three seniors from Lafayette grabbed it on Kings Highway. We're going up there and we're going to get it back."

"High school seniors? Jesus, Bobby, they'll be twice our size."

"Goddammit, Ventura, get the fuck down here," he yelled up at the window.

"I don't know if we want to tangle with high school kids, Bobby," I said.

"What do you mean you don't know? What if it was your fucking bike?"

I didn't have a bike.

"Nicky, I'm getting really pissed," he yelled again.

And he was.

"Where's Tony?" I asked.

"Stop asking a million fucking questions and get a stick or

something because when I drag that asshole Nicky down here we're going to Kings Highway."

"I don't want to go, Bobby. It's Tony's bike, so where's Tony? And you're too riled up, you need to calm down."

And then he walked down the steps from Nicky's front door and hit me between the legs with the baseball bat he was holding.

The swing was more Ben Hogan than Mickey Mantle.

And then, in the dream, he said, "You're going to die for this, Frankie."

But Frankie was my brother's name.

I held myself where Bobby had hit me with the bat.

Then I felt myself getting aroused down there.

I opened my eyes and found my wife with her hand down there.

"Look who is back and rearing to go," she said.

"I guess the operation went okay," I said.

"Sure feels like it."

"Do you think I should try to get out of this bed?"

"What's the rush?" Maggie said, and she climbed into the bed beside me.

I must have fallen asleep again.

My father walked into my room.

"How was the game, Dad?" I said, "I was looking for you and Frankie on the TV."

"Come downstairs. Your mother and I need to speak with you."

"What is it?"

"Just come down, son."

I followed him down the stairs into the living room. My mother was sitting on the sofa. Her eyes were red. My father sat beside her and wrapped his arm around her shoulder. I rushed over to Dad's vacant TV chair, wanting to grab it before Frankie came in. Come to think of it, where was Frankie?

"Where's Frankie?" I asked.

Dad and Frankie had stopped into the A&P on Stillwell

Avenue on their way home from the ballgame. My father always carried his service revolver, even when off duty.

When they came to the checkout, a young neighborhood kid was pointing a gun at the cashier as she filled a paper sack with money from the register. Dad drew his weapon and told the boy to give it up before it was too late, and then it was too late. The kid pointed the gun toward my father and my brother and the gun went off.

"Frankie was killed, John," my father said.

"Was it Bobby Leone?" I asked, shaking.

"No, of course not," he said. "It was a boy from the high school. A squad car picked him up on Kings Highway."

"It's my fault," I said.

I should have gone to that game.

I should have gone with Bobby to Kings Highway.

I should have left Dad's chair empty for Frankie.

I woke up and found Sam sitting beside the hospital bed.

"We got the guy who shot you."

"What was his beef?"

"He thought you were someone else. He was gunning for someone named Frankie Johnson who walks a dog exactly like yours in the same park and who happened to be sleeping with the shooter's wife."

"*You're going to die for this, Frankie.*"

"Huh?"

"That's what I heard, before the gunshot. I thought he was calling *my* name, I thought I knew the voice. I was hearing something else. How'd you find him?"

"He killed Johnson this morning. I heard the surgery went okay."

"Yeah, want to see me get up and walk?"

"I was hoping you'd do that little tap dance you do."

"Is Maggie around?"

"Saw her on my way in. She's gone to fetch the kids. She looked somewhat disheveled. You guys didn't decide to do some catching up here in the hospital bed?"

"I'm not sure."

"Don't tell her that."

* * *

A week later we had just finished dinner when I asked my father if he would take a walk with me around the block. What I wanted was a stroll down memory lane. Maggie said she'd have the coffee and dessert ready when we got back.

Charlie wanted to come along but Annie, in all her teenage wisdom, sensed that I needed to be alone with Dad and she corralled her little brother at the front door, bribing him to stay with the promise of a chocolate éclair.

"Dad," I said, as we moved away from the house.

It was good to be walking.

"Yes, son?"

"The day Frankie died, the day of the World Series game."

"Yes."

"The kid who shot Frankie, he was one of the kids who stole Tony Baretta's bike earlier that day," I said. "Bobby Leone wanted me and Nicky Ventura to go with him to find them."

"And do what, get yourselves shot?"

I guess not.

We were quiet during the rest of the walk, but it was good just to be at his side.

When we returned to the house, the pastries and the espresso were laid out as promised. Annie, I should say Anne, gave me a quick peck on the cheek and said she was meeting her friends at the Kent movie theater on Coney Island Avenue.

"How are you getting there?" I asked.

"Connie's mom."

"Don't let me find out differently."

"Okay, I won't let you find out," she said, and ran out laughing.

I had to laugh also.

Maggie had a legal brief to complete, so she apologized and moved to her study.

My father and my son busied themselves with dessert.

"Dad," Charlie said.

"Yes."

"Remember when I was little and I got lost at the camp place?"

How could I forget?

"Yes, son."

"How come when you found me you called me Frankie?"

"Did I?"

"Yeah. You said, *Thank God, Frankie, I thought I would never see you again.*"

"I guess it was my special way of telling you how glad I was to find you, son."

"Oh, okay," he said.

"He reminds me a lot of Frank, Jr.," said my father, reaching for a pastry.

"Grandpa, the éclair is mine," Charlie said. Then he looked over at me and added, "But I'll share it with you."

I left them to it and took the dog for a walk in the park.

Christians
Tom Franklin

1887

It was August, so she had to bury him quick. Soon she would be able to smell him, a thing she didn't know if she could endure—not the live, biting odor he brought in from a day in the fields but a mixture of turned earth and rot, an odor she associated with decaying possum and coon carcasses, the bowl of a turtle she'd overturned as a girl and then tumbled away from, vomiting at the soup of maggots pulsing inside.

It was late afternoon. He lay on his back on the porch, covered by a sheet stained across the torso with blood, the sheet mapped with flies and more coming, as many flies as she'd seen gathered in one place, a revival of them, death calling like the Holy Spirit. In her left hand she held his hat, which the two men had thrown to the ground after they'd rolled him off the wagon and left him in the dirt.

She hadn't wailed at the sight. Hadn't flung herself on the body or swiped her fingernails at their implacable faces as they watched, the two of them, one young, one old. She hadn't even put her hand over her mouth.

They told her they'd kept his gun. Said they meant to give it to the sheriff. Said like father like son.

"Leave," is all she'd said.

And she herself had dragged him up the steps, holding him under his arms. She herself had draped him with their spare bed sheet and turned her rocking chair east to face him and sat rocking and gazing past him—past the corpse of him and its continents of flies—to the outreaching cotton so stark and white in the sun she could barely look at it, cotton she'd have to pick herself now that her son was dead.

* * *

Sheriff Waite came. He got down off his horse and left the reins hanging and stood in the yard. He studied the drag marks, the stained dirt. His green eyes followed the marks and paused at the blood on the plank steps and the gritty line of blood smeared across the porch. He watched the boy under the sheet for nearly a minute before he moved his eyes—it seemed such an effort for him to look at country folks—to her face. In the past she'd always had trouble meeting town men's eyes, the lust there or the judgment (or both), but now she sat rocking and staring back at him as though she understood a secret about him not even his wife knew. His hand went toward his nose, an unconscious gesture, but he must've considered it disrespectful for he lowered the hand and cleared his throat.

"Missus Freemont."

"It was that Glaine Bolton," she said. "Him and Marcus Eady."

Waite stepped closer to the porch. Behind him his tall handsome horse had sweat tracks down through the dust caked on its coat. It wiggled its long head and blinked and sighed at the heat, flicked the skin of its back and the saddle and the rifle in its scabbard.

"I know," Waite said. "They already come talked to me. Caught me over at Coffeeville." He moved his hand again, as if he didn't know what to do with it. "How I was able to get here so quick."

She folded her arms despite the heat, nestled her sweating breasts between them.

"They give me his pistol," Waite said.

She waited, and his face became all lines as he got himself ready to say it out loud. That there would be no justice. Not the kind she wanted, anyway.

Since it was so easy to look at him now, she did it, reckoning him in his late forties. If she hadn't been so brimming with hate, she'd have still considered him fine-looking, even all these years later. His shirt fit well at the shoulders, his pants snug at the hips. He was skinnier than before. One thing she noticed was that his fingers weren't scarred from cotton, where nail met skin, the way hers and her son's were. Had been.

"You see," Waite began, "it's pretty generally known where your boy was going." He flapped a hand at her son. "When they stopped him."

"'Stopped him?' That's what you call what they done?"

"Yes'm."

She waited.

"He was going to shoot Glaine's daddy."

She waited. She realized she'd quit rocking and pushed at the porch boards with her bare feet until she was moving again, whisper of wind on the back of her neck, beneath her bun of brown hair. She heard her breath going in and out of her nose.

Waite suddenly took off his hat and began to examine the brim, the leather band sweated through, then turned it over and looked into the dark crown shaped by his head. "Way I hear it," he said, "is your boy and Travis Bolton had some words at the Coffeeville Methodist last week. I wasn't there, see. I'd been serving a warrant down in Jackson." When Waite came forward she heard his holster creak. He set a foot on the bottom step, careful not to touch the blood, and bent at the waist and rested his elbows on his knee. "But I got me a long memory, Missus Freemont. And the thing I told you back then, well, it still stands."

Bess had a long memory, too.

She'd been sixteen years younger. Sixteen years younger and almost asleep when that *other* wagon, the first one, had rattled up outside. She rose from where she'd been kneeling before the hearth, half in prayer, half for warmth. Another cold December day had passed, she remembered, rain coming, or snow. It was dark out, windy at intervals, the rocking chair on the porch tapping against the front wall. A pair of sweet potatoes on the rocks before her all the food they had left.

A horse nickered. She pulled her shawl around her shoulders and held it at her throat. Clay, not two years old then, had been asleep under a quilt on the floor beside her. Now he got up.

"Stay here, boy," she told him, resting a hand on top of his head. He wore a tattered shirt and pants given by church women from the last county they'd lived in, just over a week before. Barefooted, he stood shivering with his back to the fire, hands behind him, the way his father liked to stand.

On the porch, she pulled the latch closed behind her and peered into the weakly starred night. Movement. Then a lantern raised and a man in a duster coat and derby hat seemed to form out of the fabric of darkness. He wore a beard and spectacles that reflected the light he held above him.

"Would you tell me your name, miss?" he asked her.

She said it, her knuckles cold at her throat. She heard the door open behind her and stepped in front of it to shield Clay.

"This is my land you're on," the man said, "and that's one of my tenant houses y'all are camped out in."

Bess felt relief. *He's only here about the property.*

"My husband," she said. "He ain't home."

"Miss," the man said, "I believe I know that."

Fear again. She came forward on the porch, boards loose beneath her feet, and stopped on the first step. The horse shook its head and stamped against the cold. "Easy," the man whispered. He set the brake and stepped from the seat into the back of the wagon, holding the lantern aloft. He bent and began pushing something heavy. Bess came down the first step. Behind her, Clay slipped out the door.

The man climbed from the tailgate of the wagon and took a few steps toward her. He was shorter than she was, even with his hat and in his boots. Now she could see his eyes.

"My name is Mister Bolton," he said. "Could you walk over here, miss?"

She seemed unable to move. The dirt was cold, her toes numb. He waited a moment, gazing past her at Clay. Then he looked down, shaking his head. He came toward her and she recoiled as if he might hit her, but he only placed a gloved hand on her back and pushed her forward, not roughly but firmly. They went that way to the wagon, where she looked in and, in the light of his lantern, saw her husband.

E. J. was dead. He was dead. His jacket opened and his shirtfront red with blood. His fingers were squeezed into fists and his head thrown back, mouth opened. His hair covered his eyes.

"He was stealing from me," Bolton said. "I seen somebody down in my smokehouse and thought it was a nigger. I yelled at him to stop but he took off running."

"Stealing what?" she whispered.

"A ham," Bolton said.

Bess's knees began to give way, she grasped the wagon edge. Her shawl fell off and she stood in her thin dress. Bolton steadied her, his arm going around her shoulders. He set the lantern on the floor of the wagon, by E. J.'s boot.

"I am sorry, miss," Bolton said, a hand now at each of her shoulders. "I wish..."

Clay had appeared behind her, hugging himself, his toes curling in the dirt.

"Go on in, boy," she told him. "Now."

He didn't move.

"Do like your momma says," Bolton ordered, and Clay turned and ran up the stairs and went inside, pulling the door to.

Bolton led Bess back to the porch and she slumped on the steps. He retrieved her shawl and hung it across her shoulders.

"My own blame fault," he said. "I knew y'all was out here. Just ain't had time to come see you. Run you off."

No longer able to hold back, Bess was sobbing into her hands, which smelled of smoke. Some fraction of her, she knew, was glad E. J. was gone, glad he'd no longer pull them from place to place only to be threatened off at gunpoint by some landowner again and again. No more of the sudden rages or the beatings he gave her or Clay or some bystander. But, she thought, for all his violence, there were the nights he got only half-drunk and they slept enmeshed in one another's limbs, her gown up high where she'd pulled it and his long johns around one ankle. His quiet snoring. The marvelous lightness between her legs and the mattress wet beneath them. There were those nights. And there was the boy, her darling son, who needed a stern hand, a father, even if what he got was one like E. J., prone to temper and meanness when he drank too much whiskey. Where would they go now, she asked herself, the two of them?

"Miss?" Bolton tugged at his beard.

She looked up. It had begun to rain, cold drops on her face, in her eyes.

"You want me to leave him here?" Bolton asked her. "I don't know what else to do with him. I'll go fetch the sheriff directly. He'll ride out tomorrow, I expect."

"Yeah," Bess said. She blinked. "Would you wait...?" She looked toward the window where Clay's face ducked out of sight.

"Go on ahead," he said.

Inside, she told the boy to take his quilt into the next room and wait for her.

When she came out, Bolton was wrestling E. J. to the edge of the wagon. Bess helped him and together they dragged him up the steps.

"You want to leave him on the porch?" Bolton huffed. "He'll keep better."

"No," she said. "Inside."

He looked doubtful but helped her pull him into the house. They rolled him over on a torn sheet on the floor by the hearth. In the soft flickering firelight, her husband seemed somehow even more dead, a ghost, the way the shadows moved on his still features, his flat nose, the dark hollows under his eyes that Clay would likely have as well. She pushed his hair back. She touched his lower jaw and closed his mouth. Tried to remember the last thing he'd said to her when he left that afternoon. His mouth had slowly fallen back open, and she put one of the sweet potatoes under his chin as a prop.

Bolton was gazing around the room, still wearing his gloves, hands on his hips. Abruptly, he walked across the floor and went outside, closing the door behind him. When he came back in, she jumped up and stared at him.

In one arm he held a bundle.

"This is the ham," he said, casting about for somewhere to set it. When nowhere seemed right, he knelt and laid it beside the door. "Reckon it's paid for."

He waited a few moments, his breath misting, then went outside, shutting the door. She heard it latch. Heard the wagon's brake released and the creak of hinges and the horse whinny and stamp and the wheels click as Mr. Bolton rolled off into the night. She went to the window and outside was only darkness. She turned.

Her fingers trembling, Bess unwrapped the cloth sack from around the ham, a good ten-pounder, the bone still in it. A pang of guilt turned in her chest when her mouth watered. Already its smoked smell filled the tiny room. She touched the cold, hard surface, saw four strange pockmarks in its red skin. Horrified, she used a fingernail to dig out a pellet of buckshot. It dropped and rolled over the floor. She looked at her husband's bloody shirt.

"Oh, E. J.," she whispered.

The next morning, as Bolton predicted, Waite arrived. She left Clay in the back, eating ham with his fingers.

"I'm the sheriff," he said, walking past her into the cold front room. He didn't take off his hat. His cheeks were clean-shaven and red from wind and he wore a red mustache with the ends twisted into tiny waxed tips. The silver star pinned to his shirt was askew, its topmost point aimed at his left shoulder.

Moving through the room, he seemed angry. When he saw E. J.'s old single barrel shotgun he took it up from the corner where it stood and unbreeched it and removed the shell and dropped it in his pocket. He snapped the gun closed and replaced it. The door to the back room was shut, and glancing her way, he pushed aside his coat to reveal the white wood handle of a sidearm on his gunbelt. Pistol in hand, he eased open the door and peered in. The little boy he saw must not have seemed threatening because he closed the door and holstered his pistol. He brushed past Bess where she stood by the window and clopped in his boots to the hearth and squatted by E. J. and studied him. He patted the dead man's pockets, withdrew a plug of tobacco and set it on the hearth stones. Watching, she felt a sting of anger at E. J., buying tobacco when the boy needed feeding. In E. J.'s right boot the sheriff found the knife her husband always carried. He glanced at her and laid it on the rocks beside the plug but found nothing else.

Waite squatted a moment longer, as if considering the height and weight of the dead man, then rose and stepped past the body to be closer to her. He cleared his throat and asked where they'd come from. She told him Tennessee. He asked how long they'd been here *illegally* on Mr. Bolton's property and she told him that, too. Then he asked what she planned to do now.

She said, "I don't know."

Then she said, "I want my husband's pistol back. And that shotgun shell, too."

"That's a bold request," he said. "For someone in your position."

"My 'position.'"

"Trespasser. Mr. Bolton shot a thief. There are those would argue that sidearm belongs to him now."

Unable to meet his eyes, she glared at his boots. Muddied at the tips, along the heels.

"I'll leave the shell when I go," he said, "but I won't have a loaded gun while I'm here."

"You think I'd shoot you?"

"No, I don't. But you won't get the chance. The undertaker will be here directly. I passed him back yonder at the bridge."

"I can't afford no undertaker."

"Mr. Bolton's already paid him."

Bess felt her cheeks redden. "I don't understand."

"Miss," he said, folding his arms, "the fact is, some of us has too little conscience, and some has too much." He raised his chin to indicate E. J. "I expect your husband yonder chose the right man to try and rob."

She refused to cry. She folded her arms over her chest and wished the shawl could swallow her whole.

"I have but one piece of advice for you," the sheriff said, lowering his voice, "and you should take it. Travis Bolton is a damn good man. I've known him for over ten years. If I was you I would get the hell out of this county. And wherever it is you end up, I wouldn't tell that young one of yours who pulled the trigger on his daddy. 'Cause if this thing goes any farther, even if it's ten years from now, fifteen, twenty years, I'll be the one that ends it." He looked at E. J. as he might look at a slop jar, then turned to go.

From the window, she had watched him toss the shotgun shell onto the frozen dirt and swing into his saddle and spur his horse to a trot, as if he couldn't get away from such business fast enough. From such people.

"Travis Bolton's a good man," Waite repeated now, these years later, putting his hat back on. "And it ain't that he's my wife's brother. Which I reckon you know. And it ain't that he's turned into a preacher, neither. If he needed hanging, I'd do it. Hanged a preacher in Dickinson one time, least he said he was a preacher. Didn't stop him from stealing horses. Hanged my second cousin's oldest boy once, too. A murderer, that one. Duty's a thing I ain't never shied from, is what I'm saying. And what I said back then, in case you've forgot, is that you better not tell that boy who killed his daddy. 'Cause if you do, he'll be bound to avengement."

"Wasn't me told him," she said. So quietly he had to lean in and ask her to repeat herself, which she did.

"Who told him, then?"

"The preacher's son his self did."

Waite straightened, his arms dangling. Fingers flexing. He looked at her dead boy. He looked back at her. "Well, Glaine ain't the man his daddy is. I'm first to admit that. Preacher's sons," he said, but didn't finish.

"Told him at school, Sheriff. Walked up to my boy in the schoolyard and said, 'My daddy kilt your daddy, what'll you say about that, trash.' It was five years ago, it happened. When my boy wasn't but thirteen years old. Five years he had to live with that knowing, and do nothing. Five years I was able to keep him from doing something. And all the time that Glaine Bolton looking at him like he was a coward. Him and that whole bunch of boys from town."

Waite took off his hat again. Flies had drifted over and he swatted at them. He rubbed a finger under his nose, along his mustache that was going gray. "Thing is, Missus Freemont, that there ain't against the law. Young fellows being mean. It ain't fair, it ain't right, but it ain't illegal, either. What is illegal is your boy taking up that Colt that I never should've give you back and waving it around at the church like I heard he done last Sunday. Threatening everbody. Saying he was gone kill the man killed his daddy, even if he is a preacher."

Last Sunday, yes. Clay'd gone out before dawn without telling her. Soon as she'd awakened to such an empty house, soon as she opened the drawer where they kept the pistol and saw nothing but her needle and thread there, the box of cartridges gone too, she'd known. Known. But then he'd come home, come home and said no, he didn't kill nobody, you have to be a man to kill somebody, and he reckoned all he was was a coward, like everybody said.

Thank God, she'd whispered, hugging him.

Waite dug a handkerchief from his back pocket and wiped his forehead. "Only thing I wish," he said, "is that somebody'd come told me. If somebody did, I'd have rode out and got him myself. Put him in jail a spell, try to talk some sense into him. Told him all killing Bolton'd do is get him hanged. Or shot one. But nobody warned me. You yourself didn't come tell me. Travis, neither. And I'm just a fellow by his self with a lot of county to mind. One river to the other. Why I count on folks to help me. Tell me things."

He looked again at her son, shook his head. "If he'd had a daddy, might've been a different end. You don't know. But when a fellow says—in hearing of a lot of witnesses, mind you—that he's gone walk to a man's house and shoot him, well, that's enough cause for Glaine Bolton and Marcus Eady to take up a post in the bushes and wait. I'd have done the same thing myself, you want the truth. And if your boy come along, toting that pistol, heading up toward my house, well, miss, I'd a shot him too."

A fly landed on her arm, tickle of its air-light feet over her skin. Waite said other things but she never again looked up at him and didn't answer him further or take notice when he sighed one last time and turned and gathered the reins of his mount and climbed on the animal's back and sat a spell longer and then finally prodded the horse with his spurs and walked it away.

She sat watching her hands. There was dried blood on her knuckles, beneath her nails, that she wouldn't ever wash off Blood on her dress front. She'd have to bury her boy now, and this time there'd be no undertaker to summon the preacher so it could be a Christian funeral. She'd have to find the preacher herself. This time there was only her.

She walked two miles along unfenced cotton fields wearing Clay's hat, which had been E.J.'s before Clay took it up. She didn't see a person the whole time. She saw a tree full of crows, spiteful loud things that didn't fly as she passed, and a long black snake that whispered across the road in front of her. She carried her family Bible. For no reason she could name she remembered a school spelling bee she'd almost won, except the word "Bible" had caused her to lose. She'd not said, "Capital 'B,'" to begin the word, had just recited its letters so her teacher had disqualified her. Someone else got the ribbon.

Her Bible was sweaty from her hand so she switched it to the other hand then carried it under her arm for a while. Later she read in it as she walked, to pass the time, from her favorite book, Judges.

Her pastor, Brother Hill, lived with his wife and eight daughters in a four-room house at a bend in the road. Like everyone else, they grew cotton. With eight sets of extra hands, they did well at it, and the blonde stepping-stone girls, less than a year apart and all blue-eyed like their father, were marvels of efficiency in the field, tough and uncomplaining children. For Bess it was a constant struggle not to covet the preacher and his family. She liked his wife, too, a tiny woman named Elda, and more than once had had to ask God's forgiveness for picturing herself in Elda's frilly blue town dress and bonnet with a pair of blonde girls, the youngest two, holding each of her hands as the group of them crossed the street in Coffeeville on a Saturday. And once—more than once—she'd imagined herself to be Elda in the sanctity of the marriage bed. Then rolling into her own stale pillow which took her tears and her repentance. How understanding God was said to be, and yet how little understanding she had witnessed. Even He, even God, had only sacrificed once.

Girls. Everyone thought them the lesser result. The lesser sex. But to Bess a girl was something that didn't have to pick up his daddy's pistol out of the sideboard and ignore his mother's crying and push her away and leave her on the floor as he opened the door checking the pistol's loads. Looking back looking just like his daddy in his daddy's hat. A girl was something that didn't run down the road and leap sideways into the tall cotton and disappear like a deer in order to get away and leave you alone in the yard, trying to pull your fingers out of their sockets.

She stopped in the heat atop a hill in the road. She looked behind her and saw no one. Just cotton. In front of her, the same. Grasshoppers springing through the air and for noise only bird whistles and the distant razz of cicadas. She looked at her Bible and raised it to throw it into the field. For a long time she stood in this pose, but it was only a pose, which God saw or didn't, and after a time she lowered her arm and walked on.

At Brother Hill's some of his girls were shelling peas on the porch. Others were shucking corn, saving the husks in a basket. Things a family did in the weeks the cotton was laid by. When they saw her coming along the fence, one hopped up and went inside and returned with her mother. Bess stopped, tried in a half-panic to remember each girl's name but could only recall four or five. Elda stood on the steps with her hand leveled over her eyes like the brim of a hat, squinting to see. When Bess didn't move, Elda came down the steps toward her, stopping at the well for a tin cup of water, leaving the shadow of her house to meet Bess so the girls wouldn't hear what they were going to say.

"Dear, I'm so sorry," Elda whispered when Bess had finished. She reached to trace a finger down her face. She offered the tin.

"I thank you," Bess said and drank.

Elda touched her shoulder. "Will you stay supper with us? Let us go over and help you prepare him? I can sit up with you. Me and Darla."

Bess shook her head. "I can get him ready myself. I only come to see if Brother Hill would read the service."

The watchful girls resumed work, like a picture suddenly alive, when their mother looked back toward them.

"Oh, dear," Elda said. "He's away. His first cousin died in Grove Hill and he's there doing that service. He won't be back until day after tomorrow, in time for picking. Can you wait, dear?"

She said she couldn't, the heat was too much. She'd find someone else, another preacher. Even if he wasn't a Baptist.

It was after dark when she arrived at the next place, a dog-trot house with a mule standing in the trot. There was a barn off in the shadows down the sloping land and the chatter of chickens everywhere. This man was a Methodist from Hattiesburg, Mississippi, but he was prone to fits and was in the midst of one then, his wife said, offering Bess a cup of water and a biscuit which she took but didn't eat. Though Bess couldn't recall her name, she knew that here was a good woman who'd married the minister after her sister, his first wife, had died of malaria. Been a mother to the children.

In a whisper, casting a glance at the house, the woman told Bess that her husband hadn't been himself for nearly a week and showed no sign of returning to his natural, caring state. She'd sent the young ones to a neighbor's.

As Bess walked away, she heard him moaning from inside and calling out profane words. A hand seemed to clamp her neck and she felt suddenly cold though her dress was soaked with sweat. God above was nothing if not a giver of tests. When she thought to look for it, the biscuit was gone, she'd dropped it somewhere.

The last place to go was to the nigger preacher, but she didn't do that. She walked toward home instead. She thought she smelled Clay on the wind on her face before she came in sight of their house. For a long time she sat on the porch holding his cold hand in hers, held it for so long it grew warm from her warmth, and for a spell she imagined he was alive. The flies had gone wherever flies go after dark and she fell asleep, praying.

She woke against the wall with a pain in her neck like an iron through it. The flies were back. She gasped at their number and fell off the porch batting them away. In the yard was a pair of wild dogs which she chased down the road with a hoe. There were buzzards smudged against the white sky, mocking things that may have been from God or the devil, she had no idea which. One seemed the same as the other to her now as she got to her knees.

Got to her knees and pushed him and pulled him inside and lay over him crying. With more strength than she knew she possessed, she lifted him onto the sideboard and stood bent and panting. He was so tall his ankles and feet stuck out in the air. She waved both hands at the flies but most were outside, only a few had got in. She closed the door, the shutters, and moved back the sheet to look at his face. For a moment it was E. J. she saw. Then it wasn't. She touched Clay's chin, rasp of whisker. It was only a year he'd been shaving. She built a little fire in the stove, heated some water, found the straight razor and soaped his cheeks. She scraped the razor over his skin, rubbing the stiff hairs onto the sheet that still covered his body, her hand on his neck, thumb caressing his Adam's apple. She talked to him as she shaved him and talked to him as she peeled back the stiff sheet and unlaced his brogans and set them side by side on the floor. She had never prepared anyone for burial and wished Elda were here and told him this in a quiet voice, but then added that she'd not want anybody to see him in such a state, especially since she'd imagined that he and Elda's oldest daughter would someday be wed. Or the second oldest. You could've had your pick of them, she said. We would've all spent Christmases together in their house and the sound of a baby laughing would be the sound of music to my ears. His clothes stank, so she unfastened his work pants and told him she'd launder them as she inched them over his hips, his knees, ankles. She removed his underpants which were soiled and covered his privates with the sheet from her bed. She unbuttoned his shirt and spread it and closed her eyes then opened them to look at the wounds. Each near his heart. Two eye-socket holes—she could cover them with one hand and knew enough about shooting to note the skill of the marksman—the skin black around them. She flecked the hardened blood away with her fingernails and washed him with soap and water that turned pink on his skin. Then, with his middle covered, she washed him and combed his hair. She had been talking the entire time. Now she stopped.

She snatched off the sheet and beheld her boy, naked as the day he'd wriggled into the world of air and men. It was time for him to go home and she began to cry again. "Look what they did," she said.

The Reverend Isaiah Hovington Walker's place seemed deserted. The house was painted white, which had upset many of the white people in the area, that a nigger man would have the gall to doctor up his house so that it no longer had that hornet's nest gray wood the rest of the places in these parts had. He'd even painted his outhouse, which had nearly got him lynched. So many of the white folks, Bess and Clay included, not having privies themselves. If Sheriff Waite hadn't come out and made him scrape off the outhouse paint (at gunpoint, she'd heard), there'd have been one less preacher for her to consult today.

"Isaiah Walker," she called. "Get on out here."

Three short-haired yellow dogs kept her at the edge of the yard while she waited, her neck still throbbing from the crick in it. She watched the windows, curtains pulled, for a sign of movement. She looked over at the well, its bucket and rope, longing for a sup of water, but it wouldn't do for her to drink here. "Isaiah Walker," she called again, remembering how, on their first night in the area, E. J. had horse-whipped Walker for not getting his mule off the road fast enough. Though the preacher kicked and pulled the mule's halter until his hands were bloody, E. J. muttered that a nigger's mule ought to have as much respect for its betters as the nigger himself. He'd snatched the wagon's brake and drawn from its slot the stiff whip. She'd hoped it was the mule he meant to hit, but it hadn't been.

The dogs were inching toward her, hackles flashing over their backs, taking their courage from each other, smelling the blood on her hands, her dress. She wished she'd brought a stick with her. She'd even forgotten her Bible this time, saw it in her mind's eye as it lay splayed open on the porch with the wind paging it. She hadn't eaten since they'd brought Clay back, and for a moment she thought she might faint.

She stamped at the dogs and they stopped their approach but kept barking.

In all, it must have been half an hour before Walker's door finally opened, the dogs never having quit. She lowered her hand from her neck. The reverend came out fastening his suspenders and put a toothpick in his mouth. He looked up at the sky as if seeking rain. A man entirely bald of hair but with a long white beard and white eyebrows and small rifle-barrel eyes. He whistled at the dogs but they ignored him and ignored him when he called them by name.

She thought it proper for him to come down and meet her, but he never left the porch.

"This how you treat white folks?" she croaked at him.

"I know you," he said. "Heard why you here, too. And you might try tell me the Lord God, He expect me to forgive. But I been in there praying since you first step in my yard, Missus Freemont, since them dogs first start they racket, and I been intent on listen what God say. But He ain't say nothing 'bout me saying no words over your boy soul. If He wanted me to, He'd a said so. Might be them dogs stop barking. That would tell me. The Lord, He ain't never been shy 'bout telling me what to do and I ain't never been shy for listening."

But she had turned away before he finished, and by the time the dogs stopped their noise she had rounded a curve and another curve and gone up a hill and then sat in the road and then lay in it.

Lay in it thinking of her past life, of her farmer father, widowed and quick to punish, overburdened with his failing tobacco farm and seven children, she the second oldest and a dreamer of daydreams, possessed he said by the demon Sloth.

Thinking of the narrow-shouldered, handsome man coming on horseback seemingly from between the round mountains she'd seen and not seen all her life, galloping she thought right down out of the broad purple sky onto her father's property. The young man taking one look at her and campaigning and working and coercing and at last trading her father that fine black mare for a battered wagon, a pair of mules and a thin eighteen-year-old wife glad to see someplace new. Of crossing steaming green Tennessee in the wagon, of clear cool rainless nights with the canvas top drawn aside, lying shoulder to shoulder with her husband, the sky huge and intense overhead, stars winking past on their distant, pre-told trajectories, the mules braying down by the creek where they were staked and she falling asleep smelling their dying fire, his arms around her.

E. J. Ezekiel Jeremiah. No living person knows what them letters stands for but you, he'd said.

Ezekiel, she'd repeated. *Jeremiah.*

Out of the wagon to jump across the state line (which he'd drawn in the dirt with his shoe), laughing, holding hands, and going south through so much Alabama she thought it must spread all the way from Heaven to Hell. Slate mountains gave way to flatland and swamp to red clay hills, and they ferried a wide river dead as glass then bumped over dry stony roads atop the buckboard pulled by the two thinning mules. Then the oldest mule died: within two months of their wedding.

E. J. not saying anything for a long time, staring at the carcass where it lay in the field, hands on his hips, his back to her; and then saying why the hell didn't she tell him her daddy was trading a bum mule.

For days and mostly in silence they paralleled a lonely railroad until it just stopped and there were nigger men hammering alongside white ones and the ring of metal on metal and tents speckling the horizon and octoroon whores hanging their stockings on what looked to be a traveling gallows.

For two months he laid cross-ties and flirted (and more) with the whores. Then they departed on a Sunday at dawn when he was still drunk from the night. She had a high fever and from inside her hot lolling head it seemed they were slipping off the land, ever south into an ooze of mud.

Then clabbertrap railroad or river towns on the landscape, she expecting a baby and sick each afternoon, staying with the wagon and reading in her Bible while he walked to town or rode aback the remaining mule to find a game of blackjack or stud and coming out more often than not with less money than he'd gone in with, her little dowry smaller and smaller and then things traded, the iron skillet from her grandmother for corn meal and her uncle's fiddle—which she could play a little—for cartridges. E. J. had begun to sleep with the pistol by his head and his arms around his coat, the wagon always covered at night now, as if he'd deny her the stars. Waking one morning to a world shelled in bright snow and that evening giving birth to the squalling boy they called Clay, after her father who, despite herself, she missed.

Where we going? she'd asked E. J. and he'd said, To a place I know of.

Which, eventually, was here. The cabin that belonged to Travis Bolton. Who lived in a large house four miles away and who killed E. J. for a ham and then said she and Clay could stay on in the cabin, if they wanted to, and not pay rent, and pick cotton for him when harvest time came.

Some thoughtful part of her knew it was killing E. J. that had let Travis Bolton hear God's call. That made him do whatever a man did, within his heart and without—papers, vows—to become a preacher of the gospel. She imagined him a man of extravagant gestures, who when he gave himself to Christ gave fully and so not only allowed her and her boy to work and live on his land, in his house, but did more. On the coldest days she might find a gutted doe laid across the fence at the edge of the property. Or a plucked turkey at Christmas. Not a week after E. J. had been committed to the earth by Brother Hill, a milk cow had shown up with the Bolton brand on it. She'd waited for Mr. Bolton or his hand Marcus Eady to come claim it, but after a day and a night no one had and so she'd sheltered it in the lean-to back of the house. Aware she could be called a thief, she'd wrapped Clay in E. J.'s coat (buckshot holes still in it) and carried him to the Bolton place. Instinct sent her to the back door where a nigger woman eyed her down a broad nose and went fetched Mrs. Bolton who told her Mr. Bolton meant for her to use the cow so that the boy might have milk. Then she shut the door. Bess understood that Mrs. Bolton disapproved of her husband's decision to let them live in the cabin. To let them pick cotton alongside the other hired hands and tenant farmers, to pay them for the work of two people even though she was a sorry picker at first and Clay did little work at all in his early years. Nights in the cabin's bed with Clay asleep against her body, Bess imagined arguments between the Boltons, imagined them in such detail that she herself could hardly believe Mr. Bolton would let *those people* stay in their house, bleed them of milk and meat and money. Bess's own father would never have let squatters settle in one of his tenant houses, had in fact run off families in worse shape than Bess's. If you could call her and Clay a family.

When she woke, she knew God had spoken to her through Jesus Christ. In a dream, He had appeared before her in the road with a new wagon and team of strong yellow oxen behind Him, not moving, and He had knelt and pushed back the hair from her eyes and lifted her chin in His fingers. She couldn't see His face for the sun was too bright, but she could look on his boots and did, fine dark leather stitched with gold thread and no dust to mar them. She heard him say, Walk, witness what man can do if I live in his heart.

She rose, brushing away sand from her cheek, shaking sand from her dress, and started toward Coffeeville.

She had walked for two hours talking softly to herself when she heard the wagon behind her and stepped from the road into the grass to give way to its berth. The driver, a tall man dressed in a suit, tie and derby hat, whoaed the mules pulling it and touched the brim of the hat and looked at her with his head tilted. He glanced behind him in the wagon. Then he seemed to arrive at a kind of peace and smiled, said she looked give out, asked her would she like a ride to town. She thanked him and climbed in the back amid children, who frowned at one another at her presence, the haze of flies she'd grown used to. A young one asked was she going to the doctor.

"No," she said, "to church."

175

She slept despite the wagon's bumpy ride and woke only when one of the children wiggled her toe.

"We here," the child said.

Her neck felt better, but still she moved it cautiously when she turned toward the Coffeeville Methodist Church, a simple sturdy building painted white and with a row of tall windows along its side, the glasses raised, people sitting in them, their backs to the world, attention focused inside. In front of the building, buggies, horses and mules stood shaded by pecan branches. Women in hats were unrolling blankets on the brown grass that sloped down to the graveyard, itself shaded by magnolias. From out of the windows she heard singing:

Are you weak and heavy laden?
Cumbered with a load of care?
Precious Savior still our refuge,
Take it to the Lord in prayer.

The children parted around her and spilled from the wagon, as if glad to be freed of her. The man stood and set the brake, then climbed down. He had a cloth-covered dish in his hand. "Here we are," he said, and put down his plate which she could smell—fried chicken—and offered his hand. She took it, warm in hers, and the earth felt firm beneath her feet.

Tipping his hat, he began to make his way through the maze of wagons and buggies and up the steps and inside. She stood waiting. The song ended and more women—too busy to see her—hurried out a side door carrying cakes, and several children ran laughing down the hill, some rolling in the grass, and from somewhere a dog barked.

Two familiar men stepped out the front door, both dressed in dark suits and string ties. They began rolling cigarettes. When the young one noticed her he pointed with a match in his hand and the other looked and saw her too. They glanced at one another and began to talk, then Glaine Bolton hurried back inside. Marcus Eady stayed, watching her. His long gray hair swept back beneath his hat, his goatee combed to a point and his cheeks shaved clean. He lit his cigarette, and trailing a hand along the wall, he moved slowly down the steps and off the side of the porch and along the building. When he got to his horse he stroked its mane and spoke softly to it, all the while watching her.

The front door opened and the man who stepped out putting on his hat was Sheriff Waite, wearing a white shirt and thin black suspenders. He stood on the porch with his hands on his hips. She was holding onto the side of the wagon to keep from falling, and for a moment Waite seemed to stand beside his own twin, and then they blurred and she blinked them back into a single sheriff

He had seen her. He glanced over at Marcus Eady and patted the air with his hand to stay the man as he, Waite, came down the steps and through the wagons and buggies and horses and mules, laying his hands across the necks and rumps of the skittish animals nearest her to calm them. When he stood over her, bent as she was, she came only to his badge.

"Missus Freemont," he said. "What are you doing?"

"My boy needs burying," she said. "The Lord led me here."

For a moment, as he watched her, Waite held in his eyes a look that doubted that such a lord existed any more. What did he see in her face that made his own face both dreadful and aggrieved? What a sight she must be, bloodied, rank, listing up from the camp of the dead to here, the sunlit world of the living, framed in God's view from the sky in startling white cotton. She clung to the wagon's sideboard and felt her heart beat against it, confused for a moment which of her men it held. More people had come onto the porch in their black and white clothes and were watching, stepping down into the churchyard. A woman put her hand over her mouth. Another hid a child's face. Marcus Eady had drawn his rifle and levered a round into its chamber. Glaine Bolton emerged red-faced from the church, pushing people aside, and pointed toward Bess and Waite, the sheriff reaching to steady her. The man last out was the preacher, Travis Bolton, and now she remembered why she had come. It was for her boy. It was for Clay. At the church Bolton raised his Bible above his eyes to shade them so he might see.

Then he pushed aside the arm of his son trying to hold him back and left the boy frowning and came through the people, toward her.

Mall Rats
Britni Patterson

Screams echoed in my ears, to the point I could no longer distinguish one voice from another. Bodies crashed in frantic collisions and took off running again. Tears and blood had both been shed. It was my third day of surveillance in the Five Oaks mall KidZone play space, and I'd already picked out the mother I'd assault if I could get promised a quiet cell.

Lupita, an adorable seven-year-old blackmailer, tugged on my arm. "Aunt Justice," she said. "I want a smoothie."

I bent down to look her in the eye. "We talked about this. I'll get you a smoothie after we're done here, when it's time to go get your brother."

She sighed heavily. "Promise? Because this is boring."

"Smoothies are only for the full two hours," I said. She'd held us up for a smoothie every day. "We've got possibilities, and I've got to pay attention. Go play." She sighed again, and rolled her eyes, before taking off to join the group of kids determined to scale the lighthouse on top of the slide.

Five Oaks had hired the Givens Detective Agency, which consists of my twin sister Mercy and me, to find out who was stealing strollers. So far, sixteen parents had reported their stroller being stolen while they were at the KidZone, along with their shopping bags and personal items. The mall wanted it stopped, and the security cameras weren't helping, because they couldn't tell which strollers were being stolen in the scrum.

My phone beeped with a text message.

Mercy: "Good target approaching. Stroller has Belk bags, one Apple bag. Stroller looks expensive."

My twin sister Mercy was playing cripple in a wheelchair up on the skywalk, with a sketch pad theoretically getting filled with drawings of the darling children at play. I say "playing" because while Mercy is a genuine paraplegic, she's also a genius and the brains behind the Givens Detective Agency. She doesn't consider herself crippled in any sense of the word and usually reacts with violence to any pity, condescension, or other forms of insensitivity the public tends to offer people in wheelchairs. She also doesn't usually position herself in public as a target for the stares and whispered comments. In this case, she reluctantly agreed the wheelchair would let her hang out up on the skywalk all day with her binoculars without being suspicious.

Me, I had to change my look six times a day. My skin was getting raw from going from full make-up to bare, to somewhat made-up and back again, and my scalp hurt from the wigs. I was constantly sweating from standing under the skylight which did nothing to mitigate the Texas sun in July. I'd also had to borrow four children from our lawyer's younger sister, who was more than happy to avail herself of free babysitting and a hundred bucks a day rental fee, even if it meant she had to drive to the mall four times a day to trade kids out. Right now, I was watching Lupita while wearing my "skank mom" look: a black wig, Kardashian-sized sunglasses, and studded blue jeans with high heels under a cleavage-displaying tank top. I hoped our culprit didn't need chasing while I was wearing it. The jeans were about ten pounds too tight, thanks to the unfortunate proximity of Cinnabon to the KidZone.

We'd determined most of the stolen strollers were pricy, the kind with features like digital temperature display and built-in pedometer, double padded straps with racing harness, or one-touch stroller collapse function. It had been startling to find out how much people could spend on a stroller. But the strollers targeted were also those loaded up with shopping bags, particularly from the higher end stores.

With a casual yawn, I looked over to check out the stroller approaching. The woman pushing it did not match the stroller. Her hair was frizzy and pulled into a messy ponytail, and she looked tired, in worn blue jeans and a Canada hoodie, but the tired look was explained by the bouncing toddler and the baby in the stroller.

My phone beeped.

The text from my sister read, "Probably shouldn't let her climb the lighthouse."

I looked over at the lighthouse. Lupita was six feet off the ground, bare toes splayed on the inch-wide rim as she reached for the next rim. She had a good grip on another knob, but she was two inches too short to go any higher.

"Lupita!" I yelled. "Get down from there!"

She pretended she couldn't hear me, though I saw her head cock in my direction.

I rolled my eyes, much like Lupita, before turning my gaze casually back to the strollers. The one Mercy had spotted was gone.

"Lupita!" I yelled. "Upstairs to Mercy! Now!" I waited only long enough to make sure Lupita heard me before I vaulted over the barrier wall. My phone rang. I yanked it out and thumbed it on, as I spun around, looking for the stroller.

"Heading towards JCPenney," said Mercy's voice. "I've got eyes on Lupita. The suspect is wearing black pants, purple top, brown hair, black ball cap, sneakers."

"Got her. Call George," I said. George was head of mall security and our liaison. Mercy had one of the mall security radios in her chair. I took off running again, despite both the jeans and the heels, focused on the lady casually but quickly pushing a stroller into JCPenney's. Why couldn't she steal the stroller during my yoga instructor look? Yoga pants and sneakers were much more conducive to chasing people.

Unfortunately, the sound of my heels on the slick tile floor alerted our suspect. I saw her look over her shoulder at me, and then she took off like a rocket.

"She's running!" I said into the phone.

We'd scoped out JCPenney and Macy's for exits beforehand, because they were the closest stores to the KidZone with exits to the outside. We were lucky she went into JCPenney's because there was only one exit on the ground level. We didn't think she'd try to manhandle a stroller up the escalator. Too slow, and too much attention.

Mercy was watching the way we came in, so I turned and ran for the exit, ducking through the bedding and kids' section, to find George blocking the doors. It wasn't hard for him to block things with his six-foot-four frame, bulked out with what our dad used to call wrestler's fat, a skim layer of pudge hiding solid muscle.

George was a former Army Ranger and retired police officer who ran his crew of mall cops like a professional task force. He had gotten shot and nearly killed by a wannabe bank robber high on coke about six years before. After that, his wife demanded he find something else to do, and George figured after twenty years of putting up with his hazardous career choices, he owed it to her and their three kids. The mall paid him twice as much as the San Antonio Police Department, but I suspected he secretly missed the adrenaline rush, because he'd been way too excited to set up the sting operation with us.

"See her?" I asked.

He shook his head. "Your sister passed on the description, and my guys are heading to the front of Penney's. I've got another one on the upper level in case she takes the escalator." I nodded. We kept watching the store, but five minutes later, there was no sign of her.

"Ditching the evidence," said George. "She's gonna try to walk out or wait us out."

"I'll go see if I can flush her," I said. "Two bucks she's in the bathroom changing into whatever was in those shopping bags."

George nodded, and lifted his walkie-talkie. "JCPenney Loss Prevention, be advised we have a shoplifter in the store. Suspect is female, brunette, was wearing black yoga pants, purple sleeveless shirt, black ball-cap, and black sneakers. Please support."

I headed out into the store. Loss prevention officers are supposed to look like ordinary shoppers, but it wasn't hard to spot them as the radio call went out, and their heads all popped up like meerkats. They all started moving into positions that set up roadblocks throughout the aisles. I poked my head down the bathroom hallway. A very large man wearing a jacket that said "SECURITY" was leaning against the emergency exit. One of George's.

"Anyone come this way with a stroller in the last fifteen minutes?" I asked.

He shook his head. I turned back into the store. I was in the men's section. If she had turned away from the exit, she would have hit the men's section first. The other dressing rooms were all the way across the store. The only other person in the area was a man standing near the register, wearing a black wool topcoat, a dress shirt open at the collar, dress pants, and patent leather shoes that gleamed. He was holding a pack of underwear and looking around with a frown. I went past him and into the dressing room.

There was a stroller down at the end, parked in front of the last dressing room.

"Hey," I called, "You might as well come out. The place is locked down!"

Silence answered.

I pulled my Taser out of my pocket. The mall contract stipulated no firearms so my beloved Beretta was home in the safe. I moved down to the last door, and knocked on it. It swung open, revealing our former suspect. Her eyes were lifeless and her jaw was distended from the tie stuffed into her mouth. I reached out for a pulse, even though the unnatural purple color of her face told me there wasn't much point. Finger-shaped bruises stood out on her neck. She looked like a discarded doll, limbs awkward and twisted into uncomfortable angles.

"Drop it!" someone screamed behind me. I saw the man who'd been standing at the counter now standing behind me, pointing a Taser at me. He lifted the radio in his other hand to his mouth. "I've got the suspect cornered in the men's fitting rooms."

"Let me show you my license," I said, "I'm a private detec—" was about as far as I got before he zapped me. I screamed, because getting Tasered hurts like a son of a bitch and because I was falling and couldn't catch myself. I was grateful for the carpet, but I could have done without falling next to the body.

"I'm a private detective contracted by George Racalle." I said through numb lips, without moving. "Don't shock me again."

"Loss Prevention to George Racalle, we need the police. There's a private detective in here says she's with you, and I found her kneeling over a dead body!"

Great. The next ten minutes didn't get any better. George came running in to vouch for me and help me up. Mall Security herded everyone out and set up a guard around the door.

I sat in the chairs outside the fitting room. Mercy and Lupita arrived shortly afterwards, Lupita sitting on Mercy's lap. Lupita gave me a hard hug, but didn't say anything until the paramedics went running by.

"Is she going to be okay after all?" Lupita asked.

"What? Oh, I don't know, honey. I know they're going to try to help her," I said, giving Mercy a dirty look for telling Lupita our suspect got killed. Mercy squeezed her hand and gave me a dirtier one back.

Mercy muttered to me, "When we came in to find you, one of George's men tried to stop us at the door and told us a woman had been found dead."

I rolled my eyes.

The police replaced the mall cops and started herding everyone in the store together.

George came over to sit next to me, wringing his hands together as he inspected the carpet, his powerful shoulders hunched with defeat.

"Sorry about the Taser," George said, eventually. "He's loss prevention. He says he saw the...person and freaked out."

"Uh huh," I said.

"So, Homicide is here. They've locked down the store. No one goes in or out until the cops interview everyone. They're holding off until they hear your statement," said George. His jaw was tight as he ground the words out. There'd just been a murder in his mall. There were going to be so many questions. The loud ones from the press, and the quiet ones from the owners who signed his checks.

"She was gone when I went in. I didn't see anyone coming out," I said.

"Don't tell me, tell them. I've already been informed the *real* police will be investigating this matter," said George, bitterly, looking down at his knotted fingers, white at the knuckles.

Mercy and I exchanged looks. Usually cops liked working with ex-cops, though there were always some who would resent George trading brotherhood for money and personal safety.

"We'll get you our report as soon as possible," Mercy said.

"Who's here from Homicide?" I asked. If I was lucky, it wasn't Lieutenant Conley, who was both head of Homicide and a great kisser. If we were extra lucky, it wouldn't be Sergeant Montoya, who was carrying a torch for Mercy. They both got really annoyed when we got involved in their murder cases. We were catastrophically unlucky.

"Detective Peña," said George.

Detective Peña was one of those snide, misogynistic assholes that make other cops annoyed to be wearing the same uniform. We hated his guts, and he hated ours right back, especially since the fact we were involved with two of his superior officers meant he had to be respectful.

"Tell the paramedics I feel overly warm," I said. "Probably feverish with no-talk-to-jerks-itis."

"You wouldn't believe what it takes to keep it down to seventy-eight in here, when it's a hundred plus outside," said George, defensively. He wasn't really listening as he watched the cops work with worried, wistful eyes.

"I called Susanna," said Mercy, to me, "to come get Lupita."

"I'm sorry I asked about the smoothie," said Lupita. "I thought you were dead."

I wiggled my fingers. "Totally not dead. And you were great. Jumbo smoothie for sure."

Her face brightened. "The one with the *Frozen* cup and the Olaf bendy straw?"

"Sure thing," I said. Kids.

Detective Peña made his way over to us. He had a square

face with mean eyes too close together, and the tightly pinched expression of a hemorrhoid sufferer. His shirt also was twenty pounds too small and badly ironed.

"Miss Givens," he said, with a nasty emphasis on "miss."

"I'd like to get your statement now."

I glanced over at Lupita. "Here? Now?"

"Now," he said. Jerk.

"We were hired to discover who was stealing strollers from the KidZone. We realized a stroller was being stolen, and I chased after the stroller into JCPenney. We coordinated with George Racalle to prevent the suspect from leaving through the exits. We waited near the exits, but the suspect didn't appear. I went to look for the suspect, and found someone, ah," I looked at Lupita, "...hurt, in the men's fitting room. I started to check for signs of life, when a loss prevention officer came in and precipitously Tasered me before I could show him my license."

He waited. I waited. He broke first.

"That's it?" he asked.

"That's it."

"You didn't see anyone come out of the fitting room?"

"No."

"You aren't sure your suspected thief is the dead woman?"

Lupita winced. So did I.

"There's a resemblance, but I never got a good enough look at either my suspect or the victim to be certain. Especially because her face was all..." I made a vague gesture with my hand, while looking sideways at Lupita. "But I'm sure the cameras caught her."

"Right, right," said Peña, staring down at his notebook. "Well, we'll get the surveillance footage. I'd like you to wait around while I interview the other people in the store."

"Lupita's mother is coming to pick her up in twenty minutes," Mercy said.

"I'll have an officer escort her back to reclaim custody of her child," said Peña. Super jerk. Susanna was going to freak out when she got here, and a cop was waiting to take her to her child.

Thirty minutes later, a white-faced Susanna had picked up

Lupita, along with enough cash to get jumbo smoothies for herself and all four kids, plus a "sorry your kid got mixed up in a murder" bonus. Mercy, Peña, George, me, and the head of JCPenney's loss prevention team, a large man named Cecil who was sweating copiously through his polo shirt and looking really nervous, were squeezed in the surveillance booth. Peña was distinctly unhappy to have us come along, but he needed us to identify the suspect. Mercy had managed to run over his foot in the elevator.

"Time stamp should be around eleven forty-three," I said. "That's when I began chasing the suspect into JCPenney's."

Cecil clicked around on the screen, and the video feed of the mall entrance popped up. We saw our suspect look back over her shoulder, and then take off running. We saw her turn sharply towards the men's section before she went off screen. A few seconds later, I appeared on the same screen. I stopped, looked around, and then headed straight.

"That's unfortunate," said Cecil, with the air of someone trying to give bad news slowly.

"What's unfortunate?" Peña demanded.

"Well, we had a short in the wiring to those cameras about two months ago. The entire men's section is blind. We have to have corporate-approved security technicians come to do any repairs. We told them we just needed an electrician, but nope. Work order has to be reviewed, approved, and then performed by a pre-approved vendor, the nearest of whom is in Houston. We have an appointment for them to come out and provide an estimate next month."

Peña was so quiet that I was sure he was having a stroke.

"You're telling me we don't have camera coverage of the critical area?" he said.

"That's what I'm telling you. Men's wear isn't a big target for loss, so it's not a priority."

Mercy frowned. "Any other areas with electrical issues?" she asked.

Cecil pulled a handkerchief out of his pocket and mopped at his forehead. "Luckily, no."

"I'll ask the questions," snapped Peña. "This is a *professional* investigation, and you need to keep quiet unless you're answering questions or giving a statement. No one here is interested in your opinions."

The expression on Mercy's face told me Peña had just made a bad, bad mistake. We'd been trying to play nicely with the police department, given our personal relationships with two of their members, but if he wanted to play who's-the-bigger-bitch games, we had him outnumbered.

"Of course, Officer," said Mercy with an expressionless face.

"Detective," said Peña.

"Of course," she said again, this time through gritted teeth. "George, why don't we leave De-tect-ive Peña with Cecil. I'm sure he would like to have a long conversation with him about other camera angles, and this is a very small space."

George looked at Mercy's bland expression, and nodded, "Of course." He was smarter than Peña.

We were barely at the end of the hall leading back into the store, when Mercy said quietly, "George, can you find out if those cameras could be sabotaged?"

George looked thoughtful. "You're thinking the thefts and the cameras are related?"

"I'm thinking our thief didn't hesitate at all to turn into the men's section, instead of going straight for the exit or the restrooms, or even into the kids section where she'd be less conspicuous. Also, the timing is suspicious."

"Yeah....Yeah. And who would be dumb enough to commit murder in a mall, with cameras everywhere, unless they knew the cameras weren't working," said George, slowly.

Mercy nodded, hiding her impatience well. "So find maintenance and see how hard it would be. Then we'll know if we're looking at specialized electronics knowledge or someone who cut a bunch of wires."

George got on the radio, and we stepped out onto the sales floor again.

We could see two groups of people herded together by several officers on the floor below. The loss prevention people were all wearing expressions of resignation. The real shoppers looked confused and annoyed.

Mercy stared at the groups. I looked down at them too. Most of the loss prevention officers were women, wearing either sundresses or khaki shorts with the polo shirts JCPenney was currently promoting. There were two other men besides my Taser-buddy in the coat. One was dressed like he was scheduled to shoot eighteen holes that afternoon, and the other one was in beach wear, Bermuda shorts and a T-shirt, with teeth so white I could see his smile across the store against his tan.

Mercy murmured, "Is it that easy?"

"What?" I asked.

She gave me an irritated look. "Seriously?"

"What," I said, surprised. "You've picked the murderer out of the line-up?"

"Haven't you?" she asked.

I stared at her. "Seriously?"

She ignored me, tapping her chin. "Well, let's say I know which one I'd recommend for further questioning. But I want to make sure George gets the credit."

"Which one?" I asked.

George came up behind me. "Maintenance is pulling up the electrical info. We'll have to get the manager's permission to look at the security specs."

"What's the total take on the stroller thefts so far?" Mercy asked.

"Market value of all the items? Around twenty-three thousand. Street value, half that. They got a diamond pendant and some Bose speakers that account for most of it."

"Is there any way to track if the items stolen in the strollers were returned to the stores?" Mercy asked.

George blinked. "Maybe. You're thinking the merchandise was returned?"

"If the receipts were in the bags, it'd be easy," I said.

George smiled. "And returns are logged. Evidence. But that won't link our stroller thief to whoever she's working within the mall. It could be anyone!"

Mercy's lips tightened with annoyance, and she said

carefully, "I think her accomplice would have to be someone in loss prevention in this store."

George stared. "You lost me."

"She wheels the strollers into JCPenney's. If Loss Prevention meets a shopper and marches them off to the back room where there are no cameras, and the employee entrances, who's going to notice? Also, they have access to the back areas of the store, and the badge to use the employee entrances. And if loss prevention walks by carrying a lot of merchandise, who's going to say anything, especially if it's from another store? The clerks can't leave their station, and they're constantly under watch since they handle money. The thief rolls up to their accomplice, and they decide what to do with their gains out of sight. But then the thief gets busted by us, and she runs straight for her accomplice. He panics and kills her to remove the link to him."

"You're saying him," said George.

"Men's section, remember? The loss prevention officers have to blend in."

"You've got more than that," said George suspiciously.

"Yes. One of them changed his clothes to hide the fact that he was involved in a struggle."

"How do you know that?" I asked.

Mercy pinched the bridge of her nose, before gesturing angrily towards the groups of people. "Look! It's as plain as the nose on your face!"

"Maybe the nose on *your* face," I said, lamely. When you're identical twins, insulting each other's looks doesn't quite work.

"I don't see it either," admitted George.

"It's July. It's a hundred and two degrees outside. It's seventy-eight degrees in here. Why the hell is someone who has to walk around a store all day long wearing a coat? It's not a uniform, no one else is wearing one," said Mercy. "And if he's going to be prissy enough to wear a coat, why isn't he wearing a tie? I'm betting his tie is the one in the victim's throat. He probably had to put the coat on because the struggle trashed his shirt."

George stared at my Taser buddy.

"Think that's enough for you to beat Peña to the punch?" asked Mercy.

"Yeah. Yeah, it is. I'll call you." George was practically running towards the fellow officers, his radio up to his ear. We watched as George made his way downstairs and whispered urgently to the officers herding people. The cops began drifting towards our friend in the coat. We watched as his conversation with the fake golfer and beach boy faded under the realization the police were paying attention to him, and the exact moment he decided to run. He made it four steps before he got mashed under six hundred pounds of cop.

We managed to get out of the mall after writing up our statements, because Peña was so pissed off at having his thunder stolen by a "mall cop," he had forgotten all about making us miserable.

"I got Tasered," I said, plaintively, on the way home.

Mercy sighed. "Fine. We can stop and get milkshakes."

I left rubber on the turn into Burger Boy.

It came in a *Frozen* cup with a bendy straw.

Driftwood
Sean Doolittle

Late in the afternoon, I approached three local boys cleaning fish on the beach, and for sixty pesos each they told me where to find the crooked old gringo I described for them.

His name was McNamara. At least that was the name I'd been given. The boys on the beach called him *El León*. He'd been a cop in San Diego, and now he lived here; beyond that, I couldn't separate the facts entirely from the stories I'd heard. But I found him just where the village boys had promised, in a sling chair beneath a palm-thatch awning, half a mile's trudge up the sand.

Attached to the awning was a sunblasted Airstream trailer. The trailer perched on cinderblocks amidst the dune grass, looking out on the Sea of Cortez. The man in the chair watched me until I came to stand just beyond his line of shade; he was somewhere in his sixties, with broad heavy shoulders and skin like saddle leather, his hair and beard as bleached and shaggy as the palm thatch overhead. His open shirt exposed a solid round belly, a tangle of chest hair like wiry fur. *El León.*

I said, "Are you McNamara?"

He appraised me without expression, a bottle of beer sweating on his knee.

I shaded my eyes with the back of my hand. "My name is Randall. Donald Randall. I understand that you're...I was told you'd be expecting me."

Silence. I started to think about how far I'd come when McNamara gave a small nod toward the empty sling chair at his left. While I accepted the seat, he opened the stained white lid of the cooler between us and rummaged in the ice for another beer. He twisted off the cap and handed me the bottle. The chilled wet glass felt good in my hand.

When he tipped his bottle, I did the same. The thin local beer quenched my throat like rain on a dry creek bed. The waning sunlight threw long shadows, casting the open water in a coppery sheen. McNamara's feet were bare, his toenails thick and yellow, ribbed like mussel shells.

He finally said, "Donald Randall. People call you Don?"

"Sometimes, but I prefer Donald."

"So tell me, Don," he said. "What brings a nice white schoolteacher from Kansas City all the way to Mexico just to kill a man?"

I offered to buy him a meal somewhere in the town. McNamara just waved a hand and sent a skinny brown boy into the water. Five minutes later, the dripping boy returned with his hands flapping, a gyrating fish gripped by the tail in each. McNamara handed the boy twenty pesos and sent him away. Then he cooked the fish over knots of mesquite on a rusty grate behind the trailer.

We ate tacos pescados together in the chairs. The fresh fish tasted exceptional, bedded on some kind of relish that started with a cold crunch and left my mouth burning. I hadn't realized I was so hungry; McNamara ate what he wanted and left me the last of his share.

"Never seen him before," he said, wiping his fingers on his cutoff chinos as he scrutinized the photograph I'd given him.

"Down here he goes by Young," I offered. "Malcolm Young."

McNamara chuckled at that. "If there's a *norteamericano* in five towns with a fake name that obvious and I haven't met him, it's because there aren't any." He handed back the photograph with a soft grunt. "Where do the ladies come in?"

"The little girl in the picture is my granddaughter. The older is her mother." I held the photo in my fingers, hoping he'd ask to look at it again, sensing that he wouldn't. "They're coming home with me."

McNamara sat a moment, then made a lazy gesture with

his beer bottle in the fading light. "Hell, I don't know why I asked. Whoever got you this far is out of touch."

"How do you mean?"

"How I mean is, whatever you want me to do for you, I don't do it anymore."

Then why did you cook me dinner? I thought. But I said, "I only need your help finding them."

"You found me just fine."

"Not without help, I can promise you."

"Like I said." His tone was dismissive yet not impolite. "Out of my sphere."

"I was led to understand that your sphere extended past the immediate area."

He opened a new beer as if changing the subject.

I felt myself getting anxious. "I'm certain that they're somewhere on this side of the peninsula."

"This side of the peninsula?" Another chuckle. "So, not much ground, then."

I raised the photograph. "I have copies."

Now the chuckle became a laugh. "Christ. You're an earnest hombre, I'll give you that. Tell me something: if you find him, what then?"

"If you help me that far, then I take it from there."

"Uh huh."

"Listen, Mr. McNamara," I said. "I understand that it's probably difficult for you to take me seriously."

"Oh, I'm taking you seriously. It's imagining any of this going well for you that's difficult." McNamara sipped his beer. "No offense."

Before I could reply, the same boy who'd brought us the fish reappeared, this time carrying an armload of driftwood. He dropped to his knees, dumped the wood aside with a clatter, and dug a hole in the sand just beyond our awning. He lined the hole with dune grass, then piled in some dry limbs. In no time, he'd produced a fire and vanished once more.

It was pleasant here, I thought. Full dark soon, and already the air on the beach seemed a few degrees cooler. The fire crackled and popped as it grew, sending motes of spark and ash into the dusky sky. The smoke smelled peppery and sweet.

After a long silence, McNamara said, "Out of curiosity, how exactly do you plan to accomplish this mission? Run the sonofabitch over with the rental car?"

"I'm not sure I understand."

"Don't take this the wrong way, but you don't strike me as the type of fellow who smuggles a weapon over a border."

On that point he had me. "Now that you bring it up," I said, "I guess I could use your help in that area as well."

McNamara shook his head slowly. I might have taken it for a gesture of reproach if he hadn't been smiling.

Well after sunset, with no moon overhead, the beach seemed to produce its own muted light. We walked inland, away from the water, into the dunes and the dark.

McNamara carried a small duffel bag in one hand, a spotlight in the other. Far behind the trailer, a few hundred yards out in the scrub, he killed the light and dropped the duffel in the sand. The bag landed between us like a bundle of heavy tools.

"Pick what you like," he said.

I looked at the sky, imagining a starry drape pulled over a clear dome. "I'd rather get your recommendation, if you wouldn't mind giving one."

I couldn't tell if the next sound McNamara made was another chuckle at my expense or a sigh. I heard another soft grunt as he stooped, followed by the quick, musical scrape of a zipper separating flaps of nylon. In a moment, he offered me a six-shot revolver with a chip in the handle, a frayed strip of duct tape pressed over the rear sighting bracket.

"Simple," he said. "No safety, no sliding parts. Walk up close, squeeze the trigger, done. That's my recommendation."

I took the gun and looked at it. I felt the weight of it in my hand. Even at arm's length, I could smell the smell of it: oil and fireworks.

"'If you want noise suppression," McNamara added, "then we gotta go back in the bag."

"Simple is probably best," I said.

"Couldn't agree more. Now. Would you like some advice I won't make you pay for?" When I didn't answer, he added, "Side note, this offer would represent a rarity."

"Then I accept," I said. "Please."

"If I'm any judge of current fashion," he said, "and I like to think that I am, that picture you showed me is two decades old if it's a day. Am I ballpark?"

I felt myself nodding in confirmation. Part of me was listening to what McNamara was saying. The rest still pondered this heavy thing in my hand. It seemed blunt to me. Stunted in some way. Ugly.

"So this little undertaking of yours, no pun intended. You've been at it a good long while."

Squeeze the trigger, done. What would that feel like? I nodded again.

"Trust me when I tell you: it's a young man's game."

"You don't think I'm capable. I recognize that."

"That's not the point."

Now I looked at him. His craggy, shaggy features had become clearer to me in the dark. Standing face-to-face like this, he only came up to my chin.

"The point is—and, honestly, I gotta say, I think you probably know this already—guys get to be our age, they have something they didn't have before."

"Arthritis?"

"The benefit of understanding."

This time, I nodded consciously. It took more effort than I might have expected. "I'm curious to know what you think I probably understand."

McNamara's tone seemed almost kind. "That those girls in that picture don't exist anymore. The guy in that picture doesn't exist anymore. *You* don't exist anymore. And that's why it doesn't matter."

Maybe he was right, I thought. Maybe I did know that already.

"The river's gone under the bridge, amigo. Take my word on it." He shrugged. "Revenge doesn't feel like anything."

I let out a long, slow breath. I took another look down at the gun. Another look up at the encrusted sky.

After a moment, I handed the gun back to him.

"Still," I said, "can you show me where the bullets go?"

Somewhere in the duffel bag, McNamara assured me, there was a box of ammunition that went with the ramshackle pistol.

While he knelt in the sand, rummaging, I took the coil of guitar string out from my pocket. While he cursed and reached for the spotlight, I slipped my fingers into the steel rings now affixed to either end of the wire.

"Bingo," he said.

As McNamara straightened, but before he had a chance to turn, I slipped the guitar string over his head, gripped the rings, and yanked back sharply, with all my might. He barked in surprise, dropping the gun in a powdery puff of sand.

I heeled back, pulling him off balance. As we fell together, McNamara flailed with his other hand. Capsules of lead and brass clicked and scattered in the scrub around us as the box of rounds flew. With both hands free, McNamara began to claw: at the air, at me, at the wire biting his throat. He gagged, then sputtered. Then he roared.

El León.

I held on like a bullrider at his sudden surge of effort. Clearly he still had too much air to work with. I pulled back on the wire until my wrists and biceps ached, crimping his roar to a croak.

He'd had me pegged from the beginning, of course: I was not now, nor had I ever been, the type of person who smuggles contraband into a foreign country. The guitar string I'd purchased from a street-corner mariachi a hundred miles north of here. I'd harvested the rings from a pair of souvenir keychains shaped like sombreros.

Turtled on his back, his full weight atop me, McNamara groped with his hands and thrashed with his legs. My best guess at functional length had been a touch past the mark, I discovered; at the base of his skull, my fists had already met each other at the knuckles, and I could pull them no closer together. I crossed my wrists one over the other and pushed in opposite directions instead.

McNamara writhed and spat. I bore down with all I had. My hands had gone numb. My shoulders trembled. McNamara clutched and scratched. I had sand in my eyes, raw gouges on my face. McNamara wheezed. I began to roar myself with the effort of this. To my own ears, it sounded more like a scream.

All at once I became aware of a slippery warmth on my wrists. At the same time, distantly, I registered that the resistance in the wire had seemed to give an inch. I bore down harder.

McNamara's wheezing turned to a sucking, gurgling sound. I felt new warmth patter my neck, soak into my shirt, and I bore harder still. I wondered if I should have bought a thicker string.

Finally, as he began to weaken, I pried my hands open and shoved out from under him. I had just enough strength to crawl to my feet.

McNamara had just enough strength to turn over in the sand, then push himself up to all fours. He stayed that way a few moments, still spouting from the neck, panting like a dog.

Pretty soon he began to sag. Pretty soon after that it was over.

I paid the same three boys six hundred pesos each to bury him in the dunes and bring me a change of clothes.

At least I thought they were the same three. The smallest of them I now identified as the one who'd brought us fish and fire. Even in the dark I recognized his eyes.

When they'd gone off to their chores, I walked back to beach, toward the low red corona in the near distance. There, at the hole in the sand just beyond McNamara's awning, I picked up a gnarled, arthritic-looking limb of driftwood and threw it onto the pile of glowing coals.

While the fire grew, I stripped out of my blood-sodden clothes. The flames threw undulating shadows as they climbed. The driftwood crackled and popped. In the background, the surf along the shoreline whispered and shushed.

I added more wood, then tossed my clothes on the fire. The stained fabric sizzled, and blackened, and fell in on itself.

I looked at the photo of my wife and daughter in the rippling firelight.

Had I honestly expected McNamara to recognize the three of us? After twenty years' time?

If he had, I'd have let him live longer, I thought. Not comfortably, but longer.

But I'd been a much younger man on that family vacation, it was true. And, in fairness, I'd had quite a beard.

Before they'd been taken—before I'd mortgaged all the stars in this sky to pay the horrid price his men had never intended to honor—one of my girls had hated that beard. The other had loved it. And if, after the twist and torque of these many years since, I myself could no longer remember with absolute certainty which of them had taken which side on that point, what could I possibly have expected of a man like McNamara?

I made a careful crease in the print. I folded the crease back on itself, sharpening it with my thumbnail. I gently tore the bearded man free of the photograph and dropped him onto the last of the fire.

I stood awhile longer, watching the torn man bubble and melt. I tucked the remainder of the photograph into one of my shoes and set them safely aside. Then I walked down to the water.

He'd been right, I thought, as I waded naked into the surf. Revenge didn't feel like anything.

But the night sea felt warm, this close to the shore. Even invigorating. I swam out against the tide, into the cooler water, wondering how far I could get before the boys on the beach returned.

A Good Name
Rob Brunet

Perko Ratwick stood frozen in place. He was pissed as hell it was Mongoose who found him out, and scared like a deer facing oncoming headlights. The lunk had shown up unannounced at the barn Perko was wiring as a grow op. His plan to produce a quarter ton of skunk weed four times a year was about to go up in smoke. Anger battled fear inside him, and his chest burned like he'd swallowed live charcoal.

"Rules is rules," Mongoose said. "You run a grow op behind everyone's back, you's out on your ass." Like getting kicked out of the Libidos Motorcycle Club was an option. Like it wouldn't mean painting a target on Perko's back. Like maybe there'd be a severance package.

"It's experimental," Perko said, scrambling. "A pilot project. Thinking we could bring production in house."

"We don't grow pot. We sell it."

"Ever heard of vertical integration?"

Mongoose crinkled his forehead, visibly struggling to figure out whether he'd just been insulted.

Perko said, "We bring the means of production under our roof and we control quantity, quality, scheduling, the whole shebang." He walked his fellow Libido around the barn, pointed out the hydroponic drip lines, the rack-mounted lights on pulleys. "State of the art," he said. "Something to be proud of."

"Until we gets busted." Mongoose may have been unable to wrap his head around a lot of things but avoiding unnecessary risk was pretty basic around the MC. "That's why we farm this shit out."

"I set things up after the Nghiem thing tanked."

"The gook running suburban ops?"

"Right." Perko told him how the guy had left him in the lurch when two of his residential grow ops got busted, how Perko had decided to go it alone, grow his own supply for the New York buyers he had lined up. "It's sanctioned," he lied. "Surprised you didn't know."

He watched Mongoose process that information. Plenty of side deals went on in the gang and a lot happened on a need to know basis. Still, the bulky biker would have expected to be in the loop on something this big. He said as much, telling Perko he didn't like the idea of him running a grow op on his own. "Besides, we go back. You oughtta have told me."

"I was gonna."

"So why didn't ya?"

"I just did."

Mongoose drew his lips into a tight smile and shook his head. "Unh-unh. No ya didn't. I found out, didn't I?"

"What's the difference?"

"Difference is you didn't tell me and I don't believe you told no one else neither. I can tell when someone's shitting me."

Perko started to argue the point then dropped it. There was no clean exit. As soon as Mongoose outed him, he'd be toast. Even if the gang let him stay, the trust was shredded. The optics were all wrong. He said, "What if I cut you a slice?"

"Sounds like a bribe."

"Call it what you want. I was gonna bring this deal inside anyway. Wanted to get it nailed down tight first is all."

Mongoose asked, "How much?"

Perko knew he'd want half, but if he gave it up too easy, even Mongoose would smell something off. "Ten points," he said.

"Fifty."

"Thirty."

"Lemme think about it," Mongoose said. "Meet me at the Cue 'n Cushion at six."

On Perko's list of people who deserved to die, Marty "Mongoose" Muldoon occupied the top spot. Had done so for a long time. What started as raw anger at their first dealing grew to a simmering hatred over a decade and a half of meting out punishment to more deserving souls. That one would die at the hand of the other was an eventuality he'd long accepted, and he had no doubt Mongoose felt the same way. Any surprise felt by either man would be at the timing and nature of his killing, not at its perpetrator.

Much as the men knew one would do the other someday, neither was in a rush. The lack of urgency wasn't complicated. They worked shoulder to shoulder in the Libidos Motorcycle Club, earning as one did and protecting the brand, so to speak. More often than not, Mongoose's brute strength came in handy, and Perko repaid him with a cunning the larger man failed to comprehend. The twin threats of violence and incarceration inherent to their line of work meant they were worth more to each other alive than dead.

Until Mongoose snagged Perko's pudgy fingers crammed in the cookie jar.

He'd had every intention of announcing his sideline to the club house once the clones were planted. Kick in like a good soldier. But he needed to make up for hiring Nghiem in the first place. Half the gang had been opposed to using the Vietnamese grower. They claimed it was about local roots, not racism. Perko couldn't tell the difference and didn't see why it mattered. Either way, it was on him when his supply fell through, and it didn't much matter whether it was the Libidos or the New York Skeletons who made him pay—it was coming out of his hide.

Twenty minutes after leaving Mongoose, he let himself into a marina a couple miles from the Libidos club house and stole a two-ton hand winch. He found the perfect pair of oak trees on Fire Route 63. The hard-packed gravel road offered a seven-minute run of twists and rises no back country biker could avoid gunning. He hooked the winch assembly to the eight-inch oak on the south side of the lane and tested the length, walking the quarter-inch cable across. Perfect. Four feet to spare. He cranked it back into the winch and left the assembly hanging there.

A quick run up to the end of 63 confirmed the three cottages there had yet to be opened for the season. No chance that'd happen on a Wednesday. For the next few hours, this road belonged to him. As far as places to die, he thought, a man could do worse. It made him feel downright benevolent. What biker *wouldn't* want to check out on a glorious spring ride at dusk?

He stopped again at the death spot and drew the cable taut across the narrow road. He picked the place where he'd park to watch the kill. See things through to the end. Trust no one and leave nothing to chance. Hard rules to follow and costly to ignore. Mongoose himself had been instrumental in teaching Perko that lesson when they'd first crossed paths in high school.

Perko had started selling weed after getting ripped off one time too many as a teenage consumer. He and two friends pooled eighty bucks to score a lid. In the morning, before class, they gave the cash to a dealer from the next grade. The guy told Perko and his pals they'd have their bag of weed after second period.

Second period came and went, and so did third. Finally Perko caught up with the guy in the stairwell just before lunch. Confronted, the seller shrugged and fished a tiny baggie of pot out of his pocket. It couldn't have been worth more than twenty dollars. "Here, take it," he sneered.

"This ain't no eighth," complained Perko.

"No shit, Sherlock. You didn't give me a chance to cut it."

"Cut it?"

"Toss in some shake. What else?"

When Perko demanded the guy give their money back, the dealer laughed and walked away, leaving Perko slack-jawed clutching a couple joints worth of bud. One moment, he'd been humming "All the Young Dudes," convinced he was about to become a cool kid with enough grass to show off. Next, he was backed flat against a locker by his two pals who were convinced it was him who'd done the stealing.

When school let out that afternoon, he was still reeling from the betrayal. He felt like a punk loser. All around him, kids were shouting, laughing, high-fiving each other and calling out their plans for Friday night. Hands stuffed in his jacket pockets, Perko kicked a stone down the sidewalk, not even flinching when it ricocheted off a car parked at the side of the road.

"Hey, Ratface. Yo, Perko!" The shout came from a beefy red-haired kid, Marty Muldoon, one of the roughest kids in the school. It would be years before Marty earned the Mongoose moniker. No one in school would have dared call him by anything but his real name.

That Friday afternoon, Muldoon was sitting on the steps in front of the electrical building across the street from school with three hangers-on. "Cmon up, man. We's just sparking."

Perko perched himself on the steps, and everyone smiled silent hellos. Their lopsided grins told him they'd been smoking all afternoon. Laying on his best chill, Perko said, "Hey, man. Is it the weekend, or what, eh?"

The stoners looked at Muldoon who smiled at Perko with laughter in his eyes. He handed him the joint. "Here, you's gonna light it."

Perko shook like a squirrel with an acorn. Muldoon had to be the most happening tough guy in Grade Eleven. He had failed at least one year and was built like a brick shithouse—prime material for the football team that practiced behind the school, but Marty preferred to hang out on Front Campus smoking Export A. Nobody ever dared pick a fight with him, it being common knowledge his mean streak ran deep. Some said he'd had something to do with the mysterious disappearance of another shit disturber last semester. Even teachers cut him a wide berth.

No doubt about it, Marty Muldoon was the kind of guy you wanted on your good side. And here he is sharing his pot with me, Perko thought. On a Friday. In front of everyone. Maybe I'm not a loser, after all.

He hauled deep on the joint. "Thanks...Pfft." He coughed. "This is some good green." His voice came out all pinched and he gagged, spewing smoke.

"Can't hold it in, Ratface?" Muldoon scoffed. The other guys snickered.

Perko turned red and drew his neck into his shoulders. When the joint came round again, he was careful not to take in too much. He nodded, squinting a bit, and passed it along quickly.

"Y'know," said the boy who would one day become the biker known as Mongoose, "buddy of mine gave me this pot a couple hours ago." He was talking like normal even with his lungs full of smoke—man, was he cool. He snorted. "It's from your buy, Ratshit. This here's my cut. My cut of *your* pot. Ain't that a riot?" He laughed, belching pot and spittle in Perko's face. It was all Perko could do to keep tears of shame from welling in his eyes. He did his best not to tremble when the joint came round to him again; it burned his fingertips as he sucked sparks down this throat, resolving there and then to become a tough guy—feared and respected. Whatever it took.

When the young men found their way into the same gang, there had been the occasional fight, but mostly they put their fists to better use. More than once, Perko burned Mongoose, and a couple of times he got caught at it. He took a pounding or two and bided his time. When Mongoose's temper landed him in the drunk tank, Perko celebrated. When the biker's inability to remember a plan meant Perko himself got locked up for running black market cigarettes to Toronto, he spent seven weeks plotting revenge. The transgressions were mutual and multi-layered, and while none had come close to triggering fratricide, they combined to create a lightness of spirit in Perko Ratwick as he set out to lure Mongoose to his final ride.

He found him waiting in the pool hall off Water Street. For six p.m. on a weeknight, the joint was surprisingly busy, but no one bothered the six-foot-four biker about the table he was shooting alone. Perko could tell the beer he was nursing was far from his first.

"Shoot for the tab?" Mongoose suggested.

"Fat chance," said Perko, "but I'll buy the next round if you let me pick your brain a minute." He picked up a cue and waived the waitress over while Mongoose racked the balls.

"What you wanna know?"

Playing it dumb to the bone-headed goon almost gave Perko a twinge of guilt, but he suppressed it easily enough. Mongoose hadn't exactly left him with many options. He could trust the guy not to rat him out—and give up a huge chunk of profit while he was at it—or he could deliver a knock-out blow to a relationship grown damn costly. Once the balance tilted to the darker path, Perko's ability to manipulate using bold-faced lies went into overdrive. He said, "Suppose we needed to move a whack of weed in a hurry."

Mongoose made the break, sunk the three ball and lined up his next shot. "Yeah, so," he said, "we partners now?"

Perko waited until he was ready to sink the two, sitting alone in front of the corner, before saying, "I'm talking a hundred kilos. Serious skunk." He watched Mongoose choke the shot, then walked around the other side of the table where the waitress was delivering two beers. He handed her a twenty and waved her off, making sure Mongoose noticed the size of the tip.

"We gots time, right?"

Perko said, "Naw. I'm talking now."

"Another grow?"

Perko nodded.

"Shit, how much pot you putting out?"

"Keep it down," Perko said. "You want the whole bar listening in?" He took a shot, purposely missing and leaving his opponent with a couple easy balls. "So you gonna help move my product?"

"Our product."

"Whatever."

Mongoose squinted. "Didn't you say you had a buyer in New York?"

"Had an amazing crop. Wound up with extra." Only Mongoose would be stupid enough to believe he'd have managed to keep not one but two operations off the radar. For a moment, Perko thought maybe he'd gone too far. He needn't have worried.

"A *shit ton* of extra." His elbow shaking, Mongoose stepped away from the table for a swig of beer before taking his shot. "Alls I'm saying is if you's gonna ask for help, you gotta let me have a look." Greed working its wonders.

Perko stifled a grin at his opponent's scratch. "We'll see." He banked the nine into the center pocket and got ready to drop the eleven.

It took another three turns for Perko to clear the table. Rather than set up for the eight ball, he deliberately hooked himself sinking the twelve and made a big deal of the scratch when he missed his final shot. He actually watched Mongoose's chest swell, as if winning with all seven of his balls still on the table were as good as it gets.

Outside the bar, having a smoke, Mongoose pressed again. "I gots connections, y'know. Good ones."

Perko made like he was thinking on it. He said, "Maybe I could run you up there day after tomorrow. I'm heading over there now, but my grower's a little tense."

"Who're you using?"

"Some punk. Doesn't matter. Less he knows...you know the drill."

Mongoose scratched his thigh and looked like he had more to say. Perko snapped his helmet chin strap into place. As he rode away, he checked his rear view mirror for what he knew he'd see: his fellow Libido kick starting a machine half his size. The bait was set.

Perko slowed three times on the way to Fire Route 63, always halfway up a hill, to make sure Mongoose remained on his tail. Once he was sure he'd seen him turn off the main road, he sped up, riding the last two miles faster than felt safe. He worried that Mongoose would notice the dust cloud cease at the final turn-off where Perko planned to hide, letting the other biker round the corner into the cable, tight as a cheese slicer.

While frowned upon, Perko knew killing a fellow gang member wasn't strictly against the rules. Funerals outnumbered retirement parties as far as send-offs went around the clubhouse. And internal rivalries were as valid as any other. Mongoose himself had been known to argue in favor of thinning the herd from time to time.

If anything, snitching was a worse crime. It's what made him certain Mongoose wouldn't have said a word about the grow op yet. The special hatred the gang reserved for snitches could easily backfire. Even Mongoose could figure that out. Still, the last thing Perko wanted was to be booted out alongside him. Sharing ignominy wouldn't make it less bitter.

The pull-out he'd chosen was near the bottom of a vale, scrub growing close on both sides of the road. He slowed his Harley and had the brakes on three quarters when a brown blur appeared in front of him. He leaned hard left and felt the bike skid out from under him. The hot metal clipped the deer, taking out its legs. The animal did a graceful flip, eyes wide open. *Just like a freaking deer,* Perko had time to think. The bike scraped into the ditch but Perko's own forward movement was cut short when the deer plopped onto his midsection, knocking the wind out of him. Reflexively, he reached up to feel his helmet, thankful he'd snapped the chin strap. He tried moving his legs and was pretty sure he saw the deer's flank shift from their pressure. Then he blacked out.

He came to staring up at Mongoose on his bike.

"You's not dead?"

Perko blinked. "Guess not."

"Killed a deer, looks like."

Perko asked him to help get it off him. Mongoose cut his engine and got off the bike, but stood there looking at him, like he wasn't sure what to do. "You's probably wondering why I'm here," he said.

Perko started to say no, then realized they had a problem. He wondered how long he'd been out, whether there was a chance Mongoose had spotted the cable at the top of the next rise. There's no way he would have seen it at speed, not this near dusk, not until the last second. But lying there, looking past the man and up the hill, he could see just make out the line. He forced his eyes away from it and asked again, "Get this son of a bitch off me."

"See, way I figure, they's no way you'd have a grow already done, ready to harvest." Mongoose placed his foot on the deer's carcass, adding a good amount of his own weight to the pressure on Perko's stomach. "'Cause the Nghiem bust only happened like four weeks ago. Ain't no way you'd have a harvest. You'd be more like where I found ya this morning, just about ready to plant."

Even through the haze of fresh pain, Perko marveled at Mongoose's reasoning. It wasn't exactly rocket science, but this was a guy who counted anything more than a hundred dollars by sorting bills into piles by denomination.

"So I's thinking you must be trying to put one over on me…"

Perko grabbed an antler with both hands and tugged, but all he managed to do was turn the deer's face toward this own. Same caught-in-the-headlights stare. He wondered if he'd wear that look the day he died. He wondered if would be anytime soon.

"And I's thinking that ain't no way to treat a partner, so I'm gonna tell the gang about your grow and let the chips pile up where they may."

"Fall."

"What?"

"Chips fall where they may."

"Yeah, so."

Perko started to laugh.

"What's so funny?"

"I'm just remembering that night outside The Boathouse. The night you got your name."

Mongoose stared, uncomprehending.

"I could've killed you." Perko wheezed. "Can't really breathe here."

Mongoose lifted his leg off the deer. Grabbed its hind legs and pulled it off his fellow Libido. Perko lay there a moment before rolling onto his side and slowly pushing himself into a sitting position. Everything worked. Hurt like hell, but stuff worked. Had he not been slowing down…

"What you saying, Perks?"

"The snake."

They'd been sleeping next to their bikes on the granite slab outside their favorite roadhouse, killing the last few cans of warm beer, watching a bunch of university kids dance on the roofs of a couple houseboats docked there for the night.

"The rattler."

"Weren't no rattler, Mongoose."

"Were too. A real Massasauga Rattler, leopard spots and all."

Perko shook his head. "I was there, remember?"

Libidos legend held that Marty Muldoon had wrung the neck of a rattler and roasted it in its own skin as a midnight snack.

"Fact is," said Perko, "I know well as you it was a pint-sized water snake. Not a venomous fang in its mouth."

Spittle bubbled at the corners of Mongoose's mouth.

"And I know 'cause it was me put it in your sleeping bag."

Mongoose had flopped around the fire like a badly hooked pickerel while the harmless creature slithered around his legs. He cried out for Perko to shoot the damn thing.

"It was tempting," Perko said. "'Course I'd likely have shot your balls off trying to kill it."

"I killed the sucker myself."

"You crushed it, Mongoose. Landed on it and squished it dead, squealing like a schoolgirl."

"You put it there?"

Perko said, "And I never said squat. Let you take 'Mongoose' as your nickname like you were some kinda snake-choking thug."

Mongoose looked down on him, smeared with deer blood, crumpled on the road. "I oughtta kill you now."

"Now why would you do that?" Perko pulled a deck of smokes from an inside pocket. He held a flattened cigarette with his teeth and passed the pack to Mongoose while he fished in his jeans for a lighter.

"For the snake."

"I ain't never told," said Perko. "And you kill me now, you lose the five points on my grow op."

"Half," said Mongoose. "Or I kills you and take the whole thing."

"You might. 'Course then you'll have some explaining to do around the club house."

"Like you don't."

"Stopped in earlier today, right after I left you at the barn. Told the guys I'd run them over tomorrow for a look. Making good on the whole Nghiem thing."

"But I's the one found you out."

"Nice of you to keep your mouth shut for a whole afternoon."

"Ain't no snitch."

"Exactly, Mongoose, and neither am I. Which is why you get to keep your good name."

"And five points."

"I knew you'd see it my way." Perko prodded the deer with his foot. "Help me clean this sucker. Barbeque season's around the corner."

The Sevens
Kristin Kisska

"One persistent theory surmises that the [Seven] society was founded when eight students planned to get together for two tables of bridge but only seven showed up."
—Wrapped in Mystery, *The University of Virginia Magazine*

April 10, 1905

My new spring Oxfords are stiff, causing each step to scuff the brick walkway. Shadows chase me down the colonnade, but no matter. The moon is waxing, and the heady scent of early spring flowers lightens my mood and my step. Luck courses through my veins this evening.

We fellows don't normally play bridge on a Monday night, but most lectures have been cancelled due to Dr. Alderman's inauguration as our first college president. We're all expected to participate in the ceremony on Thursday, though I suspect few University of Virginia students were invited to his installation banquet afterward in the Rotunda.

A glance at my pocket watch confirms my tardiness. But the chaps will wait. Tonight, we're playing for pipe tobacco, the finest a university student can afford—or can't—depending on one's means. Father wouldn't approve of my whittling away my allowance on games of chance, but he needn't know. Two tables. Stiff competition, but those thirteen tricks will be mine unless Maddox fleeces me again.

The wooden steps of Hotel C creak as I rap the brass knocker. Laughter seeps under the black door along with a sudden cheer which gets louder as it opens. Hamilton flashes his dimple, betraying that he's already been sampling spirits. He searches beyond me then lets me in.

"Ashby, old boy, you're late. Come in. Come in." Hamilton slaps me on the back before helping me out of my

213

overcoat. Spring has taken its time warming the Charlottesville air this year. A fire crackles and both card tables are set together in the parlor. I reach for a glass of brandy on the credenza before joining the other Third Year fellows.

Stucky, sporting his motoring clothes to make us jealous of having his father's Oldsmobile here at school, holds open a box of cigars for me to select from. "How's tricks? We're still waiting on Maddox and Walker. Did you see them on your way over?"

"Did not. I daresay the rain forecast will give the organizing committee a headache if they're required to relocate the inaugural festivities inside. Maddox isn't responsible for the torchlight procession Thursday night, is he?"

Big changes are at hand now that we will finally have a proper president. Dr. Alderman is planning to usher The University into modern times. He wants to expand The University and establish an endowment. I've even heard rumors that Dr. Alderman has visions of enrolling women as students of higher education. There's a great deal of excitement in the air over the possibilities for growth, but there's an undercurrent of anger, too. Not everyone on Grounds welcomes change.

"Maddox is a bigshot on the committee along with Robert Tate and a few other students. Not sure about Walker." Hamilton, our resident dandy, brushes an invisible speck off his sleeve and adjusts his cuffs. "But if it does rain during the inauguration, a spot under the colonnade will be as hot as a two dollar pistol. And I wager the *Hot Foot Society* will try to sell those tickets."

"That secret society is as crazy as a bedbug! The faculty loathes their bacchanal parties. Last month they stole students' chamber pots for their *Ski*-king coronation." Stucky's face shifts to accommodate a wide grin, crinkling the pink scar next to his eye—a trophy he earned as The University's short stop during a game last season. It is a rare spring night for him to not have a baseball game or team practice scheduled. "I'll take your wager, Ham. I hope you

chaps brought fine tobacco. The tricks will be mine tonight."
Not if I can help it, Stucky. Stick with baseball and driving that automobile. After lighting my cigar, I chide, "Gentlemen, I suggest you save your bets for our card game—"

Heavy banging on the front door echoes through the parlor, halting our conversation. Hamilton reaches the door first. A draft ruffles the fire, casting eerie shadows against the walls as the door creaks open.

Walker remains outside and leans over to catch his breath. His dark hair, normally slicked back, is disheveled, his voice raspy with exertion. "Maddox is deathly ill...he can't stand...stomach cramps...delirious." He wipes his mustache with a handkerchief before standing upright. "Send for the doctor. And be quick!"

Without our overcoats or hats, Hamilton and I race behind Walker to Maddox's room. Stucky leaves to fetch the doctor in his automobile. The other three remain behind at Hotel C to tend the fire lest we return to join a bucket brigade.

"Is it tuberculosis?" Hamilton asks, his voice shrill with nerves. The disease has plagued Virginia in recent months. Rumor around Grounds is that one of our classmates passed away earlier today.

"He seemed quite fine during our Greek lecture this morning. And I don't recall hearing him cough." Walker doesn't slow down as he answers the question, so Hamilton and I walk at a fast clip, chasing him. "I stopped by after supper to collect him for bridge. He didn't answer, but his door was unlocked. Poor fellow could barely sit up in bed. He was talking to ghosts in the room. Kept telling them to go away. He thought I was Dr. Alderman."

As we turn the corner of the East Range, we see someone slumped on the ground in front of his door. We run up to him and find Maddox in his night shirt, shivering in the fetal position, and lying in a pool of vomit.

We help Maddox stand up, but he collapses again despite our support. My pulse throbs in my ears, so I can barely hear Walker's orders.

Though I cover my nose, I can't help but gag. The three of us drag Maddox into his room. He moans as we hoist him into bed. With the glowing embers the only source of light, his face is as white as the painted columns of the Rotunda. Despite the chill in the room, he's drenched with sweat.

The odor inside is rank and laced with a sickly sweet aroma. Hamilton pulls open a window, and the gust of crisp air sends papers cascading off the desk.

A knot twists in my stomach as I try to keep busy and helpful. I fill the wash basin with water and wipe Maddox's face. When I fold his sleeves up to wash his hands, I nearly drop the cloth. On his forearm is a coin-sized burn scar, but he's in no condition to answer my queries. Though the twisted brown skin is long past blistering, I avoid touching it so as not to cause him more discomfort.

He rocks his head back and forth. His whisper is hoarse. "Alderman...Alderman...Thursday..."

"Poor old chap is worse than I thought." Hamilton clucks as he stoops to collect the books and pages of scattered lecture notes. He uses a nearby teapot as a paperweight. "Don't worry, Maddox, Dr. Alderman will take the oath of president even if there is a little rain on the horizon."

"...Alderman..." Maddox squints and grits his teeth as another spasm attacks his stomach. His pallor is fading still.

Where is the blasted doctor? I try to keep my expression neutral, but I can't resist cocking my eyebrows when Walker's eyes lock on mine. I help Maddox sit up enough to sip some water.

"I hope Stucky drives fast." Walker, clenching his jaw, turns to stoke the fire and add a log.

Maddox leans over, retching into a chamber pot. When he relaxes, he points towards the door, his voice ebbing. "...Thursday...must...protect...Alderman..." Then his arm drops to his side. His head falls back, his eyes close, and his breathing turns shallow. I rest his head on the pillow.

But his words haunt me. "Must protect Alderman? You don't think he means Dr. Alderman is in danger, do you?"

Walker shakes his head. "I told you. Maddox is delirious. Earlier he was mumbling about the significance of Alderman's inauguration falling on Thomas Jefferson's birthday and something about the Rotunda fire."

"That disaster was ten years ago. I think the old boy's chock-a-block." Hamilton, never one to resist the temptation of a nip of whiskey and a lark, laughs as he picks up the wicker chair that had tipped over.

"I thought so at first, but I found no spirits when I arrived to collect him. Perhaps he'd returned from an afternoon spent visiting pubs." Of course. Walker, who keeps a fatherly eye on all of us, would have already searched for liquor.

A bang on the door precedes Stucky, who bursts into the room with the doctor in his wake.

The four of us step outside to allow the doctor a measure of privacy. When smelling salts fail to rouse Maddox, the doctor confirms that he's unconscious. The doctor barks questions about the symptoms we'd witnessed. We hover outside the door waiting, except Walker, who stands a few yards away stroking his mustache and stares into the night.

"Do you think he has tuberculosis?" Hamilton blurts out, wringing his hands as the doctor approaches us.

"No." Shaking his head, the doctor mops his face with his handkerchief. His voice is grave. "Gentlemen, I believe he's suffering from some form of contamination. I'm concerned for your friend's life. We must get him to the hospital immediately."

Within moments, we carry Maddox out to the idling Oldsmobile. With two beeps of his horn, Stucky lurches out of the alley to drive Maddox and the doctor to the University Hospital.

Quiet descends on Maddox's room in the wake of his departure. Walker, Hamilton, and I return to search his room for something, anything, that could be considered toxic.

"Could he have food poisoning? Perhaps he ate mushrooms?" My question is only answered by shrugs, as no evidence of food is present.

Instead, I flip through the papers on Maddox's desk. All of them seem to be related to organizing this Thursday's festivities: an itinerary of distinguished alumni scheduled to arrive in two Pullman cars first thing Thursday morning, a presentation of a banner, the schedule for Alderman's inauguration, the menu for the installation banquet, a list of the toasts, the logistical plan for the evening's torchlight procession on the Lawn, and a copy of the letter requesting Stonewall Band to play "The Good Old Song" on the Rotunda steps. Even a fireworks display, including one in the shape of Thomas Jefferson and one in the image of Dr. Alderman, is planned for Thursday night over the Rotunda.

Maddox certainly has a great organizing responsibility on his hands. I'm surprised he even considered a night of cards. Seven hundred students, plus faculty, alumni, and important visitors—all told, thousands of people—will be present to witness Alderman's inauguration—the first president ever at the University of Virginia, despite the fact eighty years have passed since our founding. Until this past autumn, the Board of Visitors governed the faculty, which has merely been acting under Thomas Jefferson's legacy.

As I straighten the pages and place them back on the desk, Saturday's issue of *College Topics* slips from the pile. A small handwritten note is scribbled above the headline. The scrawl might as well have been hieroglyphics. It was illegible. I hand the newspaper to Hamilton. "Can you read this?"

He adjusts the paper at different lengths, but can't decipher the shorthand note either. Walker grabs the paper and holds it close to the burning embers. He looks up at us.

"Monday. Midnight. Amphitheater."

A single gas lamp from across the amphitheater flickers in the gusty night. According to my pocket watch, it's nigh midnight. Hamilton, Walker and I are hiding in the shadows. An earthy draft whips around me, causing me to shiver.

No one else is here. Not a soul. Could we have misunderstood Maddox's note? How the devil did he get caught in this tangle—and what, precisely, is this tangle all about?

I try to control my breathing so the steam from my mouth won't reveal my hiding spot. When Stucky returned from the hospital, the lads were gathered at Hotel C. Maddox still hadn't regained consciousness. The doctor's blood test found traces of toxins. Based on his severe reaction, the doctor suggested he'd been poisoned.

There is no more upstanding and decent man than Charles Morgan Maddox, the Third. He's well mannered, comes from a respected Williamsburg family, and we've spent many fine hours joking and debating together over cards and brandy. He could teach some of these college fellows a thing or two about diplomacy.

Only once did I witness him lose his temper, when he chastised a poor First Year student who argued against charging students admission to our baseball games. I thought for sure they would settle the matter with fists.

So who would want to kill him?

A crunch of wet gravel makes my pulse sound in my ears. I hold my breath. Two men climb down the grassy terraces to the bottom level of the amphitheater. Their faces are hidden in the darkness; no detail betrays any identity. Someone approaches them from the opposite side. A paper-wrapped package, about the size of a brick, is passed from the two men to the individual. They part without a word, each leaving toward different directions.

Ice water floods my veins, yet I resist the urge to call out and stop the men lest they scatter and run. After signaling to Hamilton and Walker to follow the other two, I follow the man carrying the package.

Tiptoeing so as to keep my Oxfords from squeaking, I keep a sizeable distance between me and my mark. I track him down the Lawn's brick path toward the Rotunda.

With his derby pulled low and his collar stretched high, I can't make out his face. My pulse is a metronome, keeping time with each click of his heels echoing through the hollow colonnade.

After passing the final pavilion, he pauses behind a column. Within a heartbeat, the lights of the Rotunda are extinguished, and all falls silent on the Lawn save a weak chorus of crickets chirping. He descends the steps to the

Rotunda's underground passageway. I race the length of the Lawn, the slick grass muffling my footsteps.

A nearby oak tree offers a better vantage point, for I dare not enter behind him. The shadow of his hat passes along a series of demi-Palladian windows of the passageway before he disappears from sight entirely. My watch ticks the seconds.

Though dark inside, I detect movement through the glass paneled door at the top of the Rotunda's steps. Then nothing.

Five minutes.

Eight minutes.

Dear God, what is this man doing inside? My heartbeat throbs in my ears. I fear I may have to sneak in after him.

I glance yet again at my pocket watch. Ten minutes have passed since he entered.

Woosh. The heavy underground door closing heralds his exit. Clicking footsteps follow, but I've yet to see—there! A silhouette skates by the remaining semi-circular windows, emerges from the quasi-underground tunnel, then disappears into the inky darkness of night.

I follow him at a distance down the exposed brick path. It's flanked by serpentine walls on the left, shielding one of many pavilion gardens, but I ignore the intoxicating aroma of spring in bloom. His pace quickens. His hands are empty and swing like pendulums by his side.

A quiet student boarding house along Rugby Road accepts his key. After the second-floor windows brighten, I sneak into the mudroom entryway. Next to the coat rack sits a bank of wooden mail bins, one for each tenant. Each has a few letters waiting for their owners except one that stands empty. Above it, the label reads a student's name I recognize.

R. P. Tate.

Walker and I climb the Rotunda's circular staircase to the top. Every creak of the floorboards shifting under our weight alerts the ghosts of The University's past that we are not where we ought to be. Just a few hours ago, the room was charged with students researching and studying. But now, the air is still, and we are the only beings disturbing the settling dust.

As he and I enter the Dome Room, illuminated by nothing but the penumbra of the smoky clouds drifting above the oculus, Maddox's nearly incoherent words of warning repeat in my mind "must...protect...Alderman..."

Dark forces have most definitely been at work around Grounds.

Earlier, when I left Tate's residence, I ran the mile back to Hotel C. As I approached, several other fellows were returning as well.

"We found the poison!" Stucky shouted as he and another fellow charged into the parlor. "It's Lily of the Valley. A bud was stuck to the inside of the teapot in Maddox's room."

These flowers have been blooming rampantly throughout the pavilion gardens of late and would account for the heady floral smell around Grounds. According to the botany textbook we consulted in the pavilion's library, it's also highly toxic. Stucky and another fellow left immediately to report the news to the hospital. Hopefully, this information would help the doctor treat Maddox. Poor chap.

Hamilton had yet to return from following one of the men at the midnight rendezvous, so Walker offered to help me search for Tate's package inside the Rotunda.

Now as our eyes adjust to the darkness, the Dome Room edges into view. White columns, supporting three levels of book shelves, stand perfect sentry around the perimeter of the cavernous round room. In the center is a circular desk of reference books and card catalogs. Polished reading tables and wooden carrels are strategically positioned throughout the space. Opposite the stairs, on a pedestal overlooking the very heart of his Academical Village, is the white marble statue of the Third President of the United States, author of the Declaration of Independence, and The University's founder, Thomas Jefferson.

We split up to search for Tate's package, whatever it may be. Walker climbs to the two upper levels encircling the room with book cases.

My knees begin to ache as I crawl along the edge of the

lowest level of the room, checking under each desk and behind each bookshelf. But it is penance for the vengeance burning within my soul. How could a man hurt a fellow student—nay, anyone—and call himself a Virginia gentleman? We sons of the Old Dominion answer to a higher call.

Somehow Maddox must have stumbled on Tate's plan, whatever hell he's been brewing. They've been meeting regularly these few months since Christmas as both served on the inauguration organizing committee. Who else would be more intimate with each detail of The University's first president's inaugural events than the students organizing the festivities?

Tate. And he isn't working alone. There are at least two others. Maybe more.

But why now? Alderman accepted the appointment by the Board of Visitors, moved to Charlottesville after serving as president of Tulane University, and has been functionally acting as president since the academic year began last August. He has been president in all things but title for the past eight months.

In less than three days' time, April 13th, the Dome Room will be the stage for Dr. Alderman's inauguration. It will also be Thomas Jefferson's birthday. What a sacrilege to defile our University's first president on our founder's birthday! Or, perhaps that was the point.

"Ashby, do you see that? Behind his feet." I glance up at Walker. He's leaning over the second level banister and pointing towards the statue below.

I approach the life-sized sculpture, but in the semi-darkness, Mr. Jefferson's full-length marble cloak is all I discern. Squatting, I try to maneuver around the back, but the space isn't large enough for me to enter. Instead, I reach behind the base and pat blindly, until...

Voila!

Carefully, I extract a brown package, which was all but hidden from view from those on the lower level. This must be what Tate hid. It's wrapped in paper and sealed closed with wax. In the dim lighting, I can't quite make out the embossed stamp. I rip the paper, taking care not to damage the seal.

Inside are what looks like a dozen loose cigars. Each is wrapped in red tinted paper with a wick. No. Not cigars. Candles? But a pungent sweet smell—similar to the heavy odor in Maddox's room—soon causes me to gag.

No!

I hold the bouquet of sticks away from me as if I'm carrying a coiled serpent ready to strike. My eyes widen as I consider the resulting nightmare if these were lit inside. The chaos. The smoke. The fire.

"What the devil! Is that what I think they are?" Walker, who just a moment ago had been hovering over the banister above me, rushes down the stairs to my level.

"Dynamite."

The two tables in the parlor of Hotel C are still arranged by the fireplace, but the cards have yet to be shuffled or dealt. Dawn is mere hours away, and what few morning lectures are still scheduled will commence soon thereafter.

But we still have work to do.

Stucky returned from the hospital with an update. Maddox is still in critical condition, but the doctors were able to administer an antidote to counteract the poison. He sent a telegram to Maddox's family informing them of his condition.

"It's true!" Hamilton bursts into the parlor. The draft sends playing cards scattering around the room until the front door shuts. "Tate's gang is plotting to kill Alderman."

"Slow down, Hamilton. Start from the beginning."

He leans over and unbuttons his collar, his cheeks ruddy from having run all the way here. "I followed one of the men back to a flat after the midnight exchange. There were others waiting in the room, but the curtain wasn't fully drawn. I listened from outside."

All six of us surround Hamilton's tall frame and wait for him to continue. I'm incredulous that any student of the University of Virginia would ever resort to premeditated violence. But one of our friends was poisoned mere hours ago, and Walker and I found explosives stashed for uses unknown.

"Do you know their plans for Dr. Alderman?"

"Yes. Just like for Maddox, they were grinding more Lily of the Valley. Since they mentioned something about the toasts, I think they intend to poison his coffee at the inaugural banquet. They mean to warn all who attend that no one should ever be appointed to replace Thomas Jefferson as The University's figurehead. They are members of a secret society—"

"Oh, those *Hot Foot* hoodlums have gone too far with their antics!" Stucky slams his fist into his hand. I hold his shoulders back as he looks ready to either punch a hole in the wall or grab his baseball bat and go hunting for Tate.

"Keep your shirt on, old boy. Not the *Hot Foot Society.*" Hamilton takes a deep breath, clearly irritated that he'd been interrupted. "This is a different secret society. They call themselves the *VTJs.* It stands for *Viva Thomas Jefferson.* Based on bits of their conversation tonight, I gather they've been meeting since Alderman arrived last August. They vow that Thomas Jefferson is the only qualified leader of our University. Past, present and future. No other mortal can take over his vision for Virginia."

Guffaws ripple throughout the room as we crowd even closer around Hamilton.

"But Mr. Jefferson died eighty years ago. How do these idiots expect him to lead our University?" I shudder at the lunacy. Not only are they dangerous, they're a gang of rebellious fools.

Hamilton shrugs as he adjusts his cuffs. "I suppose the same way The University has always managed since 1826, with the Board of Visitors' guidance over the faculty."

We barrage Hamilton with questions, but he holds up his hands to quiet us, at first relishing the attention. Then his voice turns grave. "It's not as simple as the *VTJs* merely not wanting any president to serve The University. They object specifically to Dr. Alderman's vision. He wants to grow The University. To make scholarships available. To admit laborers, women and..." He shuts his eyes and swallows before continuing. "...Negros. The *VTJs* refuse to accept their gentry sons graduating from their beloved alma mater next to those of lower birth and circumstances."

"The Civil War ended forty years ago. The Confederacy lost!" Walker, normally so proper we tease him about being retained as the next professor after graduation, is scuffing his foot against the floor boards, perhaps trying to dig Tate's grave one splinter at a time. "And to resort to violence in the name of Thomas Jefferson. Blasphemy!"

I catch snippets of angry comments from the other fellows. "...we can't let Tate get away with this...criminals...alert the police..."

"Wait!" I interrupt the rumblings filling the room. "What do you think Tate intended to do with that the dynamite Walker and I found hidden in the Rotunda?"

Hamilton's face turns ashen. "Gods' teeth! One of the *VTJs* mentioned that the fireworks display after the torchlight ceremony would be déjà vu, and then they all laughed. They must intend to ignite the dynamite during the fireworks program."

Only the crackle of the glowing embers pierces the silence as I'm sure each one of us recalls the photographs of black smoke billowing from the Rotunda ten years ago. Construction of the new building was completed only a few years before we arrived as students at The University.

In fact, the very statue of Thomas Jefferson where we found the dynamite survived the fire only because students wrapped it in a mattress and carried it out of the burning building, chipping the hem of its marble cloak in the process. My stomach twists at the thought of Tate's thugs destroying the Rotunda.

An unanswered question stabs at my mind. How the devil did Maddox discover Tate's plan?

Dashing outside to the place where I'd stowed the dynamite, I retrieve the paper wrapper and bring it back inside to the lamplight. I adjust the angle to inspect the wax seal. It's embossed with an imprint: a circle with the script letters T and J entwined in the center and around the perimeter is written the motto, *Rebellion to tyrants is obedience to God.*

Hamilton looks over my shoulder. "That's Thomas Jefferson's personal seal. I saw it on other papers. The *VTJs* must be using it as their society's sign..."

Hamilton's words fade as a chill runs down my back. I've seen this seal before.

"Ashby, you look like you've seen a ghost." Walker snatches the wrapper from me to look at the seal.

I shake my head, reluctant to verbally acknowledge it. "Maddox was a *VTJ*."

Adamant denials and swears swirl through the room, but I stand firm.

Rather than meet their glares, I roll up my sleeve and point to my forearm. "He has a scar of Thomas Jefferson's personal seal—the same seal that was on the dynamite—burned into his skin, right here. I suspect Tate and the others are branded as well. Maddox was the chairman of the student organizing committee." My gut churns with unease. "Did he help plan Dr. Alderman's murder? But he..."

My head throbs. I'm unable to reconcile how Maddox, my classmate and friend, could commit such an atrocity.

Walker strokes his mustache and finishes my thought for me, his voice barely as loud as a whisper. "I gather Maddox had a change of heart so Tate poisoned him. He begged us to protect Alderman."

Stucky slams his fist on a table. "We must foil Tate and his men!" Placing his hand in the center of our group, we wait. "Walker? Will you join me to protect Dr. Alderman?"

Walker places his hand on top of Stucky's. One by one, the other men follow suit, and finally Hamilton; a circle of righteous and justifiably angry Virginia gentlemen.

"Ashby?"

All dozen eyes are trained on mine. But only Stucky's is laced with challenge.

I hesitate—not from fear or lack of purpose—then I nod once as I place my hand on top of the others.

"We seven men are on our honor to protect Dr. Alderman—nay, the University of Virginia—from sabotage. Let's together start a *new* secret society."

* * *

The wooden brush in my hand is steady, despite a night of no sleep and no supper. The white paint glows against my canvas, the brick walkway at the foot of the Rotunda. Walker, Hamilton, and a few others are keeping watch for early risers so we can scatter and hide if someone approaches. Morning will break soon and students will be milling about the Grounds to go to class.

Our vote in Hotel C was unanimous. We weren't confident we knew all the particulars of Tate's plan to disrupt the inaugural festivities. Could there possibly be more nefarious elements we have yet to discover? We would be more effective scouting the Grounds anonymously. We are Third Year class members, so we blend within The University. And we wish to be of service both now and after we graduate.

We seven have each pledged to take our secret—our membership in this secret society—to our graves, thus the number seven I'm painting on the brick walkway in front of the Rotunda.

We drafted two anonymous letters. The first was addressed to the police department alerting them of the murder attempt on Maddox and Tate's plans for disrupting inauguration day. We listed every detail we'd collectively unearthed while investigating and included the package of dynamite we found in the Dome Room. Walker left this letter outside Tate's boarding house door while Hamilton rang the police alerting them to a suspicious package.

At this very moment, Stucky should be climbing in through Alderman's office window and leaving our second letter on his desk for him to find this morning.

April 11, 1905

To Dr. Alderman:

Thomas Jefferson once said, "One man with courage is a majority." As president, you have been tapped to lead the University of Virginia, and to realize our founder's brilliant vision of his Academical Village.

To some, this change is painful, but we will never tolerate violence, particularly as a means to express an opinion. The

Charlottesville police have been informed of a plot to murder you and to destroy the Rotunda during your inaugural festivities. While we are relieved to have uncovered this plot before these students were able to act on it, we cannot be confident we've unearthed the complete plan nor identified every member of the gang.

We seven Virginia men will remain vigilant on your behalf, but please be on your guard this Thursday and beyond. Unlike other secret societies, ours is a beneficial organization. Each of us vows to protect The University from harm—both within and without. Let our sign—the number seven nested within the symbols of alpha, omega, and infinity—be a talisman to ward off evil and promote the welfare of Mr. Jefferson's university.

Should you ever need our help, leave a note at the statue of Thomas Jefferson in the Rotunda.

Sincerely,
The Seven Society

Old Friends

B.K. Stevens

"Steal his hat," I said.

I pointed to a tanned, stocky Texas-type sitting at the far end of the cafe, talking on his cell phone, face turned toward the street as he half-watched cars drive by. His hat, a sure-enough cowboy hat, sat on the table next to him. Vince took thirty seconds to look him over, to glance at other diners chatting quietly at small, glass-covered tables set out on the sidewalk. He shook his head.

"No fair," he said. "Stealing's a crime. You can't ask me to commit a crime."

I shrugged. "It's not much of a crime. It's just a hat. And you don't have to keep it forever. If he sees you taking it, give it back and make up some excuse. But I bet he won't notice. He hasn't stopped talking or looked away from the street in at least five minutes."

Vince gritted his teeth, stood up, and squared his shoulders. "Sheila and Carol were right," he said. "We should've stopped doing this years ago. Okay. Here goes."

I had to admire his style. He walked off unhurried but unhesitating, passing tables without looking at them, not glancing down or breaking stride even when he reached out casually with his left hand and slid the hat off the table.

But Texas-type saw it. I heard his indignant "Hey!" and saw him stand up to snatch the hat back, watched Vince talking and gesturing and smiling. People at the nearest tables turned to listen. Finally, Texas-type sat down again slowly, his eyes still fixed on Vince, his mouth still locked in a scowl. Vince headed back to our table, moving more quickly now.

"Damn," he said as he slid into his chair, "that was humiliating. Thanks a bunch, Ken."

"At least he didn't call the police," I said. "What did you tell him?"

He cringed. "That I wasn't trying to steal his hat, that I just admired it and wanted to look at it in a better light for a moment."

"Pretty smooth," I said, impressed. Cool October sunlight poured down uninterrupted on almost the entire café, but Texas-type sat directly under a massive oak tree—still plenty bright, but arguably a few degrees shadier than the rest of the place. I saw a brisk young server heading toward us, carrying a small basket of rolls and crackers. "Look, I know that was a rough one. Let me buy you a drink, make it up to you."

He raised an eyebrow. "At lunch? All right. If you're paying, let's be decadent."

He ordered a dirty martini, and I ordered Jim Beam on the rocks. Our server didn't flinch, but I bet we'd shocked her. She looked like the sort of sensible, health-conscious young person who's been brainwashed into good behavior. Well, I don't usually drink at lunch, either. But today was special. I reached for a menu.

"They have a great New York strip here," I said, "and incredible fried fingerlings. You should try them."

"No thanks. That's a little heavy for lunch, don't you think?"

"Maybe. But I'll make up for it at dinner. Sheila's turned into a fanatic. Everything's got to be organic and locally sourced, whatever the hell that means. These days, she never cooks anything but poached fish and grilled vegetables. Or sometimes grilled fish and poached vegetables. If I want real food, I have to get it at a restaurant."

"If a hunk of red meat is your idea of real food." He smiled at the server. "How's the trout and watercress flatbread, Elise? Pretty good? Then that's what I'll have."

He watched her walk away before turning to face me again. "Your turn. Truth or dare?"

We'd been playing this game since middle school. Back then, the dares had usually been physical challenges—hold your breath for two minutes, run up and down the stairs five times without stopping, climb a ladder using only one hand.

In college, the dares often involved drinking a certain number of shots, sometimes of mildly disgusting substances. Now, our dares tended to be tamer. Always, though, we'd both taken the game absolutely seriously. Neither of us had ever let the other one win by turning down a dare or refusing to reveal a truth—and I know I'd never lied, and I'm willing to bet Vince never had, either. In the old days, we'd sometimes kept at it for hours, because neither one of us wanted to look weak by saying we should stop. Eventually, we'd agreed to limit the games to five rounds. Then, three years ago, our wives had ordered us to cut them out altogether. We were in our thirties now, for God's sake, they'd said. We shouldn't still be doing something so childish, so ridiculous, so dangerous. So we'd promised to stop.

That time, we *had* lied. Vince and I had grown apart over the years, but we still got together, secretly, every six months or so, so we could play.

I took a roll from the basket and started slathering it with butter as I thought about my choice. I knew Vince wouldn't go easy on me, not after the dare I'd just given him. Whatever I picked, he'd look for a way to retaliate. "Truth," I said.

"Coward." Vince thought for a moment. Then he sat forward. "How much do you weigh, Ken?"

"Ouch." I put down the roll. "As of this morning, two-oh-four."

He didn't hide his smirk. "I wondered if that first digit had rolled over. You better watch it, buddy. You're not even six feet, and you've got a pretty small frame. You're running a serious risk of—"

"That's enough," I cut in. "*I'm* the one who's supposed to be telling the truth. Not you."

He laughed, Elise brought our drinks, we toasted old times, and he asked about Sheila.

"She's doing great," I said. "Looking great, too. *She* hasn't put on weight. She never does. Still not a trace of gray, either. Most women we know have started coloring their hair, but she hasn't had to."

"Lucky thing for you. She'd never get a blonde that rich from a bottle."

"No argument there." I folded my hands on the table, leaned forward, and looked up at him. "Vince, let me say again how sorry we are about Carol. Even though you were separated, it must've hit you hard."

"Yeah, it did." He let his shoulders droop, let out a deep sigh. "I still had feelings for her. And when they told me that she was dead, that she'd slit her wrists, I couldn't help feeling guilty. I should've reached out to her, helped her somehow, stopped her."

"Hell, how could you have known she was thinking about doing something like that? I sure didn't. I had a drink with her just a few days before she did it, and it never occurred to me. I mean, I could tell she was feeling down, sure, but suicide? Never crossed my mind."

Vince started unwrapping a cracker. "You had a drink with Carol?"

"Yeah, she called me out of nowhere, suggested we meet after work. Anyway, we shouldn't dwell on all that. Your turn. You want to play it safe, choose truth this time?"

He looked at me, and his eyes narrowed. "No. Dare."

"Suit yourself." I sat back in my chair and thought for a moment. "Okay. Stand up, shout 'Cowabunga!' and then chug both of our drinks without taking a breath in between."

"Oh, man." He grimaced, then raised an eyebrow in appeal. "Shout?"

"Well, say it loudly. No fair whispering it so I'm the only one who can hear."

He didn't look happy, but he did it, and he did it with gusto. People at nearby tables chuckled; one man raised his own glass in salute. Vince sat down again, blushing.

"Nice job," I said. "I'll reward you by springing for a second round."

"A second one? At *lunch*?"

"Well, you couldn't really enjoy the first one, and I barely got to taste mine. And your office is only a few blocks away—you walked here, right? So you don't have to worry about driving under the influence."

"Only about falling asleep at my desk this afternoon. That's all right. Work's been going great—I'm the golden boy these days. Nobody's going to begrudge me a nap." He shot me a smug look. "Your turn again. Ready to take your chances with a dare?"

I tilted my head to the side, then shrugged. "No, let's stick with truth."

"Afraid I'd get back at you for those last two, huh? Okay." He sat forward in his chair. "Leaving Impact Communications after all those years—was that really your idea? One hundred percent?"

He knows how to pick them, I thought. But I had to tell him. The middle-school code of honor demanded it. "Not one hundred percent, no. My sales were down. Bruce called me into his office, and we agreed I should start looking around for other opportunities. Within two months, I'd found one. I've been very happy at TripleCom. I'm doing well."

"As well as you were doing at Impact five, six years ago?"

I gave him an arch look. "That sounds like a separate question. You can save it for the next round."

"Don't think I need to." He sat back and grinned. "I think you just gave me my answer."

Elise brought us our lunches. "That smells amazing," I said, unrolling the white cloth napkin and grasping the oak-handled steak knife nestled inside. "Thanks, Elise. And I promised my friend another round of drinks."

This time, her left eyebrow quivered. "Right away, sir," she said, and scooped up our empty glasses and scurried off.

Vince dusted a chunk of garlic off his trout. "You made it sound like the drinks were my idea."

"Did I? Sorry." I cut into my steak. The juices had set nicely—the folks here know what they're doing. I hate it when plates get bloody. "Does it really matter? You weren't thinking of making a move on her, were you? I know you're single now, but she's a brunette, she's short, and she's wearing big glasses. Not really your type, is she?"

"No, she's not my type. And of course I wouldn't make a move on her. She looks like she's still in college. But it's embarrassing."

"Sorry," I said again. "Well, let's move ahead. How about picking truth this time? I know those dares were rough on you, and I've got something I want to ask you."

He looked up quickly. "Dare," he said. "But maybe you can make this one a little less rough."

"Okay." I scanned the other tables. "That woman sitting alone and reading, at the table next to the door—Ms. Cool Young Professional. Ask her what her favorite color is."

Vince glanced at her, and his glance settled into a gaze. She was tall and slender, probably in her late twenties, with thick, soft blonde hair that curled up gently an inch or two below her shoulders. "Okay," he said. "I don't mind this one."

"But no fair saying I dared you to do it," I said. "You have to just ask her, without making any excuses."

"Of course not. That's always the rule." He smoothed his hair into place, stood up, and sauntered over to her table.

I watched him and didn't even try to suppress the envy. He'd always been taller and better looking than I am, but now he was noticeably thinner and more fit, too. And he looked five, maybe ten years younger, even though we were almost exactly the same age. Plus he had charm. Vince had always had charm.

It didn't seem to be working on Ms. Cool Young Professional, though. Vince rested his hands on her table, leaned in to an intimate distance, turned his smile up to full, and started talking. She looked up from her book and stared at him but didn't smile back, didn't speak. He kept talking, leaned in closer, smiled harder. He was wheedling. Even from that distance, I could tell he was wheedling. Finally she said something curt, turned her body away from him, and fixed her gaze on her book again. He stood there for another few seconds, smile frozen on his face. Then he hunched his shoulders up briefly and walked back to our table.

He sat down and lit into his flatbread. "Blue," he said. "Her favorite color's blue. What a bitch."

"So you two didn't hit it off? Sorry. I thought you might. She's a lawyer, too."

Vince looked up sharply. "You know her?"

"Not really, no. I've never spoken to her. But I know who she is. Ashley Graham. We both eat lunch here often, and I've seen her with other people from Lambert and Steinberg. She's the new associate."

"And now she thinks I'm some kind of stalker." He dunked a sprig of watercress into horseradish sauce. "So if we ever meet up professionally, it's gonna be damn awkward. Thanks, Ken. This is turning into a really fun lunch."

Elise came back with our drinks, and Vince grabbed his from the tray and downed half of it with one swallow. Elise's left eyebrow quivered again, but she retreated without a word.

"Want to try a fingerling?" I asked, holding out my plate. "They're really crispy outside and really flaky inside and—"

"No, I don't want a damn fingerling," he said, too loudly. The couple at the next table stared, and he lowered his voice. "Your turn. Come on, Ken. Take a dare. Why won't you choose dare for once?"

And why won't you choose truth for once, I thought, even when I keep humiliating you with dares? I bit into a fingerling. Crispy outside, flaky inside, just like I'd said. Delicious. "I'm not in the mood for a dare," I said. "Truth."

He took a big bite of trout, made a face, and chewed rapidly. "All right," he said after he'd swallowed. "How much did you lose at poker last month, Ken? Or did you somehow manage to come out ahead for once?"

Good one, Vince, I thought. Another direct hit. "No, I didn't come out ahead last month. It's been a long time since I came out ahead. And I don't keep exact figures on how much I lose. Keeping exact figures gets depressing. I'd say I lost somewhere around a thousand. That's about typical."

"Wow," Vince said. "That's a lot to flush down the toilet every month, especially since you aren't bringing in as much as you used to. I'm sure Sheila's dental practice is doing well—it always has—but even so. That kind of loss, month after month, has gotta be doing serious damage to any long-term plans you two might have."

"Oh, I've got lots of long-term plans for Sheila and me," I said. "I just hope they all work out. I love her, Vince, and I depend on her. She's a dynamo—I've never known anyone else who works as hard as she does, anyone else half as determined to succeed. She's carried me through lots of little crises, and I'm sure she always will."

"That's touching," Vince said. "Faith. That's always touching. Well, good luck to you." He picked up his second martini and drained it.

"Thanks." I sawed off another hunk of steak. "Round four. Almost done. Why not choose truth this time? You don't have anything to hide, do you?"

He shrugged. "You're not in the mood for choosing dare, and I'm not in the mood for choosing truth. Let's get this over with. Dare."

I took my time chewing, looking around the café. Elise was at the next table, refilling water glasses for three well-dressed older women who looked like they were having a post-retirement get-together. I swallowed. "Call Elise over here and ask her to take the bread basket away. Say it's giving off a bad aura, and you can't have that kind of negativity around you right now. And keep a straight face while you're saying it."

"Oh, for Pete's sake. She'll think I'm crazy."

"No, she won't. She'll just think you're being silly. I'm sure she's heard customers say stuff a lot weirder than that. Anyhow, what does it matter? You said you're not interested in making a move on her."

"No, I'm not." He gave me a long, hard look. "I can do a lot better than Elise."

"I'm sure you can," I said. "Go ahead, Vince. Have fun with it. I can't wait to see how she reacts. And I can't wait to see if you can keep a straight face."

"That's easy." He took a deep breath, then lifted a hand to catch Elise's eye.

She stepped over to our table. "Can I get anything for you? How's your flatbread?"

"Oh, it's fine," he said, keeping both his face and his voice carefully neutral. "Very tasty. But could you take the bread basket away, please? It's giving off a bad aura, and I can't have that sort of negativity around me today."

Elise's head jerked back, and her eyes got huge. "Of course, sir. If that's what you both want."

She looked at me, and I lifted my shoulders helplessly. "Whatever makes him happy. But maybe first I'll take one more roll to—"

"No!" Vince pulled the basket away as I started to reach for it. "I tell you, those things are disturbing my chakras. I want them gone. And you've had enough rolls, fat boy. Back off. Elise, get that pit of depravity out of here."

This time, she didn't speak, just took the basket from him and sped away. As soon as she was out of sight, he started laughing. I took a long swig of Jim Beam.

Still chuckling, he wiped a hand across his forehead. "I actually *did* have fun with that. Oh, man! Did you see her face? And I kept *my* face straight the whole time—I stayed absolutely in character. Come on, Ken. Admit it. I did a great job."

I put down my glass and gave him a sour look. "You did a great job. But I'm not sure 'fat boy' was really necessary."

"Oh, sorry." He leaned forward over the table, letting his face sag into an exaggerated expression of remorse. "Did I hurt your tiny little feelings? What a shame. Then again, maybe you've earned it, considering all the nasty stuff you've thrown at me today."

"You haven't exactly gone easy on me, either. Anyway, this game shouldn't be about getting revenge. It should be about having fun. Every dare I've given you has had a humorous element to it. I can't say the same for your questions."

He lifted a shoulder in acknowledgement. "Then see what sort of funny stuff I can come up with. Or can't you take a dare?"

"Maybe I can't," I said. "Truth."

He didn't hesitate for even a second this time. "How's your marriage, Ken?"

I took a bite of potato. It had gotten cold. "Not so great," I said. "It's not that we argue. We've hardly ever argued. Sheila's not the type. She hates drama. These days, though, she's—well, she's polite. She's always been polite, but these days she's *just* polite. Sometimes, I get the feeling she's staying with me mostly for Matthew's sake. And he's only a few years away from college. Sometimes, I wonder if once he leaves, Sheila might consider another option."

Vince toyed with another sprig of watercress but didn't eat it. "You think she's got another option?"

"Definitely," I said. "She's having an affair. I know that for a fact. But I also know that, deep down, she still loves me. We've had some problems, though, and now this other option has come along. I think he's someone thinner and more successful, someone who doesn't gamble. I think he's someone who looks like the answer to everything that's ever made her feel dissatisfied with me. I think this other option is dazzling her, distracting her from how much she really loves me. I even think I know who he is. You want me to tell you his name?"

"That's all right," Vince said. "That's all the truth I can handle right now. And I'm sorry it's so rough with you and Sheila. I know it must hurt. But sometimes, when things have run their course, it makes sense to move on. It's hard at first, but in the long run, everybody's better off. Carol couldn't understand that, and I'll always regret it. I think if she'd hung on a little longer, she would've been fine. She would've found someone new, she would've shrugged off the past, and she would've moved ahead with her life and been happy again. You know?"

"I know. You're probably right." I cleared my throat and looked up at him with a determined smile. "Last round. What do you say, Vince? Time for a little truth?"

"No, let's not go there." His face grew heavy with pity. "Dare. Do your worst, Ken. Maybe this game *is* about revenge sometimes, and maybe sometimes that's okay. Whatever you tell me to do, even if it makes me look like an absolute maniac, I'll do it."

"Okay." I dropped back against my chair and looked around the café. "I don't know. I don't feel especially creative right now. But all right. Here's something. Stand up, lean across the table, and take my tie off me while saying, 'I have to! I have to! I have to!' And no, you don't have to shout it, but you have to say it loudly enough for the people at the next few tables to hear. And then you have to run across the café, shimmy up the oak tree behind Texas-type, and hang the tie from the lowest branch."

Vince grimaced. "Damn. You *do* want revenge. If the senior partners hear about this, I'll have a lot of explaining to do. But I said I'd do it, and I will. And you'll still have one turn left. Get ready for a question about your sex life."

"If you complete this dare," I said, "I'll answer any question you like. Or who knows? Maybe I'll choose dare this time."

"You can't take a dare anymore," he said. "You don't have the guts. All right, old man. Here goes."

He took a deep breath, stood up, leaned across the table, and grabbed my tie. "I have to! I have to! I have to!" he said, and brought his hands to my throat as he started to undo the knot.

"What's wrong with you?" I shouted. And I picked up my steak knife and plunged it deep into his chest.

His eyes filled with confusion. I forced the knife in deeper and twisted it. I had to make sure it found his heart.

It did. His body collapsed on top of me, and I pushed it away. The blood spurting out across my plate disgusted me.

I fell back against my chair, pressed a bloody hand against my forehead, and wept. I didn't have to force the tears. Vince was my oldest friend, my dearest friend, and his death broke my heart. But some things have to be done. As I wept, Elise dropped her tray, and Texas-type ran over to help. Ms. Cool Young Professional grabbed her cell phone from her purse to call 911, and the retired ladies at the next table cried out in alarm. All down the length of the café, other people at other tables were standing up, pointing, talking.

I hoped they were talking about all the strange things Vince had done during the last hour, about how much he'd had to drink, about how erratic and out of control he'd seemed. All that would help when the police arrived, when I told them that Vince had been deeply disturbed since his estranged wife committed suicide, that he'd seemed to reach his breaking point today, that for some reason he seemed to blame me for Carol's death, that he'd started to strangle me. Of course, I wouldn't tell them that when Carol and I had a drink a few days before she slit her wrists, she had confided in me about the longstanding affair between her husband and my wife. I wouldn't tell them she'd said that's why she'd decided to leave him.

I never would've realized they were having an affair, not on my own. But Carol was a lot smarter than I am. Luckily, Sheila thinks she's a lot smarter than I am, too. I'm pretty sure she doesn't suspect I know the truth. Even if she does, even if she suspects that's why I killed her lover, I don't think she'll say anything to the police. Seeing his father arrested for murder would be too upsetting for Matthew, and she really loves that boy.

Maybe I'm wrong. Maybe it won't work. But without Sheila, my life isn't worth much anyhow. So I'm willing to risk it.

Who says I can't take a dare?

Life Just Bounces
Graham Wynd

In her small flat on the west side Madeleine waited, checking the mobile phone in her hand every few seconds as if looking at it might hurry along some news. The day had got off to a bad start and it wasn't getting any better. You'd think it being her birthday would be awesome enough. She tried to ignore what was behind the couch or think about what it meant. That should be easy enough.

Nonetheless, weird thoughts filled her head. She remembered how in novels people were always wringing their hands. She wondered what that actually looked like. It seemed as if it would be strange. When she thought of wringing something, it required two hands so how could you wring your hands both at the same time? At least she was holding the phone so it kept her from actually trying it.

I must be nervous though, Madeleine concluded. *I hope she gets here soon.*

The doorbell rang and she bounced out of her chair, running to the door to open it, almost breathless not so much from her dash to the door, but from the pent-up terror and excitement. She may have been holding her breath, too. Maybe since she woke up.

"I'm so glad you've come!"

Claire swept in with her usual breezy air. "Hello, darling!" She leaned in to kiss Madeleine, not noticing the pinched look on her best friend's face. This was normal for Claire, who carried adventure with her everywhere and had no need to look for it in anyone else's life. Something was always happening, about to happen, or had just happened to this young woman, so she always had something exciting to say. It was one of the things Madeleine liked best about her normally. No doubt about it, Claire was fun. But this was not a normal day.

"You would not believe the traffic! Madness. And I could not find a place to park. Three times around the block before I could squeeze into a spot. Braille parking to the rescue again."

"Claire, I have to ask you—" But it was clear that Claire had not heard her hesitant start. As Claire bounded for the sofa, she followed her with a heavy heart and slower steps.

Claire did not seem to notice her friend's mood. Then again, you wouldn't expect an express train to stop on a dime. You had to wait for the brakes to squeal a little first. "Oh my God, did you see the pictures Adele posted on Facebook today, I swear that woman will never—"

Or you could pull the emergency brake. "Claire!"

"What?!" Claire finally took in her friend's pale face and twisting hands. Madeleine still held the phone in her hands. Even though the summoned help had arrived, she squeezed it between her fingers as if she might hope to wring further help from the mute machine than just Claire. She was agitated enough that Claire finally remarked upon it. "What's wrong?"

Madeleine tried to smile, but her lips refused to cooperate. They wanted to tremble instead. Her blinking eyes did their best to hold back the tears that wanted to start. Madeleine knew if she let even one fall they would not stop for a good long while. Best to keep things on a humorous note. "Ah...well...you know how people say 'friends help you move—'"

Claire made a tiny gasp. "Oh my God, you're not moving again?! I cannot do it, cannot! It took me ages to finally get all that horrid newsprint off my fingers and I couldn't help it if the china broke anyway because I thought I had wrapped it carefully, but I guess I got distracted—"

Madeleine closed her eyes. It shouldn't be this hard, should it? But it was difficult to make headway with her friend on the best of days. She knew that. Patience was required. "Claire, you're not listening. I said, you know how people say, 'Friends help you move, but real friends help you move bodies...'" Madeleine tried to smile. Failing that she attempted to give her a significant look. She wasn't exactly sure how to give a significant look. Her face felt as if it were made from rubber and it all seemed so clownish and like clowns, not terribly funny.

Claire paused for a moment. It would have to do as far as thinking went with her. It wasn't really her strongest suit. "No, I don't think I'd heard that one before. You know, that's actually pretty funny. You should post that on Facebook. Oh my God, Adele would laugh so much at that."

Madeleine lost it. Most of the time Claire's scattered nonsense was amusing and fun. It's not like she was all that serious most of the time either. But right now was a crisis, and in a crisis, you really needed someone who could be serious at least for a moment or two.

"Claire! I mean it. I really *really* need your help."

Claire stared at her. They were doubtless words that had never been uttered to her in the entirety of her life. There had never been anyone who actually needed Claire for anything. She was by nature an accessory, someone to be added for the sparkle that she always provided, like glitter or gems. People in trouble did not consult Claire. No one in need had ever so much as required her presence. But finally the truth of the utterance got through to her. "Wait, what? Are you saying—?"

Madeleine nodded her head slowly up and down. "Yes."

The two friends exchanged a few anxious glances. Each had reason to worry about the other. Theirs not a friendship that had been tested by heartfelt bonds and longstanding hardship. Rather they had fallen into common cause mostly by chance, opportunity, and a low level of expectation easily met by a round of cocktails and a smorgåsbord of rom-coms.

Claire couldn't quite wrap her head around the possibility of it being real. "A...body?"

"Um...yeah."

It's not that Claire doubted her assessment of the situation. It was just a challenge to picture Madeleine coming up with some sort of body without warning. Not that warning would have made it any easier to picture. But that brought up a very good question. "So, um...who?"

Madeleine sighed. It was pretty obvious, surely. Then again the obvious answers were often the ones you most overlooked. It couldn't be that simple naturally. But it was. "Bill. Of course. Who else? I mean, I'm not like a random murderer or anything, you know."

Claire nodded. "No, of course not, I'd never think that of you." She paused for a moment to think the news over. "Well, *that* I can believe. You know, I tried not to talk him down, knowing you were getting it regularly if nothing else, which is important of course. I remember how things were before Bill. You were climbing the walls, darling! But yes, not the whole package, clearly. I know I may have said that a little too often."

It was Madeleine's turn to nod. "And I appreciated that and you were right, as usual. He was impossible in the end. I know that now. *Im*possible."

I should say so, Claire thought but wisely kept the words to herself. She prided herself on being generous enough not to say *I told you so* too often. Another thought struck her. "So, erm, where is he?"

Madeleine motioned with her head. "Behind here."

The two of them get up, turn around and look over the back of the sofa for a moment or two before turning back around to sit in silence for a moment.

Claire finally said, "Oh, that's reminded me." She got her mobile out of her handbag and started texting.

When she could no longer contain her curiosity, Madeleine finally asked her, "What's that all about?"

Claire put her phone back into the bag. "I needed to schedule a facial."

"Ah." Madeleine didn't know what else could be said to that.

After a moment Claire coughed and then asked, "So...what brought this on?" There wasn't much else to say after all. At least not yet. They were processing the enormity of it. Claire was big on processing. She wasn't entirely sure what it meant, to be honest. She had learned it from the movies and used it a lot, mostly as a way not to deal with things she preferred to leave alone. There were so many things she didn't feel ready to deal with. A dead Bill certainly fell under that heading.

Madeleine shrugged and sighed again. "Well, a lot of things, but—well, mostly my birthday. You know what he got me for my birthday?" Madeleine's birthday had been the day before but with one thing and another going on and Claire's inability to keep dates straight in her head it was only today that they were actually going to go out for a drink. Or had planned to do so later, which is why Claire was a bit puzzled when Madeleine had called so much earlier than planned. However she took it as a given that people were eager to spend as much time with her as they could and didn't give it much more thought.

"What did he get you?"

Madeleine lost the harried look she had worn and her face looked as annoyed now as it probably had done the day before. "A frying pan."

Claire shook her head. This would be the stuff of legends when all the rest of it had blown over. In all her days, she had not heard anything to rival it. "The mind boggles."

Madeleine looked relieved. If there had been a moment of doubt, it swiftly disappeared then. The mind indeed boggled at such incomprehensible buffoonery. It sounded like the start of a joke, not a crime. "I was flabbergasted, I can tell you. I think it would have been all right I suppose, but he got all on his high horse about how it was 'an encouragement of my artistic side' and a 'premium item' to boot."

"Premium item!" Claire gaped. "And yeah, his kind only gets interested in your 'artistic side' when he gets the payoff, like when Tommy wanted me to take up pole dancing—'for my health', you know."

They both laughed at that. The idiocy of men could not be overestimated. At least the men they knew. Rumors of more astute men reached them at times. Life continued to disappoint.

The reality had begun to sink it. That led to curiosity. "So, how, uh—" Claire didn't know quite how to ask it. She had sense enough to realize that it could be delicate drawing out details from what must have been an emotionally charged incident.

Madeleine blanched. It was obviously distasteful to remember the particulars. Nonetheless, she went on. "Well, you know I was excited, first gift from the boyfriend, and I picked it up and I thought, funny, you know. 'Cause it was really heavy."

Claire nodded. "Funny."

"Yeah, funny, but I unwrap it and it's this Le Crueset frying pan. Green. Huge. Heavy. And I say, what am I meant to do with this? And he says, it's to encourage my—"

"Artistic side." The two of them said the words in unison and then burst out laughing.

"Yeah, and I say, I express my artistic side when I pick up the phone and call out for some takeaway. And he says, maybe you need to express a little more artistic qualities, and so I said you got any complaints about me, and then he goes off on this fantasy of home cooking and 'domestic arts' that's right out of some 1950s Technicolor film."

Claire shook her head. "Totally retro. Too many lad mags for that one. And should I imagine some drinking may have been involved here as well?"

"Well, just a gallon or so of gin. Oh, my head this morning!" Madeleine put a hand to her forehead in memory of the hangover.

"Not as bad as his though," Claire added just to be truthful. And it struck her as funny, so to speak.

Madeleine winced. "Ouch!"

Claire rushed to apologise. "Sorry, couldn't resist."

"I don't quite know how it came about exactly." Madeleine raised her hands up in a gesture of helplessness. "I mean, I was furious and we were both saying all kinds of things we'd never be able to take back and I just sort of saw red and shrieked a lot and he was shouting in that way that goes right through your brain pan and it was just the last straw when he said he was going home to his mum who knows how to cook and take care of a man so I bashed him one on the noggin and down goes Blaze."

For a moment they were both silent. Madeleine looked

ready to burst into tears but mastered her emotions at last and added, "I didn't really think he was dead, you know. I didn't really think that."

"No, of course not. You're not heartless." Claire was unwilling to believe that any friend of hers could be such.

Madeleine squeezed her arm with gratitude, then smiled. "Although there is something terribly satisfying about whacking someone on the head with a frying pan. I can see why they always do it in cartoons."

"Makes sense. The sound alone is aces."

Madeleine smiled, but the happiness faded. "But when I got up this morning, there he was yet. So I called you."

Claire nodded. "You need a cool head in a crisis."

"So how do you get rid of a body?" Madeleine looked hopefully at her friend. It wasn't so much that she thought Claire a mastermind of some kind, just that she had no real ideas herself.

Claire did her best to look thoughtful. "I know I've seen them do it in films and television, but off the top of my head..."

"And films always seem to be about it going wrong." Madeleine nodded quickly. "I wish I knew someone to ask ...someone with experience."

Claire snapped her fingers. "Google! You can find anything on the internet."

They both got their phones out and started tapping. Madeleine looked at her friend. "So, erm...what do we look for?"

"Well...how to get rid of a body?"

They both typed away. Claire made a face. "Oh, my God—that's disgusting!"

"What?"

Claire showed her the screen and they both shrieked.

"Oh God, turn off the images!" Madeleine looked askance at her own phone. "That's really disturbing."

"No kidding!" Claire said, feeling a bit scarred by the lingering image. "Who knew this CSI stuff was real." There was more typing and a lot more wincing.

Madeleine finally said, "I hate to say it, but looks like dismemberment is the way to go."

Claire agreed. "Nine out of ten body disposers recommend it." It helped to keep some humor in the situation.

"Yes, but how do we—you know...do it?"

Claire squinted at her screen. "Preferred equipment seems to be samurai sword or chainsaw. How're you fixed for those?"

Madeleine rolled her eyes. "Oh, if only I hadn't sent my samurai sword to the cleaners yesterday!"

"Well, what do you have on hand?"

Madeleine made a quick mental survey. "I have...no, let me think. I don't..."

"Do you have any kind of heavy equipment? Apart from the frying pan, of course."

She thought it over. "Define 'heavy'."

"Well, I think weight has to be a part of it. But sharpness, too." She took a quick look behind the sofa. "Yeah, sharpness will be necessary."

"Well, let me think. Or better yet, let's have a rummage."

Both of them got up from the sofa and begin to rifle through the various drawers and cabinets in the small galley kitchen. They pulled out a variety of objects of dubious applicability to the task: a hand mixer, rolling pin, blender, electric knife, eliminating most of them before finally deciding on a couple of items each that seemed potentially useful and laying them on the coffee table in front of the sofa. There was a meat tenderizer, the two largest knives she owned, and some weird thing with a handle that her mother had given her years ago and she'd never figured out what it was for.

"I have a bad feeling I've just been in a movie montage," Madeleine muttered. "And without a punchy theme tune."

"I have severe doubts about this."

Madeleine looked up with her mouth open. "What do you mean? You gotta help me. You just have to!"

"No, no, I mean, I don't think we have the right equipment."

Picking up the largest knife she had, Madeleine had to agree. They just weren't properly equipped for the deed. "This is sharp enough, don't you think?"

"Well, probably. I guess."

"I think I have a sharpener somewhere..."

Claire sighed. "Okay, maybe it's sharp enough, but what about heaviness? It's got to be heavy, right?"

"Do you think heaviness is that important? What about speed? I seem to remember that speed adds to the sense of heaviness, if you know what I mean. It was in math class. Or science maybe. There was a formula."

Her friend frowned. "Maybe, but do you think you can have as much speed as a chainsaw?"

"Probably not." Her face fell. Then she had a thought that mitigated the disappointment somewhat. "But a samurai sword isn't as fast, surely. Speed has to count for a lot. They're speedy. Bill loves those samurai movies. And hopping ghosts, but I think that's Chinese. Samurai—that's Japanese right?"

Claire looked completely lost at that. "I suppose a samurai sword's not heavy, but it's got a good heft and you can swing it pretty fast. You have to go through bone, you know. It's wicked sharp."

"I guess you're right."

They both considered the matter for a moment or more. Outside the traffic noises got louder as the day wore on.

"Oh, I know!" Claire's face shone with pleasure at actually coming up with a solution.

"What?"

She grinned. "We could jump on it."

"Jump on it?"

"To make it heavy."

"Ah." Madeleine didn't seem entirely convinced.

"Shall we give it a go?" Claire was eager to see her idea in action.

"Well...I suppose so."

They went behind the sofa with the big knives and stood awkwardly for a moment looking down at the body that had been Bill.

"Where do you suppose we should, ah...start?" She couldn't stop her thoughts from jumping to the stain the blood would leave on the carpet. Amazing that Bill could be such a mess even dead.

Meanwhile Claire had been taking inventory. "I say hands. Start small, work our way up. Learn as we go. It's a process." She sounded almost eager.

"Yeah. A process."

"Left or right?"

Madeleine didn't know if it mattered, but suddenly having to choose made the whole thing seem absurdly difficult. "Erm..."

Claire could tell her friend was dithering. It was the same way she was with menus. "Let's say left. Okay?"

"Right. Left."

"Right?" Clare raised an eyebrow inquiringly.

"No, left. Just, you know—it's a lot harder when I'm not mad at him."

Stay on task, Claire thought, her assistant manager training kicking in. "Yeah, I can believe that. But if we start here—" She bent to move his arm. And was unprepared for what she felt: movement. "Hey!"

Bill groaned. The two friends jumped back and looked at each other. Like guilty school kids they hid the knives behind their backs.

With supreme effort, Bill rolled onto his side and put a hand to his mashed face. "My head! I can't believe I drank so much." His fingers stuck in the drying blood on his temple. "Ow—hey! Did I fall down?"

Madeleine and Claire spoke in unison and with complete conviction. "Yes."

Bill groaned again. "Damn, it really hurts."

Madeleine had regained a little color in her face. "Shocking behavior, just shocking. I was appalled and disgusted. And on my birthday, too."

Claire breathed in deeply and let the air back out again. "Let that be a lesson to you, young man. As you reap, so shall you sow."

Bill made another painful groan. "Help me up, baby." The two women grabbed his arms and dragged him into a more or less standing position. He weaved and winced. They led him around the sofa and let him drop to the cushions.

"Maybe we should get you to emergency services. You might need an x-ray or something," Madeleine said, trying to think how it would look.

"Yeah, being drunk may have saved you from serious injury, but it's not doing your liver any good. You should mind your drinking. It's causing you awful harm." Claire clucked her tongue.

"Well, you don't have to beat me over the head with it," Bill complained feeling sulky.

The two friends laughed and laughed.

Death of a Bible Salesman
Sarah Shaber

I was closest to the door when the bell rang, so naturally I was the one who opened it.

"Are you the lady of the house?" the man asked. He was a small person, I had to look down to speak to him.

"No," I said, "I'm one of her boarders. My name is Louise Pearlie. You want Mrs. Phoebe Holcombe."

"May I speak to her?" he asked. "If she's not too, well, distressed."

Distressed? What was the man talking about?

"Who are you?" I asked.

"Hiram King," the small man said. He removed his black fedora, revealing slicked-down hair with thick comb marks running through it, and held the hat respectfully over his chest. His head was slightly bowed, like an undertaker welcoming mourners to a wake. Even though today was Saturday he wore a natty black suit and tie, which just reinforced his ghoulish image.

"I hate to intrude at such a sad time," he said, "but I think Mrs. Holcombe would want to see me."

I didn't know what he was talking about. The saddest we'd been today was when the radio in the lounge blew a tube and we realized we couldn't listen to *Ellery Queen* or *The Grand Old Opry* tonight.

"I'm sorry, she's not in," I said. Phoebe and Dellaphine, our colored cook, had gone to the market armed with our weekly ration stamps and Betty Crocker's wartime cookbook. "Can I take a message for her?"

"Could I just come inside for a minute?"

"No," I said, eager to be shed of him, "just tell me what you want."

"Well," King said, placing his hat back on his head so he could lift his briefcase with both hands and click it open facing me. Inside was a handsome leather Bible cradled in red velvet.

"No," I said, "no, no! We're not buying any Bibles. We have plenty. Go away, please."

"You don't understand," King said, "this isn't just any Bible. Mrs. Pearlie's late son purchased this for her as a gift."

For a second my heart clutched. Had something happened to Tom? Last we heard, and Phoebe got a letter from him yesterday, Tom was behind the lines in the Pacific, guarding an island stocked with supplies for a destroyer group scheduled to dock and refit. And Milt had been home for weeks now.

Then I understood what had happened. Phoebe's home was a row house on 'I' Street a couple of blocks south of DuPont Circle. The house on the east side of hers, owned by the Roberts family, was identical to hers, down to the brick and trim color. The front windows met together in the center of the facade. The two houses were often mistaken for one large home. The Roberts' front window had displayed a gold star for two weeks now. Mark Roberts had died when the Allied troops landed in Salerno.

Mr. King had come to the wrong door, and he was about the pull a nasty wartime scam on the Roberts family. I grabbed King's arm.

"You little drip!" I said. "Let me guess. The soldier who bought this Bible for his mother owed money on it, didn't he, and you're going to give her the chance to pay that off so that she can treasure his last gift to her."

King snapped the case shut and pulled his arm away from me.

"I'm calling the police," I said.

"Don't bother," said Milt behind me. He must have heard the last few sentences of my conversation with King. Milt shoved his way past me, his jaw clenched tight and his eyes narrowed, his only hand reaching for King's throat. King snapped his Bible case shut and turned to run. He didn't get far before Milt was on him, grabbing him by the neck and shoving him to the sidewalk. Kneeling over King he struck him squarely in the face and pulled his fist back, ready for another punch.

"Stop it, Milt!" I screamed. Milt slammed his fist into King's face again and I saw a spurt of blood erupt from King's nose. Milt had come back from the Pacific with one arm, a drinking problem and an awful temper. I thought he might kill the man. I grabbed his arm, but he was too strong for me and tore loose, again drawing back to belt King.

"Henry!" I shouted. "Henry, help!"

I could hear Henry Post, our male boarder, clatter down the steps behind me. Between the two of us we dragged Milt off the bloodied Bible salesman. Henry held on to Milt's arm while I gripped his belt so he couldn't attack the man again. King climbed to his feet, and without saying a word to us, staggered down our walkway and out into the street, wiping blood from his face with a handkerchief.

"You should have let me hit him again," Milt said, shaking loose from us.

"He thought this was the Roberts' home," I said to Henry, explaining what had happened. "He wanted to sell Mrs. Roberts a Bible, supposedly bought by her dead son. I'm going to call the police."

"Don't bother," Milt said. "He won't come back to this street again, if he knows what's good for him."

I told Phoebe and Dellaphine what happened when I helped them unpack the groceries they'd bought at the Western Market. Their purchases were predictable, to say the least. Henry wouldn't eat offal, and I hated fish, so our meals were mostly chicken and macaroni dishes with an occasional meat loaf or pot roast. We were entitled to a little butter and sugar and more margarine and honey. We grumbled plenty about food rationing, especially the shortage of beef and sugar, but we were still better off than most people in the rest of this world at war. We canned lots of home grown vegetables, the bounty from our Victory garden. Our hens laid plenty of eggs, although that would slow down during the winter. We were hardly starving.

"Before the war people never thought of doing such awful things," Phoebe said, shaking her head over the Bible salesman's nerve. "Imagine taking advantage of Marjorie Roberts' grief like that. Her only son dead, and some grifter moves in to cheat her out of a few dollars."

"Mrs. Roberts' husband has gone back to his job up north now too, Miss Phoebe, did you know?" asked Dellaphine. "And her daughter had to go back to her man and her babies. Mrs. Roberts be all alone next door."

"Did you call the police?" Phoebe asked, turning to me.

"No, ma'am," I said. "I'm sure he didn't give his real name, and after Milt decked him I doubt he'll turn up in this neighborhood again."

Phoebe frowned. "Milt hit him?"

I'd hated to tell her, but when she saw the bruises on Milt's knuckles she'd know soon enough.

"He overheard the conversation we had at the door."

"How angry was he? Had he been drinking?"

"He was furious," I said. "But I haven't seen him take a drink today. He simmered down quickly once Henry and I stopped him."

I could see Dellaphine shaking her head as she stored the meat and milk in the Frigidaire. "Milt never had a temper when he was a little child," she said. "He was the sweetest boy."

"Well, for heaven's sake he's lost an arm!" Phoebe said. "Of course he's angry!

At six o'clock I slipped away from the house. Dellaphine didn't cook on Saturday nights and I didn't want to stay at home. I'd wind up in the kitchen making sandwiches and cleaning up afterwards. Henry took care of Phoebe's car and Milt was always willing to run errands, but they couldn't find the mayonnaise if their lives depended on it. Not that they tried real hard, mind you. Ada wasn't much better. A clarinetist with the Statler House band, she was rarely home in the evenings, but when she was, cooking was not on top of her list of things to do. She'd skip a meal before she'd go to the trouble to fry an egg. I, though, was a widow, an ordinary government girl, and the obvious replacement for Dellaphine or Phoebe when they weren't available. I kept my mouth shut, though, as I did about most of my life. I had to get along with my fellow boarders. Our lodgings were luxurious compared to most boarding houses.

And I was beginning to wonder if civilian workers could get battle fatigue. I had Top Secret Clearance at the Office of Strategic Services, where I worked for the Morale Operations Branch. We planned "black" propaganda operations in Europe meant to demoralize the German military and the German people. I'd started out as a file clerk, sure, but I'd since been promoted to a real job. I'd started bringing home a briefcase full of papers after work, which meant I needed to take NoDoz a couple of evenings a week to get my paperwork done. So what with coping with lack of sleep, Milt's anger, Ada's dramas, and Dellaphine's arguments with her grown daughter Madeleine, sometimes I just wanted to be by myself for an hour.

Our block had a long, wide alley called Dove Court that divided the buildings between 'I' and 'H' street. If an alley could be considered private, this one was. It had just one narrow entrance from the street. Residents used it to get to their garages, stow trashcans and bicycles and whatever else they wanted off the main street. At night only the lights that filtered out of the windows of homes and small businesses lit the alley.

I crossed it almost every Saturday night, escaping to a little restaurant where I could order a martini and the blue plate special without being bothered by anyone. Tonight wouldn't be one of those relaxing solitary evenings, however. Marjorie Roberts sat down opposite me in my booth.

"Do you mind?" she asked.

"No, of course not," I said. How could I turn away a grieving mother? Although Marjorie, with her thick middle and grey hair waved like a washboard, looked more like a grandmother than a mother of a young soldier. I remembered that Phoebe told me she had married late, in her thirties.

Karen, our waitress, brought me my usual martini and set it down in front of me. She was a big-boned girl with a long red ponytail. Karen was about Milt's age and lived at the end of our street with her widowed sister's family. During the day she watched her sisters' kids while the sister worked and at night she waitressed at the pub to make her own money.

"I'm so sorry about your son," Karen said to Marjorie. "I understand, my sister is a war widow. If you need anything, you know we're right down the street."

"Thank you, dear," Marjorie said.

"Can I get you something to drink?" Karen asked her.

"Fizz water with lime would be nice," Marjorie answered.

After Karen left, Marjorie studied my cocktail.

"Is that a martini?" Marjorie asked me.

"Yes," I said, "don't you want one?"

"No, I don't drink alcohol," she answered. "Honestly, you girls today are so lucky. When I was your age I wouldn't have dreamed of going out for dinner by myself, much less ordering a cocktail. But with my husband and daughter gone now, I can't sit at home and brood."

"I am sorry," I said. "About Mark."

"Yes," she said. "Everyone has been so kind. I got a letter from his commanding officer today." Her eyes brimmed with tears. She used a napkin to sop them up and it came away stained with mascara and eye shadow, revealing deep circles under her eyes.

When Karen got back to our table with Margery's drink, we both ordered the special, ham croquettes with mashed potatoes and baked beans.

Before she went back to the kitchen, Karen asked me if I wanted another martini.

"No, thanks," I said. I kept a bottle of gin in my bedroom and could fix another drink when I got home. I was pretty sure I was going to want one.

"Oh," Marjorie said, brightening, "but look what happened today! I got a gift from Mark he ordered before he left for the Pacific!" She dug around in her large pocketbook and pulled out a Bible. A Bible that looked just like the one the salesman had showed me out in front of my boarding house this morning. I felt my stomach lurch.

"See," she said, turning the pages to show me the book's glories. "It's such soft leather, with gilt-edged papers. And a bookmark that's a real silk ribbon, with that sweet little gold heart charm fastened at the end. I've got the bookmark set right here at the Twenty-Third Psalm. Such a comforting verse, don't you think?"

My neck muscles twisted into tight knots. "Marjorie," I said, "where did this Bible come from? Did you get it in the mail?"

"No," she said, "this nice salesman came to the back door. He was very reluctant to tell me the story, but I finally got it out of him. Mark bought the Bible before he left the country. He still owed thirteen dollars on it, but of course I wanted it, so I finished paying for it." Marjorie opened the Bible to the blank dedication page. "Of course Mark would have signed it and everything if he'd had the chance."

I grasped at a last straw. Maybe this was just a coincidence and Marjorie hadn't been conned.

"What did the Bible salesman look like?" I asked.

"Oh," she said. "He was wearing a nice black suit and fedora. His face was all bruised up, though, he told me he'd tripped over the curb and fallen flat."

I couldn't believe the gall of the man. He must have gone around our block to the alley entrance and knocked on Marjorie's back door even though he'd been run off our front stoop. I wished I'd let Milt beat him senseless!

Marjorie stowed her Bible back in her pocketbook and we ate our meal without mentioning the Bible again. I could hardly swallow, I was so upset and angry. What should I do? I thought about contacting the police after all, but decided not to. I didn't want Marjorie, under any circumstances, to find out Mark hadn't ordered that Bible for her. Not from me, anyway.

Marjorie left the restaurant before I did, saying she didn't want to miss *Ellery Queen*. Since our radio wasn't working I stayed to drink a cup of coffee. Karen sat down with me during her break. I couldn't help but tell her what happened to Marjorie and about the Bible salesman's visit to our boarding house, although I made her promise to keep it to herself.

"Of course I won't say anything," Karen said. "But she'll figure it out. The newspaper is full of stories about these cons. Honestly, there is no punishment too terrible for that man. When I think of what my sister went through after her husband died! If I were you I'd have let Milt beat him until he couldn't move well enough to sell Bibles ever again."

"When do you get off work?" I asked. "Want to come to my place? Our radio isn't working, but we could play gin rummy."

"I get off at nine," she said. "But I'll take a rain check on the gin rummy. I have to get up early tomorrow to take care of my sister's kids."

"I'll take another bourbon and water," Milt said, tapping the bar counter with his empty tumbler.

"You look a little shaky, have you had anything to eat?" the bartender asked.

"No, our housekeeper doesn't cook dinner on Saturdays, and none of the women are at home. I have no objections to a liquid meal. That way the buzz hits me faster."

"What happened to your hand?" the bartender asked, nodding at the blue bruises on Milt's knuckles.

"Had to teach a crooked Bible salesman a lesson," Milt said. The bartender set his fresh drink down on the bar and Milt drank half of it in one gulp.

Today he'd sensed the fingers on his left hand, the one that used to hang at the end of the arm he'd lost. He hated that. The doctors told him it was natural, but he never told anyone else, he was sure they'd think he was a crackpot. It was bad enough to start every day rolling up his left sleeve and pinning it under his armpit without then feeling that damn arm like it was there all day. And he didn't even have a purple heart to show for it, since he'd lost the arm in a jeep accident while off duty. Then there was spending all day long operating an elevator at the Pentagon, because that was the same as being a soldier, wasn't it? Serving your country? And a man only needed one arm to run an elevator, right?

On top of everything some people were getting rich off this war. Not just Bible salesmen, either. Black marketers would do anything for a buck. Hold back prime beef for rich customers, water down whiskey, hoard canned food until prices skyrocketed. And big companies like General Electric and Ford were making millions off fat government contracts. They should all be lined up in front of firing squads and shot. Or made to live with one arm.

"I'll take another," he said to the bartender.

"That's three," the bartender said.

"So?" Milt said. "Is there any law against me getting blotto?"

"It's just me here tonight, so there's no one to see you home."

"I wish I had a dime for every time I've crossed that alley at night. Unless I pass out I can find my way home."

"This is your limit, anyway," the bartender said, refreshing Milt's drink. "I'm closing at eight."

"Why so early?" Milt asked.

"In case you haven't noticed you're my only customer tonight," the bartender answered. "On Saturdays everyone goes downtown to the clubs. I don't know why I bother to open."

I was helping Phoebe fix flapjacks for everyone when the doorbell rang. Wondering who would be calling on us so early on a Sunday morning, I wiped my hands on my apron and went to answer the door.

Officer Bennett, our neighborhood cop, stood on our stoop. He had more grey in his hair than the last time I'd seen him. If all the young men weren't in the military he would have retired months ago.

Bennett removed his cap.

"Mrs. Pearlie," he said. "Good morning."

"Good morning," I said. "You're up bright and early. Would you like some coffee and flapjacks?"

"I'm here on official business," he said. "May I come in?"

"Of course," I said. I opened the door wide and he entered the hall.

"I need to speak to all of you. Would you ask everyone to join me in the lounge?"

"Ada and Milt are still asleep, and Madeleine and Dellaphine are at church."

"I don't need Ada. Or Dellaphine or Madeleine. But I must speak to Milt."

"Please have a seat," I said, gesturing to the davenport in the lounge. "I'll get everyone."

I flew down the hall to the kitchen, my imagination running wild. Why on earth was Officer Bennett here? What had happened?

Phoebe went white when I told her that a policeman was waiting for us in her lounge.

"I'll go upstairs and get Milt," Henry said. "I hope that fool boy hasn't done anything stupid."

That was my first thought too, and probably Phoebe's, that Milt had lost his temper and gotten into another fight. We all knew he'd spent the evening last night in the bar across the alley.

Phoebe brought a tray with coffee and cups into the lounge and I busied myself pouring until Henry and Milt joined us. Milt was in his pajamas and robe and looked like he had the hangover from hell. He sat gingerly down on a chair, his hand over his eyes to avoid the light. Phoebe quickly switched off the lamp on the table nearest him. I poured him a cup of coffee with my ration of sugar added to his.

"Sorry," Milt said, smiling weakly at Officer Bennett. "Drank too much last night. You know how it is."

"So I understand," Bennett answered, sipping from his own cup.

"What's going on?" Henry said, giving in to the curiosity that was eating at us all.

"I understand that a Bible salesman named Hiram King came to your door yesterday and tried to work one of those scams on Mrs. Holcombe, but she wasn't here."

"He thought this was Marjorie Roberts' house," I said.

"He was scum," Henry said. "Milt taught him a lesson. Broke his nose, I bet."

"I know," Bennett said, looking at Milt, who still had his head down, covering his eyes. The bruises on his knuckles were obvious.

"Please, Officer Bennett," Phoebe said, "what's happened?"

"The bartender at the bar across the alley found King's corpse near his trash cans when he took out his garbage first thing this morning. King'd been beaten to death, not with fists, but with a hard object of some kind. Maybe a shovel or a chunk of wood. The back of his head felt like it had been fractured, all soft like. The doc will tell us for sure after the autopsy."

Bennett's statement was met with stunned silence. Henry's mouth hung open and I felt the muscles in my neck knot. Phoebe clutched her hands to keep them from trembling. We avoided looking at Milt, but when I finally glanced at him, he showed no sign of surprise, just kept his hand over his eyes.

"Why was King even around here at that hour?" Henry asked. "We ran him off in the morning."

Bennett shrugged. "I don't know," he said. "I'm not done with my inquiries yet. We'll be interviewing everyone on the block, and searching for a murder weapon, or evidence that King's body was dragged from somewhere else in the alley, though that will be hard to tell because of the cobblestones. In the meantime I need statements from you, especially you, Milt."

"Hey!" Milt said, raising his head. "It wasn't me that killed him!"

"The bartender said you left last night in as mean a mood as he'd ever seen you after he closed his bar at eight. What time did you get home?"

"I don't know exactly," Milt said. "I blacked out. But that doesn't mean I killed anyone."

Phoebe was ashen, her hand at her throat. I could see her throat muscles moving, but she seemed unable to speak.

"Officer, I brought Milt home last night," Henry said. "I got worried when he didn't get home after the bar lights went out. So I went looking for him and found him in the alley."

"Where in the alley?" Bennett asked.

"Right outside our gate," Henry said.

"Didn't you see King's body?"

"No," Henry said. "I wasn't looking for anybody. Besides, you said it was all the way across the alley near the bar. It was dark by then."

Milt suddenly covered his mouth with his hand and gagged. He jumped to his feet and rushed out the door of the lounge. We could hear his feet pounding down the hall as he hurried toward the bathroom off the kitchen.

"What time was this, Henry?" Officer Bennett asked.

"Around fifteen minutes to nine," Henry said.

"The bars and restaurants around here close early on Saturdays," Phoebe said. "Most people go downtown on the weekend to go out."

Bennett grabbed at his back and winced as he stood up. "The police doctor isn't through with the body yet," he said. "So I don't have an estimated time of death. But if it's close to the time Milt left the bar, I'll be back. Tell him for me not to think of leaving town."

Phoebe began to cry quietly. Henry took her hand and patted it, but she pulled away from him, found a handkerchief in her pocket and covered her face with it.

I followed the policeman outside and down our walkway, catching up to him at the gate out into the sidewalk.

"Officer Bennett," I said. "I know why King was in the alley last night. When he came to our house yesterday morning he thought it was the Roberts' home, the house next door. He came back later to approach Marjorie Roberts again. But he entered the neighborhood through the alley and went to her back door. I guess he thought no one would notice him out back. Looks like he was right."

Bennett leaned up against our fence and stretched his back. "I'm getting too old for policing," he said. "At this rate I won't live long enough to collect my pension. Mrs. Pearlie, how do you know King came back to Mrs. Roberts' house?"

I told him the pitiful story of my supper with Mrs. Roberts last night.

"I think she had just received the Bible, so that would have been before seven o'clock, when I saw her at the restaurant."

"I'll go talk to her," Bennett said, looking back at Roberts' front window, where the gold star pressed against a pane of glass.

"Does she have to know her son didn't order the Bible for her?" I asked.

Bennett shook his head sadly. "I'm afraid so. I don't know how I can avoid telling her. Poor woman."

I watched as Bennett walked up Mrs. Roberts' walkway, and then I wanted to be far away from this house. I didn't want to face Phoebe, Milt or Marjorie right now. I didn't know what to think. Milt had been so angry since coming home, I could easily see him going off half-cocked if he should run into King again, especially if he'd been drinking. I couldn't imagine that he intended to kill him, but that part of it could have been an accident. Since Milt had just one arm he might need to pick up a weapon to subdue King and kill him without really meaning too. From the look on Henry's face, and the tears streaming down Phoebe's, they must think it was possible too.

Milt needed an alibi, or some piece of information that would clear him.

I wondered if anyone else could have seen what was happening in that alley last night, despite the dark. If whoever killed King made any noise, someone might have heard it. Then I remembered. Karen! She would have been heading back to her sister's house after work. At nine o'clock! If Milt killed King, it would have had to be before eight-forty-five, when Henry found him. Karen couldn't help but see the body lying behind the bar then. She had to walk right past that spot to get home.

If Karen didn't see the body, and I assumed she didn't since she hadn't called the police, maybe she had seen someone else in the alley at that hour. The real killer.

I couldn't wait for Bennett to leave Marjorie Roberts' house to tell him. Instead I took off running down the street toward Karen's sister's house. If Karen saw something in that alley last night I wanted to know about it right away.

Breathless, I dropped the knocker on Karen's door. Marsha, her sister, opened it.

"We've met," I said to her. "I'm Louise Pearlie, I board at Phoebe Holcombe's house."

"Of course," Marsha said, "come in. I'm trying to get some housework done before the work week starts." Marsha wore a faded housecoat over trousers and a blouse. She was barefoot and held a damp mop in her hand. I could see into her kitchen, where a clothesline hung with children's garments crisscrossed the room.

"Is Karen up?" I asked.

Marsha dropped her mop on the floor with a crash and put her face in her hands.

"Is everything all right?" I asked, surprised by her response.

"Oh, yes, I suppose," Marsha said, dropping her hands from her face. She wasn't crying, but she looked discouraged and careworn. "Karen took off last night."

"Took off?"

"She said she'd had it. Babysitting during the day and working at night. That the world was a terrible place and life hardly worth living since the war started. She said some people in this country were as bad as the Nazis. She looked awful tired and unhappy. She packed her bags and left right then."

"Where did she go?"

"I don't know," Marsha said. "She said she'd take the first train she could out of Union Station and that she'd let me know where she landed. Won't you sit down?"

I sank onto the battered davenport. Marsha sat down beside me.

"I'm out of coffee," she said. "Would you like some water?"

"No, thanks," I said. "I'm fine."

"I don't blame my sister for leaving," Marsha said. "She has been a great help to me, and she's had no life of her own for two years. My children are old enough to place in a day nursery now. I hope Karen finds a great job somewhere and has some fun."

"Did Karen, by any chance, say if she'd seen or heard anything when she crossed the alley last night?"

"No, except she must have run into Mr. King. He'd left by my back door a few minutes before she got home."

"Mr. King?" I said, my throat so tight I could hardly get those two words out. Karen had seen Mr. King alive on her way home? "The Bible salesman? He was here?"

"Yes," she said. "Look what he brought!"

She opened a drawer in the table sitting near the sofa and brought out a black leather Bible. A red silk ribbon with a gold heart charm dangling from it marked a passage somewhere in the New Testament.

"Mr. King said my husband ordered the Bible for me before he left for the Pacific. He said he waited a long time to come by because he hated to distress me, but he thought I might like to have it. It took all the money in my cookie jar to finish paying for it. Isn't it lovely?"

I was glad Karen had a twelve-hour head start.

267

Down Home
Toni Goodyear

The first time Andy Griffith came to arrest me I set my living room sofa on fire.

The flame-retardant fabric, with its tired colors polished to a sheen by too many years of sliding *derrieres*, sent out tornado-shaped funnels of toxic smoke before bursting into a line of dancing, pink-lavender licks. I should send that salesman a thank-you note, I thought from my hiding spot behind the wingback, a wet rag to my nose. That earnest young salesman who told me he cared too much for my safety to let that sofa leave the store without chemical treatment, good for thirty years.

Griffith dropped his howdy-neighbor smile and waved both hands at the black cloud, his big horse teeth nowhere to be found. He pulled his Mayberry sheriff shirt out of his waistband, slapped a corner of it over his mouth and nose, and scampered for the door.

"That's a mighty silly thang for a schoolteacher to do," he muffle-sputtered as he high-tailed it out of the house. "A mighty silly thang!"

"*Retired* teacher," I shouted through my rag. "And let this be a lesson to you. Don't come around here bothering people!"

"My God, Mother," Noreen cried, yanking me from behind the chair just as the fire started to get going good.

We coughed and mopped our eyes and waited on the lawn while Sam Collins, our strutting rooster of a fire chief, had his men spray-foam my sofa and chairs and my antique Carolina oak side tables, and drag them out of the house. They rolled up the burnt Persian and took what was left of that too.

"That could have been real bad, Greta," Collins said

slowly, as if talking to a slow child rather than a woman gone eighty. "You know that, don't you? *Real* bad. How did it start?"

I gave an innocent shrug. "John's pipe, I suppose. Ash must've fallen behind a cushion."

He and Noreen exchanged glances as if I wasn't there. That had begun happening a lot lately, with county officials, bank tellers, doctors, and nurses. They talked to Noreen, not to me. I'd started to become invisible after what Noreen called my "episode" a few months back, the day it had become clear to me that my little turd of a next-door neighbor, a stumpy Turk who smelled like nutmeg, was releasing parasites into my hostas. I'd called the cops on him. Nobody had believed me, not then, not since. The doctors told Noreen I was experiencing "transient paranoid disturbances" not uncommon in an aging brain. With occasional invisibility as a side effect, I guessed.

I smiled at my daughter and the fire chief and kept quiet. I'd learned not to let people know what was happening, to deal with problems myself. I *had* been smoking John's hand-worn laurel pipe before Griffith came in and ruined my evening, so it seemed a good explanation. I'd taken up smoking it after John died, filling the house with the deep, warm cherry smell that was one of the thousand things I missed so terribly.

Still.

Despite everything.

"You best take better care, Greta," Collins said, superiority squaring his thick jaw. "We were able to stop it this time. Next time you might not be so lucky."

Go tell Saint Peter, I thought, my smile never wavering. My mother had thumped into my head that it wasn't polite to tell a person to drop dead, that was God's decision after all, but inviting someone for a chat with Saint Peter, that was something the Lord could hardly hold against you. Now that I was of an age soon to be seeing my mother again, I didn't want to have to hear that particular lecture.

"Go tell Saint Peter," I said aloud, but Collins had turned away.

After the firemen left, Noreen opened all the windows in the living room and set to running the smoke-scrubbing deodorizers they'd given her. It was one of those almost-autumn evenings with a cleansing breeze, half an hour to sunset, light sweater weather after nightfall. A moment in universal time that purged the rainforest steam and ozone-red thickness of the North Carolina summer.

"I left the windows open and closed the living room doors so the rest of the house won't get chilly," Noreen said. "I'll call about the insurance tomorrow. Kenny will come over later and stay with you."

I nodded. It would do no good to tell her I didn't need Kenny to stay with me, that I was fine, that our suburban corner of the world was embarrassingly safe. Arguing with Noreen never did any good. Besides, my eighteen-year-old grandson was a good boy. I liked having him around. When he came with his pods and pads and little white earplugs and blue-cased phone thingy, it was like a tectonic plate had shifted and bumped a foreign country smack up against my house. Kenny and I spoke different languages but we were friendly aliens, intrigued by one another's eccentricities. He loved being here because he got to spend all night doing whatever he wanted with his electronics with no mother telling him to go to bed. I was sure that if Griffith ever succeeded in locking me away in that rustic little jail cell of his, the one the town drunks used as their overnight hotel, Kenny would press some buttons on his magic phone and conjure up other friendlies to spirit me away. I'd go with them to their Youngland, where electronic jolts to the synapses could wipe out troubles and start me over again like we used to do with used computer disks at school.

Reformatting the floppies, we called it then.

A week later I sat at the kitchen table, a dry martini in my hand, missing John and trying not to think about death or sheriffs.

John and I had always had one martini each night before supper, spicy heat to burn away the cares of the day. We'd drink, then eat while we watched old sitcoms on cable TV. It was John's weakness. He loved old sitcoms, and I loved the clarity of his laughter, so for fifty years I sat beside him and watched. But he also loved when I read aloud the old stories and poems I taught to high schoolers. The Last Leaf. All in green my love went riding. Quoth the raven, nevermore. When he died—almost a year ago it was now—from anaphylactic shock brought on by going gaga and eating peanut butter crackers, it was an ending worthy of T. S. Eliot: Not with a bang, but a whimper.

I was sipping my drink when I heard the jiggling of metal tools in the front door locks, first the knob, then the dead bolt. I'd never seen Griffith do anything fancy with hardware. In Mayberry he just fiddled around with fishing reels and once or twice cleaned a rifle out of the gun case in his sheriff's office. He was what my grandson would call low tech. But I knew it was him nonetheless. It seemed he could now get into my house anytime he wanted. There were unseen rips in the fabric of reality, honest-to-god holes that had opened up when John died.

I put down my drink and ran—quick-shuffled was more the truth of it—to the laundry room off the kitchen. John's .22 Ruger pistol was stored in the top cabinet behind the detergent. After Griffith's first visit, I'd loaded the magazine and laid it alongside the gun. Now I slapped it into place like John had taught me, flipped the safety, and cocked the slide.

"You're not taking me, Andy," I swore softly, edging my way around the doorframe with the gun pointed toward the ceiling like they did in the movies.

I inched forward in the small hallway, then stopped and listened, trying to still the rush of my breathing. Everyone knew Griffith was smart, long on worldly wisdom and common sense. No use trying to put him off with any addled old-lady tales, I'd have to do this the hard way.

I edged around the corner of the doorframe and peered into the kitchen. The island was in front of me, table and chairs beyond. I saw nothing out of the ordinary. No shadows, no movements.

Bending at the waist, I scuttled to a spot behind the island. Somehow, I managed to get down on one knee. Thank God the natural fattening that had stricken most of my friends didn't run in my genes. I was on the almost-too-thin side. Still, I knew I couldn't stay in this bent-leg position for long.

I peered around the island. No one. Only a soft vibration of air that pricked the hairs on my arms.

I held onto the countertop and struggled to a standing position. When the circulation in my leg returned, I maneuvered around the island with the gun at the ready, and made my way, slowly, to the foyer.

The front door was closed, locks still in place. I must've been mistaken, no one was coming that way.

From the hall behind me, I heard the familiar sound of the basement door opening.

I whirled.

"Now there's no sense goin' on this way, Miss Greta," Griffith drawled in that quiet way that had inspired the adoration of generations. He walked casually toward me, his hands in his pockets. "I'd say it was time we settled up, wouldn't you?"

I didn't wait to find out what would happen next. I pointed the gun in his general direction and fired. Eyes closed, I squeezed the trigger over and over, spending the ten bullets in the magazine, until finally the slide froze open, the chamber empty.

The sudden silence was as frightening as the blasts.

I didn't look to see what I'd hit. I jumped into the nearby coat closet, closed the door and held the knob, pulling it hard toward me. I waited silently in the dark, straining to hear. If Griffith came for me now, there would be no way to stop him, not without more bullets, and those were in the laundry room, a run I'd never make.

But he didn't come.

I waited and listened but he didn't come. Had I scared him off? Had any of the bullets struck home?

I eased the door open and peered out. The hallway was empty, the menacing vibrations gone. The house was silent. Settled. When I talked myself brave enough to come all the way out, I found no body, no blood on the hallway floor, no sign of invasion. Just my ten bullets lodged helter-skelter in the drywall and basement door.

I went to the laundry room and reloaded the gun, then searched the house to make sure he was really gone. I spent the rest of the night with spackle and wood putty. If Noreen asked about it, I'd tell her I'd had the urge to freshen things up, to fill in the dings and scratches and then repaint.

She'd shake her head and sigh as usual, but that didn't matter.

At bedtime, I hid the Ruger in the bedside table under my summer scarves.

The next night was Thursday, my regular supper with Kenny. I made his favorite meal, meat loaf and mashed potatoes with buttered green beans and peach pie. Our habit was to eat before the television, sharing whatever old shows were airing on cable. I set us up in the den this time—the living room was still a wasteland.

Say what you will about television, it had always been one of the ways our family bonded. When Noreen was attending the local college she'd bring home new friends, freshmen far away from home, and they'd fill their plates with chicken casseroles and salad and plop down on a blanket in the living room for a carpet picnic with *Star Trek* reruns.

"It doesn't get any better than this," they'd say, giving each other high fives.

Between John and me, Kenny had grown up comfortable with old TV shows, stories, and poems. I watched him now as he happily squirted ketchup onto his meat loaf. His sweet, sandy-haired beauty reminded me so much of the young John, slim and handsome with an autumn-colored glow, his clear eyes open and affectionate. Tender, like his grandpa. The only negative comment my husband had ever drawn from his employers in all his years as a banker was that he was sometimes too soft on people.

"I believe I can live with that, Greta," he'd tell me with a wink.

Kenny found the remote and flipped to the usual channel. It was time for *Gilligan's Island*. He'd watched it often with John, their contagious laughter lightening the house.

We ate and watched and giggled.

"What's next?" I said.

"The *Andy Griffith Show*. It's an episode with Ernest T. Bass. We loved that guy."

As I headed to the kitchen for the pie, I heard the whistle of the show's opening credits, saw in my mind the familiar picture of Andy with fishing pole, Opie skimming rocks.

I looked around cautiously as I plated our dessert. Everything was quiet. Would the show act like a siren call? I didn't want Griffith to make an appearance while Kenny was here. I wasn't sure we should risk the viewing. On the other hand, I knew he wouldn't hurt the boy. It was me he wanted. And if I told Kenny about it, he wouldn't have to be frightened, whatever happened. I was sure I could trust him not to tell anyone, but, if he did, Noreen would just write it down in her little book for the doctor and tell Kenny not to worry, old people sometimes went a little dodgy.

I pulled a carton of vanilla ice cream from the freezer and dropped a healthy dollop on each slice of pie.

We watched and chuckled as Ernest T. Bass tried to win a new girlfriend. Kenny smacked his leg in delight. When the show was over, I reached for the remote and turned down the sound.

"That Andy, he's the perfect lawman, isn't he?" I said. "We should run over to Mount Airy sometime, it's not too far. TV Land has put up a statue there. They have a Mayberry Days festival. We can visit the museum."

Kenny raised his forkful of pie. "I'll drive us."

I smiled. There were still things for which a grandmother was useful, and getting to drive her around was one of them.

"That would be fun." I paused. "Kenny, if I asked you to keep a secret, you'd do that, wouldn't you?"

"Sure. What is it?"

"It's something important. It would have to stay just between us. No one could ever know."

He stopped eating and looked at me, waiting. I reached out and touched his cheek. He was so young.

Then I told him. I told him Andy Griffith had showed up twice already, wanting to arrest me, maybe even kill me if I fought back too hard.

Kenny's brow darkened. I couldn't tell how much of it was kneejerk anger at anyone who would threaten his family, and how much was instant fear and confusion.

He slowly put down his fork and took a breath. Then he said evenly, "You know Andy Griffith's dead, don't you, Grandma? Granddad told me he died some time back."

I nodded. "I know. But he's still after me."

He sat back in his chair. As he studied my face, the etchings of distress slowly faded to a mix of sadness and affection. He let out a little sigh and cocked his head like a sparrow. He seemed to be considering just how loopy his ancient grandmother might be.

When he spoke, his tone was gentle. "Even if that was possible, Grandma, why would Andy Griffith come after you?"

There it was, the big question.

I stared down at my hands. Two specks of wood putty sat on the nail of my right thumb. I poked at them with the edge of my fork.

"He blames me for your grandfather's death," I said quietly.

Kenny blinked. "Why would he do that?"

"I don't know. I guess he thinks I shouldn't have kept those crackers in the house anymore, even though we always had some on hand, ever since we were married. Cheese for John, peanut butter for me. I kept mine over the refrigerator, away from everything else. All those years we never had a problem. It never crossed my mind he'd go after them."

I thought I was talking calmly, but I felt a hot tear move down my cheek.

Kenny saw it too. He came and sat beside me.

"Granddad had dementia. He didn't know what he was doing."

I sniffed. "That's why Andy wants to arrest me. It was my job to watch over my husband."

My grandson put his arm around my shoulder and hugged me to him. "Andy Griffith doesn't want to arrest you, Grandma. No one can watch another person every minute. My friend's little sister broke her arm trying to climb out of her crib because no one thought she was ready to try. It's not your fault Granddad died."

I dipped my head to his and for several minutes we sat there together, our foreheads touching in silence, mourning the loss.

"Come on," he said finally, patting my hand. "Let's have another piece of pie."

No more was said of it, not that night, nor in the morning before he left.

It was near the witching hour when Griffith showed up the next night. Despite the lateness, his uniform looked fresh. As usual, he had no pistol on his hip, no weapon of any kind.

I sat up in bed, reading Frost. Miles to go before I slept.

Griffith came in quietly and plopped himself down at the end of my bed as if it were his natural place. "I'm afraid this has gone on long enough, Greta. We've got to go now."

I put the bookmark in my book and laid it beside me on John's pillow.

"You're not taking me, Andy," I said. "I won't go. I'll fight you."

He shook his head. "Now, I'm sorry to hear that, 'cause I think coming along with me is exactly what you want to do."

I didn't answer. My eyes strayed to the wall behind him and the picture of my wedding day—John and I at his family's lake house, the little gazebo down by the dock. We'd sparkled in linen whites, me with pink-red flowers, his tie the same color, coveting each other like we were strawberries smothered in whipped cream. If I closed my eyes I could still smell him in the air.

Griffith sat watching me. His patience was unnerving.

"This isn't going to stop, is it, Andy? You're never going to quit haunting me."

He gave me a sad smile. "'Fraid I can't. It's my job."

The simple, relentless truth of that struck me like a beacon, illuminating my future. We would have to continue this farce forever, he and I, running in and out of doors, ducking bullets, setting fires. There would be no other way to carry on.

I felt the knot of resolve in my stomach start to unravel.

"How did you know, Andy?" The calm in my voice surprised me.

"Helps to be dead, I reckon." He crossed his legs and cupped his hands over his knees in a relaxed pose, like we were two friends chatting on a back porch. "Why did you do it, Greta? Why commit murder after such a good life?"

"It was for him," I said, my voice low. "I did it for John."

Griffith's warm brown eyes caught mine. "Now that's just not true, Greta. You know that, don't you? You got worn out. People make an awful mess when they get worn out, even feed peanut butter to a man with a deadly allergy."

I laid my head back against the headboard. From the hallway I heard the tick of our wedding clock, the one John's uncle had given us, the one we'd called the "sometimes clock" because it would sometimes chime this hour, sometimes that. It was even more perfect now, the hit and miss of it, the crazy mixed upness of time—time that had taken John and left a creature in his place. Someone John had never met. If he had known him, he would have despised him.

As much as I did.

God help me, as much as I did.

"I'm afraid we've got to do what's right now, Greta," Griffith said. "I've got to take you with me."

I reached over and opened the bedside table drawer. The gun was cold and heavy in my hand as I drew it out and pointed it at his heart.

"Sorry, Andy, I can't let that happen. I'd never be able to stand that folksy little jail of yours, with that annoying deputy and Aunt Bee's tacky doilies on the nightstand."

He cocked his head and treated me to one of his famous

mock-hurt grins. "Now that's just not nice, Miss Greta. That just ain't kindly at'all."

"No," I said sadly. "It isn't."

He leaped forward to grab my arm, but it was too late.

I turned the gun to my temple as the sometimes clock struck twelve.

On the Ramblas
Robert Lopresti

Tourists wandered down the Ramblas like sheep waiting to be fleeced.

Josep looked at that beautiful street, crowded with fascinating people and overstuffed stores, and all he could see were bulging purses, unzipped backpacks, and dangling cameras.

It was an occupational hazard.

He sighed. A pickpocket should be happy on an evening like this, warm and fine. The high season was beginning and tourists were flocking to Barcelona, begging to have their money and possessions removed by skilled artists like himself. And yet, ever since he had left the Plaza de Catalunya for his city's main tourist street, he had felt nothing but melancholy.

Because only foolish amateurs worked alone. The best pickpockets worked in teams, with specialists to distract the marks, others to watch the cops, and one to make the actual graceful dip.

Josep knew that as well as anyone. In the decade since he began his career he had worked with some of the finest teams in Catalunya, first as a boy apprentice, then as muscle, and lately as master touch artist.

Now all that was gone, because he had forgotten an ancient rule. *Never mix business with romance.*

Romance. He looked at two birds sitting in a cage on his left. In this part of the Ramblas the whole pedestrian section, wedged between two lanes of traffic, was crammed with animals for sale. Were those two droopy birds mates, or just strangers pressed together by a salesman? They certainly didn't seem happy together.

Of course, that was true of many couples. Josep considered

the human twosome examining the birds. From their appearance, they were American, in their forties, and wealthy.

The man, overweight and perpetually frowning, had an expensive camera in a leather case on his back. The woman, thin and jittery, had the telltale bulge of the money belt under her silk shirt.

If his team had been with him, Josep would be smiling now, directing them with a gesture here and a nod there, smoothly guiding each member into position around their prey. But alas, he was alone.

Frank stared at the cage in disbelief. "Is that a *pigeon?* They sell pigeons here?"

"It looks like one," Helen agreed. She had lost her page and was shuffling through the guidebook.

"For the good Lord's sake, I could go through Capitol Square and scoop up enough pigeons in an hour to get rich here."

His wife rolled her eyes. "Can't you ever take your mind off business, Frank? We're on vacation."

"We're here to see the sights, aren't we? Right now the sight in front of me is a pigeon, a flying rat." He turned to the next group of cages and his eyes went wide. "And those are *real* rats, for the good lord's sake!"

"I think they're hamsters. Or guinea pigs."

"Do people here *eat* these things?"

"Don't be silly, Frank. They're pets."

"Huh." He scowled. "Well, don't get any ideas about taking 'em home. I don't want to try to explain those critters to Customs."

"I'm just looking at them, Frank."

"Don't look too close. I know how you love to pick up strays."

"You're being unreasonable."

"No? How long did it take you to find someone to take care of our cats and dogs while we took this trip?"

Helen thought about that and decided not to answer. "Just relax, Frank. I'm not buying anything."

"Well, open that dictionary on your phone and look/ for *hamster*. If it shows up on a menu I don't want to make any mistakes."

Helen sighed. This trip was turning out like so much of her married life: great in theory, shaky in practice. Frank had found Madrid too hot, Toledo too steep, and now he found Barcelona too much of all kinds of things.

She was determined not to let him spoil the trip for her, but that took almost superhuman effort.

"Let's keep walking," she said. "There are some lovely little stores down the hill."

"More shopping," said Frank. "I can hardly wait."

Josep hated the sudden hesitancy he was feeling. Having no one to watch your back felt like standing in the street naked.

It was humiliating to go solo after managing a team. And what a team it had been! Pasquale could smell a cop fifty meters away, and his broad back could block any number of prying eyes. Pasquale's brother Pere could throw a seizure that would fool a doctor. And Merce was the greatest distraction a thief could hope for.

Ah, Merce. That had been the problem. If Josep hadn't fallen in love with her or at least hadn't been foolish enough to permit her to join the team...

It had seemed like such a good idea. She was smart, she was beautiful. She could make any tourist forget the warnings about keeping an eye on his belongings at all times. While she chatted with a man, leaving him staring in dazzled delight, Josep could empty the target's pocket in peace. And the work made her so happy, so excited. That was even better than the profit.

But disaster had struck. Merce decided she wanted to be the pickpocket *herself*. Josep had tried to explain that she was all wrong for that role—not because she was a woman, he hastened to add, or that she lacked the wit to learn the most delicate art, but because she was so beautiful. A pickpocket's duty was to be *unnoticed,* the one thing Merce could never be.

It was like asking one of the human statues here on the Ramblas to pass through a crowd unseen. His tourists were watching one of those performers now. It was the perfect time to make his approach, but a herd of less promising targets blocked the way.

"What's *he* supposed to be?" Frank asked.

They stood before a skinny young man dressed in cardboard armor, painted silver. He wore pale white make-up and a very phony gray beard, and he stared at the evening sky without moving a muscle.

"I think he's Don Quixote," said Helen. "Remember the statue in Madrid?"

"Oh, yeah. So this guy's imitating a statue. What's his racket?"

As if in answer, a bald man dropped a Euro into the metal box sitting on the pavement in front of the phony knight. When he heard the clink of the coin the young man leapt into action, pulling a wooden sword from his belt and waving it dramatically. He bowed to his benefactor and tried to kiss the hand of the bald man's lady friend. The woman pulled away with a giggle and Quixote heaved a heart-broken sigh.

"Mimes," said Frank with disgust. "Beggars in make-up."

"Well, I think it's cute."

"They're cluttering the street, keeping—just a minute. I got a call" He opened his cell phone with expert skill. "Mike? What time is it there? One p.m. That's right, we're seven hours ahead."

"Frank," said Helen, sounding calmer than she felt. "Please put that thing away. We're supposed to be on vacation."

"Won't be a minute. Talk to Quixote. Mike? Tell 'em to lose five percent or we're gone."

Talk to a mime, Helen thought. *I've been doing that for years.*

* * *

284

Josep trailed his tourists into the Boqueria, the open-air farmer's market. What was wrong with those two? They clearly had money and enough free time to visit Barcelona, yet neither of them seemed happy.

All *he* needed to make him happy was beautiful, delightful Merce. Alas, she had run off to start a new romantic and professional relationship with Pasquale. Naturally Pere had deserted with his brother, leaving Josep, who taught them all their trade, to start from scratch.

Put it out of your mind. He was directly behind the tourist now, close enough to empty those bulging pockets. The big man was still braying into his phone.

Now.

"Frank, look at this," said the wife. She pointed to a big slab of meat on a butcher's counter. "Is that beef or pork?"

Amazingly, the tourist turned to look. As he put his phone back into his belt his hand actually *brushed against* Josep's.

Josep had to step back and suck in air. He stared at his own hand, which was trembling, actually trembling. Surely he wasn't losing his nerve, not after all these years?

"Beef or pork," said Frank, "either way it's E. coli waiting to happen. I like my meat rare, but not that rare."

He looked around at the countless booths and tables. "Raw meat next to raw fruit. Don't they have any health rules around here?"

"You're always complaining about government regulations. I would think this would make you happy."

"Not if it's gonna make me sick." He shuddered. "I don't want Montezuma's Revenge."

"Montezuma was Mexican, Frank. He didn't like Spaniards any more than you do."

"Then he *would* want revenge, wouldn't he? Let's get out of here."

They strolled down the Ramblas, past countless makeshift booths selling arts and crafts. "Flea market crap," Frank announced.

Helen was examining a scarf on one of the tables. It tightened in her hands as she eyed her husband's neck.

Wait until they reach the statue. Nothing distracted Americans better than that.

Now that he had a plan, Josep felt better. He wasn't hesitating, just anticipating the perfect moment.

He let out a breath he hadn't realized he was holding. What a beautiful evening it was.

Frank and Helen stood in front of the massive monument supporting a column with a statue on top. Beyond them was a plaza that ended in the harbor. "So, who's on the shaft? Quixote again?"

Helen checked her guidebook. "It's Columbus!"

"What's he doing here? He's American."

His wife rolled her eyes. "Remember Ferdinand and Isabella? They paid for his ships."

"Oh, yeah. Think they charged interest?"

She sighed. "Take a picture, Frank."

"Sure." He yanked out his new toy. "Stand in front of the lions. Try to look Spanish."

Josep stood beyond their view while the man took pictures. At last the big complicated camera went back into its case, and the couple turned toward the sea.

Now. He took a deep breath and stepped forward.

Someone shouted on the other side of the monument. Two men were swearing in lively Catalan. The taller one backed up, fists windmilling in furious circles. The shorter man practically leapt in the air as he flung curses at his opponent.

Everyone stopped to stare.

It's my team. Pasquale pushed his brother violently away, but Pere came back swinging in wide dramatic uppercuts that had no chance of connecting.

Josep looked around and sure enough, there was Merce,

her lustrous black hair covered with a scarf, slipping up behind the Americans. As if a scarf could hide her glorious eyes or magnificent form!

Naturally she had picked the same target. Who had taught her?

And now her slim hand dove deep in the tourist's back pocket, fishing out the wallet that was supposed to belong to *Josep*. The injustice struck him like a blow to the chest.

He shouted his rage in three languages. *"Lladre! Ladron! Thief!"*

Merce jerked back as if the tourist were electrically charged. Her hand still clutched the fat man's fat wallet.

Both tourists turned around, looking for the shouter. They spotted Josep immediately. The woman was the first to see Merce, a stunned look on her face, the prize in plain sight.

To Josep's astonishment the American woman smacked Merce on the nose with a perfect right cross. The beautiful girl hit the street backside-first and sat there, glaring at Josep.

Then she looked past the monument to her companions, but Pasquale and Pere, forgetting everything Josep had taught them, had taken to their heels at the first sign of trouble. The various bystanders, who had watched as if the events were more street entertainment, backed up to let the men rush past.

Josep was pleased to see that Merce, at least, kept her wits about her. She spun the wallet between the tourists as hard as she could. Both of them turned to watch it hit the monument and flop to the ground. By the time they looked back, Merce was on her feet and moving like a deer.

She ran, Josep noted with great satisfaction, *away* from Pasquale and Pere. The cowardice of the brothers, he was certain, had terminated both the love affair and the partnership.

Of course, that didn't mean Josep's situation had improved. He couldn't go home tonight; one or more of the trio would certainly be hoping for revenge.

And worse, the Americans were on the alert now. He didn't dare go near them.

* * *

"Did you see that?" said Frank. "She had my wallet in her hand." He stared at the thing, now resting in his own. He leaned against the monument for support.

"She had it until I knocked her down. *Pow!*" Helen shook her head in amazement. Her self-defense classes, combined with her fury at Frank, had turned her into a warrior. She rubbed her bruised knuckles and relished the pain.

"These damned foreigners..." said Frank. For once he was lost for words.

"Don't stereotype." She felt *empowered.* She had defended her family and won. What a story to tell back in Raleigh! "Remember, it was a Spaniard who warned us—and there he is!"

Josep needed every bit of self-control not to flee. *They don't know I was involved. The devil! I was not involved!* Innocence was a new and disconcerting experience.

The woman rushed over, a smile on her face. "You! Señor. You warned us, didn't you?" She grabbed his hand with both of hers, shaking it enthusiastically.

Josep had no choice but to see where this trail led. "Yes, *señora.* I am so sorry that this should happen to you in Catalunya."

"I thought this was Barcelona," said the man.

"Hush, Frank. Catalunya is the region. Like a state, except they have their own language, don't you?"

Josep nodded, still trying to pry his hand loose. "We do, a very old and beautiful language. I am sorry about what happened, but if you will excuse me—"

"Oh, you can't leave." She looked at her husband. "Think of all the trouble he saved us, Frank. The money, the credit cards—" Her eyes widened. "Oh, that girl wouldn't have stopped with his wallet, would she?"

Josep nodded. "These *lladres,* thieves, they will take your camera, your cell phone, your passport...."

He watched with deep interest as the man tried to lay hands on half-a-dozen parts of his body at once. The American slowly relaxed as he found everything in its place.

"I guess we do owe you something." He opened his wallet.

Josep had to make a quick calculation. *Take the small prize or gamble for a bigger one?*

He rolled the dice. "No, señor. I cannot take your money, not for doing what any good man would."

"How about if we buy you dinner?" asked the woman. "We've heard so much about tapas, and we were wondering which of these restaurants—"

Josep made a sour face. "No, no. These are all for, how you say, tourists."

"I knew it!" She looked at her husband triumphantly. "See, Frank, a native can point us to the authentic places. Oh, the girls will be so jealous."

She turned back with a smile. "My name is Helen, by the way. This is Frank."

"And I am Josep. If you wish, I would be honored to show you the best tapas bar in all Barcelona."

Arnau's may or may have not been the best, but it was very good. And old Arnau would remember that Josep had brought him business, but forget about him completely if the police came inquiring.

When Josep led his charges into the smoky, crowded bar, deep in the Gothic District, Arnau nodded his gray head but gave no hint he had ever seen Josep before.

Josep ordered a bottle of very good wine and several raciones —the largest plate size—of the specialties of the house. The Americans paid the inflated charge without a murmur and followed him to the back where he spied an empty table barely big enough for the tapas. Somehow they squeezed in and for a few minutes there was contented silence as they grazed.

"What do you call this one?" Helen asked. "It's like a quiche, but firmer."

"That's tortilla, señora."

"The hell it is," said Frank. "I've eaten in Mexican restaurants all over the U.S. of A. and never had a tortilla that looked like that."

Josep shrugged. "I don't know what they do in Mexico. In Spain, this is tortilla."

"Whatever you call it, it's good," said Helen. Even Frank couldn't argue with that.

During the second glasses of wine Helen asked about Josep's past. He told his usual tale, about coming from a small town in the north.

"What brought you to Barcelona?"

"Ah, I am looking for a job. I used to have a good one in a big factory near the border. We made bags. Bags? From cows."

"Leather." Helen smiled.

"*Sí*, leather. Beautiful, beautiful bags. Little ones for your arm, big ones for travel. But the factory closed."

"Why was that?"

Time to guess. If these people were leftists the correct answer was that a big corporation had moved all the jobs to Asia.

But the odds were on the other side. "The government closed us down." He shrugged and poured wine. "They said the water from the factory was killing fish downstream. Little fish that is no good to eat, no use for anything."

Frank stopped with a handful of bread-and-tomatoes halfway to his mouth. "You hear that, Helen? The damned environmental regulations are destroying business *every-where.*"

Josep hid a smile behind his glass.

By the time the second bottle of wine was empty, so were the plates. "Do you know where we can get a taxi, Josep?"

"There's a plaza not so far from here, Frank. I will lead you to it."

"Can we give you a ride?" Helen asked.

That brought up a thought he had been dreading. "Ah. I am afraid I have nowhere to go tonight."

She looked concerned. "Are you homeless, Josep?"

"I have a place but..." He decided on something near the truth. "One of those people who tried to rob you, I think he lives in my neighborhood. If I saw him..."

"Maybe he saw you," said Frank. "You think he might want revenge?"

Josep shrugged, magnificently stoic. "Very likely."

"That's awful," said Helen. "Frank, we should have called the police."

"No, no," said Josep hastily. "Please don't. I know this sort of fellow. In a day or two he will forget me and think of some other mischief to make. But I dare not go home tonight."

Helen's eyes went wide. "Frank..."

The man seemed almost panicky. The conversation that followed made little sense. "No, Helen. He's not a stray dog."

"I don't mean back to the *States*. But he needs a place to stay tonight."

"Maybe we can give him something toward a room."

"You *know* the hotels are full. The clerk said—"

"I remember." Frank scowled pulled out his phone. "I'll call the concierge. Maybe he has—"

Helen wore the sweet smile of a winner. "If it weren't for Josep, you wouldn't *have* that phone, would you?"

They told him three times and he still thought his English must be at fault.

But it was true. The taxi released them in front of the most expensive hotel in Montjuic. "We can't let you sleep on the street just because you rescued us," Helen explained. "Besides, Frank insisted on booking a suite, so there's plenty of room."

If he had wandered in alone he would have been corralled by security before removing his tattered coat. With these Americans, however, he was invisible. They all walked through the marble lobby without a glance from anyone.

On the sixth floor Frank opened a door which led to the fanciest hotel room—no, *suite*—that Josep had ever seen. "It's wonderful," he said, and meant it.

Frank seemed to have forgotten them. He shed his jacket and turned to a laptop computer that sat on the desk.

Helen smiled. "On the rare occasions I can pry my

husband away from home he insists on traveling first class. It is nice, isn't it?"

Josep could see a scanner, an expensive briefcase, other things he didn't recognize, but knew were expensive. "Wonderful," he murmured again. "Helen, would you mind if I look at the bedroom? Such a fancy hotel."

"Of course," said Helen, playing hostess. She led the way into the next room.

Josep memorized the location of each piece of luggage. The in-room safe sat on a small table in the walk-in closet. It was the type that opened with the swipe of a credit card.

Helen led him back into the sitting room. "You can sleep on the couch out here. I believe there are extra sheets and blankets in the closet."

"You are too kind, Helen. You too, Frank."

"Don't be silly. It's the least that we could do."

Frank was still mesmerized by his computer screen. "How about some wine?"

They split a bottle from the fridge in the kitchenette. Frank was still burrowing through his email but Josep entertained the woman with stories about the history of Barcelona, some of them even true.

Eventually Helen dragged her husband away. "Come on, Frank. We need to let the poor boy get some sleep."

"Okay," he said reluctantly. "Sleep tight, Josep. And hey, thanks for your help tonight."

"It was a pleasure."

As he settled in on the couch, Josep ran the plan through his head. The busy day and the wine should put the Americans quickly to sleep. He would wait an hour and then slip into the bedroom.

He had seen Helen put her purse on the night table. From the purse Josep would retrieve a credit card to open the little safe. It was a shame not to hunt for Frank's wallet—the bait that started the whole adventure! —but that would be on the far side of the room and, as he used to tell Merce and the others, it was foolish to be greedy.

On the way out he would scoop up the computer and whatever else he could carry. He would be long gone before the tourists awoke.

Josep smiled. With the loot he could move up the coast to Figueras or Gerona and acquire a new string of co-workers. By the time his students were ready for the big city, darling Merce and her friends would have moved on to some new grudge.

He stretched out on the couch, and studied the painting on the wall above him. It showed a *dehesa,* one of the oak forests near the Portuguese border, the source of the best ham in the world. All through the autumn the pigs wandered freely through those woods, fattening contentedly on acorns, unaware of their future.

Which made him think of his hosts in the next room. Not that they would be slaughtered, no. All he wanted was their money.

Josep closed his eyes, but made sure he was not comfortable enough to fall asleep. For the first time in a week, he was happy.

In the bedroom, Frank and Helen argued quietly, so as not to disturb their guest.

"For the good Lord's sake," Frank muttered. "You must be out of your mind, picking up strangers on the street. We could be robbed in our sleep."

"And why are we a target? If you hadn't insisted on bringing every fancy gadget you own, no one would have tried to rob us at all."

In the morning it would turn out they were both right. And oddly enough, that would make each of them happy.

ABOUT THE CONTRIBUTORS

J. L. ABRAMO was born in the seaside paradise of Brooklyn, New York on Raymond Chandler's fifty-ninth birthday. A long-time educator, journalist, theatre and film actor and director, he received a BA in Sociology at the City College of New York and an MA in Social Psychology at the University of Cincinnati. Abramo is the author of the Jake Diamond mystery series including *Catching Water in a Net* (recipient of the MWA/PWA Award for Best First Private Eye Novel), *Clutching at Straws*, *Counting to Infinity*, *Circling the Runway* and the prequel *Chasing Charlie Chan*—as well as the stand-alone crime thriller, *Gravesend*. Abramo is a member of the Mystery Writers of America, International Thriller Writers, Private Eye Writers of America and Screen Actors Guild. Abramo lives in Denver, Colorado. For more information, please visit: http://www.jlabramo.com/.

J.D. ALLEN had a normal happy childhood traveling the country with her Air Force father. She was in Texas several years after he passed. Longing for trees and following a suspicious male, she moved to the Midwest where she attended Ohio State University and earned a degree in forensic anthropology with a minor in creative writing. Over the years, she's taken cover working in a morgue, as a midnight gas station attendant, a used car salesmen, and a software testing project manager. In 2007 J.D. disappeared from her normal corporate environment and began a secret mission to infiltrate the publishing industry. Although published in several genres, J.D.'s most excited about getting her stories about PI's, cops, bounty hunters, and serial killers out of her head. She's also know to help teach other writers the basics of crime scene investigation, what Hollywood gets wrong in forensics, writing skills, the art of public speaking, and pitching a manuscript.

LORI G. ARMSTRONG left the firearms industry in 2000. The first book in her Julie Collins series, *Blood Ties*, was nominated for a 2005 Shamus Award for Best First Novel. The first book in the Mercy Gunderson series, *No Mercy*, won the 2011 Shamus Award for Best Hardcover Novel and was a finalist for the WILLA Cather Literary Award. Lori also writes under the pen name Lorelei James, and is the *NY Times* and *USA Today* Bestselling author of contemporary western erotic romance. Lori lives in western South Dakota.

"A Good Name" is a prequel to **ROB BRUNET'S** novel *Stinking Rich*, published by Down & Out Books, which asks, What could possibly go wrong when a backwoods biker gang hires a high school dropout to tend a barn full of high-grade marijuana? Plenty, it turns out. Drug money draws reprobates like moths to a lantern. Brunet's short fiction has appeared in *Ellery Queen Mystery Magazine*, *Thuglit*, *Shotgun Honey*, *Out of the Gutter*, and numerous anthologies. He teaches creative writing at George Brown College and lives in Toronto with his wife and two children.

P.A. DE VOE is an Asian specialist and cultural anthropologist, which accounts for her being an incorrigible magpie for collecting seemingly irrelevant information. While she's published extensively in the social sciences, she's now entered another exciting world: writing contemporary and historical mysteries and crime stories. Her first cozy mystery, *A Tangled Yarn*, is set in a deceptively peaceful Oregon coastal town. Presently, P.A. De Voe writes two historical series highlighting 14th and 15th Century China. *Hidden* is the first novel in her YA historical adventure/mystery trilogy—the *Mei-hua Ancient China trilogy*. Set in 1380, a young bi-racial woman finds her once safe world turned upside down when her father is falsely accused of treason. *Lotus Shoes, a short story from Ancient China* is a prequel to the Mei-hua trilogy. The *Judge Lu Ming Dynasty Case Files*, is a series of short stories modeled after crime stories written throughout several hundreds of years by

Chinese magistrates themselves. P.A. (Pam) De Voe lives in St. Louis, Missouri, with her husband and Sophie a feral cat who, once she came inside, never left. Pam's daughter and son-in-law live in Wisconsin. You can learn more at http://padevoe.com.

SEAN DOOLITTLE is the critically-acclaimed author of *Dirt, Burn, Rain Dogs, The Cleanup,* and *Safer.* His latest book is *Lake Country,* recipient of the 2013 ITW Thriller Award for Best Paperback Original. He lives in western Iowa with his family and served as co-Toastmaster, with Lori Armstrong, of Bouchercon 2015: Murder Under the Oaks.

TOM FRANKLIN is the author of *Poachers: Stories,* the title novella of which won the Edgar Award. His novels are *Hell at the Breech, Smonk,* and *Crooked Letter, Crooked Letter,* which won the *L.A. Times* Book Prize for Mystery/thriller and the UK's Golden Dagger Award for Best Novel. Most recently he collaborated with his wife, writer Beth Ann Fennelly, on *The Tilted World,* a novel. He lives in Oxford, MS and teaches in the MFA program at the University of Mississippi.

TONI GOODYEAR is a former journalist, winner of the North Carolina Press Association Award for features. Other past careers include ghostbusting (yes, really). Her short stories have appeared in *The Killer Wore Cranberry: Room for Thirds, Kings River Life Magazine, Carolina Crimes:19 Tales of Lust, Love and Longing,* and the Sisters in Crime/Guppy anthology *Fish or Cut Bait.* She holds a Ph.D. in Psychology from the University of North Carolina at Chapel Hill.

ROBERT LOPRESTI is the author of more than fifty short stories, including twenty-five in Alfred Hitchcock's Mystery Magazine. He has won the Derringer Award (twice), and the

Black Orchid Novella Award. His latest novel, out this year, is *Greenfellas*, a comic crime novel about a mobster who decides to save the environment.

KRISTIN KISSKA used to be a finance geek, complete with MBA and Wall Street pedigree. A member of the James River Writers and Sisters in Crime, Kristin is now a self-proclaimed *fictionista*. When not writing suspense novels, she can be found on her website~ *about.me/kristin.kisska* or Tweeting *@KKMHOO*. Her short story, "A Colonial Grave" will be published in the *Virginia is for Mysteries II* anthology in February 2016. Kristin lives in Richmond, Virginia with her husband and three children.

ROBERT MANGEOT lives in Nashville, Tennessee with his wife, cats, and trusty Pomeranian. His short fiction appears here and there, including in *Alfred Hitchcock Mystery Magazine, Mystery Writers of America Presents Ice Cold: Tales of Intrigue from the Cold War, Lowestoft Chronicle*, and *The Oddville Press*. His work has won contests sponsored by the Chattanooga Writers' Guild, *On The Premises*, and Rocky Mountain Fiction Writers. He currently serves as chapter Vice President for Sisters in Crime of Middle Tennessee. Read more about him at http://robertmangeot.com/.

MARGARET MARON has written thirty novels and two collections of short stories. Winner of the Edgar, Agatha, Anthony, and Macavity as well as Lifetime Achievement Awards from Malice 2014 and Bouchercon 2015. She has served as national president of Sisters in Crime and of MWA, which named her Grand Master in 2013. (www.MargaretMaron.com)

Author and popular speaker **KATHLEEN MIX** writes stories of romance and suspense. She has developed software ranging from submarine combat control systems to a database devoted to the feeding habits of storks. But as an avid sailor and licensed charter captain, she'd always longed to sail off into the sunset. When she realized that dream, she began her second career writing sailing and travel articles for national magazines. One day, while anchored in the Virgin Islands, she turned to writing fiction and found her true love. Since then, she's written nine novels of romantic suspense. Kathleen now sails on Chesapeake Bay. Her latest book, *Sins of Her Father*, is available from Entangled Select Suspense. Excerpts from her books and pictures of her boat can be found on her website at http://www.kathleenmix.com.

BRITINI PATTERSON was born and raised in a small border-town in the armpit of Texas. Growing up with a West Texas family prone to "swappin' yarns" gave her a love of telling stories, and the ability to laugh at anything. Through a series of hysterically bad decisions that somehow ended for the best, Britni now lives in North Carolina, having married a paramedic who keeps ruining her best murder ideas with "reality", with two mostly adorable children. Her third book in the Justice & Mercy series will be published September 2015, following the eponymous *Justice & Mercy* and *A Thousand Deadly Kisses*. A short story collection of her Rosa Parks short stories is coming soon. Find her on Facebook or Twitter for discussions about drag queens, Syfy movies, other people's books, freaky human tricks, and occasionally, information about upcoming releases.

KAREN PULLEN'S first mystery novel *Cold Feet*, published by Five Star, will soon be followed next year by a sequel, *Cold Heart*. She edited the Anthony-nominated *Carolina Crimes: 19 Tales of Lust, Love, and Longing*. She lives in Pittsboro NC. www.karenpullen.com

RON RASH teaches at Western Carolina University.

KAREN SALYER lives and writes in upstate South Carolina. A native Tennessean, she received a pony and a Classic Press edition of *The Gold Bug and Other Tales of Mystery* on her tenth birthday. The horse obsession has since faded; however, her love for reading, writing, history, and of course, Mr. Poe, continues to grow. She is a member of Mystery Writers of America, Sisters in Crime, and the Short Mystery Fiction Society. Ms. Salyer has not quit her day job in insurance, and she is currently working on a sequel short story featuring a teenaged soldier Poe in Charleston.

SARAH SHABER is an award-winning mystery author from North Carolina. Her historical mystery series begins with *Louise's War* (2010) and stars Louise Pearlie, a young widow working for the Office of Strategic Services in Washington, DC, during World War II. Her Professor Simon Shaw murder mysteries are available as ebooks. She's also the author of a stand-alone horror novel, *Blood Test*, and editor of *Tar Heel Dead*, a collection of short stories by North Carolina mystery writers.

ZOË SHARP spent most of her youth living aboard a catamaran on the northwest coast of England. She opted out of mainstream education at the age of twelve and wrote her first novel at fifteen. She began her crime thriller series featuring her ex-Special Forces trainee turned bodyguard, Charlotte 'Charlie' Fox, after receiving death-threats in the course of her work as a photojournalist. She has now written ten books and a novella in the Charlie Fox series, numerous short stories, a standalone crime thriller, *The Blood Whisperer*, and has just finished a supernatural thriller called *Carnifex*. Her work has been nominated for awards on both sides of the Atlantic, been optioned by Twentieth Century Fox TV, used in Danish school textbooks, turned into a short film and has inspired an original song. She is currently working on another standalone set in the Lake District, a collaboration with John Lawton, the next in the Charlie Fox series, and developing a second career as an international pet-sitter. She says sleep is very over-rated.

B.K. (BONNIE) STEVENS has published almost fifty short stories, most of them in *Alfred Hitchcock's Mystery Magazine.* Some of her stories have been nominated for awards such as the Agatha and the Macavity; another won a Derringer from the Short Mystery Fiction Society; one made the list of "Other Distinguished Stories" in *Best American Mystery Stories 2013*; and another won a suspense-writing contest judged by Mary Higgins Clark. Her first novel, *Interpretation of Murder,* published by Black Opal Books in April, 2015, is a traditional whodunit that offers readers glimpses into deaf culture and sign-language interpreting. Her second novel, *Fighting Chance*, is a martial arts mystery for young adults. It will be published in October, 2015, by The Poisoned Pencil / Poisoned Pen Press. She's also published three nonfiction books (Holt, Harcourt, and Behrman House), along with articles in *The Writer* and *The Third Degree.* She blogs at SleuthSayers and also hosts The First Two Pages. B.K. and her husband live in Virginia and have two grown daughters. Website: http://www.bkstevensmysteries.com.

ART TAYLOR (editor), author of *On the Road with Del & Louise: A Novel in Stories,* has won two Agatha Awards, a Macavity, and three Derringers for his short fiction in addition to being twice named a finalist for the Anthony Awards. He teaches at George Mason University and writes frequently on crime fiction for both the *Washington Post* and *Mystery Scene.* www.arttaylorwriter.com.

A writer of bleakly noirish tales with a bit of grim humour, **GRAHAM WYND** can be found in Dundee but would prefer you didn't come looking. An English professor by day, Wynd grinds out darkly noir prose between trips to the local pub. Wynd's novella of murder and obsessive love, *Extricate* is out now from Fox Spirit Books; the print edition also includes the novella *Throw the Bones* and a dozen short stories. Visit https://grahamwynd.wordpress.com/ for more.

OTHER TITLES FROM DOWN AND OUT BOOKS

See www.DownAndOutBooks.com for complete list

By Anonymous-9
Bite Hard

By J.L. Abramo
Catching Water in a Net
Clutching at Straws
Counting to Infinity
Gravesend
Chasing Charlie Chan
Circling the Runway (*)

By Trey R. Barker
2,000 Miles to Open Road
Road Gig: A Novella
Exit Blood
Death is Not Forever (*)

By Richard Barre
The Innocents
Bearing Secrets
Christmas Stories
The Ghosts of Morning
Blackheart Highway
Burning Moon
Echo Bay
Lost

By Eric Beetner and
JB Kohl
Over Their Heads (*)

By Eric Beetner and
Frank Scalise
The Backlist (*)

By Rob Brunet
Stinking Rich

By Milton T. Burton
Texas Noir

By Dana Cameron (editor)
Murder at the Beach: Bouchercon Anthology 2014

By Tom Crowley
Vipers Tail
Murder in the Slaughterhouse

By Frank De Blase
Pine Box for a Pin-Up
Busted Valentines and Other Dark Delights
A Cougar's Kiss (*)

By Les Edgerton
The Genuine, Imitation, Plastic Kidnapping

By A.C. Frieden
Tranquility Denied
The Serpent's Game
The Pyongyang Option (*)

By Jack Getze
Big Numbers
Big Money
Big Mojo

By Keith Gilman
Bad Habits

(*)—Coming Soon

OTHER TITLES FROM DOWN AND OUT BOOKS

See www.DownAndOutBooks.com for complete list

By William Hastings (editor)
*Stray Dogs: Writing from the Other
America* (*)

By Matt Hilton
No Going Back (*)
Rules of Honor (*)
The Lawless Kind (*)

By Terry Holland
An Ice Cold Paradise
Chicago Shiver

By Darrel James,
Linda O. Johnston
& Tammy Kaehler (editors)
Last Exit to Murder

By David Housewright
& Renée Valois
The Devil and the Diva

By David Housewright
Finders Keepers
Full House

By Jon Jordan
Interrogations

By Jon & Ruth Jordan (editors)
Murder and Mayhem in Muskego

By Bill Moody
Czechmate
The Man in Red Square
Solo Hand (*)
The Death of a Tenor Man (*)
The Sound of the Trumpet (*)
Bird Lives! (*)

By Gary Phillips
The Perpetrators
Scoundrels (Editor)
Treacherous (*)

By Gary Phillips, Tony Chavira
& Manoel Maglhaes
Beat L.A. (Graphic Novel)

By Robert J. Randisi
Upon My Soul
Souls of the Dead (*)
Envy the Dead (*)

By Lono Waiwaiole
Wiley's Lament
Wiley's Shuffle
Wiley's Refrain
Dark Paradise

By Vincent Zandri
Moonlight Weeps (*)

(*)—Coming Soon

CPSIA information can be obtained at www.ICGtesting.com
Printed in the USA
LVOW11s1220011115

460619LV00005B/689/P